Praise for Patricia Gaffney and her novels

"Patricia Gaffney . . . is one of the finest writers to come along in years."

—*Romantic Times*

To Love and To Cherish

"Magnificent! Powerful, beautifully written, and as deeply moving as it is richly romantic . . . destined to become a classic."

—Mary Jo Putney

"A beautiful story that tugs at the heartstrings. A powerful tale of love and faith."

—*Romantic Times*

To Have and To Hold

"Compelling and sophisticated."

—Virginia Henley

"Patricia Gaffney writes with power and passion."

—*Romantic Times*

Forever and Ever

"Simply glorious."

—Nora Roberts

"Lovely writing and a story that is honestly and passionately told."

—*Romance Forever*

continued . . .

Outlaw in Paradise

"Lively, exceptionally well-written."

—*Library Journal*

"Sophisticated, humorous . . . a delightful, mature romance that brings readers a unique look at the Wild West."

—*Romantic Times*

Crooked Hearts

"With a lyrical voice and keen wit, Patricia Gaffney weaves compelling stories that echo in the human heart."

—Nora Roberts

"Absolutely marvelous. . . . It's been a long time since I read a book this wonderful. I loved it."

—Joan Johnston

"Poignant, and exciting. An unforgettable read. There have never been two more wonderful and memorable larcenist lovers."

—*Romantic Times*

"Heartwarming and delightful . . . the best matched hero and heroine since Hepburn and Tracy . . . pure pleasure."

—Elaine Coffman

"Wickedly delightful. You'll never meet two more outrageous, endearing characters."

—Margaret Brownley

"Sexy, funny, and wildly entertaining."

—Arnette Lamb

"A refreshingly unique and humorous romance."

—*Affaire de Coeur*

"Fabulous . . . unusual and beautiful, warm and witty . . . one of the funniest and most entertaining stories I've read in a long, long while."

—Rebecca Paisley

The Saving Graces

"Anyone who's ever raised a glass to toast her women friends will love this book—its raw emotion, its rueful humor, its life lessons."

—*Times-Picayune*

"This ode to the friendships between women could easily become the northern version of *Divine Secrets of the Ya-Ya Sisterhood*."

—*Booklist*

"A jewel of a book and every facet sparkles."

—Nora Roberts

"Rich, lovely . . . an intimate portrayal of friendships through the eyes of four unforgettable women. I hated to put it down!"

—Michael Lee West

Sweet Everlasting

"A romance of immense beauty and emotional power . . . exquisite!"

—*Romantic Times*

"A beautiful, tender love story, evoking your senses and stirring your emotions. It will renew your faith in unselfish love."

—*Rendezvous*

Wild at Heart

"Delightfully different . . . *Wild at Heart* brims with laughter and passion."

—*The Literary Times*

"Wonderful and enlightening. . . . Ms. Gaffney once more stretches the boundaries of the genre as only a premier writer can do."

—*Romantic Times*

To Love
and
To Cherish

Patricia Gaffney

NEW AMERICAN LIBRARY

New American Library
Published by New American Library, a division of
Penguin Putnam Inc., 375 Hudson Street,
New York, New York 10014, U.S.A.
Penguin Books Ltd, 80 Strand,
London WC2R 0RL, England
Penguin Books Australia Ltd, 250 Camberwell Road,
Camberwell, Victoria 3124, Australia
Penguin Books Canada Ltd, 10 Alcorn Avenue,
Toronto, Ontario, Canada M4V 3B2
Penguin Books (N.Z.) Ltd, Cnr Rosedale and Airborne Roads,
Albany, Auckland 1310, New Zealand

Penguin Books Ltd, Registered Offices:
Harmondsworth, Middlesex, England

Published by New American Library, a division of Penguin Putnam Inc.
Previously published in a Topaz edition.

First New American Library Trade Paperback Printing, February 2003
10 9 8 7 6 5 4 3 2 1

 REGISTERED TRADEMARK—MARCA REGISTRADA

Set in Fairfield Light

Printed in the United States of America

PUBLISHER'S NOTE

BOOKS ARE AVAILABLE AT QUANTITY DISCOUNTS WHEN USED TO PROMOTE PROD-
UCTS OR SERVICES. FOR INFORMATION PLEASE WRITE TO PREMIUM MARKETING
DIVISION, PENGUIN PUTNAM INC., 375 HUDSON STREET, NEW YORK, NEW YORK
10014.

For Midge. I miss you.

I

EVEN ON HIS DEATHBED, Lord D'Aubrey was a hard man to love.

God, give me patience and humility, prayed Reverend Christian Morrell, who was in the business, as it were, of loving the unlovable. Leaning over the bed but not touching it—ill as he was, the elderly viscount still bristled when anyone except his doctor got too close—Christy asked his lordship if he would take the sacraments.

"Why? So I can go straight to heaven? Do you think I'm going to heaven, Vicar? Eh? Think I'm—" He ran out of breath; his parchment-colored face turned blue until he sucked in a wheezing gulp of air. By now he was too weak to cough; he kept swallowing until the spasm passed, then lay exhausted, hands limp on his sunken chest.

Christy sat down again in the high-backed chair he'd pulled as close to the bed as the old man would allow. The oil lamp couldn't penetrate the gloom in the large, spartan bedchamber; he had to squint to read his prayer book. He tried to remember that beyond the heavy draperies the noonday sun was shining on a Devonshire spring of spectacular beauty, but that vital world seemed frivolous here, a figment of a hopeful imagination. Larks might be singing outside, insects droning, squirrels scratching in the ivy; but in the viscount's sickroom, all Christy could hear was the ticking of his own watch in his pocket.

Dr. Hesselius ought to be here, he couldn't help thinking. "Send for me if you need me, but I doubt that you will," he'd told

Christy two hours ago, in this room. "He's not in any pain—they frequently aren't at this late stage. I doubt he'll live through the day. I've done all I can; old Edward's in your hands now, Reverend." Christy had nodded at that, gravely, calmly, as if the prospect didn't demoralize him.

In his own estimation, at least on good days, he was a reasonably effective clergyman, considering he was new at his calling and his best qualities were still only earnestness and perseverance. But he had numerous failings, and they had a perverse way of multiplying and combining at extreme times like this, when his deepest wish was to give comfort and consolation to the needy. Edward Verlaine offered a special challenge, and Christy despaired that he wasn't up to it.

Memories kept intruding on his best efforts to pray. In the sparsely furnished room, a dark, gilt-framed oil painting of Lord D'Aubrey's grandfather loomed conspicuously over the mantelpiece. A peculiar grayish blur under the haughty-looking ancestor's nose made Christy smile, albeit a bit grimly. He recalled the day, probably twenty years ago now, when he and Geoffrey, his best friend, had stolen into this room, giggling and shushing each other, giddy with nervous excitement. Christy hadn't really believed Geoffrey would do it, but he had: he'd stood on a chair and drawn a charcoal mustache on the scowling face of his great-grandfather. Faint traces still lingered, the charcoal having proved remarkably resistant to numerous efforts at removal. Christy wondered if Geoffrey still bore the marks from the thrashing his father had ordered for punishment—delivered by his steward, not himself, for even in his rages Edward Verlaine had kept his distance.

The words in Christy's Book of Common Prayer began to run together. He rolled his stiff shoulders, fighting off the sleepiness that kept dragging at him. He stood up and went to the window. Drawing back the curtain, he looked out past Lynton Great Hall's derelict courtyard toward the tall black spire of All Saints

Church, half a mile away and all that could be seen from here of Wyckerley, the village where he'd grown up. It was April; the gentle, oak-covered hills were a brilliant yellow-green, and the Wyck, normally a placid little river within its steep-sided banks, churned down from Dartmoor with the force of a torrent. He and Geoffrey had fished in the Wyck year-round, ridden their ponies up and down every sunken red lane in the parish, left urgent messages for each other in a crevice of the gray stone monolith at the crossroads. They'd been all but inseparable for the first sixteen years of their lives—until Geoffrey had run away. In twelve years, Christy hadn't heard a word from him.

Until six days ago, when a note had come to the rectory. "Just tell me when the bastard croaks," Geoffrey had scribbled on the back of a tailor's bill—and that only after Christy had written repeatedly to the London address he'd finally gotten from Lord D'Aubrey's solicitor. "How the hell are you?" Geoffrey had scrawled in a postscript. "You're joking, aren't you? A *minister*??"

Christy wasn't surprised that his new vocation seemed like a joke to Geoffrey, considering all the times that, as boys, they'd made fun of Christy's gentle, pious father. ("Old Vicar," the villagers called Magnus Morrell now, although he'd been dead for four years; and Christy, inevitably, was "New Vicar.") Stories of Geoffrey's wild, decadent life in London and other worldly fleshpots were hard to reconcile with competing and almost equally incredible rumors that he was a mercenary soldier, ready to take up arms for any cause that paid enough money for his services. Christy had stopped missing him—even the deepest wound heals in time—but he'd never stopped wondering what had become of him.

"How is he?"

The urgent whisper made him whirl away from the window, startled. Mrs. Fruit hovered in the doorway, twisting her arthritic fingers, her kind, wrinkled face screwed up with worry. He went to her, nodding reassuringly. She'd been the housekeeper at

Lynton Great Hall for more years than he'd been alive; now she was feeble and frail, and almost completely deaf. He touched her hands and said softly, moving his lips slowly, "No change. He's sleeping." She looked past his shoulder at the still figure on the bed, and tears welled in her faded gray eyes. Christy made a motion toward the bed, inviting her to go closer. She crept a few feet nearer and stopped, not out of fear, but out of reverence for the master she'd served for so long.

The only sign that Edward Verlaine wasn't dead already was the intermittent flutter of his yellow, clawed fingers against the heavy counterpane. Under the bedclothes, his distended abdomen was nearly as round as a pregnant woman's; by contrast, his arms and legs had shrunk to the size of a child's. His head on the pillow looked like a barely breathing skull. Mrs. Fruit drew a quavery breath, dropped her face in her hands, and wept.

Christy patted her shoulder, feeling useless, and doubly frustrated because even if the perfect comforting remark miraculously occurred to him, she wouldn't be able to hear it unless he bellowed it in her ear.

At length she recovered enough to ask if she could fetch him anything, tea or a glass of wine. He thanked her and said no, and she withdrew. He heard her blowing her nose and then the sound of her slow, careful footsteps on the stairs.

He should have asked her to stay, he realized a moment later. Mrs. Fruit was the only person he knew who had truly loved old D'Aubrey, and most certainly the only one who would miss him.

A noise from the bed made him turn. The viscount's face, yellow with jaundice, had turned on the pillow; he was glaring at him. "You." It came out an accusing croak. "Don't want you. Where's your father?"

"My father's dead, sir," he reminded him gently, leaning over the bed.

Recollection took the anger out of the old man's hard black

eyes, but a truly ghastly smile curled at the corners of his mouth. "Then I'll see him soon enough, won't I?"

Christy fumbled with his prayer book, reconsidered, and laid it aside. He hated the inadequacy he felt at this moment, and the trivial sound of all the things that came into his mind to say. He felt like a child again—like the boy who had grown up terrified of this dying wreck of a man, hating him on principle because Geoffrey, his best friend, had hated him.

He bent closer, into the old man's line of vision. "Would you like to pray?"

Out of habit, the viscount's eyes narrowed with contempt. A moment passed. He turned his face away. "You pray," he exhaled on a feeble sigh.

Christy opened his book to the Psalms. " 'The Lord is my shepherd,' " he began, prosaically enough; " 'I shall not want. He maketh me to lie down in green pastures; he leadeth me beside the still waters. He restoreth my soul—' "

"Not that one. Before that."

"The—"

"The twenty-second." His eyes closed in exhaustion, but the bloodless lips curved again, sardonic. "Read it, Parson," he rasped when Christy hesitated.

He scanned the seldom-read psalm in dismay. " 'My God, my God, why hast thou forsaken me? Why art thou so far from helping me, and from the words of my roaring?' " He read the prayer in a low voice, but it wasn't possible to soften the desperate message. " 'They cried unto thee, and were delivered; they trusted in thee, and were not confounded. But I am a worm, and no man; a reproach of men, and despised of the people. All they that see me laugh me to scorn. . . .' "

A sound silenced him; he looked up. Edward's eyes were closed, his jaws clamped in a grimace, but for all his efforts, tears trickled through his papery lids. Christy reached for one of his hands and held it tightly, while the viscount's weeping turned into weak, desolate cursing. The words became garbled as he grew more agitated. He gave Christy's wrist a feeble yank. "Do it," he muttered. "Do it, damn you."

He stared at him, baffled. "I don't—"

"Absolve me."

Christy looked down at the fierce, spidery grip the old man had on his hand. "Almighty God," he prayed quickly, "who desireth not the death of a sinner, but rather that he may turn from his wickedness and live, hath given power to his ministers to declare and pronounce to his people the absolution of their sins. Edward, do you truly and earnestly repent of your sins?"

"I do," he grated through his teeth, eyes closed.

"Are you in love and charity with your neighbors—"

"Yes, yes."

"And—will you lead a new life, following the commandments of God and walking from henceforth in his holy ways?"

"Yes!"

"Go in peace, then. Your sins are forgiven."

The viscount peered up at him in panicky disbelief.

"They're forgiven," Christy repeated, insistent. "The God who made you loves you. Believe it."

"If I could . . ."

"You can. Take it inside your heart and be at peace."

"Peace." His hand loosened and fell away, but he continued to gaze up with pleading eyes. All the hopes of his life had narrowed and funneled into this one hope: that he was loved, and that he was forgiven. Christy was learning that at the end it was all anyone wanted.

"My lord," he asked, "will you take the sacraments?"

A minute went by, and then the old man nodded.

Christy prepared the bread and the wine quickly, using the bedside table for an altar, reciting the words of the ritual in a voice loud enough for Edward to hear. He was too ill to swallow more than a tiny morsel of the Host, and he could only wet his lips on the edge of the chalice. Afterward, he lay utterly still, the flutter of the wilted lace on his nightshirt the only indication that he still breathed.

The silence that flowed back into the room was different now, Christy fancied—not quite as hopeless. He prayed for a while, then just sat in his chair, resting. His failings as a priest assailed him again; he thanked God for the sacraments, for without them he would be worse than useless. If only he could stop thinking of *himself,* stop worrying about what kind of job he was doing, stop feeling fear in the face of another's death, instead of love and true compassion for the ill and the dying—in other words, he thought wearily, if only he could be more like his father. *Lord, give me the strength to go with the dying into the dark places,* he prayed. *And help me to forgive myself when I can't.*

He opened his prayer book at random, abashed because once again, even in this dire hour, his thoughts were on himself, not the dying soul to whom he'd come to minister. "If I climb up into heaven," he read, "thou art there; if I go down to hell, thou art there also. If I take the wings of the morning, and remain in the uttermost parts of the sea; even there also shall thy hand lead me, and thy right hand shall hold me. . . ."

Time ticked past in the dim box of a room; the lamp wick began to sputter, and he rose to turn it higher. A choking sound from the bed made him turn back quickly.

Edward was trying to sit up on his elbows. "Help me . . . help . . . oh, God, I hate it . . . I'm afraid of the dark . . ." Christy put his arm around his thin shoulders, propping him up. "Geoffrey?" He stared straight ahead, unblinking. "Geoffrey?"

"Yes," Christy lied without hesitation. "Yes, Father, it's Geoffrey."

"My boy." His smile was rapturous, a little smug. "I knew you'd come." His head bobbed once and fell on his left shoulder; a long, ragged sigh rattled up from his chest, but he was already dead.

Christy held him in his arms a little longer before laying his slack torso back on the bed and gently closing his eyes. "Go in peace," he murmured, "for the Lord has put away all your sins." The unmistakable aspect of death had already seeped into the viscount's corpse; his soul was gone. Christy administered the last sacrament, the anointing of the body with oil, taking a melancholy comfort in the solemn rite. When he finished, he sank to his knees by the bed to pray, hands folded, his forehead pressed against the side of the mattress.

That was how Geoffrey found him.

II

CHRISTY HADN'T HEARD footsteps but something, maybe a change in the air, made him lift his head and look toward the doorway to the hall. A tall, dark-haired man stood in the threshold. Sallow skin, sunken cheeks, black, burning eyes in hollow sockets—for one grotesque moment, Christy thought it was Edward, returned from the dead in the semblance of his youth. But a second later, a flesh-and-blood woman materialized behind the man's shoulder, and Christy realized he wasn't seeing ghosts. He got to his feet in haste.

He met Geoffrey in the middle of the room. He would have embraced him, but Geoffrey held out his hand and they shook instead, clapping each other on the back. "My God, it's true," Geoffrey cried, his voice sounding shockingly loud after the long silence. "You've gone and become a priest!"

"As you see." His gladness gave way to concern as he took in his oldest friend's profoundly altered appearance. At sixteen, Geoffrey had been a strapping, muscular youth; when they'd wrestled together, they'd almost always fought to a draw, and on the rare occasions when Christy had won, it was only because he was taller. Now Geoffrey looked as if a well-placed blow from a child could knock him down.

But his charming, wolfish grin hadn't changed, and Christy found himself smiling back, wanting to laugh with him in spite of the somber circumstances of this meeting. "Geoffrey, thank God you've come. Your father—"

"Is he dead?" He moved around him to the bedside without waiting for an answer. "Oh, my, yes," he said softly, staring down at the still corpse. "He's dead, all right, no question about that."

Christy stayed where he was, to give Geoffrey a little time to himself. The woman in the doorway hadn't moved. She was slim, tall, dressed sedately in a dark brown traveling costume; the veiled brim of her hat cast a shadow over her face. He glanced at her curiously, but she didn't speak.

Geoffrey had his back to the room; Christy tried to read his emotion from the set of his shoulders, but the rigid posture was unrevealing. After another minute, he crossed to the bed to stand beside him, and together they gazed down at Edward's lifeless face. "He didn't suffer at the end," Christy said quietly. "It was a peaceful death."

"Was it? He looks ghastly, doesn't he? What was wrong with him, anyway?"

"A disease of the liver."

"Liver, eh?" There was no hint of sorrow in his frowning, narrow-eyed countenance; rather, Christy had the unnerving impression that he was scrutinizing the body to assure himself it was really dead.

"He asked for you before he died."

Geoffrey looked up at that, incredulous, then burst into high, hearty laughter. "Oh, that's good. That's very good!"

Dismayed, Christy looked away. The woman had come farther into the room; in the shadowy lamplight, her eyes glowed an odd silver-gray color. He couldn't read the expression in them, but the set of her wide, straight mouth was ironic.

"I think he was sorry at the end," he tried again. "For everything. I believe he felt remorse in his heart for—" This time Geoffrey cut him off with a crude, appallingly vulgar oath that made Christy blush. The woman arched one dark brow at him; he'd have said she was mocking him, but there was no playfulness in her face.

Then Geoffrey flashed his charming smile, and the anger in his eyes disappeared as if it had never been. He spun away from the bed and draped his arm across Christy's shoulders, giving him a rough, affectionate squeeze. "How've you been, you ruddy old sod? You look . . ." He stood back and made a show of examining him, head to toe. "Christ, you *still* look like an archangel!" He ruffled Christy's blond hair, laughing, and under his breath Christy caught the unmistakable odor of alcohol. He stiffened involuntarily. All the things he could have said about Geoffrey's appearance seemed either tactless or hurtful, so he didn't answer.

"Come on, let's get out of here," Geoffrey urged, guiding him toward the door. Christy resisted, and Geoffrey stopped short, adjacent to the silent, motionless woman. "Oh—sorry, darling, forgot about you there. This is Christian Morrell, an old chum from my halcyon youth. Christy, meet my wife, Anne. Anne, Christy. Christy, Anne. Shake hands, why don't you? That's it! Now let's all go have a drink."

"How do you do, Reverend Morrell," murmured Anne Verlaine, unsmiling, ignoring her husband's facetiousness.

Christy struggled to hide his surprise. Rumors about Geoffrey were always rife in Wyckerley, had been since he'd run away at sixteen and never returned. About four years ago Christy had heard that he'd married the daughter of an artist, a painter—but the next rumor had him off fighting the Burmese in Pegu, and there was no more talk of a wife. As a consequence, Christy had assumed that the marriage was just another in the colorful catalog of stories about the village's prodigal son that might not be true but never failed to entertain the natives.

"Mrs. Verlaine," he greeted her, taking the cool, firm hand she held out to him. She was younger than he'd thought at first, probably not even twenty-five. Her accent was English, but there was something distinctly foreign about her; something in her dress, he thought, or the penetrating directness of her gaze.

"No, no, it's not Mrs. Verlaine anymore, is it? It's Lady

D'Aubrey! How does it feel to be a viscountess, darling? Frankly I can't wait for someone to call me 'my lord.' Come on, we must go and drink to Father's demise. It took him long enough, but better late than never, what?" Geoffrey's arm around his wife's waist looked steely; she resisted for only a moment, then let him lead her out of the room. Christy had no choice but to follow.

Lynton Hall's best drawing room looked even drearier than usual to him, but that might be because he was seeing it through Geoffrey's eyes. "Bleeding hell," the new viscount pronounced on entering the cold, depressing chamber. "Place looks like a ruddy crypt. Light some candles, will you, Anne?" He glanced around for the bell rope, which dangled beside the marble fireplace mantel. "Does this work?" He pulled on it. Plaster dust sifted down from the ceiling in time with a faint tinkling in the distance.

Anne Verlaine went to the windows and pulled back the heavy draperies. Bright sunlight flooded the drawing room, picking out each stain in the wallpaper and every threadbare patch in the dusty carpet. Geoffrey threw his forearm across his eyes and gave a mock-pained cry. "Eh! Easy, darling, not *that* much light." His wife sent him an impenetrable look, pulled the curtains half closed, and went to the sideboard to light the oil lamp.

While Christy stood by the door, Geoffrey prowled the room, scowling at the furniture. "See anything that looks like it might hold liquor?"

"Not likely," Christy said, smiling. "Your father stopped drinking spirits when he became ill." Geoffrey cursed cheerfully. "I suppose there might be brandy or something in the kitchen."

Halting footsteps coming from the hallway made them all turn toward the door. The housekeeper started into the room, saw them, and stopped in confusion.

"Mrs. Fruit!" Geoffrey cried genially. "God's flesh and blood, you haven't changed much, have you?" She drew back, fearful. "What, don't you know me? It's Geoffrey!"

She cupped her left ear. "Geoffrey?" she quavered, smiling uncertainly. "My saints, it is you. Glory be—I thought it was your father!"

Geoffrey clutched at his chest, pretending he was stabbed. "Don't tell me I look like that blighted corpse up there, old dear!" he said playfully. "Take it back, do you hear?"

"What? Corpse?" She covered her mouth with her hands, staring at him in dread.

Geoffrey finally realized she was deaf. "He's dead!" he said loudly. "The sod's croaked!" He watched in amazement as Mrs. Fruit's wrinkled old face crumbled. "By God, she minds," he marveled, turning to Christy and Anne. "She actually *cares.*" He put his arm around the housekeeper's frail shoulders. "There, there, old thing. Go and get us some brandy, will you? *Brandy!* And have a snort for yourself, it'll do you good." He turned her around and gave her a little shove out the door.

Coming out of his shock, Christy started to go after her— but Anne was faster. "Geoffrey, for God's sake," she said in a low, strained voice, and walked quickly out into the hall. The desolate sound of Mrs. Fruit's weeping faded with the two women's footsteps.

"Why did you do that?" Christy asked, more astonished then angry.

"Do what?" Geoffrey strolled to the high casement windows, looking innocently pleased with himself. He gave another of his high, forced laughs, trying to make Christy join in. "Look at this place, will you? It's grotesque! I haven't thought about it once since I walked out twelve years ago, not once, I swear to you. And yet, now that I'm here, it's as if I'd never left. I remember every corner, every stick of furniture. Every trick of the light . . ." He trailed off, gazing into space, seeming to have forgotten what he was saying.

"Your father had let things go," Christy offered, conscious of the understatement.

"Why? Because he was sick?"

"No, his illness only lasted a few months. He just wasn't interested."

"Ha! And I thought we had nothing in common."

Christy stared at him in growing dismay. "The estate makes a fair profit, I'm told, but he never cared about reinvesting the capital in his holdings. The tenants' farms are in very bad shape, the cottages—"

"What did he do with his money?"

"Banked it, I assume." He came closer. "You could do a lot of good here, Geoffrey. Holyoake does the best he can, but he's only—"

"How much is there? How much money?"

"In the estate? I couldn't say."

Geoffrey looked as if he didn't believe him.

"He never took me into his confidence, I assure you. His lawyers will be in touch with you soon, I'm sure, and then you'll know everything."

"That's assuming he's left me anything at all," Geoffrey retorted with an unamused smile. He went to the hall doorway and leaned out, calling loudly, "Anne! Hurry and find a bottle of something, anything, and bring it back when you come!" To Christy he said, "What a trip! I'm dry as a virgin. We were on the train from London all night, then the most awful coach up from Plymouth this morning." He threw himself full-length on the worn brocade sofa. "Sit down! God, I can't get used to the sight of you, Christy. You look like a great black crane in those clothes."

Christy smiled, taking the wing chair beside him; the odor of mildew rose from it when he sat. "That's not the image I was trying to foster." He didn't say it, but he couldn't get over the sight of Geoffrey, either. The Verlaine good looks had all but vanished under a pallor of illness. His dark brown hair was already receding from a white, bony forehead, making his eyes look blacker than ever. His fine nostrils were pinched, papery; he licked his dry lips with a whitish tongue, and his eyelids were crusty, as if he'd just woken up, or as if he'd fallen asleep weeping.

"No, not a crane," he corrected himself, "a golden eagle—because of the hair. Ha! So tell me, how long have you been in your saintly calling?"

"I was ordained two years ago. I had a small living in Exminster for about a year before the bishop assigned me to St. Giles' parish."

"Assigned you? Didn't you want to come home?"

"I . . . had mixed feelings." Geoffrey laughed knowingly, but Christy doubted that he and his friend had the same reservations about returning to Wyckerley.

"And what does the *real* Reverend Morrell think about you following in his hallowed footsteps?"

"My father died about four years ago. Two years after my mother."

"Oh, Christy, I'm sorry. I really am."

"Thank you." He wanted to ask, *Why didn't you ever write? Why did you let twelve years go by without even telling me where you were?* "And you've become a soldier of fortune," he said instead, adopting the light tone Geoffrey had set. "If half the rumors I've heard are true, you've had an interesting time of it, to say the least."

Geoffrey got to his feet jerkily and started pacing the room again. "Oh, hell, yes, interesting to say the least. Say, Christy, do you still ride?"

"Yes, I've got a chestnut gelding. His name's Doncaster, and he's a great beauty."

"Do you race him?"

"No, not anymore."

"What!" Geoffrey made a shocked face.

Christy thought of the wild, reckless chases they'd run as boys; it had been their favorite sport, the rabid, abiding interest that, at the end, was almost all that had held their friendship to-gether. "The bishop frowns on horse racing among the clergy," he said with a dry smile, "so I've given it up."

"Bloody goddamn pity." He strode to the door again. "Anne! Ah—here you are, and not a second too soon." The new Lady D'Aubrey came into the room, and Geoffrey grabbed at the bot-tle she was carrying on a tray; the sudden shift of balance almost toppled the two glasses beside it. She set the tray on the table by the sofa and walked away, stopping before the cold fireplace.

"Sherry. Good God," Geoffrey said, making a face. "None for you, darling?" She turned around to murmur a refusal. She'd taken off her hat; she had reddish-blond hair, worn loose and cut shorter than Christy thought was currently the fashion. Geoffrey filled the glasses and handed one to him. "What shall we drink to? I know: to being orphans. My wife's an orphan too—aren't you, darling? Oh, yes, a poor, penniless orphan. I thought she was a rich one, you know, but that turned out to be an error of gross and tragic proportions." He tossed back half the sherry in his glass and immediately filled it again. "What? You won't drink to being an orphan? Very well, let's be more direct." He held his glass high. "To the death of my father: may his wicked soul rot in hell forever."

Christy watched him finish his drink in a few swallows and slap the empty glass on the table with nearly enough force to break it. He felt Anne Verlaine's quiet regard, and turned to look at her. Her eyes weren't silver now; they were green, and they were watching him with a strange, somber, resigned expectancy. He set his glass down untouched.

"So! Tell me the news of my beloved old home. Holyoake's still the bailey, is he?" Geoffrey reached again for the bottle.

"No, he died several years ago. Do you remember William, his son? He's the bailiff now. He's a good man, a hard worker; I think you'll—"

"Excellent, then I can turn everything over to him."

Christy frowned. "Then you don't intend to stay?"

"Good God, no. Not for long, anyway. I've applied for a new army commission—didn't I tell you? The worst mistake of my life was selling my captaincy last year. Well—" he grinned at his wife "—almost the worst. Should've borrowed the money I needed instead. Ah, but that's all water under the bridge. Do you know what the Royal Commission wants for a lieutenant colonelcy in the Foot Guards these days? Nine thousand pounds—and that's only the regulation fee; the real cost is closer to thirteen thousand. If dear Father has left me anything at all, I'll be able to pay the thieves in Mayfair off, and with luck I should be on a ship sailing to the Black Sea within the month."

This time Christy couldn't hide his amazement. "You mean—to fight? You'd go as a *soldier?*"

"What the hell do you think I'd go as, a nurse?"

"But you—" He broke off awkwardly. "I beg your pardon. It's just that I thought perhaps you'd been ill."

"Oh, really? Do I look ill?" Belligerence flashed in his fierce black eyes. But he smoothed his hair back with one hand, and afterward it was as if he'd smoothed away his anger, too. "Actually, I've had a flare-up of an old plague of mine—malaria; got it in Basutoland in 'fifty-one, fighting the bloody natives. But I'm fine now, tip-top. Dear Anne takes such wonderful care of me, my bad spells never last long. Do they, sweeting?"

Everything Geoffrey said to his wife sounded like a subtle insult. Christy could feel the tension between them, volatile as a sparking fuse. He kept searching for a sign, a glimmer of the old Geoffrey in this gaunt, sardonic stranger, but twelve years had erased every one. His brittle geniality was a mask, and under it lay something dark and unwholesome.

As for Geoffrey's wife, Christy wanted to stare at her until she made sense to him, fit into some category of womanhood he could check off and set aside, a mystery solved. She was lovely—but that was obvious; a quality much more arresting than beauty simmered under her apparently unlimited composure. It drew him in spite of the faint mockery in her eyes—he was sure now that it was mockery—whenever she intercepted his curious glance.

Geoffrey had collapsed on the sofa again, shoulders hunched, staring down into his drink; it was as if a light inside had gone out, so total was his withdrawal. Christy had to speak twice to get his attention. "I said I'll make the arrangements for your father's burial if you like, Geoffrey."

"Yes, do," he said carelessly. "Oh, are you leaving?" Christy had picked up his hat. "Don't go." He stood up, animated again, almost urgent. "Stay, can't you?"

He hesitated. "Yes, all right. For a little while, if you want me to."

"Good! Have a drink, then, for God's sake. Let's tie one on, Christy, just like old times. Remember the night my father was away in Tavistock, and you and I drank up all the gin the stableboy had hidden in his tack? I've never seen anybody so drunk as you were that night. You wanted to ride that bay horse you had—what was his name?"

Christy grinned, abashed. "Piper."

"Piper! You wanted to bring him in the house and see if he'd eat supper with us at the dining room table. Ha! Remember? Here, drink your drink."

Geoffrey tried to press the glass into his hand, but Christy set it down and reached again for his hat. "I'm sorry, I have to go."

"What? But why?"

"I've got a meeting with the vestry and the churchwarden that I've put off twice already. They'll be waiting for me at the rectory. After that, I have Evening Prayers."

"But you just said you'd stay!"

"I thought you might need me," he explained, feeling awkward again. "That is . . . in my professional capacity."

"Oh, you thought—" Geoffrey threw back his head and roared with laughter. "You thought I needed *spiritual comfort!*"

Christy felt his face getting warm. He couldn't look at Mrs. Verlaine this time, but he imagined her steady, measuring gaze on him; she was probably marveling over her discovery of a quaint, amusing specimen of English country life she'd only read about in books until now.

"I'll speak to Dr. Hesselius on my way home," he said, trying not to sound stiff. "There are some women in the parish who will take care of everything as far as your father's—body is concerned, so you needn't concern yourself about that."

"Oh," said Geoffrey, pretending dismay, "I've offended you. I'm sorry, truly I am."

"No, not at all." At that moment he realized Geoffrey was drunk. Mrs. Verlaine had turned her back on them and was staring out the window, apparently not listening anymore.

"Come to dinner tomorrow night," Geoffrey said impulsively. "There's a cook here, isn't there? Or Anne could make us something, she's wonderfully handy that way, aren't you, love?"

"I'm sorry," Christy said quickly, "I already have an engagement."

"Oh, have you?" Unaccountably, Geoffrey sounded hurt. "Another time, then."

Christy put his hand out to shake. "Come and see me at the vicarage."

"See you at the vicarage?" He repeated it blankly, as if he'd forgotten what they were talking about. Then his eyes cleared. "Yes, I'll do that! That'll be a treat, won't it? Like old times again, only it'll be *you* in your father's study, behind that enormous desk, won't it? You can offer me canary wine, the way he used to with his visitors." His face was unnaturally alive now, his voice too loud. He threw his arm around Christy's shoulders and started to walk him out the door.

Christy held back. Anne had turned around. He said formally, "It was a pleasure meeting you, Lady D'Aubrey."

His formality seemed to amuse her. "Thank you for coming, Reverend Morrell. It was kind of you. I hope—"

"Oh, say," Geoffrey interrupted, "you don't expect Anne to go around visiting sick cottagers now, do you? Wife of the lord and all that?" He laughed. "But, darling, what fun! Lady Bountiful of Wyckerley. Oh, it's *perfect.* I've wondered for years what your true calling might be, and now it seems you've found it!"

Her cheeks pinkened; that and the deliberate relaxing of her clenched hands at her waist were the only signs of emotion, but Christy felt disproportionately relieved: at last, the beautiful Lady D'Aubrey had given a little of herself away. She recovered instantly and said good-bye to him in a cool, controlled voice. He made her a short bow while Geoffrey snickered—laughing at both of them now, he suspected. She turned away quickly; the last he saw of her, she was reaching for his untouched sherry glass and drinking down the contents without stopping. Afterward she shuddered, as if she'd drunk poison.

III

Lynton Great Hall

7 April 1854

    Geoffrey buried his father today. Buried, not mourned; I saw satisfaction in his eyes, but no grief. I thought of my father, and how little he truly cared for me. I always knew it, and yet I loved him with a blind, uncritical passion that amazes me now. Who was that girl? Where has all that fervor gone? Burned up along with my other childish wants and needs. It's unimaginable now, that I could have felt things so strongly.

    Although I can guess, I don't really know why Geoffrey hated Edward Verlaine so bitterly. He won't tell me—something else that's none of my business. The old man wouldn't give him money, that I know. I finally threw away the note he sent to me after that first endless winter, when Geoffrey had disappeared and I was four pounds and six shillings away from being thrown out of the flat in Holborn. I remember what he said, though: "Do not write to me again, Mrs. Verlaine. Geoffrey's financial problems ceased to concern me years ago, and his marital ones never did. I think you must be a very foolish girl; otherwise you would not have made your bed anywhere near my son's. Since you have, I wish you luck lying in it. But I doubt that you'll survive, much less prosper. Certainly you'll get no help from me."

A very foolish girl indeed, especially if foolishness is measured by credulity and optimism. By that yardstick, I've become quite a wise woman in my old age.

The turnout for Lord D'Aubrey's funeral was, to say the very least, light. Most of the people who came weren't there to mourn the old viscount, I suspect, but to gape at the new one. Mrs. Fruit did the lion's share of the weeping, enough for a whole congregation. But I mustn't make a joke of her; her grief is genuine, and no less painful, I'm sure, for being limited exclusively to herself. The Archangel (Reverend Morrell; Geoffrey's nickname for his friend has stuck with me, because the man truly does resemble Michael or Gabriel in a Renaissance painting, or even more, one of Blake's copper etchings)—the Archangel presided over the funeral service, and when it was time for the eulogy, he skirted the knotty problem of finding enough nice things to say of the deceased to fill up half an hour or so by talking about the English tradition of community reverence for great country squires in general, not this particular community's for this particular squire. The little ceremony in the churchyard might have been touching, except that Geoffrey's impatience was too obvious by then and the reverend had to make short work of his "ashes to ashes" speech. When it was over, he kindly invited us to take tea with him at the vicarage. By then there were no other mourners. Clearly Geoffrey wanted something stronger than tea, so he sent me home alone in the carriage. For all I know, he and the Archangel are swilling brandy and soda at this very moment, while they wax nostalgic over old times.

But I don't think so. Reverend Morrell—Christian;

what an apt name. Was his calling ordained from birth?—
will have no part of Geoffrey's macabre toasts and refuses
to laugh at his bitter jests. I thought English clergymen
toadied to the gentry, but so far this one does not. Impossible to imagine them as friends, companions. Did they go
fishing together? Loll in hayricks and swap boyish dreams?
Snicker over the charms of the village maidens and exchange exaggerated tales of manly conquests? Geoffrey
would swagger, and lie, and seduce. But the Archangel?
Easier to see him striding about the countryside perform-
ing muscular but unpretentious good works. Fording a
swollen stream to save a drowning lamb, perhaps. Yes, I
can picture it.

My new home is a stone manor house with a river
running past it, barely fifty yards from the front door. I'm
quite taken with the river, which is called the Wyck and
flows right through the village alongside the main street,
spanned at intervals by old Roman stone bridges—lovely
arches; I'd love to paint them. The house has a courtyard
that's gone to seed, a dozen outbuildings in bad repair. The
terraced gardens were beautiful once, it's easy to see,
dropping down steeply behind the house and meeting
open parkland; but now they're a wilderness of vines and
tangles, and they make me feel tired just to look at them,
outside my sitting room window.

I call it my sitting room. It's not; my proper sitting room
is downstairs, a staid affair with flocked wallpaper and too
much furniture. But this is my refuge and my sanctuary,
the sort of room I longed for in Battersea Road, because
there wasn't even any turning-around room in that dreadful flat. Lynton Great Hall has thirty-nine rooms, more or
less. My sitting room is a half-garret on the third floor,
miles from the servants' bedrooms, accessible only from a

set of narrow, dangerous steps leading up from the never-used gallery. There's a fireplace, thank God, but I would hide myself away up here without it, summer or winter, because I'm safe here. (I feel safe, I should say—I shall see how safe I am.) I sit in my soft leather chair with my writing desk in my lap, scribbling or reading, sketching sometimes. The world is literally at my feet, for the windows—two of them, south- and west-facing—start nearly at the floor. If not for the trees, I wonder if I could see the south Devon coast on clear days. I've brought all my books up and set them on the mantelshelf. (The viscount's library was a great disappointment; apparently he stopped reading anything new around 1825.) I can't bring myself to ring for the girl if I want tea, or the post, or a clean handkerchief; six flights of steps to and from the basement kitchen are too much even for a viscountess to ask. This is a drawback, but I put up with it willingly in exchange for my safe solitude.

But sometimes my solitude . . . no, I won't write that.

The lawyer came yesterday. Hedley is his name, a dry old stick of a man very much out of Dickens's *Bleak House*. His news was mixed. There's money in the estate, perhaps quite a lot, but old D'Aubrey put it in so many different trusts and accounts that it's going to take some time before Geoffrey can get his hands on it. Hence, much ranting and storming about last night. I think of the time, not so long ago, when Geoffrey's rages terrified me. But terror numbs eventually. Now I listen and watch as if from behind a thick stone battlement, uncaring, although not always unscathed.

So, I suppose we are rich. It's what he's always wanted. Too late to make him happy, though, I think. What will it make me? Not happy. I cannot see a picture of myself here in this place in six months' time, or a year from now. Cannot imagine it.

Geoffrey will go off to fight in the war in the Crimea now that he's got the price of admission, or soon will have. But I wonder if they will let him fight this time. He's much stronger, but he still looks bad. Why does he crave it, the fighting and the killing? It's something I have never understood. But perhaps I make it more complicated than it really is.

9 April

Geoffrey took Christy Morrell to his first brothel. It was thirteen years ago, in Devonport, and the girl's name was Crystal. Or so she said. Geoffrey delighted in telling me this, I can't think why.

Exhausted today. Mrs. Fruit is worse than no housekeeper at all, a hundred times worse. Geoffrey says to let her go, but I can't. Won't. She's outlived all her people—there is no place for her to go except the charity home. My throat hurts from shouting at her, which I can hardly bear to do anyway; regardless of the circumstances, one ought not to shout at feeble old ladies. Even when she hears me, she has a truly remarkable way of botching the instruction. I asked her to fetch the housemaid (a surly, disagreeable woman called Violet; already we loathe each other) to help me take down the bed hangings in Geoffrey's room and shake the dust from them outside. No one came; I struggled along by myself until, at last, the parlor maid arrived (Susan, a sweet-natured Irish girl who makes me laugh), armed with her hearth-box full of brushes and blacking, ready to clean all the fireplaces!

I wasn't born to give orders to servants, I think. Certainly I've had no practice at it. We had maids sometimes in Italy and France, Papa and I, but I was too young to tell them what to do with any effectiveness.

I like William Holyoake. "The bailey," they call him here, which means bailiff; the estate agent, in other words. He's six feet tall, strong as a boulder, and he doesn't speak unless he has something to say. Geoffrey would never admit it, but I think he's intimidated by him. When Mr. Holyoake finished telling us everything Edward Verlaine neglected and all the repairs, improvements, and investments that must be made to Lynton Hall Farm immediately to stave off disaster, I was intimidated, too. What would he do if he knew that the new lord of the manor has no intention of becoming a good, strong squire, a man the people of Wyckerley could rely on to pull them out of the trough of neglect that was his father's legacy?

Meanwhile, I try to cope with the legacy of this house. Thirty-nine rooms! What shall I do with thirty-nine rooms? Old D'Aubrey's answer was to shut most of them up. I like the simplicity of that solution, but not the results: dry rot, mildew, and damp; mice, rats, and spiders; dust, cobwebs, and ghosts. (This last is only a surmise; but how could a stone manor house built four centuries ago not have ghosts?) Every trembling, uncarpeted floor creaks like an old man's bones, and no two corners meet plumb. Drafts blow from everywhere, without regard for conventional origins like windows and doors. The plaster is crumbling, the wallpaper peeling. All the fireplaces smoke. The windows are old-fashioned casements, hard to crank open, often painted shut; the glazing in them is so old, the world outside ripples and rolls like waves on the ocean.

For all its flaws and inconveniences, I can't help liking the house, though. The furnishings are fairly atrocious, with such things as stuffed animals in glass globes in the hall, a case of stuffed hummingbirds in the library—so cheery—and gilt-framed engravings of Lord Nelson and the Duke of Wellington gracing the dining room. But there are unexpected delights: a curtained alcove in the musty library, for instance, complete with a soft, cushioned bench and a bow window with a view of the hump-backed bridge over the river; balconies and little porches everywhere, most too rickety-looking to hazard, but one, off the center hall overlooking the parkland west of the house, perfect for watching the sunset; and of course my little sitting room under the eaves, snug and cozy, with sweeping views of pastures, sheep fences, and hedgerows, narrow clay-colored lanes arched over with trees, the stone spire of All Saints Church rising black and tall from a gap in distant oaks. Except for Ravenna when I was a little girl, the longest I have ever lived in one place was two and a half years—in Rouen, when Papa had a patron in the Comte de Beauvais. I can only imagine what "home" feels like, therefore. Could it be this tolerant fondness I've acquired for Lynton Hall, the sort of charitable, forgiving affection one feels for an eccentric relative? I won't set too much store by these pulls at my heartstrings, however. I can never see myself putting down roots, here or anywhere. I think I wasn't meant to have a home.

How lugubrious that sounds. I'm weary. I'll bank the fire and go down to bed now, and hope I don't meet my husband in my new house.

11 April
Heard my first bit of village gossip today: all the unmarried ladies are mad for the Archangel, and regularly bombard him with cakes and scones, mufflers and gloves, slippers, pressed flowers, bookmarkers, antimacassars—

anything they can think of to bring home to him the pitiful meagerness of his lonely domestic circumstances. Two sisters, Chloe and Cora Swan, daughters of the blacksmith, are the fiercest competitors, but the mayor's daughter, Miss Honoria Vanstone, is no slouch, and not a few interested observers have put their money on her (figuratively speaking, one assumes). My informants were Mrs. and Miss Weedie, elderly mother and middle-aged daughter, genteel ladies of Wyckerley, who paid an old-fashioned call on me this afternoon. All the above gossip was couched in the most respectful and discreet terms, of course, but one reads between the lines and draws one's own conclusions. I was welcomed to the neighborhood by these two ladies with much kindness and not a little awe (the latter most amusing and disconcerting), not to mention a large jar of pickled eggs—"with biscuits and tea, a great boon to the digestion." Once their timidity began to wear off, we had quite a jolly chat. At the end of the allotted twenty minutes, they invited Geoffrey and me to tea after church next Sunday. I was vague. *Must* I go to church? How seriously am I to take my new role of lady of the manor? Geoffrey offers no guidance; it's all a joke to him. I suppose it's a joke to me as well—and yet, the Weedies' kindness to me was real, and for a few minutes I did not feel as if I were in disguise . . .

A little money has come from the lawyer, four hundred pounds or so, I think. Geoffrey took it and went away this morning, to Exeter to buy a horse. So now I am alone. I can never decide which is worse—being alone, or being alone with my husband.

13 April

This is not a tragedy, this is only the beginning of a night. But on evenings like this I understand perfectly what drives people to drink. Everything is heightened, sharper, exaggerated, as the time crawls by. At six o'clock, the night to come seems endless, and unhealthy thoughts fester in the mind. Who will speak to me? Will I write a letter? Would William Holyoake sit down and talk with me for ten minutes, for an hour? But I don't ask him to; as dreadful as this solitude is tonight, I can't bear the thought of speaking to another living soul. But—then again—I must hear a human voice, or see a face, or watch someone walk across the courtyard. I must get out of my own mind.

No. I can't speak to anyone, I'm utterly unfit for conversation. They would think me odder than I am, even mad. Well, perhaps I am. Maybe this is how it starts. If I must go on and on like this forever, I would rather be mad. My life is becoming a desolation. I'm in an absolute hunger for warmth, sympathy, some small kindness.

I'm afraid of losing my hold on the here and now, of sliding farther and farther away from the commerce of my daily life and ending in some dark room, screaming. Absurd! Oh, but I long for a drug that would make me sleep now, deeply and dreamlessly, until dawn. Morning birds, rude sunshine, everything full and unexperienced—then I would have my courage back. But now I fear this dusk, these dark thoughts, dying, death, my end. Oh, God, what shall I do?

Nothing. Open a book, call for tea. Endure.

Footsteps on the stairs: a timely interruption. I hope it's—

IT WAS SUSAN. "M'lady," she said, patting her chest, panting a little from the climb, " 'scuse me fer interruptin', but I thought you did ought t' know that Reverend Morrell's come to see 'is lordship."

"Reverend Morrell? He's here, now?" A glance at the mantel clock told her it was almost nine o'clock.

"Well, 'e might still be here. See, ma'am, Violet answered the door an' put 'im in the blue parlor, but then Mrs. Fruit come an' told 'im 'is lordship's away an' you was indisposed—which is what you said when you wouldn't come down to supper."

"Then—he's gone?" Her chair scraped sharply on the floor when she stood up.

"Well, 'e were talkin' to Mrs. Fruit when I come up to tell you, so I can't say but what 'e might still be here. Shall I—do you want me to—"

"I'll go myself." Anne brushed past Susan in the doorway and hurried down the narrow steps, wondering at her own urgency. As starved as she was for human contact, she was also profoundly unfit for it tonight. Besides, what could she and the Archangel have to say to each other? She slowed her steps as she neared the blue parlor, hoping he wasn't there.

He wasn't.

Her heart sank; the heaviness of her disappointment amazed her. Violet was pulling the heavy draperies across the windows on the other side of the room. "Where is Reverend Morrell, Violet?"

"Why, 'e left, m'lady. Mrs. Fruit was just now walkin' 'im to the door."

"The courtyard door?" The maid nodded. "When?"

" 'Alf a minute ago."

Anne gathered up her skirts and rushed back down the hall the way she'd come.

The housekeeper was nowhere in sight. Anne threw open the courtyard door and started down the two shallow steps. Under the gatehouse arch twenty yards away, Reverend Morrell heard the door hinges creak, and whirled around; in the pale light of a thin quarter moon, the white of his shirt gleamed as bright as a candle. For a long second, neither of them moved. Then, in unison, they started toward each other, and met in the center of the weedy flagstone courtyard.

"Reverend Morrell," she said, nearly as out of breath as Susan had been. "I'm glad I caught you. They just told me you'd come—forgive me for not greeting you." They touched hands briefly, Anne wearing her blithest social smile.

He wasn't in clerical garb tonight—his sober suit looked brown or dark blue, it was hard to tell in the murky light. What would she have taken him for, she wondered, if she hadn't known he was a minister? A barrister? No, he was too . . . vigorous, too physical for such a sedentary occupation. Not a scholar either, for the same reason, although his face was intelligent enough for it. An architect, perhaps. Yes. A master builder, the sort of man who constructed churches rather than preached in them.

"It's very late," he was saying apologetically. "I really came to see your husband, just to ask him a question. When Mrs. Fruit said you weren't feeling well, I didn't want to disturb you."

She'd forgotten how consoling his low voice was. "No, she was mistaken. As you can see, I'm quite well. Won't you come in? Now that you're here—"

"Thank you, I'd better not." He peered at her as if he didn't believe she was quite well, and she wondered how he could know. If she cried so much as one tear, her eyes always gave her away, but tonight she hadn't been weeping. "I didn't know Geoffrey was away," he explained. "I only wanted to ask him a question about his father's gravestone."

"Ah." She folded her arms and took a step back. Now that she knew he wasn't staying, she couldn't decide whether she was glad or sorry. "I suppose he's left all of that to you, the details about the stone and the epitaph and so on." She made her voice sympathetic, inviting him to complain of the imposition, or to say something about how typical it was of Geoffrey.

But he declined the invitation. "Yes," he said mildly, "and now the stonecutter wants to know what to carve on the headstone."

Something made her say, "And do you really imagine, Reverend Morrell, that Geoffrey would care?"

He raised his eyebrows. "Maybe not," he admitted after a moment. "But I had to ask."

"Yes, I suppose. Perhaps I can advise you, then. If you left it to Geoffrey, I'm afraid he might suggest something profane."

She thought he smiled slightly at that. Just then the house cat, an overweight tabby called Olive, sidled out of the shadows under the archway and began to rub her rotund sides against the vicar's ankles. He bent and picked her up. The lazy animal straddled his muscular forearm and let all four legs go limp, nuzzling his hand with her cheeks and purring like a machine. Anne smiled to herself, imagining Reverend Morrell with birds on his shoulders, a squirrel or two at his feet, maybe a lamb in his arms: St. Francis of Wyckerley.

"What epitaph would you advise, Lady D'Aubrey?" he asked lightly. The shameless cat arched her back voluptuously when he scratched behind her ears.

"Mmm, something simple and unambiguous, I should think. What you want to avoid is the suggestion that Geoffrey had any actual fondness for his father. 'Rest in peace' would probably cover it. Or—in your line of work, I suppose you would prefer *'Requiescat in pace?'*" Why was she talking like this? She was almost baiting him—she reminded herself of Geoffrey!

His fine eyes measured her in that steady, tolerant way which would undoubtedly earn him a place in heaven. She reached up to pet Olive's head; their fingers touched before Reverend Morrell moved his hand back, out of reach. "When will Geoffrey return?" he asked, ignoring her facetious question.

"I really couldn't say. He went to an auction in Exeter to buy a horse. I thought he might have mentioned it to you."

"No, he didn't, but I've been away myself."

"Tending to your flock in the nether regions?" Now, that really was too much. She bit her lip. "I beg your pardon, I'm not fit for company tonight. It's—I have a headache," she fabricated, "and that always makes me insufferable. Don't pay any attention to me."

"Is there anything I can do to help you?" The gentleness in his voice alarmed her, but not as much as the understanding in his eyes. The last thing she wanted was to be understood by Christian Morrell.

"Not unless you're a physician as well as a priest," she said shortly. "Thank you for your concern, but I assure you my ailment is physical, not moral. At least for the time being."

He set Olive on her feet carefully and straightened. "I'm sorry. I won't keep you any longer."

Immediately she regretted her words—again—but she had no hope of detaining him now. And why would she want to, really? Her ambivalence was making her tired. "Good night, Reverend. I'll tell Geoffrey you came. If some sentimental fit seizes him and he decides he wants something kindhearted chiseled on his father's stone"—even now, she couldn't shake off this childish sarcasm—"I'm sure he'll let you know."

"I'm sure." He made her a slow, deliberate bow—she'd have called it an ironic bow, except she didn't think irony was in the vicar's straightforward lexicon—and left her in the darkness.

. . . "Is there anything I can do to help you?" he asked me. Which means he believes I need help. God, I hate

33

that, loathe the thought of him feeling sorry for me! It's why I sent him away, wanted him gone, wasn't even polite to him. Now I'm paying for the mortal sin of rudeness, because I'm alone again. And tonight is one of those nights when solitude is absolute hell.

IV

MISS SOPHIE DEENE was leading the children's choir in the second verse of "O Sons and Daughters, Let Us Sing!"

> That Easter morn at break of day,
> The faithful women went their way
> To seek the tomb where Jesus lay.
> Alleluia!

The shrill but sweet voices filled the church, which was packed this Easter morning, and brought smiles to the faces of many in the congregation, anxious or indulgent depending on the hearer's relationship to the little choristers. Miss Deene herself, pretty in a flowered blue frock and a little white jacket, was looking happier and more relaxed with every chorus, and Reverend Morrell recalled how worried she'd been all week about her debut as precentor of the children's choir. He made a mental note to compliment her after the service—that is, if he could get anywhere near her; Sophie had more beaus than any girl in Wyckerley, and most of them were sitting in the nave right now, beaming at her with lovesick adoration.

> That night the apostles met in fear;
> Amidst them came their Lord most dear,
> And said, "My peace be on all here."
> Alleluia!

From his chair in the presbytery, Christy gazed out at his congregation. He knew everyone, of course, some better than others, because he'd lived his whole life among them. What troubled him was that, even after a year as their vicar, except for a few, he still knew the people best as neighbors and friends, not as parishioners. Christ the Good Shepherd was his model, but the men and women to whom he regularly administered the sacraments of communion, baptism, and marriage could in no way be called his "flock." Last night he'd had a dream—he remembered it now for the first time, his memory tripped by the sight of Tranter Fox, one of his favorite but also one of his most recalcitrant parishioners, sneaking into the service late and sidling belligerently into a back pew. Tranter had figured in the dream by standing up in the middle of Sunday service and shouting out with aggrieved wonder, "Say, *you* ain't Reverend Morrell!" Christy had looked down in horror and seen that, instead of his vestments, he was wearing the old buckskin trousers and kneeboots he used to wear when he raced his horses. "No, it's me," he'd insisted, "it's Christy, you know me!" He held up his Bible, solid proof of his calling, and before his eyes it metamorphosed into a magazine edition of Edgar Allan Poe's "The Masque of the Red Death." He couldn't remember the rest—mercifully; the congregation had probably tarred and feathered him, chanting "Imposter! Imposter!" all the while.

> When Thomas first the tidings heard,
> How they had seen the risen Lord,
> He doubted the disciples' word.
> Alleluia!

The trouble was, more often than not he felt like an imposter. "This is natural," Reverend Murth, his favorite professor at theological college, had assured him in a long letter just last week. "Be patient, Christian. Soon enough the great burden of pastoral enlightenment will fall on your shoulders, and you will understand how to minister as one who bears in himself the wounds of Christ." So far, Christy couldn't see any signs of it. The gentle shadow of his father followed him everywhere, unintentionally reminding him of who the real vicar of All Saints still was, at least in the minds and hearts of those who had loved him.

Christy fingered the edge of the page of notes he'd folded and slipped inside his Bible. His teachers had frowned on the practice of carrying notes into the pulpit; a sermon should sound spontaneous, they'd decreed, even if the minister had spent hours memorizing it. All very well in theory, but Christy had learned through painful experience that his sermons went on forever when he preached them without notes—and sometimes even with them—and the primary emotion they summoned from his hearers was relief when they were finally over. He was afraid that even his concise, carefully reasoned, most philosophical discourses failed to persuade anyone to change his behavior, much less his mind, at least not for long. The mind was like a pendulum: a forceful sermon might move it from its habitual position, but sooner or later it always swung back into place.

The sound of slow footsteps on stone made him look up. Every head in the church swiveled to watch the couple moving up the center aisle of the nave at a pace that, depending on one's point of view, was either sedate or indifferent. If the Viscount and Viscountess D'Aubrey didn't quite look to the manor born yet, it wasn't, at least on Geoffrey's part, for lack of trying. His new lordship wore an Oxford gray coat and trousers with a bright and no doubt deliberately provocative cornflower-blue waistcoat and a wilting clutch of violets stuck in his buttonhole. He'd worn black to his father's funeral and had warned Christy afterward that it was for the last time. "Better to scandalize the neighbors than play the hypocrite," he'd declared, lips curling in the characteristic sneer Christy was learning to dread.

The neighbors might be scandalized—it didn't take much to

shock the people of Wyckerley—but avid curiosity was the dominant expression on their faces at the moment. Lady D'Aubrey, at least, was in suitable mourning; she wore the same plain black gown she'd worn to the funeral, with the same veiled black hat. Today she'd pinned the veil back, though, as if in defiance of the fascinated stares she must have known she would receive. Her odd, inimitable foreignness was on display again, and Christy attributed it to something more than her rather eccentric jet jewelry or the fact that her clothes looked more European than English. He couldn't define it more precisely than a certain worldliness in her manner, and he felt frustrated because the key to the intriguing essence of her still eluded him.

He broke off from his own worldly speculations, realizing the choir had piped its last alleluia. The members were taking their seats in the chancel and the congregation was training on him those looks of passive expectancy that always unnerved him. The pulpit was an ornate Jacobean affair at the top of four steps, surrounded by a carved mahogany rail; it was impossible not to feel that something special, something beyond the powers of an average human being, was required from anyone with the temerity to mount those steps and face the waiting audience, armed with nothing but a Bible and a handful of scribbled pages.

He chose Corinthians instead of Colossians for the Epistle, and St. Mark's story of the first Easter for the Gospel. The message he wanted to convey in his sermon was a simple, compassionate one, that although faith was a gift that had been given by God to all men, even Christ's disciples were amazed and astonished by his Resurrection, which he had prophesied to them again and again. How understandable, then, that so many people today, who had never known Jesus as a man, lacked true faith in him as the Son of God and the Savior of all mankind. Lack of faith was not a sin in and of itself, he argued, but simply a failing, a misfortune that could be overcome by prayer, perseverance, and God's help. Today was the day we celebrated God's love, the day when the gift of faith was there for the taking.

After half an hour or so, Christy had finished his prepared sermon. But he was reluctant to stop; he hadn't truly touched them yet, hadn't quite said what he really meant. Against everything he knew, including his own better judgment, he began speaking *ex tempore*, repeating earlier points, rephrasing them slightly. He had done this before and knew it was futile, and yet he couldn't bring his sermon to a close until the message of the Resurrection in all its hope and glory had been communicated.

Hopeless. Once again the lesson of diminishing returns had eluded him, for with every sentence, every passing minute, he heard himself falling farther from the goal. At length he summed up, and when he finished, he imagined a silent but unanimous sigh of relief.

His sense of failure weighed on him for the rest of the service. As he consecrated the bread and the wine, though, it came to him that in one way his dismal sermons kept things in proportion: since the Eucharist was the centerpiece of the service—indeed, of the Anglican faith itself—at least his parishioners were in no danger of losing proper perspective due to the brilliance of his oratory.

Fortunately, God in his wisdom had made an Easter morning glorious enough to persuade the sourest skeptic of the truth of the Resurrection. Feather-pillow clouds floated high in an azure sky, and the song of birds in the treetops sounded like the very soul of joy. Shaking hands with his parishioners on the church steps, Christy felt both humbled and relieved, knowing that the petty weaknesses and failings he agonized over every day were actually, in the true scheme of things, utterly insignificant. The Lord had a Plan—on a day like this, it was easy to believe it—and the well-meaning incompetence of one country parson was hardly likely to endanger it.

"Hell of a sermon, Reverend Morrell," Geoffrey told him, the bright gleam in his eye the only indication that he was being facetious. "Your words were an inspiration. I'll go forth and sin no more."

"Then my sacred ministry is a success," Christy returned with the same fatuous solemnity. In church, he'd thought Geoffrey looked healthier than he had a week ago at his father's funeral; but out here in the inconsiderate April sunshine, that proved to be an illusion. His cheekbones stood out like blades in his gaunt face, and the set of his mouth looked pained and unnatural. But he was sober for once, and Christy supposed that was something.

He made a short bow over Lady D'Aubrey's hand and asked how she was settling into her new home.

"Quite well, thank you. Except for the sad circumstances that brought us to Wyckerley, we're extremely pleased with our new situation."

He was certain now that her perfect, friendly propriety was a mask. But what did it conceal? Sadness? Contempt? Smiling politely, she complimented him on his sermon, the altar flowers, the music. When she turned away to speak to Dr. Hesselius, he felt a curious stab of dismay, noticing that she greeted the doctor with exactly the same bland, impenetrable courtesy with which she'd just treated him.

More well-wishers were waiting to shake his hand. He praised Miss Pine and Mrs. Thoroughgood on the beauty of the flowers they'd painstakingly arranged at dawn this morning, and he thanked Sophie Deene for a splendid job with the choir. Tolliver Deene, Sophie's father, invited him to supper next Friday, and he accepted gladly. Tolliver and his brother-in-law, Eustace Vanstone, owned the two largest copper mines in the district. Deene was a thoughtful, educated man, and Christy always enjoyed his company. Pretty Sophie was an agreeable companion, too, not only because she was easy to look at, but because her brand of flirtation was lighthearted and pleasurable, not exhausting.

"Fine sermon today, Vicar," Dr. Hesselius told him with every evidence of sincerity, while he fumbled in his waistcoat pocket for the pipe he'd been longing to smoke for the last hour and a quarter.

Christy smiled and said thanks, recalling the doctor's half-closed eyes and slack jaw toward the end of his discourse. But then, Dr. Hesselius always looked tired. Some people blamed it on too many patients, while others said it was because he'd recently married a woman who was twenty years his junior.

"Oh, yes, indeed," Lily Hesselius agreed, showing her teeth and widening her kohl-black eyes at Christy admiringly. "I don't know when I've heard a more stirring and *invigorating* talk, Reverend Morrell."

Mrs. Ludd, Christy's housekeeper, called young Mrs. Hesselius a brazen hussy. She was from the big city—Exeter—and consequently an alien; her extroverted manner didn't sit well with some of the more reserved residents of St. Giles' parish, and her interest in her husband's friends, perhaps his male friends in particular, had been taken by some for indiscretion—at best. Christy didn't judge; he liked her and was inclined to take her vivacious goodwill at face value.

More pleasantries were exchanged, and then the doctor and his wife moved away. Captain Carnock took their place. "Good talk, Vicar. Lost you there at the part about free will and the cosmology of good and evil, though," he boomed. Captain Carnock was a recent arrival to the neighborhood, only four years or so. "Still, ruddy good show and all. Keeps 'em thinking, what?"

Christy thanked him, taking a half step back from the captain's broad, imposing belly. He wasn't in uniform—he'd retired from the 4th Queen's Own Hussars several years ago—but his military bearing was still so prominent that he gave the impression of being in stripes and brass insignia no matter what he wore. "Mayor Vanstone tells me you'll be joining him on the bench at the next petty session," Christy mentioned.

"Yes, and I know at least one man I've got to thank for it." His homely face broke into a grin and he clapped Christy hard on the arm. "Vanstone told me you put in a word for me with the old viscount before he passed. That smoothed the way, sir, and I appreciate it."

"I told Lord D'Aubrey I thought you'd make a fine magistrate, which is nothing but the truth," he demurred. "It was he who passed your name to the lord lieutenant."

"All the same, I doubt I'd have succeeded without your help."

Christy smiled and shook his head, but said no more. Old D'Aubrey had grown increasingly remote in his advancing years; at a time when the county needed a new justice of the peace, he was too isolated from the people to have any idea as to who might fill the vacancy. Christy knew Captain Carnock to be outspoken, upright, and shrewd, and had merely passed that information along to his lordship before his last illness had incapacitated him completely.

The captain reached for his hat and snatched it off, and Christy turned to see Miss Weedie at his elbow. "Oh, I beg your pardon," she said softly, "I didn't mean to interrupt."

Captain Carnock made her a smart military bow, declaring, "Not at all, dear lady, not at all, we'd finished our talk. Good afternoon to you, Vicar. Ma'am." Bowing again, he pivoted and went down the steps, his back straight as a musket barrel.

For as long as he could remember, Christy had thought of Miss Jessica Weedie as an old maid, even though she couldn't have been any older than he was now when, twenty years or so ago, she'd first taught him his letters in the village school. She was shy and awkward, and filled sometimes with a strange, restless energy; she called herself, with disarming accuracy, "a bit of a mess." It wasn't that she looked particularly spinsterish; in fact, there was still something girlish in her tall, gawky figure, even though her yellow hair had begun to streak with silver. The old maid quality came from an acute reserve of manner and a timidity that intensified around members of the opposite sex. She was blushing now, her smooth cheeks glowing a pretty shade of rose. "I beg your pardon," she repeated, twisting her gloves in her hands. "I only wanted to remind you about our little tea party this afternoon, Reverend."

"I hadn't forgotten for a second."

The blush deepened. She leaned a little closer. "I'm afraid there might be a tiny problem." Christy raised his eyebrows. "My mother and I paid a call on Lady D'Aubrey last week, to welcome her to the neighborhood and so forth. We were just going to leave our cards and go away, but she invited us in, and we had quite the most wonderful chat. And then—I don't quite know what came over her, but Mother invited Lady D'Aubrey to tea. And—she said yes!" Christy said that was interesting news. "Yes, yes," she agreed distractedly, "it was very kind and condescending of her, I'm sure. Mother actually invited *Lord* D'Aubrey as well, but he can't come. He says he has business to conduct."

"On the Sabbath?" Christy exclaimed, making a shocked face. "I'm joking," he assured her when her eyes went wide as saucers; he'd forgotten that Miss Weedie took every word he said—or anyone else said, for that matter—in complete earnest. She smiled with embarrassed relief. "But I don't understand," he confessed. "What exactly is the problem?"

She moved an inch closer; her soft voice dropped a note lower. "Mother"—she made an infinitesimal movement of her head—"has just invited Mayor Vanstone and Miss Vanstone to join us!"

"Oh?"

"Now I'm not sure what to do. Miss Pine and Mrs. Thoroughgood would stay away if I asked them, but I don't like to."

"No, of course not." Miss Pine and Mrs. Thoroughgood were her two best friends. Christy frowned, at a loss. He bent over her solicitously. "And so—?"

"It's just—it's just that—oh, I'm afraid there's not going to be enough to eat," she blurted out in a rush.

He had to stop himself from smiling; he'd expected a much worse catastrophe than this. "I'm sure there's nothing to worry about."

"If it were anyone but Miss Vanstone, I wouldn't be concerned. But you know what she's like, she's always—" She broke off, mortified. "Oh, goodness—I didn't mean that unkindly, I do assure you! Why, I've nothing but the highest regard for Miss Vanstone, a woman of great substance and rectitude, really quite an asset to any gathering, and certainly a most honored guest in my mother's house at any time—"

He took pity on her and interrupted, even though he was interested in knowing how many more virtues the good Miss Weedie, given her head, would have attributed to Honoria Vanstone. "Set your mind at rest," he said consolingly. "I promise I won't eat a thing—"

"Oh, *no*—"

"—because Mrs. Ludd will make me a nice sandwich while I'm changing clothes. I'll have it just before I leave for your house."

"Oh, dear, oh, dear . . ."

"And if things get really sticky, we'll tell Lady D'Aubrey to lay off the sponge cake. A *joke*," he said hastily when Miss Weedie went white. "Don't worry," he repeated, patting her arm, "your party will be a great success, I'm sure. How could it fail to be with two such kind and cordial hostesses?"

She smiled with pleasure—it was pathetically easy to please Miss Weedie—and pressed her fingers over his in a quick, grateful squeeze. "Bless you, Reverend. I know I'm a silly old woman." He opened his mouth to deny it, but she said, "I'd better go," and started to turn away. "Before Mother invites anyone else," she threw over her shoulder softly. Christy looked for a sign that she was teasing, but couldn't see one.

Residents of Wyckerley liked to boast that no two houses in the village looked alike. Certainly the cottages in Hobby Lane, where the Weedies lived, bore only a passing resemblance to each other. Some were granite, a few were brick; some had slate roofs, others were colorfully thatched with Dartmoor heather. Many were of sturdy Devon cob but varied widely—some might say wildly—in the color the householder had chosen: buff-washed, blinding white, pink, pale green, gray-blue. Primrose Cottage, the Weedies' little house, had been painted crocus yellow in 1834, the last year of the late Mr. Weedie's life. In the intervening twenty years it had dimmed and mellowed through stages of saffron, lemon, and flax, and now it glowed a soft, creamy shade of dusty gold, as faded and gentle as the two ladies who lived inside its flaking walls.

Christy turned in at the gap in the trim hedges and started up the cinder path to the door. Bees buzzed among the columbine and blue forget-me-nots in the carefully tended garden, and the mild air was sweet with the odor of wallflowers. Violets and primroses tumbled from window boxes and clay pots set back from the path. The old thatch on the gables and jutting eaves of the cottage roof sprouted reeds and emerald-green mosses, and draped the upstairs dormer windows in graceful curves, like a woman's bonnet. Christy heard voices through the open front door; they broke off when he entered, ducking his head in the low doorway.

"Reverend Morrell!" Miss Weedie hurried toward him, both hands extended in welcome—as if they hadn't spoken barely an hour ago. He saw relief in her face, and deduced that entertaining the Vanstones single-handedly had become something of a strain. But she wasn't alone, he saw at a glance: her mother was sitting in her usual place in the inglenook, peering shortsightedly and smiling at him; and Miss Pine and Mrs. Thoroughgood, the Weedies' constant companions, were puttering around the tea table, trying to make themselves useful. They stopped puttering long enough to greet him. Eustace Vanstone was standing beside the window, looking dignified and mayoral with his legs spread, hands clasped behind his back. He greeted Christy with one of his hearty professional handshakes, but his first words sounded peevish. "I heard D'Aubrey's not coming."

"No, he had some business to attend to, I gather," Christy confirmed. The mayor scowled, and Christy suspected he was feeling duped. Instead of a golden opportunity to ingratiate himself with the new heir, his new patron, the man to whom he would now be in debt for every political favor that came his way, he was obliged to waste an entire afternoon being polite to a roomful of women (Christy excepted), with no one worth trying to impress except Lady D'Aubrey, a poor substitute for her now powerful husband.

"Yes, I believe he had business to discuss with Mr. Deene," Miss Weedie said helpfully. That reminded her— "Your niece did a wonderful job with the children's choir today, Mayor. They sounded like angels, everyone said—"

"Geoffrey's talking to Tolliver?" Vanstone interrupted sharply. "What about?"

"Why, I have no idea," she faltered, realizing belatedly that she'd added insult to injury by revealing that the absent viscount was at this moment conducting business with the mayor's brother-in-law. Deene and Vanstone might be friends, but it was no secret that they were also rivals.

"Miss Vanstone, you're looking well," Christy put in for a diversion, taking the mayor's daughter's limp hand and bowing over it. Honoria didn't get up from her padded wing chair, the seat of honor in the small, cramped parlor, and he wondered whether she would relinquish it when the real guest of honor arrived. He doubted that she had ever set foot in the Weedies' modest cottage before, or that she would have now if the new viscountess weren't coming.

"Good afternoon, Vicar," she said, batting her dark eyelashes. At twenty-six, Honoria was skating perilously close to the thin ice of permanent spinsterhood, and the knowledge didn't agree with her. Lately a look of discontent had begun to settle in her sharp features, souring an aspect that before had merely seemed tart. Close in age, they had been "Honoria" and "Christy" in their careless youth, acquaintances and schoolmates if not friends. Sometime between his departure for theological college and his appointment to the benefice of All Saints Church, though, they'd retreated from first-name familiarity and grown formal with each other. Which was ironic, Christy thought, considering that Honoria, unless he was grossly mistaken, had romantic designs on him.

He sat down in a rush-bottomed chair that looked familiar— he thought it belonged to Mrs. Thoroughgood, who lived across the street—and set about making himself agreeable to the decidedly mixed group the Weedies had invited, out of innocent good faith, to their home. Once Lady D'Aubrey arrived, it would undoubtedly become even *more* mixed, but everyone stole glances at the noisy eight-day clock on the mantelshelf anyway, impatient for her arrival.

At three o'clock she still hadn't come, and the brilliance of the conversation had definitely dimmed. Christy had exhausted his store of ministerial chitchat and listened to all the opinions Mayor Vanstone had about the war with Russia to which a man ought to have to listen on Easter Sunday. Miss Weedie was in an agony of indecision over whether to pour the tea now, out of deference to the important guests she already had, or continue waiting for the most important guest and risk offending all the others.

It didn't help that her mother, whose mind wasn't as sharp as it had been, kept asking from the inglenook, "Is it time, Jessie? Why don't you pour out now, dear?"

At half past three, quick footsteps sounded on the cinder path, and seven heads turned as one toward the door. Pink-cheeked and windblown, carrying her hat in her hand, Lady D'Aubrey stepped over the threshold, giving the open door a humorous little rap with her knuckles. "I beg your pardon," she said breathlessly to the group at large, "I'm most terribly sorry for being late. You'll think me extremely foolish, but the truth is—I've been lost!"

Everyone stood up and exclaimed in astonishment and concern; Miss Weedie apologized, as if her ladyship's misfortune were her fault.

"I was ready to come at half past one—much too early—and so I decided to go for a walk. I'm still not quite sure how I did it, but somehow I ended up at a sort of canal, I think, only it was abandoned, the water stagnant and weed-choked. A most melancholy place, but—beautiful, you know, with reeds and wild-flowers and—" She broke off with a little grimace, as if telling herself to stop talking. Christy had never heard her say so much at one go before, and realized she was flustered. She looked very young and almost carefree, for once, with her reddish hair awry, her fringed black shawl dangling rakishly from one shoulder.

Honoria took it upon herself to explain that she must have walked south and stumbled upon the northern tributary of the Plym, used for barge traffic to and from Devonport years ago, but silted over now and abandoned. Her ladyship said she thought that was very likely it, and then Miss Weedie, with an air of fearful bravery, plunged into the formidable social task of introducing her to everyone.

She accomplished it flawlessly, and everybody sat down, Anne in Honoria's old chair at Miss Weedie's insistence. An awkward silence ensued. Eustace Vanstone, who had met Lady D'Aubrey at her father-in-law's funeral, began to say grave and ponderous things about the honor her presence brought to their humble little community, the regrettably long time it had been since a lady had graced the manorial hall, particularly one as charming as she, and so on and so forth. Her ladyship murmured suitable things back.

Honoria said it was wonderful to have Geoffrey home again. "Oh—I mean Lord D'Aubrey," she corrected herself with a self-conscious simper. "*That* will take a bit of getting used to, won't it?"

"You and Geoffrey were friends, then, before he went away?" Anne inquired politely.

"Oh, yes, certainly. I was a little younger than he, of course, but one never forgets the friends of one's childhood."

This was news. Honoria had been about thirteen when Geoffrey had run away for good, and Christy knew for a fact that they'd never been anything at all to each other, much less friends. He recalled a conversation with Honoria a few weeks ago, when she'd pressed him for information on Geoffrey's whereabouts. Naturally he hadn't told her about his unanswered letters to the London address, but Honoria had learned a great deal about Wyckerley's prodigal son via the uncannily accurate village grapevine. "I hear he's cavorting in London without a care in the world," she'd tsked, "while his father lies at death's door. I for one think it's absolutely shocking." Today she seemed to have gotten over the shock, and the new viscount, notwithstanding a great *cavorter*, was clearly an acquaintance she was ready to acknowledge.

"Do tell us what Geoffrey's been doing for the last twelve years," she invited, leaning toward Anne confidentially. "We hear such *odd* things."

"Well, you know, he's been active in the military."

"Oh, yes. As a captain, I believe?"

"Yes, until he gave up his commission last year due to an illness."

Honoria waited for her to elaborate. She didn't. "I believe I heard that he served in Africa," she went on after a pause.

"Yes, although that was before we met."

"And in Burma, I think?"

"Yes. And India, and New Zealand," she added in a dry tone.

"My goodness! How fortunate we are to have such a *patriotic* Englishman for our new lord," Honoria smirked. "Do you have family in England, my lady?" she inquired next.

"No, I've no family. My father died shortly after Geoffrey and I were married."

"I'm so sorry. And that was—?"

"Four years ago."

"Ah, I see. And so, when Geoffrey—his lordship; I *do* beg your pardon—when his lordship was away in India or Africa or wherever it might have been, you stayed in England quite alone?"

The other ladies shifted and cleared their throats, uncomfortable with Honoria's bold prying. "Quite," Anne answered, looking at her directly. "I lived in London, by myself, in our house." The arch of one sleek eyebrow asked as eloquently as words, *Is there anything else you'd like to know?*

Honoria colored slightly and closed her lips.

Tea was served. Miss Weedie poured while Tabby, the housemaid the Weedies shared with Miss Pine, passed cups and saucers. "She's not what you might call a *treasure*," Christy recalled Miss Weedie confiding in him once, "but she does try." Lady D'Aubrey was given a tiny table from which to take her tea, while the others made do with plates on their laps. The cream toasts and green pea pie occupied everyone for a few minutes, so that the lulls in the conversation weren't uncomfortable, but soon afterward the silences grew awkward again. The Weedies and Miss Pine were clearly overwhelmed by the eminence of their guest, and even Mrs. Thoroughgood, normally a hard woman to dissuade from sharing her voluble opinions, seemed too intimidated to initiate a subject. Christy was about to introduce some innocuous topic when Anne herself broke another nerve-wracking pause.

"Tell me about Wyckerley," she said, aiming the question at her hostess. "Have you lived here always?"

"Oh, yes," Miss Weedie answered brightly. "I was born in this house, and so was my father. Mother's the foreigner: she came from Mare's Head."

"That's the next village over," Mrs. Thoroughgood put in, passing her empty plate to Tabby. "My husband was a foreigner too, from Crediton; that's on the other side of the moor. He passed away some years ago."

"I was born here," Miss Pine worked up the courage to say, "and so were my parents." She was a small, dark, wrinkled old woman with nervous hands and intense black eyes. She lived in two rooms in her own small cottage and rented the other two out to boarders.

"We're all great friends," Mrs. Weedie said unexpectedly from the inglenook. "How long have you and I known each other, Miss Pine?"

"Fifty-one years, Mrs. Weedie. We met the day you came to Wyckerley to marry Mr. Weedie."

Mrs. Thoroughgood was warming up. "Oh, yes, we're great friends, all four of us. Jessica's the baby, we like to say." Miss Weedie bowed her head in acknowledgment. "We meet in one of our houses at least three afternoons a week, rain or shine, for tea or sewing, or just a nice gossip. I don't believe we've missed a day in ten years."

"Why, we missed the third and the fifth of February in fifty-two," Miss Pine corrected timidly. "Don't you remember? Jessie had the grippe, and we were afraid we'd all catch it."

The ladies nodded and laughed gently, their affection for each other obvious. What Mrs. Thoroughgood hadn't mentioned, Christy thought to himself, was that all four of them were as poor as churchmice, getting by on the minuscule livings and stipends left by their various male relatives. Constrained by good manners, fiercely proud of their independence, there was only one subject they never discussed at their thrice-weekly gatherings: money.

"Will you do any renovations to the Hall, do you think?" Honoria broke in, bored and wanting attention. "Lord D'Aubrey—the new lord's father, that is—invited Papa and me to tea last Christmas," she continued, with an air of satisfaction that came from knowing that no one else in the room except Reverend Morrell could make *that* claim. "I must say, I couldn't help noticing how . . . how . . ." She stumbled as an idea of where her tactlessness was leading finally dawned on her.

"How run-down the place is," Anne finished for her, smiling faintly. "It's true, the viscount's first priority doesn't seem to have been domestic comfort. My husband and I haven't discussed any changes to the house yet. From what Mr. Holyoake tells me, there are many things that need tending to more urgently than the Hall."

That was Mayor Vanstone's cue to fill her ear with a recitation of as many improvements and pet projects for the district as the social nature of the occasion permitted. While he spoke, Christy studied Anne over the rim of his cup, trying to fathom exactly what it was about her that intrigued him so. Geoffrey had told him that she'd lived much of her life in Italy, where her father had made a modest living as a painter. That made sense: her accent was British and so was her roses-and-cream complexion, now that she'd lost what he thought of as her city pallor; but everything else about her was emphatically un-English, from her dress to her hair to the way she listened when someone spoke to her—alertly, directly, without affectation or excessive demureness. The clothes she wore were respectable but a trifle odd, a little off, not quite what Christy imagined was the fashion in London nowadays, and she wore them with a careless panache that fit with his—perhaps naive—image of impoverished bohemianism on the Continent. For that and a number of other reasons, he couldn't get over how little she resembled his idea of any woman Geoffrey would have married.

Did they love each other? His curiosity was inexplicably strong, stronger even than the tense, ambiguous atmosphere he'd observed between them warranted. Geoffrey, for all that Christy had loved him, had never struck him as a deep man, or even a particularly thoughtful man, and his adult career as a perennial soldier had surprised everyone in Wyckerley except Christy. And although they'd parted when they were only sixteen, Geoffrey's predilection for coarse, undemanding women was already well established. Unless he'd radically changed, his choice of Anne Verlaine for a wife made no sense. She was lovely, yes, but subtly so, and her sexuality was anything—everything—but overt. Her social smiles were frequent and reassuring, but she never laughed, never; in fact, the longer Christy knew her, the more unthinkable it became to imagine her gay or exuberant, playful or silly, convulsed with helpless hilarity. "Tragic" was too strong a word to describe the fine, elusive essence of her—he hoped; yet beneath her limitless composure he sensed the soul-sick desperation of a life gone out of control.

Mrs. Thoroughgood was speaking to him. "I say, have you given Lady D'Aubrey a tour of the church yet, Vicar?" He said that he hadn't. "It dates from Norman times, you know," she told Anne, whose interest appeared genuine. "You can see the Norman influence in the chancel arch and the carvings on the pillars, but most of the rest was added later."

"Our village was named by the Saxons in the seventh century," Miss Pine said softly. "We've been invaded by the Celts, the Romans, the Saxons, and the Normans."

"'Wic' is Old English for hamlet," Mrs. Thoroughgood contributed. "Reverend Morrell must take you through the rectory as well. It's a lovely old house, as fine as any of its kind in England."

"Elizabethan," Miss Pine chimed in.

"I look forward to it," said her ladyship, smiling across at Christy.

Old Mrs. Weedie, who had been following the conversation only intermittently, got up suddenly from her place by the fireplace and sidled toward the door to the scullery. On the way, her hand grazed Christy's shoulder, and he thought she murmured, "Follow me." Her surreptitious tone prompted him to stay seated until Honoria launched a new topic, the sad state in which the old lord had left the once-beautiful gardens at Lynton Great Hall. Then, as inconspicuously as possible, he got up and followed Mrs. Weedie into the passage.

She was already at the far end of the pantry, bending over the shelves, running her hand along the stacked foodstuffs and crockery. The frail curve of her back made him think of the time, not so long ago, when she had been tall and upright, a vigorous, no-nonsense woman. Now, every day, she depended more and more on her self-effacing daughter, and the change frightened both of them.

"Here it is." She pulled a folded piece of paper out from between two flour bags. "If you mail it, it'll get there," she told him, pushing the paper into his hands, her eyes gleaming with the thrill of conspiracy.

He looked down and saw the name "Robert James Weedie" scrawled on the outer fold, but no address. Perplexed, he asked, "Who is it?"

"*My son,*" she said in a fierce whisper. "I've never written to him before. I was wrong not to. They need guidance at that age. Bobby—"

"Mother?" The casual trilling note in her voice couldn't disguise Miss Weedie's anxiety.

The old lady put her finger to her lips and pressed the letter in Christy's hand to his waistcoat. "Put it away and don't tell Jessie," she warned. "She disapproves. More tea, Vicar?" she asked in her normal voice, ushering him past her daughter in the narrow passage without looking at her.

Christy only had time to give Miss Weedie a reassuring smile and a quick shake of the head. Later, he would decide whether she needed to know that her mother was writing letters to a son who had been dead for thirty years.

Shortly after that, Lady D'Aubrey said she had better be going. Everyone stood up. Amid the thanks and farewells, Christy surprised himself by asking if he might walk back with her to the Hall. She thanked him and said she would like that very much.

V

16 April—Easter Sunday

Reverend Morrell is the first clergyman I've known—not that I've known very many—who listens more than he talks. I think he has no idea of the effect he has on people when he does speak, either—another appealing quality. It's fascinating to watch the faces of the four old ladies (I call them that, and it's not fair; Miss Weedie is not old) when they look at him; they listen intently, hanging on every word he utters. It's no wonder they love him, he is so very kind to them. He told me a little of their history as he walked home with me this afternoon, and the very real affection he has for them shone in his face like a soft light. I like them, too—who would not? Particularly Miss Weedie—Jessica. She's a gentle woman, nervous and high-strung, anxious to please. I can't help wondering if she ever had hopes of something more than the companionship of women and the satisfactions of self-sacrifice. If so, she seems to have forgotten them. And if she's lonely, she's much too well-bred to let it show.

But I don't think she will be my friend. She and the others will maintain the social gap they think is between us, in spite of anything I could do to bridge it. The irony is that it's a false gap, this peeress-commoner nonsense.

The *real* gap is even wider; it's the one that separates goodness and simplicity (theirs) from emptiness and ennui (mine).

Honoria Vanstone, on the other hand, would be my friend in a minute if I wanted her to be. But alas, I can't like her. She reminds me of a mistress Papa had in Aix-en-Provence—Mademoiselle Bected was her name. Bected the Affected, I called her. Miss Vanstone might be slightly less insincere, but I doubt she's any less ambitious. Reverend Morrell would probably find excuses for her, mitigating influences such as her self-important father, or the lack of strong female guidance—but I am not nearly so charitable. I see a stiff-necked, humorless woman who dislikes and distrusts me even while she tries to ingratiate herself with me. Perhaps being Lady D'Aubrey won't be quite so tiring after all if it means I can lord it occasionally over the likes of Honoria Vanstone.

Now, that's a petty notion. What would the Archangel think if he knew I harbored such mean sentiments toward one of his flock? He watches me when he believes I'm not looking. I can't begin to imagine what he thinks of me, what kind of woman he's decided I am. Fallen? Lost? In need of saving? All of those, I suppose, and too far gone even for the best efforts of the very Reverend Morrell.

I must call him Christy, he says. His coloring is so fair, I always know when he's blushing. He has a big, strong-boned head, almost bust-like, and fine silver-blue eyes, gentle, not cold, in spite of their icy color. A good-humored mouth, very expressive. I see tolerance in his face, a deep sympathy for other people's pain and uncertainty. And he's the opposite of pompous. He strikes me as a man who could forgive anything in others, perhaps not as much in himself. Today he made me think of Rubens' painting *Daniel in the Lion's Den*. Only it's not Daniel he looks like, it's the lion in the middle, the standing one with the gorgeous mane and the fierce but worried look in his yellow eyes.

In church, giving his interminable sermon, he was so very earnest, so heartbreakingly sincere, I felt almost like weeping. Most unusual, not like me at all; I still can't quite account for it. And no doubt I would have been crying for myself, not him. I wonder what he would think if I told him the truth: that I have no religious faith at all, that his God is as apocryphal to me as Zeus or Apollo are to him. Would he try to convert me? What an amusing prospect. There was a mesmerist in Papa's artist circle one summer in Aix who attempted to hypnotize me, but without success; I remained disappointingly wide awake and rational. As I would, I'm afraid, if Reverend Morrell tried his Anglican catechism on me.

Too bad. Faith in God must be a very comforting thing. A merciful analgesic. A painkiller for the soul. Yes, it's too bad.

5 May

They delivered Geoffrey's horse today. He calls it Devil, even though it came with another name; Cupcake, for all I know. At any rate, Devil is a black stallion with a white blaze on its nose and two white socks. He's "a real cracker," and racing him against Reverend Morrell's horse has become Geoffrey's latest idée fixe. Are ministers allowed to run in horse races? Probably not; too worldly, I should think.

Geoffrey's captain's commission hasn't come yet (which is why he has time on his hands to entice innocent clergymen into sinful pursuits). The English army hasn't fought in a real war in thirty years, and the men at the top, says

Geoffrey, are all doddering veterans of the Peninsula. In my (unspoken) opinion, that's to his advantage, since I can imagine only senile old men allowing him into their ranks during wartime. But he looks better lately, and he isn't drinking so much. I suppose he's a good soldier when he's healthy. God knows he loves it; the only time he seems truly alive is when he's recounting the gory particulars of some battle he's fought. So I watch the mail as anxiously as he does, and offer consolation when he's disappointed. Better that only *one* of us is completely miserable, after all, and for now Geoffrey has a better chance than I of climbing out of this hell we call our life together.

Sorry for myself today. Unattractive quality. I shall try to do better.

Mr. Holyoake is beginning to get an inkling that the new lord of the manor may not be the radical improvement over the old that he'd hoped for. Poor Geoffrey: he comes ill-equipped to manage twenty thousand acres of corn, cattle, sheep, and apple orchard, not to mention the men and women who labor on the land for him. What's really needed here is a sort of working viscount, something between a peer and a squire—but alas, that man isn't Geoffrey. At first Mr. Holyoake, in his innocence, came to him with questions about steam threshers and zigzag harrows, crop rotations and imported proteins to fatten the stock. He comes no more, the futility of it having been borne in on him rather forcefully the afternoon Geoffrey passed out while he was speaking. Now (unfortunate man!) he actually directs his questions to *me*—questions about whether we can afford a new corn dresser or if the dairy parlor needs a new roof, how much to ask for our oats at the Corn Market next month. I listen to his slow, measured opinions, pretend to weigh them, and then agree with him. It's a polite fiction we uphold religiously, and then we part ways with identically furrowed brows and, I don't doubt, troubled minds.

In spite of my crushing ignorance, I find myself unexpectedly delighted with the beauty of this countryside, the rural peacefulness, the wary kindness of the villagers. I've lived in pastoral settings before, but never so intimately; I was a visitor, my father's daughter, and ironically, his painting distanced me further by making the countryside *other*, an object to be studied and measured and then *rendered* in oils or pastels. But here I am, in a sense, of the land, even a caretaker of it (albeit a spectacularly stupid one), and when I'm not quaking with fear of the responsibility for it, I feel strangely exhilarated. Oh, I shall make an abysmal lady of the manor if—when—Geoffrey goes away and leaves me alone! And yet I'm almost looking forward to it. By default, I will be the only one with responsibility for this sprawling country fiefdom. That thought terrifies me; if I believed in God I would be on my knees, praying for strength and guidance. Well, well, I will simply do my best, and hope I don't bring plague and famine down on these good people.

Mayor Eustace Vanstone paid us a visit yesterday. He reminds me of a sleek gray fox with his silvery hair and bony, ascetic face, his cheekbones as sharp as knives. He is a perfect politician, and if he has his sights set on higher game than mayor and local magistrate, I would not be at all surprised. I enjoy watching him flatter Geoffrey, while he runs his thumb and forefinger down the two ends of the elegant mustache that overhangs his upper lip. He ruled Wyckerley, I gather, when the old viscount, for all intents and purposes, abdicated, and now he fears being displaced by the new regime. A groundless fear, as he'll soon discover, but in the meantime it's amusing to . . .

A STEP ON the stair, heavier than Violet's or Susan's, made Anne look up from her writing desk and listen, her muscles tense, fingers whitening around her pen.

"Anne? You up there?" Geoffrey's voice from the landing sounded querulous.

She reached for a clean sheet of paper and slid it over the one she'd been writing on. "I'm here," she called back, and a moment later Geoffrey appeared in the doorway. He wore riding clothes and he smelled of horse and sweat. He had a drink in his hand, but she couldn't tell if he was drunk.

"So," he greeted her, thin lips curling in his mocking smile. "This is where you've been hiding."

She slumped a little, and draped an apparently negligent wrist over the arm of her chair. She didn't answer.

He walked to the south window and peered out, straightened, went to the fireplace mantel, trailed a finger across the line of books she'd put there. She recognized his mood from his movements. He was restless and bored. When he was bored, he could be dangerous.

"I want you to invite Christy Morrell for supper," he said abruptly, coming to a halt in front of her.

"When? You mean tonight?"

"Yes, why not? Send him a note, ask him to come."

She regarded him in silence for a few seconds. "Very well," she said slowly. "It's short notice; he may not come."

"I know that," he snapped. "Invite him anyway. I feel like seeing him."

His voice had a cranky, childish tone that was relatively new; he'd begun using it about the time they'd left London, she recalled. She wondered if he could hear it himself. He'd put on more weight in the last week or so; in fact, he ate like a starving man at the few meals they shared together, stuffing food into his mouth until he almost choked. Making sure her voice stayed flat and neutral, she asked, "Geoffrey, are you still taking your medicine?"

Instead of answering, he started humming. Something soft and tuneless; it sounded like a nursery rhyme. He walked around until he was behind the chair. She didn't move. "The little blue pills and the little gray pills," he said in a soft, singsong voice. The chair shifted a fraction as he leaned his weight against it. "What are you writing?"

She looked down and saw that she'd nearly covered the blank page with X's, black and militant-looking, hostile as an iron fence. "Nothing. I'm not writing anything." At the moment she felt his hand on her hair, she stood up. Papers fluttered; her little writing desk clattered to the floor. She flushed with embarrassment, but her heart wouldn't stop pounding. Geoffrey's dark eyes searched her face. He tried to smile. When she saw his lips tremble, she had to turn away.

Beyond the west window, a fiery orange sun was sliding toward the dark treetops. The lonely colors of the sky, opal and shell-pink over shadow-black oak leaves, made her chest ache. She closed her eyes and gripped the hard edge of the casement as the old misery welled up inside, familiar as a favorite nightmare. When she opened her eyes, she saw that Geoffrey was beside her. Controlling an involuntary start, she turned to him and stared straight ahead, just over his left shoulder.

His dark eyes were either gentle or hopeless, she couldn't tell which. "Anne," he said on a tired sigh. "Do you know what you look like, here with the sun on your hair?" She made no answer. "I thought you were pretty when we first met. Thank God, I thought, at least she's not a hedgehog."

She tried to laugh, but couldn't manage it.

"You've changed since then. Bloody unfair of you, darling.

You're not pretty anymore. You're beautiful." She heard him swallow, and kept her eyes off his face. "Your hair . . . you know, I always loved your hair. It's the color of poppies, red and gold, and the sun's made a halo around it."

She whispered, "Don't."

"I can remember how your skin feels. Even softer than it looks. When I touched you—" He lifted his hand.

She flinched as if he'd struck her.

The wistfulness in his eyes vanished. Both hands came up and clamped down hard on her shoulders. "Damn you," he whispered, and pushed her back against the wall. Her head struck the sharp window frame; she cried out. He covered her breasts with his hands and kneaded them hurtfully, cursing her, mashing her with his body against the wall. "You're my wife, my wife," he kept saying, while she pulled at his wrists and struggled against him. He moved one hand to the back of her neck and yanked her head back by the hair. His breath was foul—when he kissed her, she gagged.

He let go of her at once. She saw the hurt and horror in his face before she could mask her revulsion.

"I'm sorry," they said at the same instant.

She reached for him, but he jerked back, and she remembered that her pity was the thing he despised about her the most.

She stood motionless while the sound of his footsteps on the stairs faded and silence seeped back into the room. Her eyes darted to the shadowy corners, searching out comfort from the familiar: her sewing basket on the table, the frayed green and blue rug she'd brought from London, her father's watercolor self-portrait on the wall, the jar of daffodils she'd picked this morning. She'd taken to talking to herself lately. She said aloud now, "It's still mine," and wrapped her arms around herself when her voice came out high and frightened. "He didn't spoil it," she whispered. "My sanctuary. Mine."

To prove it, she gathered the scattered papers from the floor and stacked them neatly in her writing case. She resumed her seat. With a hand that shook only a little, she wrote a note to Reverend Morrell, inviting him to dinner.

VI

"... JESUS DOES NOT offer us a doctrine. He offers love, and love allows us to see beyond death. For death is nothing but a horizon, and a horizon is nothing but the limit of our vision. Love helps us see beyond the visible to the invisible, and to feel—"

"Reverend Morrell, Charlie's touching me with his foot."

Christy didn't look up from the sermon he was trying to write. "You boys only have five minutes left to complete your essays," he said in his schoolmaster voice. He crossed out "and to feel" and wrote, "to the very source of its counterpart, God's love for us."

"Reverend Morrell, Charlie's shaking the table."

He closed his eyes briefly and laid his pen down. He took out his watch, the old pinchbeck repeater his father had given him on his twentieth birthday. Before he could open it, it chimed five times, and immediately Charles and Walter Wooten slapped their books shut and scraped back their chairs.

"Have you finished?" Christy asked, eyeing the ink-stained papers they slid onto a corner of his desk.

"Yes, sir," they assured him, fidgeting, eager to be off. Charles was thirteen; his brother Walter was twelve. In another year they would go off to school in Exeter. That is, if Christy's twice-weekly tutoring in Latin, geography, and mathematics had the desired effect. They were normal, decent boys, neither bad nor brilliant; he liked them, but he might have forgone the lukewarm thrill of tutoring them had he not needed the extra three pounds a month Mr. and Mrs. Wooten paid him for the privilege.

"What's your assignment for Monday?" he quizzed them. "Walter?"

"To finish the *Aeneid* and write a page on Mezentius and Lausus."

"Charles?"

"To finish the *Aeneid* and write two pages on Nisus and Euryalus."

"Correct. All right, you may go now. *Walking*, not running. And don't forget your Sunday school assignments!"

They called back a glib promise in unison and disappeared down the hall. He heard Mrs. Ludd admonishing them for some new infraction, then the slamming of the door, and finally blessed silence. He took up his pen. "Faith is living with an emotional acceptance of those things to which we give intellectual assent—by acting as we believe. As we believe, so we become. With faith in life, life becomes more worthy of faith. With faith in ourselves, we accept ourselves more readily. With faith in God, we can feel more at home in the universe. Human doubts—"

"Warden Nineways is here to see you, Vicar."

He looked up sharply. "What? But this is Friday," he protested. "This isn't our day to meet."

Mrs. Ludd folded her arms, unimpressed. "Well, he's here all the same. Got his big book under his arm, looking like Saint Peter at the gate. Shall I fetch him in, then?"

Christy put his head in both hands and pressed hard, as if he could squeeze the exasperation out of it. When he looked up, his housekeeper was still there, bland-faced, waiting for his answer. "Yes, of course," he grumbled, "show him in. Don't bring him any tea, though, or he'll just stay longer."

She smirked. "Forgot to tell you—Swan sisters stopped by while you was with Wootens." Christy groaned, and the smirk widened to a grin. "Don't you want to know what it was this time?"

"No." He took a moment to tidy his desk. "All right, what?" he grumped, humoring her.

"Little doilies they made with their own two hands, cunningest things you ever did see. Said they're for going over all the chair arms in your study. I told 'em you'd be thrilled pink, an'd probably want more."

"How thoughtful," Christy said, rolling his eyes. His housekeeper got immoderate glee out of the ingenious campaigns of his female parishioners, who were bent on convincing him that his living arrangements were inadequate and what he really needed was a sturdy, doily-making wife.

Chortling, Mrs. Ludd went out to fetch the churchwarden.

Thomas Nineways was a small, round, deceptively mildlooking man who took his duties as warden of All Saints Church with deadly seriousness. A right-facing cast in his right eye was responsible in part, but not completely, for his unfortunate resemblance to a frog, a circumstance in which a small proportion of the congregation—generally young boys under the age of thirteen—took enormous and uncharitable delight. Entering the study, he put his bulky church ledger on the edge of Christy's desk and sat down in the chair he offered. "Before we go over the book entries for last week, there's a little matter of business I'd like to discuss with you, Reverend," he said portentously.

"Certainly." Christy hoped the matter wasn't the restoration fund for the Saint Catherine window. Subscriptions were lagging, and Thomas was upset. He honestly couldn't understand why people didn't care much about refurbishing two stainedglass depictions, side by side, of Saint Catherine being broken on the wheel and beheaded.

"Two things, actually. First, about Maundy Thursday."

"What about it?"

"Some members of the vestry have expressed an interest in reviving the tradition of feet washing."

Christy set down the pen he'd been fiddling with. "In what?"

"Feet washing. It used to be done on the Thursday before Easter to commemorate the new *mandatum,* or commandment, Christ gave his disciples at the Last Supper."

"Yes, but that was—"

"It flourished until the time of William III, who didn't care for the practice."

"No, and personally—"

"Some of us think it's time to revive it. Only among the men, of course; we don't think it would be seemly among the women."

Christy had a vision of bare-legged parishioners sitting on the altar rail, washing each other's feet. "Who in the vestry is calling for this, ah, innovation, Thomas?"

"Oh, a number, quite a number, growing all the time."

"Yes, but who, exactly?" *It's nobody but you and Brakey Pitt. Admit it,* he thought crossly.

"Well, Brakey Pitt's one. He's the most vocal, you might say. There's others too, but they're more reticent, like."

I'll bet. "Well, Thomas, I can say that I'll definitely give it some thought. Is that all?"

"No, it isn't," he said severely. "The second thing is the matter of Tranter Fox. I have it on good authority that he was inebriated in public last Saturday night."

"Was he? I didn't think Tranter was much of a drinking man. What was the occasion?"

"I'm sure I couldn't say. The point is, it was after midnight, so it was the Sabbath, and some people are wanting to know what you're going to do about it."

"What *I'm* going to do about it?"

He nodded vigorously. "You're the vicar."

"That's true. I'm not the constable."

"But it's a violation of ecclesiastical law to be disorderly on the Sabbath," Thomas insisted. "And that's not all. At Easter service, I had to get up three times and wake the man up out of a sound sleep."

"Not during the sermon, I trust."

The warden didn't crack a smile. "I know your habit of leniency in matters like this, Vicar," he said with heavy disapproval, "so I don't expect you to take action. I'm just bringing it to your attention. That's my duty, and I try never to shirk my duty."

Christy rubbed his eyes. "You're a conscientious man, Thomas, and that's a fine quality in a warden of the church. Let me ask you something. Before Easter, when was the last time you saw Tranter Fox at a Sunday service?"

Nineways ran a hand over his iron-gray hair, which he wore in a short, bristling crop. "I'm not sure. A month or two ago? I can't exactly call to mind—"

"It was Christmas Eve."

"Christmas Eve! Well, there you are, aren't you? If that doesn't just go to show—"

"And you know I've been trying for over a year to get Tranter to come to services more often. Now, Thomas," he said reasonably, "do you really think I should reprimand him the first time he sets foot in the church after staying away for four months?"

The warden tried to look thoughtful, as if he were considering the question. But Christy suspected that what he'd really like to see was some good old-fashioned justice, with Tranter chained up in the stocks and pelted with fruit by irate villagers. "I'm sure I can't say about that one way or the other," he begrudged at last. "I just think it bears watching. That's all I'll say, it bears watching."

"And I know I can rely on you for that. Now, shall we have a look at the ledger?"

But they'd barely begun when Mrs. Ludd interrupted again, this time with a note. "Sorry, Vicar. Footboy up to Hall brought this for you."

"Excuse me," Christy murmured to the warden, who had sat up straighter when he'd heard the word "Hall" and was dying to know what the message said. *The Reverend Christian Morrell,*

Vicarage, All Saints Church, was written on the envelope in a light but decisive hand—not Geoffrey's. Christy opened it and read the one-sentence invitation inside. "Geoffrey and I would be delighted if you would join us for dinner this evening, at any hour that suits you." It was signed simply "Anne Verlaine."

He looked up. "Is the boy waiting for a reply?" Mrs. Ludd nodded. He pulled a sheet of paper from his desk drawer. Mimicking her ladyship's informality, he wrote, "Thank you. I shall come at six-thirty. Christian Morrell."

The pleasantest thing that had happened to him all day was the opportunity to fill his face with sincere-looking regret and say to Warden Nineways, "I'm frightfully sorry, Thomas, but I'm afraid I've got to go out."

Lynton Great Hall lay a scant half mile beyond the last cottage at the bottom of the High Street, close upon the banks of the Wyck and nestled in the hollow of a miniature valley. The people of Wyckerley spoke of going "up to Hall" even though topographically that was an impossibility. The fact that Wyckerley overlooked the manor house instead of the other way around had never struck anyone as odd or the reverse of what might be expected, a circumstance attributable as much to the reverence in which the villagers had held their lord for close to four centuries as it was to the grandness, much faded of late, of the Hall itself. Christy knew every turn in the sunken, clay-colored lane, every tree, each new vista as the ground dropped gently away, not only in the way a man knows a road he's traveled many times, but in the minute, intimate way a boy knows the landscape in which he's grown up. Passing the familiar landmarks now, he saw a figure coming toward him on the road. Even at forty yards, he recognized William Holyoake, from his height and the breadth of his massive shoulders, the sturdy roll of his gait, and of course the black and tan sheepdog scampering at his heels. The two men came abreast, and William pulled off his hat, revealing thick, sandy hair and a ring from ear to ear in back where his hat had flattened it.

"Evening, Vicar," he greeted him in his fine tenor voice—which rang out from the choir loft every Sunday with the clarity of a bell.

"How are you, William?"

"Well and brave, sir. Are you walking up to Hall, then? If I may ask," he added diffidently, twisting his hat in his enormous fingers.

"Yes, I've been invited to dinner." They both raised their eyebrows at that, in silent acknowledgment of the fact that such a thing had never happened while the old viscount lived. "And how are you getting along with our new squire, William?" Christy asked rather boldly. It wasn't a discreet question, and William Holyoake was the soul of discretion. But they were friends, and Christy had an idea that just now William might be needing a friend.

"Well, sir," he began, and stopped. He looked off to the west, squinting into the last of the sunset, as if the answer might be hidden in the cloud formation. His powerful profile looked hard and stony, boulder-like, the nose jutting down from the broad forehead like an exclamation point. "I'm thinking it's possible that his lordship might not be a great one fer farmin'."

Christy looked down to hide his smile, but he admired William's tact. "It's possible," he agreed with similar caution. "Can you think of anything I could do to help you?"

He pondered that for a second, his shrewd blue eyes narrowing on Christy's face. "Well, sir, I don't just know. In truth, it's . . ." He halted again, weighing his words. "It's her ladyship I've been speakin' to fer guidance of late." He lowered his voice. "She's raw as a new foal, Vicar, but she's got a grea' deal o' common sense," he confided, leaning forward and tapping his temple with a gigantic forefinger. "She *means* well, I'm sayin'. There's rumors that 'is lordship means to go off to war any day, and after that we'll have only her. If you ask me, things could be worse in that event. Much worse. If you take my meaning."

"I take it very well."

"And if and when that happens, to answer yer kind question, Vicar, I'd be grateful if you could help me to . . . to . . ."

"Advise her ladyship?" he suggested, realizing William was too respectful of his betters to say such a thing straight out. "I'd be happy to do the best I can in that regard."

"Thank you, sir."

"Never mind that. Let me know when you need me, William, and I'll do whatever I can." He started to go.

"Have you seen that black stallion of his lordship's yet, sir?"

"I have, William. He's a right beauty, isn't he?"

"He is that."

"Geoffrey's keen on a race between the stallion and my chestnut, you know."

"I heard sommat o' that, sir. Well," he came right out, "will you do it?"

"I think not," Christy said, his regret undisguised. "It wouldn't be quite the thing, would it?"

"I expect not, sir." William's disappointment was the mirror of Christy's. "And it's a damn shame." His honest face turned pink. "Oh, I beg yer pardon, Vicar, my tongue said it afore my brain heard the word, and I do beg—"

"Oh, put it away, William," Christy snapped, irritated. "For God's sake," he added for good measure.

"Yes, sir," the bailiff said alertly. "Well." He put his hat on his head and smacked his hand down on the crown to anchor it. "I'll bid you a fine evening, then," he said, good humor sparking in his eyes. "A pleasure talking to you as always, Reverend Morrell."

Christy nodded and walked on, and presently the Hall's crumbling brick chimneys appeared through the new leaves of ancient oaks bordering the east front of the house. The lane turned again and the building came into full view, three E-shaped stories of pocked and weathered granite, as rugged-looking as the moor from which it had been quarried. The archway of a battlemented gatehouse provided a cold, forbidding entry, but the grassy courtyard beyond was friendlier, if only because it was in disrepair. The house lay quiet except for the cawing of rooks on the gable over the unused chapel; Christy's shoes echoed loudly on the lichened flagstones as he crossed the courtyard to the entrance, a studded oak portal with the legend "A.D. 1490" chiseled in the hard granite block overhead.

Mrs. Fruit must have been passing through the entrance hall at the moment he knocked, for she opened the door almost immediately. Rather than shout it, he mimed "Good evening," and handed her his hat. She took him into the green drawing room and said she'd go and fetch her lady. After she went away, he surveyed the room, trying to spy what was different about it. It was indefinably warmer, more lived in, and not just because of the bowls of fresh flowers on the mantel and the side tables. There were no new furnishings; if anything, there was less furniture now than the last time he'd been here. Ah, now he had it: the heavy velvet window coverings were gone, just *gone,* not replaced by anything. The bare glass should have looked naked and stark, but it didn't. It was as if not only light but fresh air as well had been allowed back into the room after years of stifling darkness.

"Good evening."

He turned. Anne Verlaine stood in the doorway with her hand on the post, her head cocked a little, studying him. He wondered how long she'd been there. She wasn't in mourning tonight; she wore a dark green gown of some soft-looking material, cut in a simpler, more casual style than was the usual fashion for entertaining dinner guests in Wyckerley. The high waist and low neck drew his attention to her breasts, which were full and lovely, in perfect proportion to her height and slenderness. With her hair up, her cream-white neck was exposed, the graceful curve unadorned by jewelry. Her arm fell to her side and she moved farther into the room, and Christy remembered to say "Good evening" back to her.

"Geoffrey will be down soon." There was a small note of doubt in her voice, though. He saw the strain in her face then, the faint but definite tension in her jaw. She gestured toward the sofa, but didn't sit down herself. "I'm glad you could come with so little notice."

He put his hands in his pockets, trying to make her relax by looking relaxed himself. "It's my pleasure. You saved me from at least another hour with Mr. Nineways, my churchwarden. He's a good, decent soul, but he'd have made some clergyman a better warden about two hundred years ago. Under Cromwell's regime, I think."

"Are you such a liberal, then?"

"Compared to Mr. Nineways, the Russian czar is a liberal."

She smiled, studying him again. "Do you mind if I ask what made you decide to become a minister?"

He stared back at her, jingling the change in his pocket, considering how to answer. Just then the maid came in with a tray of drinks. "Hello, Susan," he said, and Susan Hatch smiled back and curtsied to him. He'd forgotten she was a maid here; he knew her parents, sturdy Irish Protestants who never missed Sunday service.

"Thank you, Susan," said her mistress, dismissing her. She moved to the table on which Susan had set the tray. "There's wine and sherry," she informed him, "and whiskey, I think," she added, looking dubiously at a third decanter. She turned around to face him. "But perhaps you don't drink, Reverend Morrell. I can ring for something else. A nice glass of barley water, perhaps."

She was either testing him or making fun of him. He'd asked her once before to call him by his first name, but she seemed to enjoy the formal title. Whenever she said it, she made it sound ever so faintly ridiculous.

"I believe a little sherry wouldn't hurt," he said gravely. She lifted her elegant eyebrows. "The worst that can happen," he added as she began to pour, "is that I'll run amok and ride my horse into the house."

She looked up, arrested. When she smiled, he realized he'd never seen her smile genuinely before. Her face was transformed; he couldn't look away—even though part of him felt the familiar exasperation whenever someone was surprised to find out he was human after all, that he actually had a sense of humor.

"I'll be careful not to give you too much," she said as she handed him his glass and poured another for herself. If he'd known nothing else about her, that one unconventional gesture would have told him a great deal, for no proper English lady would serve a drink to a gentleman in her own drawing room; she would let the maid or the butler do it, or failing that, the male guest himself.

Anne looked restless, keyed up, but it must have finally occurred to her that he wasn't going to sit down until she did, because she took a seat on the edge of a damask wingback chair, and Christy sat down on the sofa across from her. "You haven't answered my question," she said. "Or perhaps it's too personal. By all means—"

"No, not at all," he assured her, at the same time feeling reluctant to go into it. She would judge him, he knew; fairly or not, he didn't know. Nor did he understand why her good opinion of him mattered. But it did. "My father was the rector of All Saints Church before me," he began. "For twenty-eight years. He—"

"Ah," she said softly, knowingly, as if that explained everything. He looked at her without speaking until she blinked and glanced away. "Sorry," she murmured. "You hadn't finished."

"My father was a good man," he went on mildly. "Deeply, genuinely religious. Something of a saint, in fact."

"How . . . trying for you."

"It was," he agreed, smiling. "When I was a boy, I found his piety embarrassing. Geoffrey and I—well, you can imagine how we made him into a bit of a joke."

She looked as if she could imagine it easily.

"After Geoffrey went away, I didn't know what to do with myself. Here I was in dull, provincial Wyckerley, with nothing but my sixteen-year-old frustrations and half-baked ambitions."

"What did you want to be?"

"Either a horse jockey or an artist."

She laughed—another first.

"Since I was too big to be a jockey, I decided to be a painter. I forgot to take into account the fact that I had very little talent."

"Oh, dear," she said ruefully. "What did your saintly father think of that?"

"He never said a word about wanting me to become a minister, never in my whole life. But my mother was another story. If he was a saint, she was a soldier. If he was an angel, she was very much a woman of this world. Not to say she wasn't good," he hastened to assure her. "But living a Christian life was harder for her, because she didn't suffer fools gladly—whereas my father saw no harm in anyone—and yet she was truly kind. Anyway, she wanted me to be a preacher from the time I was eight. She spoke of it as a given—'when you're a minister,' 'when you have a flock of your own,' 'when you have to be an example to the whole village.'"

Anne shook her head in sympathy. "It must have been a burden."

"Like a sack full of stones." Still, he thought, it hadn't been as heavy as his father's angelic example; the lightness of that airy image had weighted him down to the ground.

"And so—?" she prompted. She had her elbow on the chair arm, her chin in her hand, and she was watching him with what seemed to be complete attention.

"When I was eighteen, I left. My plan was to find work at anything, save money, then go to school to learn how to paint pictures. I'm not familiar with your father's work, I'm afraid," he digressed. "I imagine he was better known in Europe than here."

"Marginally," she said dryly. "Go on. Where did you study?"

"Nowhere you've heard of, I'm sure. I'd had no formal training, no training at all, so none of the better schools would have me. I lived in Paris for three years, two in Amsterdam. I almost starved to death. I'm not exaggerating," he said, laughing. "It was touch and go more than once."

She nodded as if she understood that, too. "And then?"

"Then . . . my mother passed away. I came home, and for the first time I saw my father falter. It was shattering to me. I'd run away at least partly to escape their power over me, and now one was gone and the other seemed helpless with despair. I felt like a child, but I was being called upon to be the strong one, to take control."

He paused, and took a sip of the drink he hadn't touched until now. She was looking at him with veiled surprise and fascination, and also as if she was getting a great deal more than she'd bargained for when she asked her simple question. But it didn't occur to him to hold back or to tell her anything except the truth, as well as he knew it.

"My father's health began to fail," he resumed. "I was his right hand. With my mother gone, I became the one he confided in, and that was a revelation." He smiled deprecatingly. "Maybe—a Revelation. From God, I mean, of my calling. I saw my likeness to my father for the first time, not just our differences. With nothing between us but love and gentleness, not resentment or immature embarrassment or superiority, I could let myself share his enthusiasms and—rejoice in our blood tie. And the things he told me then, in this new spirit of freedom and openness, were suddenly so meaningful, they couldn't be ignored."

He leaned toward her. "Sometimes I wonder now if my vulnerability, the—the tenderness in my heart during that fragile time before he died, might've tricked me, trapped me into an unwise choice. And other times, I see it as the direct intercession of the Holy Spirit. I wonder if I'll ever know which is the truth."

She didn't speak. She had her lightly fisted hand over her mouth, so he had nothing to gauge her reaction by except her eyes. Silver-green in the lamplight, they stared back at him owlishly, a trifle worriedly. At least she wasn't laughing at him.

Now he was the one who felt restless. He set his glass down and stood up. "You might be asking yourself where God is in all of that—my motives and so forth. I'm not sure myself, but most of the time I have faith that he's in there somewhere."

More silence.

"Well, I guess I've finished answering the question." She nodded slowly. He locked his hands behind his back and asked her straight out, "What are you thinking?"

"I was thinking," she said, and stopped. She looked into the middle distance, frowning a little, choosing her words. "I was thinking that you and I have something in common." She smiled at his expression, appreciating his amazement. Of all the things she could have said, that was the one he was least expecting. It struck him then that his obvious skepticism was a not-very-subtle affront. But before he could form an apology, she said, "You see, I wanted to be an artist, too. And like you, I found I had no talent for it. It was . . . one of the tragedies of my youth." She said "tragedies" with a little laugh, mocking herself, but he didn't smile. He moved closer, drawn to the sadness in her that he could see clearly for once, all the mystery gone. She lifted her head, meeting his gaze levelly. Something passed between them. Then her fine brows drew together and she said with quick temper, "Don't you *dare* feel sorry for me."

"Never."

She searched his face. She must have found what she wanted, because she looked down, a little embarrassed. "I beg your pardon. I shouldn't have snapped at you."

"You didn't."

"Yes, I did."

"All right."

She smiled, on safe ground again behind her shield of irony. "Do you know, on the whole, I believe you've turned out better than I have, Reverend Morrell."

"Maybe you haven't finished turning out, Lady D'Aubrey," he said gently.

"I have, though. Quite finished. Will you please call me Anne?"

"Anne." The honor wasn't lost on him.

"Well, now, isn't this cozy. Anne and Christy, friends together. I've waited years for this." Without stopping, Geoffrey headed straight for the drinks tray and poured out a glass of wine.

"Geoffrey, it's good to see you."

"Wonderful to see you!" He tossed off one drink and immediately poured another. "Missed you. Been thinking about you." He looked at him for the first time. "Are you allowed out like that? Christ, man, you're not in your full holy blacks!"

Christy smiled, remembering that was what he and Geoffrey used to call his father's clerical garb. "I only wear my 'full holy blacks' on grand occasions. Meaning no offense," he said for a joke, turning to Anne.

Her face shocked him. Gone were the humor and tentative friendliness, replaced by a careful blank mask, which nevertheless failed to hide a tension that verged on desperation. From that moment, the evening became hellish for Christy. Geoffrey's jokes grated on his nerves like fingers on a chalkboard, because he'd begun to hear them through Anne's ears. The forced bonhomie grew increasingly grotesque, and he found himself counting, like a temperance fanatic, the drinks Geoffrey consumed. Anne said almost nothing during the long, uncomfortable meal, during which she and Geoffrey never looked at each other. What was happening here? What was the source of this terrible unspoken strain? As green as he was, Christy had already been called upon to offer counsel to any number of troubled couples—but this went beyond any unsatisfactory marriage he'd ever encountered. There was a secret between the Verlaines, and he was beginning to be afraid that he was the last person who could help them. Because he had a stake, a favorite. His neutrality had been compromised.

When dinner was finally over, he was afraid Anne would leave. "Will you join the gentlemen for their masculine brandy and tobacco?" Geoffrey asked her, with the drawling sarcasm Christy hated. "Or do you prefer your own company, my love?"

She was ready to bolt, a polite exit line on the tip of her tongue. "Please join us," Christy said quickly, seriously. Geoffrey glanced between them and laughed. She sent her husband a look that held such contempt, Christy shivered. "Very well," she murmured, and they all three adjourned to the drawing room.

Geoffrey continued to recount childhood experiences from his and Christy's past, always flavoring them with a note of mockery or disdain. He seemed incapable of saying anything directly, unequivocally, without an edge of supposedly humorous cynicism. Christy wanted very much to know how he had gotten this way. But whenever he asked a question that might have revealed it—about his experiences in the army, the fabric of his life since they'd parted twelve years ago—Geoffrey always turned it aside with a joke.

For the third or fourth time, he brought up the subject of the horse race he was dying for them to have. His vehemence increased by the hour, and his tack this time was to taunt Christy. "You're afraid!" he pounced, as if the truth had just hit him. "You're afraid I'll trounce you and your overrated chestnut!"

Christy shook his head, unmoved.

"A hundred pounds," Geoffrey offered next. "I'll bet you could use a hundred pounds."

He laughed. "I haven't got a hundred pounds," he said candidly. "If you won, I couldn't pay you."

"It doesn't have to be for money, then," Geoffrey offered, standing in front of the empty fireplace, spreading his arms wide. "We'll just run our horses side by side as fast as we can. We won't even notice who gets to the end first."

Christy was tired of saying no. He pinched the bridge of his nose between his fingers to hide his impatience. "Listen, Geoffrey—"

"Why don't you make it a more interesting wager?" Anne put in unexpectedly. They both looked at her in surprise. She was curled up in the window seat with her arms wrapped around herself as if she were cold. She hadn't uttered a word in half an hour.

"How do you mean?" Christy asked.

"If you win, Geoffrey has to pay a hundred pounds to the charity of your choice."

"Ha!" Geoffrey exclaimed, moving toward her.

Christy asked, "And if I lose?"

She touched a fingertip to her lips; she was either thinking or disguising a smile. "If you lose, you have to preach a sermon next Sunday on the evils of gambling."

Geoffrey roared with laughter, slapping his thigh. "Perfect! Oh, God! What do you say? Come on, Christy, you can't say no, it's for charity!"

Anne was watching him. Her suggestion was outrageous. Was she laughing at him again? Impossible to tell. The arch playfulness in her face, an expression he'd never seen and had never expected to see, finally decided him. "All right," he said. "We'll race."

"Oh, capital!" To celebrate, Geoffrey poured himself a tall glass of port and drank it down without a pause. "When?" he demanded, wiping his mouth with his hand.

"Tomorrow's Saturday. I have a wedding at noon; I can't get free till three or so."

"Half past three?"

"All right. Where?"

"Why not the old route? From the Hall through the park, to Guelder mine and back. What do you say?"

Dismayed, Christy considered reneging. Geoffrey could hardly have chosen a more public race course, and he'd been hoping for some privacy, or at least a little discretion. *Oh, well,* he thought, resigned to it; *in for a penny, in for a pound.* "Right, then, I'll come at three-thirty." He stood up. "It's late—"

"No! It's only ten, it's—"

"It's late for me," he amended. "I've enjoyed myself very much. Thank you for dinner."

"I'll walk out with you," Geoffrey offered. Anne stood, too.

"Good-bye," Christy said to her. He wanted to shake hands, but she was too far away, and she made no move to come closer.

"Good night. I'm glad you came." She hesitated, looking as if she had something else to say. But then Geoffrey threw an arm around Christy's shoulders and guided him out the door.

VII

The May afternoon was warm and cloudy; it might rain later, but right now it was a perfect day for racing—dry underfoot and overcast above. A fast day, as they used to say. Still did, for all Christy knew; he'd been out of the racing world for years.

He was trotting his horse past the east front of Lynton Hall, making for the stables, when he chanced to spy Anne through the arched entrance to the courtyard. She saw him at the same time and waved. He turned his horse, ducked his head in the archway, and rode toward her.

She looked as fresh as the spring in a blue frock, flower-sprigged, with a pretty white apron. Her hands were dirty; she'd been weeding or planting something by the chapel wall. Smiling a greeting, she wiped her hands on her apron, tossing her head to throw a stray lock of hair back from her forehead. "Good afternoon, Vicar." She looked surprised to see him in his boots and buckskins, without a jacket, not even a collar for his oldest white shirt. "How was your wedding?"

"Very fine," he answered, pulling off his hat. "Everyone wept except the bride."

"Indeed!" she said with mock wonder. "And she the one with the most cause for weeping. Tell me, Reverend, do you think they'll live happily ever after?" Despite her light tone, the question was loaded with cynicism.

He answered mildly, "I pray they will."

She flared her nostrils a bit at that, but made no reply.

Moving closer, she reached up to pet the horse's neck. "What a beautiful animal. What's his name?"

"Doncaster."

"Doncaster," she repeated, rubbing his nose with a soft, open palm. "Geoffrey's horse is called Devil, you know. If he beats you, I expect we'll have to view it as symbolic of something or other."

She arched one of her lovely eyebrows at him, grinning with mischievous good humor. Christy felt a lurch in his chest. And then, to his dismay, he felt himself blushing. "Where's Geoffrey?" he asked quickly.

"In the stables, waiting for you."

He pulled on the reins, backing his horse up. "Will you watch us off?"

"No, I don't think so. But I'll have bandages and splints ready for your return." Again the wicked grin, and this time her green eyes twinkled at him.

He laughed. She was irresistible. "Till later, then."

"Good luck," she called after him softly.

He thought of knights and ladies, pledges and favors—silly, inappropriate notions that had him flushing again. This time she couldn't see him, though, which was something. Feeling extremely foolish, he spurred Don to a trot and headed toward the stables.

Geoffrey was waiting for him in the yard, pacing in his tall riding boots, impatience written in his jerky movements and the tautness of the rein with which he was pulling his horse behind him. As soon as he saw Christy, he leapt onto the black stallion's back and trotted toward him. Christy had time to wave to William Holyoake, who was standing in the stable doors next to Collie Horrocks, Lynton Hall's elderly groom. The two men waved back—and then Geoffrey lifted his riding crop high in the air and slashed it down across his horse's haunch. Devil jumped in surprise; he reared once before his muscular quarters thrust him forward with the power of a stampede. His hurtling feet sent up clouds of grit, and he was around the stable and out of sight before Christy could get his horse turned.

"Shimmering scarlet hell!" he yelled, which made Collie and William hoot with laughter. Smacking his boot heels into Don's sides, he told him, *"Go,"* and they were off.

Guelder mine lay about two and a half miles from the Hall along the old Tavistock road. Christy and Geoffrey had a different route, one they'd staked out about seventeen years ago and raced their horses over at least a hundred times. Christy couldn't remember the last time he'd ridden across the sheep pastures and moorland scrub or jumped the stream banks and stone fences crisscrossing the rough fields, but he hadn't forgotten a single turn, hurdle, straightaway, or curve in the mile-long course, and he knew Geoffrey hadn't either. Geoffrey rode flat-out at a ground-eating gallop a quarter-furlong ahead of him, using his crop freely. Devil, whose *Stud Book* name was Tandem, by Touchstone out of a Barb mare called Hermit, stood almost sixteen hands, with the long back and elegant stride of a thoroughbred racer. But he was a little top-heavy from overfeeding, Christy had noticed, a little weak-limbed from overwork. Doncaster, an English blood horse with no known Eastern lines, lacked Devil's sleek size and beauty; he had thicker bones and a bigger head, and more hair around the fetlocks. A rough coat and a kind eye. And more heart than any horse Christy had ever known. Between them, they were going to beat that Arabian Devil into the ground.

The distance between the horses didn't begin to narrow until Christy spied the tall stacks of Guelder's steam engines rising high above the trees, belching puffy clouds into the lead-colored sky. Geoffrey thundered around a curve in the sloping scree track, and Christy lost sight of him. Half a minute later, an unidentifiable wailing sound started soft and grew louder very quickly. He said, "Whoa, Don," and slowed him with his knees to negotiate the slippery turn, and when they rounded it the source of the strange sound burst into view. It wasn't wailing, it was cheering, and it was coming from at least a dozen men, miners all, clustered around the side of Guelder's engine house. They were bellowing their lungs out and waving their hats in the air, and as he galloped closer Christy distinctly heard one of them shout, "Give 'em hell, Reverend! Get 'im, Vicar, beat 'is balls off!"

Geoffrey streaked around the far end of the engine house—the halfway point—and rode straight for him. With a dozen feet separating their mounts, Christy realized Geoffrey wasn't going to give ground, that he'd ride his stallion straight into Doncaster's teeth before he'd veer off and give way. Reining sharply, breaking stride, Christy got his horse off the track in the nick of time, and Geoffrey let out a wild cackle as he flew by.

Tranter Fox was the miner shouting the profane inducements, Christy saw with no surprise as he spurred Don around the sharp engine-house curve. "On, Rev," he hollered now, jumping up and down. "Drive 'im, bleedin' drive 'im!" The glee in the little Cornishman's homely, dirt-smeared face didn't come just from the excitement of watching a horse race; it came as well from knowing he had the goods on Reverend Morrell, no mistake about it. Christy could only laugh—grimly—as he galloped past him, feeling the swat of Tranter's hat on his knee for encouragement. No matter how this race turned out, life around Tranter Fox wasn't going to be worth living for a long, long time.

Up past the slippery scree slope, he saw Geoffrey in the distance, flailing away with his crop. The black was flagging, for he was only about sixty feet ahead now. Christy bared his teeth into the wind and bent low over Don's neck, urging him on with soft-voiced imprecations, words he'd have chastised a parishioner for using if he'd heard them. The valiant chestnut understood and responded, finding new strength in the long lunge of his shoulders and his powerful hindquarters. Devil had been foaming already at the halfway turn, but Doncaster was at his peak, the heady, giddy height of his form, racing his heart out for the main job God had put him on earth to do.

The gap closed. Christy rejoiced, because he would win, and because in two more minutes Geoffrey would have to stop beating his brave, striving stallion. He urged Don over a stony stream in one strong, airy plunge, and they gained on their prey like lions in pursuit of lesser game. Now Geoffrey could hear them; he glanced back, and his mouth formed a weird, skeletal grimace. But Christy couldn't pity him. He crooned to his horse, calling to him like a lover, and his common country steed strove with all his might. Neck and neck, the horses pounded across the last open field before the park. Filled, intoxicated with the thrill of the race, the glorious winning, Christy laughed as he pulled ahead and reached out to Geoffrey with his right hand and saluted him, his oldest friend, the dearest love of his boyhood. Geoffrey's face should've warned him. He yanked hard on his left rein, and Devil, beaten and obedient, ran sinister.

No choice, nowhere to go. A low, thick coppice of hawthorn flanked the path, and one fallen beech, split by lightning halfway up, lay like the crosspiece of a lopsided H across the high crotch of its neighbor. To save his horse, Christy reined toward the highest point of the barrier. Doncaster ran through, stumbling in the sudden underbrush. Christy twisted at the last second, taking the brunt of the blow on his left temple. A sharp limb gored his shoulder, but he didn't feel it; he was already unconscious.

A jumble of voices coaxed him back from a very black tunnel, pain-filled and noisy with a sound like bees buzzing. Somebody was shouting at him. He opened one eye and saw Tranter Fox's monkey face in duplicate, his mouth moving approximately in time to words that sounded like "Bloody blinkin' 'ell. Ee surely bain't dead, Christy, or by God, I'll kill you." Somebody else had hands on his legs, and now his arms; when they got to his ribs, he let out a yell and opened the other eye.

"Cracked," rumbled William Holyoake, sitting back on his haunches. "Same as your head. Don't try to get up, Vicar; your shoulder's bleedin' pretty good and your—"

"Where's my horse?" He batted away all four of the hands that were trying to hold him down. "Where's Don?" He looked around in a panic and saw Geoffrey, standing a little ways off beside his winded black stallion. His face was ashen, his black eyes sparking with fear.

"He's all right, he's fine," he said, coming a step closer. "He ran after me. Horrocks has him, he's cooling him down."

Christy closed his eyes in relief and let William Holyoake press him back to the hard ground.

"I swear to God, Christy, I didn't see you fall," Geoffrey said quickly. "I'd have stopped if I had! I didn't know you weren't with me until I got to the end of the park. When I saw your horse trotting after me, I couldn't believe it. William was there—we came racing back as fast as we could."

Christy kept his eyes closed while he explored the egg-size lump above his ear and tried to make sense of what Geoffrey was saying. It was a lie, wasn't it? How could he not have seen him fall? But his remorse sounded so real, and the worry in his face looked genuine.

"How did it happen?" Holyoake asked, pressing his handkerchief to the throbbing gash in Christy's shoulder.

He glanced sharply at Geoffrey, who was concentrating on swatting his boots with his riding crop. "My horse shied," Christy said slowly. "I fell."

"You *fell*?" Tranter sounded incredulous. "*You* fell?"

"I fell," he repeated. He'd have it out with Geoffrey later, when they weren't in front of witnesses. "I'm not hurt badly— help me up."

They didn't want to, but he made them. The dizziness didn't last long; Holyoake's powerful arm steadied him when he swayed, and after a few more seconds he felt strong enough to walk.

"Here, take my horse," Geoffrey urged, leading the black closer. The winded stallion was taking breaths in gusts through his nostrils and heaving out his ribs to inflate his lungs.

"No, I'll walk."

"Don't be daft, take my—"

"I said I'll walk."

Holyoake and Tranter glanced at one another uneasily. Geoffrey's sallow cheeks turned red; he tried to sound casual. "Have it your way, then, old sod. Since you don't need me, I'll ride home at once. Holyoake tells me I have visitors, London friends I wasn't expecting. Come straight to the house, Christy, there's a good lad. I'll tell Anne you're coming. She's a hell of a nurse, she'll put you to rights in no time." He waited a moment, but Christy said nothing. "Well, then." He mounted his huffing stallion, saluted them with fake jauntiness, and trotted away.

With William and Tranter for crutches, Christy moved along without too much difficulty. Once Tranter realized he really wasn't mortally wounded, he couldn't resist teasing him. "Well, yer reverence, I'm that keen on church tomorrow, ee might say I'm slaverin' for it. Oh, aye, Sunday church's where I mane t' be, no mistake. Front and center, mayhap a shade early even, lest I miss a golden moment, so t' say."

"Oh, bottle it," Christy groused. Holyoake made a strangled sound that turned into a cough when the minister glared at him. "I suppose everybody in the county knows about the terms of the wager," he muttered, and neither man contradicted him. Geoffrey had even more to answer for than he'd thought.

"I shouldn't say all o' county," Tranter said presently, with mock solicitousness, "not by any manner o' manes. Nay, tes more like only the whole parish, reely."

Christy rolled his eyes. It was starting. He and Tranter had

had a good-humored battle running for years about the status of
the little miner's immortal soul if he didn't go to church more
often, stay out of the public house, and leave the ladies alone.
Christy had always considered that he had the advantage, being
the ostensible voice of rectitude and moderation, and it was vex-
ing to know he would now be on the defensive indefinitely.
"What are you doing here anyway?" he inquired irritably. "Why
aren't you at work?"

"I were comin' off my core when you an' 'is new lordship flyed
by, yer reverence. The tutmen appointed me, like, t' go an' discover which o' you'd winned, so's we could settle up our private
wagers. Speakin' for myself, I'm eight shillings out o' pocket on
account o' yer clumsiness, yer grace. Beggin' yer pardon an'
manin' no disrespect, o' course."

Christy put his aching head back and groaned.

"A spill," Geoffrey had said. A bump on the head and a
scraped shoulder. When Anne saw Christy tacking slowly across
the courtyard, supported by Holyoake and a man she didn't
know, she almost fainted.

"My God," she cried, rushing to him. His clear eyes and reassuring smile relieved her anxiety a little, but the blood staining
the chest and right arm of his white shirt did not.

"I'm all right," he told her, and when Holyoake and the other
man let go of him, he stood tall and steady as if to prove it. "It
looks worse than it is, I promise you."

"Come inside," she said distractedly, backing up toward the
door to the kitchen.

He turned to the stranger, a slight, dark, wiry individual with
a gap between his teeth and mischief in his eyes, and held out
his left hand. "My thanks, Tranter," he said gravely. "I might've
perished without you."

When they shook, the little man said, "Don't mention it, yer reverence." He made Anne a rather elegant bow and walked away. When he got to the outer courtyard door he stopped and turned around. She thought he called out "Front an' center!" before he disappeared through the archway.

"Come along," she said again, disguising her distress with briskness, leading the way down the area steps and into the short corridor that led to the kitchen. She stopped, dismayed, in the kitchen doorway: she'd forgotten that every maid in the house had been pressed into service, to provide refreshments immediately and dinner in a while for Geoffrey's uninvited guests, not to mention overnight accommodations later on. The kitchen was bedlam, with servants jostling each other for space, every flat surface covered with raw ingredients for the coming meal, and poor Mrs. Fruit shouting instructions over the din while the maids shouted back to tell her they'd heard. "Oh, ruddy hell," Anne mumbled under her breath, turning around. She saw Reverend Morrell's eyebrows shoot up, and realized what she'd said. "Oh—I'm sorry, that's—a terrible habit of mine, do forgive me—" He was smiling at her, not with saintly forbearance but with something like delight, and she subsided, relieved and embarrassed. "Come this way," she said, shepherding him and William Holyoake back the way they'd come and into the scullery. "Sit down," she ordered, pointing to a stool, and the invalid obeyed. "I'll be right back."

She returned to the kitchen for the hot water and towels she'd asked for earlier. "Violet, go and get one of Lord D'Aubrey's clean shirts from his clothes chest and bring it down to me in the scullery, please."

"The scullery, ma'am?"

"Yes, the scullery. Go along, quickly." Violet made one of her sarcastic curtseys and scurried out.

In the scullery, Mr. Holyoake was standing around looking ineffectual. When he asked if she needed him for anything more, she said no, thanked him for his trouble, and let him go. "Glad you're all right, Vicar," he said gruffly on his way out. "Don't mind saying you gave me a bit of a fright."

Christy waved his hand dismissively. "I shall be right as rain in no time. Thank you for everything, William."

"Right, then," Anne said brusquely after Holyoake was gone. "Off with this, I think, so I can clean you up. Do you need help?"

"It's only a little stiffness," he denied, unbuttoning his blood-stained shirt and shrugging out of it. They examined the wound on his shoulder together. It was extensive but superficial, and the bleeding had almost stopped. "Shallow," he judged, peering at it narrowly. "No stitches."

She agreed. "Nasty, though. I must clean it thoroughly. Let me see your head." He bowed it submissively, and she slid her fingers gently into his gold-colored hair. "That's a lovely one," she murmured, tracing the swelling with light fingertips. "Am I hurting you?"

"Not at all."

His hair was softer than she'd guessed it would be. She thought again of the beautiful, worried lion in the Rubens painting and smiled. She took her hands away reluctantly. "I believe you'll live," she said softly.

He looked up at her. His eyes were an unusual shade of ice blue. She'd seen them burn with earnestness and soften with kindness, but right now they were guilelessly wide and alert, with a particular knowledge that she thought was sexual awareness. Her own eyes dropped to his mouth, and quickly lifted away again. *Well, now,* a voice in her brain remarked. *Isn't this interesting.*

The water in the big clay bowl was still warm. She saturated a soft flannel cloth and held it to Christy's shoulder wound, bathing it as gently as possible. He flinched only once, the first time she touched him, and after that he endured it all with manly, tight-lipped stoicism. *So different from Geoffrey,* she couldn't help thinking. "What happened?" she asked to divert him. "Geoffrey said he thought you were right behind him."

"My horse shied and I fell," he said, with no tone in his voice. He closed his mouth and tightened his lips. *Why, he's embarrassed,* she thought. *Geoffrey beat him and he doesn't like it. How very interesting.* The hair on his chest was lighter than the hair on his head. Compared to Geoffrey he was a giant, thick-muscled and broad-shouldered. Yet his skin was soft and finely textured. Like his hair. She entertained a swift, lascivious thought involving his bare skin against hers, then forced it out of her mind. She tried to laugh at herself, but she was shaken. Actually shocked.

He paled a little and seemed to stop breathing while she worked on the dirtiest part of his abrasion, over the hard, rigid muscle in the top of his shoulder. "Anne, are you . . . do you . . ." He closed his eyes and said with great nonchalance, "Geoffrey's all right, isn't he? Doesn't . . . never would . . ." He cleared his throat. "You feel perfectly safe, don't you? None of my business about your marriage and all, I'm not asking that, but you—you're quite all right, aren't you, Anne?"

Her hands had gone still in the middle of his extraordinary question. All at once the motive for it hit her, and she stepped back. "What happened?" she said sharply. He looked at her in surprise. "What did he do? Tell me!"

"Nothing. I don't know what you mean."

Before she could speak again, Violet appeared in the doorway, carrying the shirt she'd asked for. "Thank you," she said tightly.

"Yes, ma'am. Will there be anything else?" Her small brown eyes narrowed avidly on the fascinating spectacle of her mistress attending to the wounds of her half-naked minister.

"No, nothing. Go and help Susan," she snapped, and Violet sent her a poisonous glance before she whirled and left. Detestable girl.

She set the flannel down in the cooling water and fixed Christy with as steely a gaze as she could muster. "He did something, didn't he? He hurt you. Why won't you tell me?"

He had the most annoying patience. "Why would you think that?" he asked, deceptively mild. He stood up, towering over her, all naked torso and big, intelligent head. "Unless he's hurt *you*. Has he?"

Checkmate. She said, "No," through her teeth. The sensitive skin of his cheeks went pink. She was beginning to love his flushes, even though this one came from frustration instead of embarrassment.

"Geoffrey drinks too much," he said combatively.

"Sometimes. Not today, though. Did he hurt you? Come, you might as well tell me."

"Why do you think he did?" he countered cagily. He was trying to be shrewd and slippery, but he was so transparent she wanted to laugh.

Without answering, she turned away, busying herself with Geoffrey's shirt while she got her face and her emotions in order. Neither of them was going to tell the other the truth, that was obvious. She would have liked to know what Geoffrey had done to him, but it wasn't worth trading any information about her own private life. She was a woman without confidantes, and had been for so long that anything else was unthinkable.

When she turned back, she saw that he'd been engaged in the same effort to disguise his feelings. Ah, poor Reverend Morrell: he lacked her years of experience; compared to her, he was a hopeless amateur.

"Lady D'Aubrey—"

"Oh, for God's sake—"

"Call me by *my* name, then!" he burst out, and his fine, irate righteousness set her back on her heels.

"All right," she said, shakily placating. "I've meant to before.

Christy." There. It sounded completely natural, and she wondered why she hadn't said it before now. General perverseness,
no doubt. "Christy," she said again, softer. An addictive name,
that irrepressible voice in her brain murmured. She held the
shirt out to him, for something to do.

He got it on unassisted, but afterward she decided to button
it for him—because his right arm was still stiff, she rationalized.
Halfway down, he said to her very quietly, "Listen to me." If he'd
followed then with something suggestive or seductive, she
wouldn't have been surprised—which summed up everything
about her frame of mind just then, didn't it? But he fixed her
with a burning blue stare and said soberly, "If you ever need
help. If you ever need anything. You know that you can come to
me, don't you? I can help. I can do something. Anne, I *will* help
you."

She nodded matter-of-factly, but inside she felt breathless.
The possibility . . . the possibility. . . . Against everything, all her
experience, she found herself almost believing him. To have a
friend, someone she could trust, someone who might really help
her. . . . It was a heady sensation, like contemplating a dive from
a great height. "Thank you," she whispered, ambivalent. Oh, but
the possibility . . .

"Stay for dinner," she said with more force. Returning to
normal, he'd think; he couldn't possibly guess at her urgency.
"You can meet Geoffrey's friends," she added—as if that were an
inducement.

"Thank you, but I'd better go. I'm not fit for company."

"Are you in pain?"

"No, not at all, I'm—"

"Then please stay." Too urgent. She forced her clasped hands
to relax. "I wish you would."

"I think I must go."

She made her voice light, made it a joke. "Ah, so you're taking back your offer of help so quickly? Please, it's just that—I've met Geoffrey's friends before. And I'd be very grateful if you would stay." She almost said his name again. *Christy.* He'd have stayed if she'd said it.

"Then I'll stay," he said.

7 May, midnight

Impossible to sleep. The rain beating against the window and gurgling in the leaky gutters isn't the culprit; it's my scattered thoughts, flying around in my head like circling rooks, repeating and repeating. And my guilty conscience.

I made an awful mistake tonight. How could I have forgotten how detestable Claude Sully and the others are, Geoffrey's so-called friends? But I hadn't forgotten; it was cowardly and selfish of me to ask Christy Morrell to stay, to help me get through an evening with those men. But I never could have foreseen how they would treat him. If I'd had any idea, I would never have imposed on his apparently limitless good nature. I'm ashamed of myself, I'm angry with him, disgusted with Geoffrey—

No, no, I'm not angry with Christy any longer—how could I be? But I was. Oh, I was. I wanted to shake him and shout in his face, "Do something! Hit somebody!" Even now, when I remember the things they said to him, my fury comes seething back and I want to beat my fists against someone's unguarded face. Sully's, preferably.

There were three of them: Sully, Brooke, and Bingham, all rotters, hangers-on, the sort of men Geoffrey is attracted to because he's smarter than they are but they have more energy (and money); they egg each other on in mob fashion and get up to loathsome "pranks" together that would shame a beastly adolescent schoolboy. Claude Sully is the worst of the lot. Because I never tell Geoffrey anything, I've never told him about the time, while he was away in Africa, I think it was, that Sully paid a call and made the slimiest, most boorish attempt to seduce me. It came to blows—I actually struck him across the face—and the worst is that I think he liked it. At least he'd got *something* out of me for his trouble, and he could leave knowing I would despise him *and* myself for a long time. And so I did.

The bloody beast.

And I set Reverend Morrell down in the midst of them, like a Christian among the lions. A cheap, easy analogy, and yet it's exactly right. He didn't understand at first what they were about. (*This* is what kills me; there's a pain in my chest, a real, true ache when I remember the surprise in his face as the truth gradually dawned on him. Why didn't he see it sooner? What kind of a minister doesn't know evil exists?) When the taunting stopped being subtle and became blatantly cruel, he didn't get up and walk out, as it seemed to me any sensible man would have done—that or start throwing the furniture. And after that, his bewilderment over their treatment of him changed to a truly infuriating patience. He literally *turned the other cheek*. The only good thing about it was that Sully grew baffled and enraged, but he couldn't show it. I loved watching his smooth, oily, insinuating facade crack and the tantrum-throwing little boy peek out. By then I was ready to give them all a good, hard smack, Christy included. There's not an ounce of Christian saintliness in me, and I'm not sorry. No, not sorry. I'm glad. I feel such contempt for Geoffrey, I don't even want to speak to him. But I probably will, because I want him to know that I found his passive complicity despicable. Christy, he says, is his best friend. Pity his enemies, if that's true.

I won't write the things they said to Christy, they're too

hateful. It was as if his very existence infuriated them. He didn't look like a minister in his buckskin riding breeches and Geoffrey's shirt, stretched tight across his chest. He looked like . . . well, I don't know what. Not anyone's idea of a country parson, anyway. But that's what he is, and Sully and the others could hardly wait to let him know that he is a joke to them, a walking relic from the prehistoric past. They asked him about his "calling," snickering behind his back when he answered them seriously. They made me feel ashamed for the times I've tweaked him a little myself, comfortable and obnoxious in my relative worldliness. He tried to engage them in an actual discussion—the fool, the fool!—but of course it was hopeless. Men like that can't debate, they can only wound and run away.

And never once did he lose his temper. That galled them to the end, and I think they were glad when he finally went away. God knows I was.

But I couldn't let him go like that, with all my anger still bottled up inside! And I wanted to know how he really felt, what was going on behind all that exasperating tolerance and forbearance. So I went after him. Told Geoffrey I was retiring, and went out the kitchen door and ran all the way around the house. I caught him on the bridge; I was out of breath, hardly able to speak at first. He thought something was wrong, he was worried for *me*—which, of course, made it hard to keep the edge on my anger. But I managed. I'm ashamed to say I berated him, but I couldn't help it. "Why did you let them do it? What kind of man are you?" Yes, I said that, and much more, as if I had the right, as if what kind of man he is has anything whatever to do with me. But I was wrought up. "Didn't you hear them? Don't you know what they were doing? They laughed at you!" Nothing; I had no better luck than Sully at trying to make him angry. "I despise humility," I said scathingly. "It's no virtue to me, it's weakness."

He said, "Do you think I'm weak?" and I thought, *Well, at least I've gotten frostiness out of him—something!* I don't remember how I answered; haughtily, though. (He's not weak, of course; I'd said it to goad him.) He said, "Do you think I don't know what they thought of me, Anne? That I sat there and didn't understand the depth of their contempt?"

"Then why didn't you react? Even Jesus got mad at the money changers!" As if I knew that story well, as if the Bible were a familiar volume to me, kept at my bedside for easy reference. It was misty on the bridge, or he'd have seen me blush. He laughed a little when I said that, and I deserved it. "The money *lenders*," he corrected.

By now I was beginning to cool down. We walked to the end of the bridge and went a little way along the bank. Everything was quiet and still except for the sound of the rushing water—such a relief after the smoke and brandy and nastiness inside the house. We stopped under the alder trees, and he said, "I've found that one of the hardest things about the ministry is the isolation. You don't know how relieved I would be if my parishioners would speak frankly about their doubts, the times when their faith fails them and they can't believe. I wouldn't be shocked; I would love to talk these things over. I'm smothering in politeness. Faith in God isn't a debate I have to win, it's a way we can understand each other."

No one talks like this, no one in my experience. I don't know what to say to him when he says these things to me. His simplicity confounds me. I *fear* for him.

He said, "It makes me sad when people can't see me as a human being. They usually come around eventually, and then it's annoying to have my humanity made into some minor revelation. Do you understand what I'm saying? I hate being a symbol instead of a person. I'm the minister, I'm Reverend Morrell; and so, depending on what your hopes and prejudices are, that makes me either a saint or a hypocrite. And I can tell you it's even harder to be adored than it is to be judged a fool."

I think he was saying he didn't mind what he'd just gone through as much as I did, because at least Sully and the others were confronting him head-on as *something*, and they certainly weren't couching it in politeness. Extraordinary. I think he's lonely.

"You're angry with me because I was so dense"—No, no, I started to protest—"and you're right." (That surprised me; I thought he would maintain that he'd done it all deliberately.) "I kept wanting to engage them, force them into a real conversation. I was naive." Here I almost nodded, then remembered to disagree politely. He said, "No, Anne, I was a blockhead."

This was *true* humility. I could hardly believe it when we both laughed, freely and—affectionately; after all that had happened, laughter seemed highly uncalled for. But it refreshed us, and that's why I told him the truth about myself: that I'm an atheist. Only I didn't like to shock him, so I cushioned the blow and said I was an "agnostic."

I don't know if he was surprised or not. But he was quiet for a minute, and then he said he would pray for me. Well, what had I expected? I didn't laugh, but I made some sound. I felt bitterness inside, and some strange disappointment in him—altogether inappropriate, of course. He put his hand on me, just a small, comforting touch on my arm. And I thought, what would he do if I made an advance? He finds me attractive, I've known that for some time. Last night, when he spoke so openly of his father and mother and his decision to become a priest, I knew I was attracted to him, too. And so, while we stood there with his hand lightly touching my elbow, I wondered what would happen if I said or did something to him—something of a seductive nature. Touched him back or—

But I didn't touch him and I didn't say anything to him. Because if I had, it would have been to test him. And then I would've been no better than Geoffrey and his wretched friends.

Then I was afraid he would try to convert me, so I said good night rather curtly. Now I can't sleep. And I wish I had told him that I admire him—for his patience with Sully, I mean. He was right not to react to their taunts; it would have served no purpose, except possibly to vent *my* anger, which is no reason at all. He's better than I am, is Reverend Morrell. But it's not because of "God"; it's because he was born that way.

VIII

"So, Christy." Teapot in hand, Mrs. Ludd stood behind the vicar's right shoulder, until he had no choice but to stop reading about war in the Crimea and look up at her. "What time did you finally come home last night?"

"Not too late. Something after midnight, I think."

"Hah! 'Twas half past two, I heard the church clock go not five minutes after you stabled your horse."

He held up his cup, and she filled it for him with steaming tea. "Why did you ask me if you already knew?"

"To see what you'd say, o' course."

Christy shook his head and tried to go back to his newspaper.

"I told Arthur, I said, 'Wake up, there's Vicar back from Bonesteels' this late, the old lady must've died after all.'"

"Arthur appreciated that, I'm sure."

Mrs. Ludd set the teapot down and moved a basket of muffins closer to his plate. "Well? Did she or didn't she?"

He sighed, laying his newspaper aside. "Mrs. Bonesteel started feeling better about one o'clock this morning. Apparently it wasn't her heart after all; it was the pickled pilchards she ate yesterday for supper."

"Well, I must say. After all that. Tsk." Mrs. Ludd folded her arms across her wide middle and clucked some more.

"Yes, I wish she'd died, too; then my evening wouldn't have been completely wasted."

Her mouth fell open. A second later she got the joke, and retaliated by thunking the vicar on the shoulder with a teaspoon. A crafty look narrowed her eyes. "How do you like your raisin muffins this morning, Reverend?"

He bit into one warily. "Fine. Why?"

"I'll be sure to tell Miss Margaret Mareton you think they're delicious." Christy groaned, and his housekeeper snickered. " 'Tis a very *special* recipe she learned from her grandmother, she said to be sure to tell you. Since you like 'em so much, I'll tell her to bring over a great cartload next time."

"You know, this isn't nearly as funny as you think it is."

That only made her laugh outright. "Oh, but it *is*." Still chortling, she started for the kitchen, but stopped when she saw, through the dining room window, a figure coming through the front gate. "My blessed saints, Christy, 'tis his new lordship, walkin' up the walk and fixing to knock on the door."

"Geoffrey?" He set his cup down and stood up.

"Shall I bring him in here or the parlor?"

"It's all right, I'll go myself." The knock came before he reached the hall. He hastened along, conscious of feeling as if a burden had lifted. He hadn't seen Geoffrey in almost two weeks, not since the night at the Hall after their horse race. Every day he'd thought he would come and offer some explanation for his behavior. He hadn't, and as the days passed, Christy had grown increasingly dejected. He'd decided to wait one more day, then confront Geoffrey himself. Thank God, now he wouldn't have to.

He surprised a worried look on Geoffrey's face when he opened the door, which he immediately hid behind a mask of facetious amazement. "Why, it's the vicar himself! I say, things are getting a bit loose when you start answering the door yourself, don't you think, Reverend? Doesn't look right. A man of the cloth has to uphold his dignity. Send the servants, man, that's what they're for."

Christy waited patiently. "Geoffrey. I was hoping you'd come," he said when the fatuous speech was over.

He sobered instantly. "Should've done it sooner," he muttered, clasping Christy's outstretched hand. "Can I come in?"

He led him back along to the dining room. Mrs. Ludd brought more tea and then left them alone, her silent, awed manner reminding Christy that she was new to Wyckerley—only ten years or so—and hadn't known Geoffrey as a boy; thus, his status as Lord D'Aubrey cowed her.

The morning sun poured through the open dining room windows, illuminating Geoffrey's sharp-edged features. Sober and calm, he looked healthier than Christy had seen him since his return. There was no manic glitter in his dark eyes and his hands were steady. A sense of purpose had replaced his restlessness, the cause of which was soon explained.

"My commission's come," he said, smiling with satisfaction. "Only a captaincy, but I'm content. And it's the Rifle Brigade, so there's no question that I'll see action."

Christy nodded as if that pleased him, but in truth, he'd never understood Geoffrey's enthusiasm for the military. "Congratulations. I'm glad for you; I know it's what you've wanted."

"Well, it didn't come any too soon—or this war, either. We're living in such revoltingly peaceful times, this will probably be my last chance to see real fighting."

Christy couldn't help himself. "Why do you like it?" he asked directly. "Is it because of patriotism?"

"Patriotism!" He barked out a laugh. "Don't be an idiot." He turned a spoon over and over on the white tablecloth. "I like it, that's all," he said without looking up. "I bloody well know what I'm doing. It's the only thing I'm any good at. Maybe you won't believe it, but there are some people who respect me for it."

"Of course I believe it." He waited, but Geoffrey didn't explain himself further. "When will you go?"

"I sail on a troop transport from Southampton for the Black Sea in three weeks. All that worries me now is that the Russians might pull back across the Danube before I can get there."

"Surely that wouldn't be the end of it."

"Oh, no," he said cheerfully, "the allies won't be content to sit back and wait for the czar to try it again. Take my word for it, they'll try to smash the Russian fleet at Sebastopol. And I mean to be there when they do."

"No point in telling you to be careful, I suppose."

"I'm always careful." A reckless gleam in his eye belied it, though.

"I'll miss you."

Geoffrey looked down again. "Can't think why. Behaved like an ass the other day. Apologize."

Christy watched him for a moment. Was it worth it to ask why he'd done it? He decided it was. "Did winning the race mean so much to you, then?"

"No," he denied—but too quickly. "Honestly, I don't know how it happened. I mean, I know *how,* but—Christy, I swear I didn't mean to hurt you."

"I believe you. But you did."

"Well, I can't take it back. Would if I could. Sometimes the devil gets into me, I guess." He gave a short laugh, trying to make Christy join in. "I don't know why I did it," he said again, more softly. "Stupid. It could've been serious. Last thing I intended." He grinned determinedly. "You have to forgive me, though. It's your job!"

Christy told the truth. "I was angry with you at first. And confused, and hurt. I couldn't understand why you'd done it. But there was never any question of forgiving you."

Geoffrey's face went beet-red with emotion. Embarrassed, he shoved his chair back and stood up, but before he could turn away, Christy caught a glimpse of the old Geoffrey, the staunch, true friend he'd loved since his boyhood. That image, gone so quickly, warmed him and unburdened his heart; the heaviness he'd been carrying for weeks because his oldest friend was a stranger suddenly lifted.

"Really came to ask you to look after Anne," Geoffrey said casually, over his shoulder, moving through the house he knew almost as well as Christy did. He paused in the open front door. "God," he breathed, and Christy looked with him past the oaks and sycamores in front of the vicarage to the quiet village green, unpopulated this morning except for a couple of mothers sunning their babies on the grass. A prosaic sight to Christy, but Geoffrey seemed taken by it. "I could almost envy you," he said unexpectedly.

"Me?" Christy blinked in surprise. "Why?"

"You've got a home."

"But you've—"

"I've got a house. And I can't wait to get out of it." He waved his arm. "He spoiled all this for me," he said, his bitterness undisguised. "I couldn't stay here without going mad. Do you remember the first time I ran away?"

Christy looked at him in surprise, thinking Geoffrey might have been reading his mind. "Yes, I remember. In fact, I was just thinking of it." He'd have said more, but Geoffrey's face closed up, indicating that the subject was closed. But the memory was indelible, as clear in Christy's mind now as on the night, more than twenty years ago, when it had happened. He'd been a child of seven or eight, playing on the floor in his father's study—his study now—on a cold, rainy evening. A loud knocking at the front door had startled him; his father had gone to answer it, with Christy at his heels.

There stood Geoffrey under the porch roof, dripping wet, rainwater indistinguishable from the tears spilling down his cheeks. Christy could no longer remember the words he'd blurted out in anger and near-hysterical desperation, but he would never forget how Geoffrey had flung himself against his father's legs and held on like a cocklebur. He was running away from home—he hated his own father and would never go back—he wanted to live at the vicarage with the Morrells. The vicar had finally pried his clinging fingers away and taken him into his study, shutting the door behind them. Christy had lurked in the hall, quaking with fear and excitement. Eventually his mother had gone into the study, too; from the staircase, he'd strained to hear their low voices. Even now he could clearly recall the pattern of the old floral wallpaper at the bottom of the steps, the muddy trail of water Geoffrey's boots had left on the oak floor; but exactly what else had happened on that rainy night was lost from memory.

At any rate, Geoffrey hadn't come to live with them. And he'd changed after that. In the nine years that remained of their friendship, Christy had never seen him cry again.

"Listen, Christy, will you take care of Anne for me?"

"Take care of her?" he repeated stupidly. "But you'll be back."

"Whether I'm back or not, watch out for her, will you? She's better off without me in any case, and Holyoake's as solid as they come as far as advice and all that. But . . . she'll be lonely. I've left her before, God knows, but never in the hands of anyone I could trust. Will you look after her?"

"Of course."

"Good. Good." He turned brisk. "Last request. Considering what happened before, you might want to say no to this, and I'll understand if you do."

"What is it?"

"Give Devil a run every once in a while. There's no one else I'd ask but you."

Christy looked at him for a moment, then threw back his head and laughed. After a couple of sheepish seconds, Geoffrey joined him. When they sobered, he said, "You're a great friend, Christy. It's not just any man I'd entrust my wife *and* my horse to."

"The honor's overwhelming." He watched Geoffrey saunter down the flagstone path to the street. "I'll see you before you go," he called, and Geoffrey waved in assent. "Give my regards to your wife *and* your horse!"

16 June

I hardly ever dream anymore, I don't know why. Tonight I did, though, and it woke me up. I was walking through a tall thicket of brake fern, the clear green fronds as high as my shoulders. I came to a gate leading into a meadow full of flowers. A man began to walk beside me, and his boots were golden bronze from the yellow pollen of buttercups. I don't know who he was, though in the dream I think I knew. After a while it wasn't a meadow anymore, it had become the hayfield Marcus Timms works as a tenant for Lynton Hall Farm, and all around us men were threshing and winnowing the wheat. We wanted to run, but the man kept my hand and we went at a slow, casual pace, always heading toward a tall hayrick at the edge of the field.

Here the dream stopped and started, stopped and started, repeating endlessly until I was nearly wild with impatience—for I knew when we got to the hayrick we would come together—make love. Someone stopped us, William Holyoake, I think, and we had to talk and talk about the harvest and the work, and some convoluted business about how much pay the itinerant workers should receive versus the parish regulars who live on the land. By now I was half-awake and forcing the dream to continue—and, as is the way of these things, it lost its innocence. But not its urgency. At last we reached our hayrick, my mysterious lover and I, and we clung to each other in the stalky, dusty pile, rolling and rolling. Our clothes disappeared. I was nothing but longing and need, I wanted him to fill me, come inside me, I wanted us to merge. It was unbearable.

My own yearning jolted me completely awake, no going back this time, no forcing the conclusion. I lay in a damp tangle of sheet and nightgown, seething and boiling, actually weeping a little from the frustration.

Who was the man, I wonder? Perhaps he was no one, merely a symbol of men in general, without whom I seem to have lived my whole life, even when I've lived in men's houses. I suppose dreams like this are natural for women, not too alarming. I'm not very old, after all, and I haven't enjoyed marital relations in four years. Not since my short-lived "honeymoon." If I lived in Italy still, perhaps I would take a lover. Here, such a thing seems unthinkably *outre*, even bizarre. Well, well, then I shall have to find something else to do with myself.

21 June

Nearly a month, and no word yet from Geoffrey. But that's nothing new. I'd thought he might scribble one of his illegible notes to Christy Morrell if not to me, but the reverend says he's received nothing. I had to look at the globe in old D'Aubrey's musty library to learn where Varna is: in Bulgaria, on the Black Sea. To the northeast is an island—or perhaps a peninsula, I can't be sure; the pock-marked globe is as old as the books, i.e., prehistoric—called Crimea, where Geoffrey expects the real fighting to occur. I read the newspapers to keep up. Quiet old England turns out to be a shade bloodthirsty: everyone is dying for a good old-fashioned war again, which they haven't had since Waterloo. The enemy seems to have been picked almost at random, as far as I can tell. The residents of Wyckerley are puzzled but proud of their new viscount for going off to keep Turkey safe from Russian encroachment (a murky and remote motive to me, but perhaps I don't understand politics) and never fail to ask me what news I've had from my husband. I say the mails are unreliable, which is certainly true, and change the subject.

Money, or rather, the lack of it, is becoming something of a problem. Geoffrey purchased half his commission on credit, and since the estate isn't completely settled yet, most of the ready cash has had to go to pay off his debt to the Royal Commission. How ironic that the Viscountess D'Aubrey is at present nearly as penniless in this great rambling pile of a house as she was when she was a mere abandoned wife in Holborn. The lawyers say the situation is temporary, so I don't worry about it overmuch. But I find it singularly unamusing that, for the second time, England's inheritance laws are playing havoc with my life.

26 June

Every day, the beauty of this place seduces me a little more. The neighborhood abounds in gloriously picturesque walks, and even though the villagers think it not quite proper of me to tramp about on my own, unescorted and unchaperoned, I do it anyway. Not to defy their conventions, but because I can't help myself—I'm lured out of the house by the droning of bees in the clover or the rising song of larks, and before I know it I'm walking in a red sunken lane, too narrow for two carts to pass abreast and nearly covered over with the leafy arching trees. Sometimes William Holyoake's dog accompanies me, but if not, I'm quite alone. I missed the clean outdoors much more than I knew, living in filthy, noisy London all those years. There's an old Roman ruin the natives call Abbeycombe, set back from the Plymouth toll road, only half a mile from here. I go there often and lose myself among the old stones, gazing up at the clouds or down at the wildflowers that spring out of the rubble. A peacefulness comes to me there; I feel as if I'm getting clean. Other times, I go to the old abandoned canal, surely the most melancholy spot in all of Devon. I'm rarely as sad as that still, lonely, lifeless place, and so it cheers me up. I've tried to sketch it any number of times, but I can never get it right.

The groundsman at Lynton Hall, a creaky, white-haired Scot named McCurdy, has banished me from the gardens for incompetence. Now I'm allowed to weed and nothing else. It's true that I have no green thumb, a minor tragedy in my life since I dearly love flowers, but if I were a sturdier person I might ask Mr. McCurdy where he gets his nerve. That ruined, overgrown series of terraces behind the house is no Haddon Hall, I could tell him, no Chatsworth, no Woburn Abbey. Someone should take it in hand. Even I, the floracide, can see the gorgeous possibilities under the bronzed and matted azaleas, the thorny, tangled vines of roses and clematis and anonymous creeper. Apparently the person who takes it in hand is not going to be me. But if it's Mr. McCurdy, I'll eat my hat.

Inside the house, I'm not quite as useless. Mrs. Fruit grows dimmer, and her housekeeping duties devolve a little more each day upon me, by virtue of there being no one else. Even so, without the ready money just now for anything except basic improvements—the leaks in the roof, for instance, and the fireplaces that smoke—there isn't that much to do. One lone woman doesn't require a great deal in the way of tending, nor does she make much of a mess. I try to think up projects for the staff—cleaning the library, airing and dusting books that haven't been opened in fifty years—but even with that, the maids have little to do by two or three in the afternoon. No one seems fazed by this idleness, so I'm left to conclude that it's been the status quo for some time.

So. After I've pretended to advise Mr. Holyoake on

farming, dairy, and sheep herd matters, after he's politely pretended to weigh and accept my advice, I'm much at my leisure. I sit in the sun, I walk along the river. I sketch and write. The villagers are standoffish—although I daresay they think exactly the same about me. Everyone is courteous, but there's an underlying servitude to their courtesy that disturbs me. "M'lady," they call me, and the laborers actually pull at their forelocks when they greet me, like feudal serfs. At the same time, I'm too reserved (enervated?) to go visiting and calling and card-leaving, all that tedious protocol one has to endure, even in this relative backwater of society, to initiate the laborious process of friend-making. The Vanstones have called on me once, and a stiff, unsatisfactory time was had by all. She is tiresome; he is ambitious. On the whole, I like him better. At least there's a sharp mind operating behind the suave mayoral smoothness. He's a handsome man in his way; hard and a bit driven, one senses, but intelligent, certainly, and probably interesting under the stiffness. But perhaps I'm too hard on Miss Vanstone ("Do call me Honoria"). She's merely inherited her father's ambition, after all; but because she's a woman, her only outlets for it are husband-hunting and social-climbing. Such is often the fate of our sex.

Honoria's cousin is a young lady named Sophie Deene, a charming, guileless, pretty girl who makes me feel like an old crone. After church last Sunday, she waited on the steps with an old school chum who was visiting from Devonport (no secrets in Wyckerley); I watched them as they stood there in the sunshine, laughing together, playfully bumping shoulders, youth and joy and innocent hope shimmering around their blond heads like auras. God, how I envied them! I went home alone, feeling sorry for myself, and spent the rest of the day wishing I were

twenty again and that the last four years of my life had
never happened. Not a new wish, and as fruitless as usual.

My only other visitor is Christy. He's come three times,
and invited me to tea at the rectory twice. Obviously Geoffrey asked him to take me under his wing. (An arresting
image; I picture myself at the Archangel's side, surrounded
by his enormous feathery arm, warm and comforting, pro-
tecting me from harm.) But even if he only comes because
Geoffrey asked him to, I look forward to his visits with impatience, and take more pleasure in his company than I
dare let on. I can come closer to being myself with Reverend Morrell than with anyone else—a huge, seductive,
powerful relief, and the last thing in the world I'd have expected. We talk about everything. So far he hasn't tried to
convert me, but he wants to know how I "got this way." I
tell him a little of my life story—not much, and only the
happy bits—and he ponders it in his careful, thoughtful
way, making no judgments. He actually *prays* for me. I
know this because he told me so, straight out, without a
blush. It gave me the queerest feeling—which I hid with a
nervous, bitter laugh. What does he say to his God about
me? I would love to eavesdrop on his monologues with the
Lord. I don't think it's pity Christy feels for me, fallen
woman though I am. No, not pity. For some reason, I do
believe he admires me. I've never been the object of admiration of a man like Christian Morrell before. I don't know
what to think of it. I think of it quite a good deal. His
frankness about his own life continues to disarm me. If
there's a dishonest or even a disingenuous bone in this
man's body, I've seen no sign of it yet. He's not like anyone
I've ever met. He fascinates me.

His house is beautiful. It's not as old as the church,
which is Norman and very impressive in its own way. The
parsonage is a hybrid Tudor-Renaissance affair built in the

late fifteenth century, with later additions that are remotely Jacobean—mullioned bow windows, a tower with
floor levels different from those of the house, and more
detail and decoration because the new parts are of sandstone rather than the hard Dartmoor granite. It's not a
quarter the size of Lynton, and much cozier, of course,
quite mellow and romantic. His study is appropriately
book-lined, but the books spill out into the hall and
halfway up the stairs. The reading lamp on his big desk
stays lit half the night, I'm sure. I imagine him sitting
there sometimes when I'm restless with insomnia, listening to my clock tick away the hours. He writes his sermons
at that desk, and I like to picture him rehearsing them to
the empty room late at night, striding up and down a bit,
gesturing in the right places. He reads a great deal, but
he's not one of those clergymen who live only to write
theological tracts, and actually *minister* only when absolutely necessary. Christy cares about every single person
in his parish, and he has no qualms about showing it.
They, in turn, adore him—why would they not? The men
admire him, the women want to take care of him, and the
girls . . . well, within the confines of a sacramentally sanctioned union (one assumes), the girls simply *want* him. I
see it every Sunday when he greets them on the church
steps, and it amuses me. In a way. But—I don't want him
to choose any of them. No, not even the lovely Sophie
Deene, and certainly neither of the silly Swan sisters, nor
Miss Mareton, nor any of the others. He's too good for
them. Much too good for all of them.

That sounds very odd, on rereading. Motherly? Good
Lord, the last thing I feel toward Reverend Morrell is
motherly. Proprietary? I suppose. I flatter myself that we
have a special relationship, and I find the thought of another woman—another *person*—hearing the things he says

to me, private, confidential, fascinating things about his hopes for his life, his fears of failure—the thought of him sharing them with another person makes me feel . . . diminished. Cheated? I might almost say betrayed, but that's too much—and—it exposes the vanity in all of this.

Reverend Morrell is not like me. He is open, generous-spirited, candid, unashamed of sharing his feelings. That's why he confides them in me, and I've made the egoistic mistake of fancying that he confides them in no one else.

On reflection, I feel slightly ridiculous.

I can't write any more.

Except that it's a good thing that I keep this journal. It helps me to see the folly in my thinking early on, and no doubt saves me from a great deal of humiliation.

IX

LAMMAS DAY, THE first day of August, fell on a Tuesday. All the Lynton Hall Farm workers were given a half-holiday, and Christy was gratified to see their employer setting an example by attending the brief church service at midday; she even joined the procession of worshipers carrying loaves of new wheat down the aisle, as an offering of the first fruits of the harvest. He blessed the loaves and gave a very short discourse on the meaning of Lammastide, distracted, as usual, by Anne's quiet presence in the manorial pew. After the service, he asked if she would wait for him a moment while he spoke to his curate on a church matter; he had a favor to ask her.

A warm wind was blowing wet gray clouds up from the coast. Midsummer had passed, but the air was still sweet and mild, with no hint of autumn yet in the sturdy breeze. Christy finished his business with Reverend Woodworth and went to look for Anne. He found her in the churchyard, prowling among the old lichen-covered tombstones. She looked up when she heard the squeal of the lych-gate latch, smiling at him as he came toward her. She wore a dark brown cape, and just then the wind snatched the hood off and ruffled her hair. He felt the now-familiar lurch in his chest and attributed it to the simple fact that she was beautiful. More so each time he saw her. It was true; she hardly even resembled the pale, tense, monosyllabic woman he'd met beside her father-in-law's deathbed four months ago.

Nothing wrong with recognizing that, was there? He wasn't *blind*, was he?

"I'm inordinately fond of graveyards," she said by way of a greeting, trailing her long white hand across the pocked forehead of a granite cherub. "I often walk in the D'Aubrey family plot, just as the sun is setting. I haunt it."

He could rarely fathom her moods. Her smiles were either brittle or soft and inexpressibly sad, and they almost never reached her eyes. She said bitter things with the soft smile and vulnerable things with the brittle one, keeping him off balance and anxious for her. "I like them, too," he told her. "I come here at night sometimes. I've never felt morbid about it."

"No, well, you wouldn't." She waved at the sea of leaning headstones around them. "The souls of all these faithful departed have gone on to their just rewards, haven't they? In fact, you'd have to say they're better off now than they were when they were among us, at least the good ones. Wouldn't you, Reverend?"

She loved to tease him about his faith. He didn't mind it; he had an idea it was as much herself she was mocking as him. "That's true. I can't say I've ever actually *envied* any of these faithful departed, however. Which must mean my faith in the ecstatic hereafter isn't as rock solid as it ought to be."

She sent him a knowing smile, acknowledging his favorite rhetorical device with her—saying what she was going to say before she could say it, thereby defusing her argument. "Aren't you going to commend me for participating in that rather pagan ritual you just presided over?" she asked archly.

"If you're referring to the blessing of the loaves, that's *traditional,* not pagan. I hope you'll join us on Plough Sunday next January."

"Plough Sunday? Don't tell me you bless a plough!"

"I do. The farmers carry it inside and set it down in the chancel, where it sits in muddy state all during the service."

"Good Lord."

"Exactly."

She laughed, a lovely tinkling sound he could have listened to forever. "What was it you wanted to ask me?"

"It was two things, actually. Have you heard of our penny readings, Anne?"

"Your what?"

"It's a misnomer; they don't cost a penny, they're free. If you haven't heard of them, it's because we haven't had any for a few years. They used to be held in the vicarage meeting room, once a week for an hour or two on Friday evenings. Mrs. Vanstone gave them. She'd usually read from the classics, but popular novels as well, or poetry, history—anything that took her fancy and wasn't too difficult, since the audience was mostly working people."

"Mrs. Vanstone? The mayor's . . . wife?"

He nodded. "She died about three years ago, and not long after that the readings were discontinued."

A look of horror crossed her face. "You aren't asking *me* to start them up again!"

"I think you'd be very good at it."

She made a disbelieving sound, not quite a snort but close to it. "Why not get *Miss* Vanstone? I should think that would be exactly her cup of tea."

"She was asked to take them over," he admitted. "They . . . weren't as popular. No one came."

"Ah."

Her tone made him feel he had to defend Honoria. "She had a different style from her mother and people didn't care for it as much. She . . ."

"She was snooty and supercilious and they loathed her?"

He sent her a look of forbearance. "She wasn't quite as natural and engaging a reader as her mother," he corrected. "Now, if you were to take them over—"

"I—"

"—you'd fill the hall every Friday night."

"Oh, rot. Well," she conceded on second thought, "I might at first, but only because they'd come to gape at me. After the novelty wore off, I'd be no more successful than the unengaging Miss Vanstone."

"Why would you think that?"

"Because I'm not good with people." When he laughed at her, she added, "Especially people in groups."

"How do you know?"

"I know." She folded her arms.

"How? Have you spoken to groups before?"

"I don't have to."

"I take it that means no." He sighed. "It gets easier," he said gloomily. "A little. Not much," he amended in a flash of candor.

Now she looked at him with interest. "Don't you like it?"

"It's not a question of liking it. Part of my clerical vocation involves preaching, which means my 'sermonic effectiveness,' as we used to say in divinity school, determines in some measure the effectiveness of my ministry."

"But, Christy, you preach a fine sermon!"

"No," he said flatly, "I do not. Anyway, we're not discussing me. I really wish you'd consider the penny readings, Anne. You could try one," he coaxed, "and if it went well, you could think about a second one."

"Why does it have to be only one person?" she fretted, nervously smacking the pockmarked cherub on the head while she spoke. "Why couldn't it be several, taking turns? Men as well as women?"

"Now, that's a fine idea! There's a meeting this Friday of the deacons and the vestry in the hall—why don't you come and suggest it? You'd be extremely welcome, needless to say. A committee could be formed, with you at its head, and the whole business could be planned in a couple of ad hoc gatherings. That's really a splendid idea. Thank you for proposing it."

She looked nonplussed. Then she began to laugh. "You know, you're not half as clever as you think you are, Reverend Morrell. In fact, you're as transparent as a glass of water."

He grinned, unrepentant. What a pleasure it was to make her laugh. "Will you do it? Come to the meeting on Friday?"

"Oh, Christy!" she wailed.

"Please."

She glared at him, weighing her choice. Now she was hammering on the cherub with her fist. "Oh, all right," she finally grumbled.

"Excellent. You won't regret it."

"I regret it right now." But she smiled when she said it. "And I'm afraid to ask you what the *second* favor is."

"Maybe you should be. It's a bigger request," he admitted.

"I refuse to teach Sunday school."

"Not that," he said, chuckling. "Can you stay a few more minutes? I'd like to show you something."

They left the churchyard and went down the narrow alley between tall hedges at the back of his house. They passed the vicarage garden on the way, neat and tidy as always, the fruit of Arthur Ludd's constant attention.

"Oh," Anne said enviously, "what a pretty garden. You're lucky to have it. Mr. McCurdy has forbidden me to work in ours."

"Forbidden you? Why?"

"I kill things. *He* says. Of course, he thinks he's Capability Brown."

He laughed again. "Have you had any word yet from Geoffrey?" he thought to ask a moment later.

"No, but that doesn't mean anything. He almost never writes to me."

"Do you write to him?"

She turned on him one of her brittle smiles. "But of course. Faithfully, once a week. I'm nothing if not a dutiful wife, Reverend Morrell."

He let that pass; when she was in this mood, prickly and sardonic, nothing he said could suit her.

He took her arm so she wouldn't stumble in the stony alley behind the house. For some reason touching her, even in this meaningless way, seemed too intimate a thing to do in silence, so he said as they went along, "I hear you've been making good progress on improvements to the estate cottages."

"Yes, well, it's a beginning. There's not enough money right now to do as much as we'd like. But Holyoake says the harvest will be good this year, and after that we'll be able to do more. Christy, what on earth was Edward Verlaine thinking of, to let things go so badly? Some of the conditions I've seen are absolutely shocking, a *disgrace*."

"He always claimed he had no monetary incentive to keep the cottages up. He said improving them would attract more families to the neighborhood, and he was afraid the increased population would raise the poor rates. So he made a deliberate choice to keep new people out and the old people in damp, unsanitary, derelict housing."

She made a disgusted sound. "That's criminal. It ought to be against the law."

"He said it was good business."

"Is this a very poor parish, then?" she asked doubtfully. "I haven't seen any real suffering yet. But perhaps I wouldn't; perhaps I'm shielded from it." She looked as if the thought disturbed her.

"There's poverty, of course. In bad years, after the poor law provisions for the district give out, sometimes private charity— my bailiwick—is all that stands between some people and the workhouse. We muddle through with the various benefit clubs the church organizes, and doles of food and clothing for the truly destitute. But I've always thought we could do more, and that philanthropy isn't the only answer."

He took her hand to negotiate the rough stile over a fence separating the church close from open pastureland. On the other side he stopped. "The grass is wet; this is far enough, we needn't go in."

She peered around, trying to discover what he could want to show her in a bare yellow field. She gave up and looked at him quizzically.

"This is glebe land—meaning the ecclesiastical parish owns it. Nearly nine hundred acres." He pointed. "It stretches south to the eastern tributary of the Plym. As you can see, it's uncultivated; it's lain fallow since the time of the sixth D'Aubrey earl—Geoffrey's the eighth."

She nodded. "Yes?"

"I had an idea that the poorest farm laborers in the parish could work it. Cultivate it and plant the crops they need to survive in the bad years—most years, for many of them."

"That's an excellent idea," she said, nodding approval. "It ought to have been done long ago."

"I agree."

"Why wasn't it?"

"Because there's no money for tools and seed. I was hoping to persuade you to donate them. At least for the first year."

She faced him, her lovely features full of surprise. He watched her without speaking, and gradually the surprise changed to thoughtfulness. She turned to gaze out across the rough, stubbly landscape, eyes narrowed, fingers lightly patting her lips. "I'd have to consult with William," she said slowly.

"Naturally."

"If he said it was feasible and he had no objections . . ."

"As a matter of fact, I've already asked him."

She raised her eyebrows at that. "Have you?"

"He's for it."

"Is he?" Suddenly she smiled, and Christy felt as if sunshine had broken through and dazzled him. "Then it's done."

He blinked at her. "Really?"

"Why not? Geoffrey won't care. I'll write to him, of course, but I can tell you now that he won't care. Oh, I'm glad for the chance to do something! I've felt so useless at times, not knowing how I could help. This is a good solution."

"You make it sound as if we've done something for you, when it's exactly the reverse."

She had an appealing, vaguely foreign way of shrugging her shoulders. She leaned back against the stile, surveying the field with a more proprietary air than before. He took the opportunity to stare at her—something he was always trying not to do. It was folly to tell himself that all she'd brought into his quiet life was friendship and frank conversation. He thought about her too much for that to be true. The days when they didn't meet seemed flat and routine to him, incomplete. He caught himself saving up stories or bits of conversation to share when he saw her. He kept her in the back of his mind, seeing the world through her eyes, thinking, *Anne would laugh at that; this would surprise her; that would put her back up.*

She turned to him suddenly. "Christy, are there so many poor people that they could cultivate all nine hundred acres productively?"

"No, thank God, not all of it."

"So the rest would continue to lie fallow?"

"Yes, I suppose."

She brooded. The wind pulled at her hair, blowing it across her cheeks. The colorless sky had leached the green from her eyes; they were smoke-gray now and narrowed in thought. "What if . . . what if Lynton Hall tenant laborers worked the other acres in the spare time I gave them? Half a day a week, say, taken out of the time they usually work on estate lands."

"You would do that?"

"I don't know; Holyoake would have to advise me. Maybe others as well—lawyers from Tavistock, Geoffrey's solicitors. Of course, the Hall Farm has to come first; I can't get around that, and it's my first responsibility. But—if the rest of this land were planted in grain crops and vegetables, and the produce sold for money that would go toward worthwhile projects in the parish— your bailiwick—wouldn't that profit everyone? The workers' lot would improve in time, so the taxes on the poor would go down, which would be to the benefit of the rate-paying gentry. Wouldn't it? Tell me if that makes sense."

"It's something I tried to persuade Edward to do, and my father before me, both of us without success. Anne," he said earnestly, "this is wonderful. It's exactly what the district needs— and has for years. You've been here a matter of months, and you've put your finger on it squarely."

He had the pleasure of watching her turn her head away in confusion. It wasn't a blush, but it was the next best thing. Her simple, straightforward kindness was so clear to him, and it drew him as irresistibly as her beauty. "Nonsense," she scoffed, pretending a great interest in the distant treetops. "It's only common sense. It may not work at all. If it does, I—we, rather, Geoffrey and I—will reap the benefits as much as anyone. Probably more."

"Maybe. I hope so. The nice thing," he said lightly, "is that you thought of it yourself. The truth is, I'd intended to suggest it to you, but not for a little while longer. My plan was to soften you up gradually." She turned back to him, obviously relieved that he was through admiring her. The humor and friendliness in her face warmed him to his bones. He lifted his hand—and dropped it abruptly, realizing he'd been going to touch her.

"I believe you've been softening me up gradually, Reverend Morrell, since the day we met," she said, quite softly.

Her words weren't as playful as they sounded. He was sure of that, but not of anything else. Neither had moved, but now they seemed to be standing too close together. She kept her gaze on his face, her gray eyes subtle as a whisper. There was no seduction in her glance, but there was awareness. He stood stock-still, afraid that if he moved he would do something irredeemable, something he couldn't take back.

She lifted her head to look at the sky, and the flash of her bare white throat dazzled him. "It looks like rain," she said calmly. He made a show of looking up at the clouds, but he couldn't see anything but her. "We'd better go. Before the heavens open."

He nodded, made some response. She gave him her hand, so he could help her over the stile. Didn't she know? Couldn't she feel the emotion sparking like a lit fuse on the surface of his skin where he touched her? No; her face was serene.

Thank God for that, ran through his mind. He flinched; best to leave God out of it, at least for the moment. Otherwise the heavens really might open up. *Fire and rain,* he thought disconnectedly. *The deluge.*

Ridiculous—he'd done nothing, committed no sin. He was still safe.

For now.

11 August

Faithful journal-keeping is easier when I'm miserable and have time on my hands. Which must mean I'm happy and busy. Impossible; I never associate those two words with myself. Reasonably content and somewhat harried. Better.

All that notwithstanding, plans to transform nine hundred idle glebe acres into productive and profitable farmland proceed apace. Tools and seed can be provided with only a minimal capital outlay, I'm assured, and already the soil is being turned and manured ("fertilized," Mr. Holyoake is always careful to say, in deference to my lady-like sensibilities); on some parcels a crop of cowpeas is to be planted, to ready it for wheat in the spring.

Getting everyone to agree on the plan—Lynton workers laboring on glebe acreage at estate expense—has proven considerably more difficult. There are more people involved in a decision of that magnitude than I realized: lawyers and bank lenders, other property owners in the district, political associates of the old viscount, church authorities—even the mayor has an opinion. I hear myself, in meetings with these men, speaking of Lynton Hall exactly as if I owned it, and using the first person singular as if, indeed, I were the lord of the manor. Sometimes I wish Geoffrey had appointed the Wyckerlian equivalent of a regent before he went away! No one, absolutely no one, is in favor of my proposal when he first hears it. I keep talking, and more often than I'd have thought possible—*mirabile dictu!*—he reconsiders and says he'll take it under advisement. By now I'm completely convinced that this is a good plan, the right thing to do morally, socially, fiscally, and every way, and I don't intend to give up until it's resolved and set in motion.

Christy's penny readings are set to begin tonight. How I let him talk me into this bit of lunacy is a mystery I expect never to unravel. I am to be the first "penny reader," an apt title, for I'm sure it describes precisely what my maiden effort will be worth. I'll read *David Copperfield* for as many nights as it takes to finish it (or until enough fruit is flung at me to make me go away, whichever comes first), after which Sophie Deene will read, then Dr. Hesselius, then Mrs. Armstrong—a widow from the village, something of a bluestocking, I gather—then back to me.

I have opening night nerves. William says, "Buck up, m'lady! Take a glass o' sommat afore you begin, and all will be well." I laughed at him. Now, two hours before my debut, the sherry decanter is looking more and more inviting. But no—I shall go to my fate undisguised with drink, and face the consequences like a man. Or, more likely, a fool.

12 August

I'm having my sherry now, for I'm celebrating. It was a success! A "rousing" one, said Christy; Mayor Vanstone, a sober man, went so far as to say "ringing." *I* say whacking, roaring, thumping, howling!! Far from throwing fruit at me, they sat in their chairs (all twenty-three of them, an unheard-of number, Christy says) as silent as fish, and at first I couldn't tell if they were spellbound or stupefied. But soon they were smiling over Peggoty, then laughing out loud, and when Mr. Murdstone appeared on the scene they began to fidget with unease and mutter worriedly among themselves. I myself had no coughing fit, no spontaneous vocal paralysis, nor did I suddenly start speaking in tongues; in fact, none of my nervous anxieties came to pass. Two hours flew by before anyone noticed, including me, and I was made to finish Chapter 5, "I Am Sent Away from Home," before they would let me stop. Then they wanted to talk about everything, and my job became trying to get them to speak one at a time.

It may have been the opportunity to stare openly for two whole hours at Lady D'Aubrey that brought them, but it's Mr. Dickens's storytelling brilliance that will bring them back next week. I'm so grateful to Christy for making me do this! The people are mostly grown men and women, all working people, rough-mannered, plainspoken, uneducated but eager to learn. It's hard to imagine Honoria Vanstone sitting in the same room with them. (I would say that to Christy, but he would think it unkind of me; I might say it anyway, to tease him.) There's a miner named Tranter Fox—I saw him once before, helping Christy after he fell from his horse in the race with Geoffrey. He's a funny little man with a broad Cornish accent; I'm quite taken with him. He calls Christy "Your Grace," and tonight he called me "Your Highness." I'm *almost* positive he knows better and is doing it on purpose. But the gleam of humor in his eye is irresistible, and when it was all over and he paid me the supreme compliment of inviting me to join him and his mates for a thimbleful at the George and Dragon, I could only laugh with the others. I daresay I'm not upholding the dignity of my rank with sufficient assiduity, and Miss Vanstone would make a far better viscountess than I. I can't help it. Tranter Fox amuses me, and I won't pretend he doesn't.

So. My first penny reading was a victory, albeit an exceedingly minor one in the scheme of things. And I'm left to ponder, alone in my room at one o'clock in the morning, why this makes me so happy.

19 August

Second reading went as well as the first. Had a cup of tea afterward with Christy in his study. Improper, I suppose, since Mrs. Ludd, his housekeeper, went to bed and left us to ourselves. I say if you can't have tea alone with the vicar, with whom can you have tea alone? No proprieties were flouted. He walked me home, and we were both snug in our beds by eleven o'clock. Our separate beds, I need hardly say.

Why did I say it, then?

28 August

At last, a letter from Geoffrey. He says he's well—I suppose I must believe it. There's cholera among the French troops, which has reduced their force at Varna and their fleet at sea to impotence. Preparations for the siege of Sebastopol go on regardless, and he thinks it will all be over in a month. His commander is Lord Raglan; St. Arnaud commands the French. "As usual," he says, "the country to whose aid we've come is doing the least. The squeamish Turks could have ended it all at Silistria if they'd stood firm." I see two disingenuities in these lines. One, we've decided to engage Russia for our own ends, not Turkey's, so it's hardly a question of coming to their aid; two, Geoffrey is delighted that things didn't end at Silistria, because if they had, he wouldn't have gotten the chance—his last, he claims—to play soldier.

At any rate, it looks like a real war this time, not the sort of skirmishing-with-the-natives business he's used to. I can't pray for him—I leave that to Reverend Morrell—so I *hope* for him. I hope he stays well, and I hope he finds some kind of peace while he wages his favorite pastime.

2 September

Another reading last night. Tea with Christy afterward. It's our habit now. I don't know how he regards them, but for me these evenings alone together are indispensable. Who would have thought it—of my entire acquaintance, Reverend Christian Morrell has become the person with whom I can most be my godless self. Astonishing.

10 September

Last night was the harvest home. I thought the sheep shearers' dinner in May was a lively affair. Ha! What naivete! It was a tea party at the Weedies' compared to the harvest home. Christy said a very nice prayer at the beginning, thanking God for the fruits of the harvest, etc., etc. After that, there were no more serious moments. There was no actual debauchery (at least not that I witnessed), but neither was there much sobriety, and precious little dignity. The great thing about the harvest home, unlike the shearing supper, is the opportunity it affords for the classic ritual of role-reversing. The employer not only has to be unstinting in the provision of great quantities of food and ale, he must also *serve at table* and in all ways see to the comfort and convenience of the guests—who, on the other three hundred and sixty-four days of the year, are mere humble laborers. No doubt that's all that prevents the affair from subsiding into complete chaos: the knowledge that everything goes back to normal on the morrow and nothing had better be done that can't be undone.

I bore my responsibilities well, I think. No one could reproach me with poor sportsmanship, and certainly not with stinginess in the meat and drink department. We're having a "St. Luke's summer," which means an abnormally warm autumn, and so the affair was held out-of-doors, on long tables arranged in a square in the courtyard. Between the full moon and the lanterns and candles all around, it was nearly as bright as day, and much more festive. There were singing and dancing to a violin and tambourine band between the courses, a bit of drunken horseplay, ribald stories punctuated with a great deal of shushing whenever I came near. I was toasted time and again for my generosity, my beauty, my cleverness, my kindness—everything but my grandmother's rheumatism. Despite all my cajoling, Christy wouldn't come inside and have a good-night toddy with me (he couldn't seem to get away fast enough, in fact; I can't think why), so at eleven o'clock I took myself off, aware that my presence was inhibiting the free expression of my other guests' good spirits—but with instructions to Holyoake that all the drinking must cease at midnight. I suppose it did, for not long afterward everyone began to toddle home, and by one o'clock there was nothing but a great mess for the maids and me to clean up.

Today I feel logy and tired, almost as though I had been among the over-indulgers last night, which I certainly was not. But I'm peaceful, too. Content. Harvest home is a good tradition. A reward for hard work; an invigorating if momentary blurring of social distinctions; an opportunity to express thanks for and satisfaction in the fruits of one's labor; a marker for the end of one season and the start of another. If we had souls, the harvest home would be good for them.

29 September—Michaelmas

William Holyoake went to the hiring fair at Tavistock today. As we discussed, he engaged only a new shepherd and an odd-job man. It means that until Lady Day, at least, the dairy will be understaffed and Collie Horrocks will have too much to do in the stables. No help for it, and we'll get along all right.

10 October

Even in Provence, I've never seen an autumn as lovely as this. From the window in my attic sitting room, the world looks like a Dutch painting, done from a palette of gold and amber and scarlet, brilliant orange and blinding yellow. Pumpkins in great piles loll in every field, and the air smells of woodsmoke. There was a frost last night, but today it's mild again, and the sky is too blue to look at. Flowers—who knew there could be so many in October? I am seduced, I am ravished by this beauty. And it's all the lovelier for being like a lover—gone too soon.

17 October

Poor Mrs. Weedie fell in her garden yesterday and broke her hipbone. Miss Weedie is beside herself. I brought food, cider, fresh bread, etc., and tried to help. They won't let me. The old ladies have rallied round like sentinels, closing ranks to newcomers and social superiors—which leaves me out on two scores. They part to let Christy in, and he hardly has to speak; he soothes and comforts just by his presence.

• Dr. Hesselius says the invalid will heal in time, but she may not walk again. Such trouble, such heartbreak. Miss Weedie does not deserve this—nor her mother, of course, but somehow, to me, it seems worse for the daughter. There's a sweetness and grace between the two of them that mesmerizes me. To have a mother like that, to know you were loved so deeply, without conditions, just for your-self alone—it touches the heart. What will Miss Weedie do when she's on her own? Where will all the love go? I want to help her—oh, I want to do something! But there's nothing to do.

Christy sees trouble and sadness like this every day, and I don't know how he can stand it.

3 November

I've neglected my journal. The habit is easily lost and hard to recover. Extremes of emotion compel me to write, I think—deep melancholy, great joy—and the prosaic pass-ing of quiet, contented days lulls me into procrastination. I must get hold of myself.

I have a little free time now because Miss Weedie, due

to the rain, cried off my invitation to tea, declining as well my offer ("too generous, too much, oh, too condescending") to send the carriage for her. She will not let me be her friend. If she knew that this hurts me, she would be mortified, and so it's impossible to take offense. I am her "better"; thus I'm beyond the scope of anything but polite civilities and correct social forms. I've almost got it now; almost accepted it.

I've had no more letters from Geoffrey, but Christy had one a few days ago and showed it to me. His regiment crossed the Black Sea without incident in the second week of September, but foul weather prevented disembarkation until the 18th. There are fifty thousand British, French, and Turkish infantry. On the 20th, they engaged the Russians and won, gaining some hill whose name I've forgotten. This was "a bloody good rout," even though three thousand British soldiers perished. Now his regiment is quartered at Balaklava, preparing for the next siege, presumably of Sebastopol.

Geoffrey's scribblings are always cryptic; I know much more of this war from the newspapers, which are full of the details of battle, both glorious and grim. I want to know how he is, the state of his health, the state of his mind. He was better when he went, had left off drinking since the long night with Sully and the others, but he was far from well. Will never be well. That he's been allowed to fight in this war at all, in any capacity, doesn't say much, to my way of thinking, for the intelligence of the men in high command.

Six o'clock! I've let the time slip past, wool-gathering. Now I'll have to hurry. Tonight's reading is half an hour earlier, by virtue of a vote taken last week. It was thought that with that addition we can finish *David C.,* and no one wanted to stretch the exciting conclusion over two whole weeks. I wonder what secondhand delicacy Christy will offer me with my tea tonight after the reading. Last week it was bacon tarts, courtesy of Miss Jane Luce; before that, "spinach tanzy," a sort of handheld souffle prepared by the irrepressible Swans. I tease him about his numerous lady admirers, which makes him roll his eyes. It's delicious.

"They'm all right an' tight now, ain't un? David an' that Agnes, livin' happily ferever after—it fair warms the cockles o' the heart, Yer Majesty, it fairly do."

"I'm so glad," Anne said, trying not to laugh, bending a little so that she and Tranter Fox could be eye-to-eye; she doubted if the diminutive Cornishman was much over five feet tall. "I hope you'll come back next week," she told him, "when we'll be starting *Ivanhoe.*"

"Weel, I ain't just so sure o' that, now."

"Oh, no? Why not?"

"No offense t' them others, Yer Grace, but we could be startin' *Ivan the Turrible,* an' I wouldn't care unless *you* was readin' it."

She couldn't help giggling at that, and Tranter Fox snickered back, delighted that he'd gotten this indecorous rise out of her. He had a gap-toothed grin and sparkling black eyes, and he was a ruthless charmer. "I'm flattered," Anne said truthfully, bowing to him.

With a cheeky wink, the little miner turned and sauntered off. He was the last to leave the vicarage meeting room. Christy, who was standing in the doorway, smiled tiredly at some jest Tranter made in parting and watched him scamper up the steps and disappear.

Alone at last, thought Anne. Aloud she said, "Well, thank God *that's* over," with humorous fervor. When Christy didn't say anything, she hastened to explain, "I'm joking—you know I'm glad you asked me to do the readings, Christy. Still, I won't deny that it's a relief to pass along the torch, so to speak. Did you hear that Mrs. Armstrong changed places with Sophie? Sophie's going to Exeter over the Christmas holiday and didn't want to break off *Northanger Abbey* in the middle." She paused, uncertain if Christy was even listening to her. He'd been quiet all evening, she realized.

She crossed the empty room to him. He was mashing his thumb against the door latch, pressing it into the bolt hole over and over, making a monotonous clicking noise. He had on his "full holy blacks," having come directly from a funeral in Princetown. His bright blond hair made a striking contrast to his dark clothes, and Anne doubted if there was a handsomer soldier in the Lord's army. "Well?" she said archly. "Shall we adjourn? I'm dying to find out what your latest conquest has made us for our tea this time." When he looked up, his somber expression brought her up short.

"It's not a good night," she said quickly. "It's all right, it doesn't matter in the least." He didn't answer, only stared at her with an emotion in his eyes she couldn't decipher. It occurred to her that she had never once asked him about their weekly tête-à-têtes; she'd taken them for granted, and now her presumption embarrassed her. "You're tired—you have such long days. I'm tired myself. We can do it next week—or not, that's fine, there's certainly—"

"No, Anne, I want to talk to you. In fact, there's something in particular I have to say to you." He opened the door wider, standing back to let her pass. She went by him uncertainly but said no more, and, in a curious state of dread, she led the way up the stairs to his study.

Mrs. Ludd brought their tea almost immediately and then retired, leaving them alone. Anne tried to make small talk. Jokes fell flat about the hopeful young lady who had prepared their feast this evening—codling tarts with churned cream. Christy ate nothing, only sipped his tea and stared into the cup, not speaking a word.

When she couldn't stand the suspense any longer, she said directly, "Something's on your mind. Tell me what it is, Christy, and let's get it over with."

He set his cup down and looked at her. "I'm finding it very hard to say this to you."

"Yes, I can see that. All I can think is that you've found out my dreadful secret," she said with a shaky laugh—"that I've sold my soul to the devil."

He couldn't even smile. He stood up and went to his desk, turned around and leaned against it—as if he needed the distance from her and the desk for support. Her nerves stretched tighter; she pressed back into her chair and waited for the blow, whatever it was, to fall.

"I won't be able to see you anymore."

"What?" she said stupidly.

"I mean—like this. The two of us, alone."

She continued to blink at him. When the words sank in, her first impulse was to laugh—bitterly, giving away her deep disappointment in him. But she curbed it and tried to make her face patient. "So, there's been talk about us," she said quietly. "I should have expected it. I've lived in small towns, but never in an *English* small town, and that's quite a different thing, isn't it? But—I have to tell you, Christy, it makes me tired to think that anyone could see impropriety in our innocent evenings. And truly, I think it's unworthy of you to give it a second's thought."

His expression only grew bleaker. He closed his eyes and rubbed them, as if his head hurt.

A thought struck her. "Oh—now I think I understand." All the bitterness disappeared. "Oh, Christy, you're doing this for *me,* aren't you? It's *my* reputation you want to protect, not yours."

She shook her head, laughing with relief. "My dear friend, don't you know me well enough by—"

"It has nothing to do with impropriety," he cut her off in a pained voice. "Nothing to do with what other people think of us. Nothing to do with you." He was gripping the edge of the desk on either side of his thighs, watching her with a tense sadness that made her heart start to pound. "Anne, it's me."

"You? Christy, what do you mean?" But then, all at once, she knew.

And he saw that she did. She could tell that it hurt him, but he said the words anyway, so there could be no misunderstanding. He said, "I care for you."

She had to close her eyes. A slow, gentle warmth filled her, soft and soothing, like healing water. *I care for you.* Excitement and trepidation came next, and she took turns thinking, *It can't be true,* and *I knew it all the time!* But it was too big, too much— she couldn't think about it now. *Later,* she promised herself fearfully, and got up from her chair.

He'd turned his head to the side. His strong profile moved her powerfully. She wanted to go to him and touch him, hold him, but the obstinacy in his features kept her motionless. And, with a sinking heart, she realized he meant exactly what he said. He was going to put an end to their friendship.

A subdued sort of panic engulfed her. "My marriage is a farce," she blurted out, the words tumbling over each other. "A farce, you must know that, must've seen it. It's a blasphemy, not a sacrament. If I . . . if I cared for you, I would not let that obscenity stand in my way."

He looked straight at her and said, "But it must stand in my way."

Oh, God. She could see it happening, the lifeline he'd flung to her being pulled out of reach, leaving her to drown in loneliness. *"Damn it,"* she whispered fiercely. "Christy, I don't like your God!"

He came away from the desk and stood straight, arms stiff and awkward at his sides. "There's nothing else I can do. Believe me, I've . . ."

He stopped, and she knew he'd been going to say, *I've prayed.* But he was afraid she would laugh at him. *Oh, Christy!* she thought.

"Anne, please don't be angry."

"I'm not angry, I'm—yes, all right, I am! I've done nothing wrong, you've done nothing wrong, and you tell me we can't see each other anymore. How do you expect me to feel?"

He shook his head hopelessly.

It was happening, he was really going to do it. "Do you think it's a *sin* to love me?" she all but taunted him. "Is that what your religion teaches you?"

"If it is," he said quietly, "the punishment is built in. I won't have to wait for Judgment Day."

She made a scornful sound. "What does that mean?"

He smiled and put his fist on his chest. "I mean that the pain is here. Now."

It took the fight out of her. She felt like crying. And she was longing for him to say *why* he cared for her, when it had begun, all the lovely, seductive details—but she knew that if even one word were spoken of that now, she would lose all hope of keeping him. Above everything, she had to leave her emotions out of it. Pretend to, rather.

"Christy," she began again, trying to sound calm and rational. She moved closer, keeping her hands clasped, so he would know she had no intention of touching him. "Do you think I could ever deliberately hurt you?"

"No, of course not. This isn't anything you've done, Anne. It's all me. I'm—"

"Wait, wait—listen to me. If seeing me causes you suffering, then I'll keep away, I swear I will, because I'd rather hurt myself than you. But—couldn't we just go on as we have? *Friends,*

Christy—friends and companions, nothing more? We wouldn't *let* it be anything more. We're both strong—you're the strongest man I've ever known! And you can trust me, I would never . . . I would never let anything happen—between us . . . oh, you know what I mean!"

He stared at a spot on the floor and said in a monotone, "I just think it's better if—"

"Anyway, what would I do without you? Who would I talk to?" She tried to laugh. "Christy, who else would put up with me?"

"That's nonsense and you know it."

"I don't know it at all! You're the only one I can be myself with. Like it or not, you're the best friend I have in England. If I couldn't see you, couldn't be with you . . ." She left it at that; the rest would sound too dire, too pathetic, and she still had a little pride left.

Christy looked miserable. He was weighing his unhappiness against hers, and she knew with a giddy, guilt-ridden surge of hope that, in such an equation, she would always be the winner. There was a long, excruciating pause she was afraid to break before he said, "All right."

But she had to hear the words. "All right, what? We can still be friends?"

He nodded. The mixture of defeat and tenderness in his smile devastated her.

"Promise?" She smiled back, on the edge of tears again.

"Yes, I promise."

Best not to let him see her relief, the full, delirious extent of it. But she was trembling inside, as if she'd narrowly avoided a catastrophe. She would rejoice later, when she was alone. "You won't be sorry," she vowed rashly, hoping it was true. He looked skeptical. She thought of saying, *Anyway, it'll go away. If you really knew me, Christy, you wouldn't like me.* But the whole subject was off limits—that was part of their bargain—and anyway, she didn't want him to know that about her. Not yet.

"Well." She turned away from him. "I suppose I'd better go home now. Before you change your mind." She made a great business of gathering up her reticule, her book, her cape—not looking at him for fear that she would see his unhappiness, or worse, his second thoughts. They said good night at the front door, both of them subdued and constrained. She wouldn't let him walk back with her to the Hall; it wasn't very late, she said, and she felt like being alone. But the real reason was because she wanted to avoid any more of the tension they were feeling in each other's company right now. And although she'd said it lightly, she truly was afraid he might change his mind.

All the way home, she told herself she'd done the right thing, that it would work out, that she would take care to see that Christy never regretted the selfless act of kindness he'd committed tonight for her sake. Once or twice, she almost convinced herself it would be possible.

But later, after she'd written it all down in her journal, the truth of what she'd done came back to haunt her.

Selfish, selfish! Why did I do it? A good woman, a *true* friend would have taken pity and let him go, not pleaded with him to let her go on hurting him. But I ignored my conscience. Christy and I established our roles a long time ago, after all: He's the saint and I'm the sinner.

Anyway, I don't care, I don't care, it worked, so I'm unrepentant. He gave in. And I know it wasn't out of weakness, but because I'd shamelessly convinced him that I needed him—indeed, that *he* would be the sinner if he threw me away. Oh, selfish! It's not true, I *am* repentant! But not enough to take back a single word. I'm miserable; I'm elated. I vow to keep my promise to the letter. *Friends,* that's all we are and all we'll ever be. I pledged it to him, and I'd die before I'd forswear myself.

But—he cares for me. That stays in my heart. I take

that hope out and hold it, look at it, stroke it, and whisper to it, like a child with a pet she's found in the wild and isn't allowed to keep. I must hide it out of sight and look at it only in the coldest times, the heartless hours. Thank you, Christy, for this extraordinary gift.

X

THE FOLLOWING FRIDAY, Christy didn't come to the penny reading. Mrs. Armstrong began *Ivanhoe* for an audience that had swelled over the last few weeks to almost thirty. Anne's turn was over, and years ago she'd read all the Walter Scott she ever wanted to, but she came to the reading anyway. To see Christy, of course—except for church on Wednesday, and then only to nod to him sedately, she hadn't seen him in a week—but also because the gatherings had become a pleasant weekly ritual for her, a time to greet the villagers and ask how they did. "Fine, m'lady," was usually all she got out of them—except for Tranter Fox—but lately she'd noticed an infinitesimal narrowing of the rigid social gap each time she came, and that was incentive enough to maintain her attendance.

After the reading, she commended Mrs. Armstrong for a job well done, exchanged a few pleasantries with Lily Hesselius, spoke to John Swan about the seeding machine she'd ordered from his blacksmith's shop—all the while keeping an eye on the door, expecting Christy to come through it at any moment. He never did. Arthur Ludd said as how he hadn't come to Evening Prayers neither, and like as not somebody in parish was sick or in trouble. Until that moment, she hadn't realized that Dr. Hesselius was absent, too. Arthur must be right.

Bitter disappointment flooded her, as if she'd drunk vinegar. Afterward, she felt guilty: she ought to be sympathizing with the anonymous sick person. But all she could think of was that she would miss Christy. Their meeting was bound to be somewhat awkward, especially at first, but she didn't care. And now that she'd lost the opportunity, she realized how very badly she wanted to see him, how much she'd been counting on it.

She wandered outside with the others, calling good night to her neighbors. It was an unusually mild night, moonlit and almost cloudless. Standing in the street in front of the rectory, she actually considered going back up the walk, knocking at the door, and telling Mrs. Ludd she would like to wait for the vicar in his study. Certainly there was nothing to prevent her from doing so; she was Lady D'Aubrey—she could say she wanted to wait for him on the roof, and no one would gainsay her. But she didn't move. After all that had happened, it seemed too forward. Almost as if she were going back on her word.

An owl gave an eerie hoot from the beech trees at the edge of the green. Anne thought of going home to her empty house, making a cup of tea and carrying it up to her empty room, drinking it in her empty bed.

It wasn't to be borne. Not tonight. She had her heart set on seeing him. Skirting the light falling on his lawn from the bow window, she moved toward the shadows in the churchyard. She would wait for him there. Just to see how he did. Just to say good night.

She'd been truthful the day she'd told him she loved graveyards. The dead were dead, and there was nothing in this moon-shadowed bone garden to frighten her. Still, she couldn't help remembering the antics of the village children on All Hallows' Eve two nights ago. Evil spirits roamed the earth on that night, the people of Wyckerley half-believed. They persecuted poor humans, whose only defense was to put on a disguise and pass for members of the spirit world. On All Hallows', the children dressed up in their parents' clothes and flew around the village, shrieking, carrying grotesque, hollowed-out turnips with candles inside, holding them up to cottage windows to terrify the inhabitants.

She smiled to herself, thinking of the thoughtful, sedate, well-reasoned sermon Christy had preached that day—All Saints', the feast day of his church and thus a fairly solemn occasion. Reconciling modern Anglicanism with still-vital holdovers from pagan rites as old as the Celts must present plenty of interesting challenges to the conscientious clergyman. She never missed Sunday service anymore, because she delighted in listening to Christy's sermons. Not so much because they were riveting drama—they weren't—but because they were a window on his mind. And she found Christy's mind fascinating.

RUFUS MARKHAM, read a low stone marker beside a border of yew trees. Or possibly MARKUS, it was hard to tell. The date of his death was 2 June 1741, but the date of his birth was too worn to read; seventeen-something, so he hadn't been a very old man when he died. In that case, he probably wouldn't mind if she sat down on his tombstone. From here she'd be able to hear Christy's step on the flagstone path to his door. Across the way, someone had a much grander stone than Rufus had, an angel's statue on a wide pedestal, with all manner of worn writing chiseled in the hard marble. Dead just the same, though, wasn't he? A mundane thought: had anyone ever visited a cemetery and not entertained it? Maybe not, but that didn't make it less true, or less subject to melancholy rumination. She let her mind drift. Her mother was buried in Reims, her father in London. She had no other relatives, at least not to speak of; there were probably cousins on her mother's side somewhere, but she had no idea where. She'd been on her own since her father's death. So, except for Geoffrey, no one else could die on her, so to speak. Which was one of those good-bad, ultimately meaningless truisms that cluttered the mind and led nowhere.

She sighed, and lifted her head to watch the moon through

the trees. Presently the church clock struck ten. She started slightly; she hadn't realized she'd been loitering here quite so long. Past the high churchyard wall, a light shone from a second-floor room in the rectory. Christy's bedroom? Perhaps Mrs. Ludd left it on whenever he was out late at night. It must be a welcome sight to him when he came home tired, sometimes dejected. The home fire burning. She sighed again, dejected herself, and not knowing why. A sound made her sit up straight.

Slow footsteps, sharp on the cobbled street, now soft on the grass. She stood, brushing at her skirts, patting her hair, aware of an airy feeling in her stomach. The lych-gate creaked on its hinges and Christy came through. He didn't see her. He moved away from her, his shoulders hunched, toward an iron bench under the giant copper beech by the wall.

Moonlight through the trees illuminated him in patches, silvering his dark-clad shoulders and even the gold in his hair. As usual, he made her think of an angel. One of the militant kind; a straight-shouldered, level-eyed, sword-wielding soldier of the Lord. Smiling, she took a step toward him—and stopped when he suddenly leaned forward and dropped his head in his hands.

Her heart began to race. Was he weeping? Irrational fear gripped her as every presumption she'd ever made about him was reversed and turned on its head. He couldn't be—*oh, please don't let him be crying,* she prayed, forgetting that she didn't believe in God. Full of dread, she crept forward. Even when gravel rasped under her shoe, he didn't hear her. She stopped a little distance from him, uneasy, not wanting to intrude on his private distress but unable to leave him now. His fingers tangled and clenched in his bright hair, making it stand on end. She felt as if she were seeing something she wasn't supposed to see. Every second she thought he would sense her presence and look up, but he didn't. At last she had to say his name, "Christy," scarcely above a whisper.

He lifted his head. She saw, to her intense relief, that he

wasn't weeping. But his face was tragic, and she remembered she had seen it that way once before, on the first day they'd met. He had been praying on his knees at Lord D'Aubrey's bedside—a strange sight, she'd thought at the time, almost embarrassing—and he'd looked up at her and Geoffrey with exactly the same expression of hopeless defeat.

Before she could say anything else, he said, "Anne," with a kind of resigned wonder, and got to his feet.

His hands at his sides looked too big, almost clumsy. She wanted to reach out and take them in hers, chafe the life back into them, do something to make him better. Not allowed. She stood still and said, "What happened?"

"Were you waiting for me?" he asked, in the same wondering tone as before.

"Yes, I— What's happened, Christy? What's wrong?"

He took a deep breath. "Tolliver Deene is dead."

"Oh, no."

"There was no warning. He collapsed at the mine office late this afternoon and died a few hours later."

Now she did take his hand, to lead him back to the bench and pull him down beside her. He put his head back against the rough bark of the tree and closed his eyes for a second, then opened them to stare up at the sky.

"How is Sophie?" she asked.

"She's completely devastated. Completely. I . . . it's . . ." He shook his head, as if the futility of words were something he was sick of thinking about.

"Was he conscious before he died?"

"Yes. He knew he was dying." He brought his hands up and clasped them across his forehead, the fingers locked. "I said all the words, all the . . . words. It didn't help."

"I'm sure it did."

"He was afraid. He didn't want to die. At the end, he asked

me why. I gave him the answers I knew—God's will, too much for us to understand, going to a better place, all that—" He squeezed his eyes shut, baring his teeth. "So he stopped asking me. Out of politeness."

Hurting for him, she sat quietly and didn't speak.

"Then he was gone, and there was nothing I could do for Sophie either. Her heart is broken. I just—watched her. Sat with her, said . . . the words. I wanted so badly to fix it for her, make everything better. Make death go away. Reassure her that all will be well, when it certainly will not."

He let his hands fall, uncovering all the bleakness in his face. She let the silence stretch between them for a moment, then laid her hand on his shoulder. He didn't look at her, but he smiled absently, gratefully. "You did your best," she heard herself say—and if she hadn't known what he was talking about before, the terrible banality of that would have brought it home with a vengeance. But he didn't sigh or flinch with impatience; he smiled again, tiredly, and gave her comforting hand a pat with his.

"You see?" she said earnestly. "I just said a stupid-sounding thing, but it consoled you a little. And you helped Sophie and Mr. Deene. You did, but you just can't see it. You were *there.* You stayed with them, you didn't run away, the way most people would've done—as I'd have done when it got too painful. 'The family should have some privacy,' I'd have said, but really I'd have excused myself because I couldn't stand it. That's what most people do, Christy, but not you."

"Because it's my job."

"Yes, exactly. And you do it well. You *do.* There *is* nothing to say at those times, you *can't* make it better. It isn't answers people need anyway, it's company. You can't cure illness or prevent death or suffering, Christy. You can just be there, holding Sophie's hand. That's all you can do."

"No, Anne," he said gently. "I'm a minister; I'm supposed to do more than that. I'm supposed to bring hope to the hopeless. I should have a vision of God's plan that's so powerful, so compelling, it comforts the dying and brings them peace. I'm God's helper on earth, his priest. I have the sacraments and I have the Bible, but unless I also have God's spirit in me, giving me the grace to say the right words, do the right things—"

"But you do," she insisted. "Oh, Christy, you don't know. You can't see it, but I can, and I'm telling you that you help everyone you meet." He laughed at that. She took his hand in both of hers and squeezed it hard. "I watch them, I see people with you. They—*light up* when you come into a room. In church, they never take their eyes off you. And I'm not just talking about all those silly girls either. I mean everybody. What I can't understand is why you don't know that everyone loves you."

He put his head down, pretending to examine their clasped hands. He was moved, and he was no good at dissembling; poor Christy, if he wanted to keep an emotion to himself, the best he could do was to hide his face.

"What are you thinking?" she asked when he didn't speak.

"I'm thinking . . . that I'm supposed to say that. 'What are you thinking?' It's what I say when people are quiet. To draw them out."

She smiled. "A fine tactic," she said softly. "I'm sure you've a hundred more and you don't even know it." He kept his head down. "Christy," she whispered. "What are we going to do with you?"

He put his other hand over hers. A light breeze blew, fluttering the tree branches, making moon-shadows in his hair. They both fell silent, and the seconds passed, and she grew obsessively aware of their touching. The texture of Christy's skin, the warmth of his big hands cradling her smaller ones. The naturalness of this intimacy. She wanted to lean down and rest her cheek on their joined hands. Just that. And stay that way for a long time. He moved, and the drawing away of his hands felt like a caress. But then he stood up, and it felt like an abandonment.

He didn't go far, just to the iron sundial, inconspicuous among the gravestones. "Watch and pray," read the inscription on the granite pedestal. "Time passeth away like a shadow." She watched him for a while, admiring his lean, muscular grace. He was an elegant man, for all that he was a soldier of the Lord in a humble country parish. And her appreciation of him was as earthly as could be. Or did she mean earthy?

The direction of her thoughts alarmed her, and so did Christy's continued silence. He had withdrawn from her, and she could only think that somehow, because of the innocent intimacy of what had just happened, she'd broken faith with him, reneged on her promise to be his friend and nothing more.

"So," she said with uncertain playfulness, "am I not allowed to hold my friend's hand when he's in trouble?"

He turned around. From here she couldn't see his face clearly. She held her breath, and finally he smiled. Her relief was so strong, she shivered with it. She patted the bench beside her. "Come back. I've decided to tell you my life story. Come, sit, I can't tell it to you if you're going to stand over me like—like God," she said deliberately, and her reward was his light laugh.

He took his seat beside her again, angling his body toward hers and resting his forearm on the low back of the bench. "Are you cold?" he asked, seeing she had nothing but her shawl.

"No. Are you?"

"No."

"Good, then you can't use that for an excuse to leave if my life story bores you."

He only smiled. Before, he'd have joked back, tried to make *her* laugh. He was guarding himself, unsure, under this new regime, of how much he could give away, how much he could take. It pained her, but she couldn't blame him for it.

"Actually," she said softly, "what I want to tell you is how it came about that I married Geoffrey." He recoiled slightly, and she knew what he was thinking—that this was dangerous territory, unwise, probably indiscreet, exactly the sort of thing he ought to avoid if he was going to save himself. "I just want to tell you, that's all," she said hastily. "It's not hurtful, it won't—harm anything. Between us, I mean."

"Tell me, then. Whatever you like. Did you meet him in England?"

She sat back. "Yes, in London. My father's brother had just died, and we'd come here to settle his estate." No—she wanted to start further back. "We'd been living in Venice and Padua, where my father had a new patron. And a new mistress," she added dryly. "Somehow they always seemed to go together."

"Your mother—?"

"Died when I was seven. She drowned in a sailing accident. My father's family had money, but they cut him off when he married her because she was 'unsuitable.' Even after she died, they didn't relent. He despised them by then; I doubt he'd have taken anything from them if they'd offered it."

"Did you always live on the Continent?"

"We lived in Ravenna until my mother died. I still think of it as home, even though I've been back only once in almost eighteen years. After she died, my father and I would come to England every few years, but for the most part we lived in Italy and France, sometimes the Netherlands. Part of his idea of himself, you see, was that he was an exile."

"Was he a good artist? I don't know his work."

"It was never shown here until just before he died. I can't say if he was good or not; I can't be objective. He wasn't as good as he wanted to be. And he wasn't very successful."

"Were you poor?"

"I guess we were, sometimes. I never felt poor. His friends were all artists, so it seemed as if everybody we knew was poor."

She paused, and after a moment Christy asked, "Were you happy?"

She studied his serious face; he was so intent on everything she said. "I didn't have what you'd call a conventional upbringing," she equivocated. This was an area she had intended to skirt. "My father had a lot of mistresses, and I was always . . . I was . . ."

"Jealous of them."

"Yes." There, that hadn't hurt so much. "And whether or not he was any good at what he did, he was completely devoted to his art. Obsessed. And so—a noisy little girl constituted a nuisance, as you can understand. An annoyance."

There was a longer pause, but this time Christy didn't fill it.

"But he was proud of me too, in his way, especially after I got older. He liked to show me off. At sixteen or so, I became his hostess. His set of friends was 'bohemian,' which meant, as far as I could tell, that they slept with each other's wives and made a virtue out of professional failure."

"You're cynical."

"Yes, I am. Haven't you noticed that about me before?" He sent her one of his bland looks, not encouraging her. "Anyway. When I was twenty, Uncle Donald died—my father's brother. He had no sons, so Papa was next in line for the inheritance, which was substantial. A fortune, in fact. We came to England, and that's when I met Geoffrey."

"How?"

"At a party. An artists' soiree. Yes, I know—an unlikely place for Geoffrey, but I didn't know that then. Nor did I know that I was to be the prize in a carefully planned and very cold-blooded seduction. Before the old viscount died, how long had it been since you'd seen Geoffrey?"

"Twelve years," he answered without hesitation. "Without a word."

"Then you must not have known that in the interim, besides

signing on to play soldier in every obscure skirmish that fired up around the globe, he spent all his money on pleasure, and all his friends' money, and all the money he could squeeze out of his father. Which was precious little to begin with, before it dried up to nothing. In short, he was desperate.

"Unfortunately for him, his dissolute character preceded him, and he was persona non grata in respectable English drawing rooms; that cut off the usual way titled ne'er-do-wells get rich— by marrying heiresses. So he set out to try a different social milieu, a first for him—the well-to-do artistic community. A comedown, I suppose, but beggars can't be choosers."

Her left hand lay palm down between them on the bench. She saw Christy start to touch her, then pull away.

"My reputation preceded me, too," she continued self-consciously. "Geoffrey knew my father had just come into a great deal of money. So I was his goal. His target."

"What happened?"

"He pursued me. It was—unreal, overwhelming. Unlike anything I'd ever experienced. He was this—*storm,* and I was standing in his path, so innocent—oh, Christy, you can't imagine how innocent I was, underneath my extremely thin veneer of worldliness." She tried to laugh. "Or maybe it wasn't innocence, just stupidity. Well, in any case, he swept me off my feet, as the saying goes, and proposed marriage within two weeks of our first meeting."

"Didn't your father object?"

"He did, yes, when he thought of it. You must understand that he was being lionized in a very small way at the time, more because he was a novelty in England—and a soon-to-be-*rich* novelty—than because anyone truly believed he was a brilliant artist. So his mind was on other things." She didn't add "as usual"; that would've sounded too pathetic.

"Geoffrey's charm can be devastating when he wants it to be, as I'm sure you know, and four years ago, when he was relatively healthy and energetic, it was at its deadliest. I found it almost impossible to resist him. He didn't seduce me—not my body, anyway. He made me believe I was the most extraordinary woman alive, that he would die if he couldn't have me, that we were made for each other. I can hardly understand it now, how I could have believed we were suited at all, two people so radically different from each other in every conceivable way—and yet I did believe it. He was like a fire, and his almost inhuman energy burned me up."

"So you married him."

"He insisted; he wouldn't have it any other way. Now I know why, but at the time I was terribly flattered. I'd have countenanced an affair—in fact, I suggested it to him, any number of times." She searched his face for a sign that she'd shocked him but couldn't see one. "Are you scandalized?"

"Would you like me to be?"

"It doesn't matter to me. I don't have to defend myself."

"Certainly not."

"But I could point out that I was raised in a setting where such things were commonplace, almost more so than conventional marriages."

"Yes, that's true," he said mildly, and she could see she wasn't going to get a rise out of him.

"Anyway," she resumed. "Geoffrey wouldn't agree to an affair; he wanted an 'honorable marriage,' he said, and I believed him. So we eloped. We did it in Scotland—very romantic, I thought. I was in a kind of daze the whole time, as if it was all happening to someone else."

"Did you love him?"

She took her time answering. "I would like to think that I did. I would like to think that I didn't give myself to someone for whom I felt only infatuation and gratitude. Twenty is not so young, and I wasn't a child. I knew him for less than a month, and during all that time he was dissembling. How could I have loved him? I think I behaved very, very stupidly. But since I've paid for it many times over, I forgave myself a long time ago."

She put her head back against the trunk of the beech tree, feeling exhausted all of a sudden. All the exhilaration she'd felt in getting this story out was gone now; it sounded sordid in her ears, and she couldn't remember anymore why she'd wanted Christy to hear it. "Do you want to know the rest?" she asked in a flat voice. "I can tell you, it doesn't get any better."

"Only if you want to tell me."

For some reason, that irritated her. She thought of saying, *Why don't you hold my hand? You held Sophie's hand—why not mine? Aren't I a suffering parishioner, too?* An ignoble sentiment, and petty in the extreme, yet she couldn't shake the childish wish that he would try to comfort her in some way besides listening to her.

"I'll speed things along," she said crisply. "When we returned to London a week after the wedding, I found out my father had died. I'd missed his funeral because they couldn't find me."

"Anne."

That one word brought tears into her throat. She swallowed them down, appalled—she *never* cried. "It was a freak accident," she rushed on, "absolutely absurd, the sort of nonsensical occurrence he'd have relished—in the abstract. He was walking past a block of flats in the Bayswater Road at six o'clock in the evening, heading for the public house on the corner. Four stories up, a woman threw a flowerpot at her husband, who happened to be standing in front of the window."

Christy bowed his head and said, "Oh, God."

"It's funny, isn't it? Geoffrey thought so, until they told him he hadn't married an heiress after all. My father hadn't made any legal provision for me yet—didn't have time—so I was left without a penny. Everything went to the closest male relative, a great-nephew who lives in Canada. His name is Mordecai."

Her hands in her lap came unclasped; she closed her eyes out of fatigue. It took an effort to finish the story. "Needless to say, the honeymoon was over. Geoffrey got drunk one night and told me the truth: he didn't love me, he'd married me for my money, and he was leaving me because I didn't have any. I didn't see him again for two years." She stood up. "Christy, I can't talk anymore."

After a moment of surprised silence, he said, "All right."

"No, no, you're supposed to argue with me! You're supposed to find the story of my life so riveting that you can't bear to wait for the thrilling conclusion."

He stood up more slowly, and for the first time she saw how weary he was, too. "I do want to hear the thrilling conclusion," he said, and the echo of her silly words in his quiet voice made her feel childish and petulant.

"It's late," she said somberly. "I've kept you too long. You must be very tired."

"It doesn't matter."

Her shawl slipped out of her hands as she was about to put it on. Christy bent and picked it up, brushing away a dead oak leaf that caught on the fringe. She turned slightly when he moved to help her with the shawl, and for a second his arm lay lightly across her shoulders. She came up to his chin, she noticed absently. When he moved away from her—sharply, too quickly—he took his body's warmth with him. For the second time that night she felt abandoned.

"Let me walk home with you, Anne."

"No. Thank you. It's not necessary."

"It's very late, you shouldn't be out by yourself."

"Nothing will happen to me. Anyway, everyone's asleep but us."

"I don't like you going home alone this late."

They argued for a little longer, but she wouldn't give in. "I've imposed on you long enough tonight, Christy. I don't even know why I told you all that."

"I'm glad you told me. Do you regret it?"

"What I regret is my own selfishness. You were the one who needed a friendly ear tonight, and for some reason I decided to burden you even more with my problems."

"You haven't burdened me, you know that."

"Ah, but that's your attitude to everyone, all of us sheep in your flock, Reverend Morrell. You ought to guard yourself better. We're heavy, and we'll take advantage of you. If you're not careful, we'll bear you down to the ground." She said it as a joke, but she could see the simple truth in it as soon as it was out. Christy would bear anything that was asked of him, and he would always think of himself last.

"I've been no help to you at all," he protested. Before she could argue, he said, "I'll keep the promise I made to you before, Anne, but I'm not easy with it. If you ever truly needed help, spiritual guidance of any kind, even the simplest counsel, I'm afraid that—under the circumstances—I'm the last man who could give it to you."

"Or the first," she shot back. The words "under the circumstances" caught her up, seemed to vibrate in the air between them. She wanted to explore "the circumstances," she realized, and immediately felt guilty. "Don't distress yourself. As it happens, I'm the last *woman* who will ever require spiritual guidance, from you or anyone else. So you have nothing to reproach yourself with. Now, good night. I won't keep you standing here another minute. Thanks for your patience with me."

"Anne—"

"And your *friendship*." She was talking too fast, saying these odd, brisk-sounding things out of a fear that he would reconsider the arrangement they'd agreed upon and abandon her for real and for good. She backed away from him before he could frame a reply, hurrying toward the gate. "Will I see you again next Friday?" Even in her own ears, her voice sounded ludicrously unconcerned, just as if everything didn't depend on his answer.

He kept her waiting, her hand poised on the iron latch of the gate, for an eternity. At last he said, "Yes," just as the clock on the church tower began to strike midnight. Under the deep, pealing tones, he didn't hear her whisper fervently, *"Thank God."*

XI

CHRISTY FLEXED HIS stiff shoulders, rubbed his tired eyes, and checked off another chore on his list: "Advent sermon." That still left "Curtis baptism; dean's visit—tell Ludd; see Weedies; thank Capt. C.; deal with Nineways." And the list didn't even include tutoring the Wooten boys in an hour, and after that, supervising the tricky negotiations he'd planned between Sophie Deene and her uncle, Mayor Vanstone, under the guise of a friendly dinner at the vicarage. Sophie was her father's sole heir, but she wouldn't attain her majority for nine months. Eustace wanted control of Guelder mine in the interim, and Sophie was just as determined to keep it for herself. Christy's job would be to work out a compromise.

In the hour between now and the Wootens' arrival, he could write a note to Captain Carnock, expressing appreciation for his generous offer of his own farm laborers next fall during the glebe harvest. Or he could think up a tactful way to handle Warden Nineways' latest lunatic suggestion, that churchgoers caught sleeping during service be required to recite the compline afterward to as many parishioners as cared to stay and hear it. Or he could consult with his housekeeper on meals and accommodations for the rural dean, who was paying a two-day visit to the parish next week. But instead of tackling any of those tasks, he got up from his desk and wandered over to the window that looked out on the rainswept churchyard.

Anne had a third-floor sitting room at Lynton Hall. She liked to write letters or read there and look out the windows at the trees and fields, the distant village. She might be there now, feeling as melancholy as he, watching slow raindrops slide down the steamy glass. She could see the spire of the church from her window, she'd once told him. She might be looking at it now through the November mist. She might be thinking of him.

He'd given up trying not to think of her. There were ways in which he was a strong man, but that kind of willpower was beyond him. Sometimes he thought that if he had just held firm to his decision not to see her anymore, he might have gotten over her by now—at least enough to function normally again. Enough to concentrate for ten consecutive minutes without thinking about her. But then again, maybe not.

He loved her. She was married to his friend, and it didn't matter at all. He had meditated and prayed for hours, and nothing had changed. He loved her.

Where was God's will in this calamity? Was it a test? What could the purpose be except to make him miserable? What would his father have done in this situation?

That was the most useless question of all, because it was impossible, inconceivable that his father would have gotten himself into this predicament in the first place. Christy hadn't asked for it, God knew, but here he was anyway, all alone, with no friend or mentor to confide in. For once he was making up the rules as he went along, not following in his father's saintly, time-tested footsteps.

He thought of the night he'd finally realized it was hopeless, that there was no use fighting any longer, or calling what he felt for Anne something more antiseptic and permissible—admiration, for example, or affection. It had happened on the night of the harvest home. She'd worn a blue gown with a crimson scarf tied around the waist. Gold rings in her ears and a jet medallion at her breast. She'd served ale from a stone jug to the laborer-guests herself and passed platters of food and baskets of bread, trifles, and fruit and cream-topped confections. Her hair had been neat and tidy, confined by combs at the start of the evening—but by the end it was free, and her face was lightly sheened with perspiration, and her rich, low laughter had grown easy to provoke. She'd looked like a well-bred gypsy to him; if there had been a bonfire in the courtyard and she'd danced around it, he wouldn't have batted an eye.

Until that precise moment, his feelings for her had been—relative to what they were now—innocent, if only because they'd been so confused. But that night she had shone too brightly, he couldn't blind himself any longer to what had been before his eyes all along. He loved her, and he wanted her. When she had asked him to stay longer, just the two of them, alone in her house—he ran away. He had no choice.

Had it been a mistake to tell her the truth? At the time, it had seemed the honorable thing to do—but what good had it done? No sooner had he confessed that he cared for her than he'd let her talk him out of his high-minded resolution to stop seeing her. The problem was his, not hers, he told himself, and besides, he still had a responsibility to her as her minister.

How she would laugh at that! Laugh harder if she knew he believed her soul was any of his business. But for him, it would be a sin to abandon her completely because his humanity had gotten in the way of his clerical duties. And that was the truth—not a handy excuse to keep seeing her. He was sure of that, because he knew exactly how painful it was to be with her.

For Anne's part, he knew she would keep her word. She called herself an agnostic, but her honor was sacred to her; and in addition, she had no temptation to be anything but honorable.

No temptation? None at all? That wasn't quite the truth. She was not completely indifferent to him. And that was at once the sweetest and the most dangerous aspect of the whole affair. He couldn't let himself dwell on that forbidden delight, because behind that door lurked the devil at work. That was brazen seduction.

He rested his forehead against the cold windowpane and prayed for strength.

Presently he heard footsteps in the corridor. Five o'clock already? But it wasn't the Wooten boys who crowded into his study a moment later. It was William Holyoake.

"Vicar, thank God you're here." Rain sluiced off the hat in his hand and puddled around his boots where he stood. His homely face, red from the cold, looked pinched and worried.

"What is it?" Christy asked anxiously. "Is something wrong at the Hall?"

"Aye."

"Is it Anne?"

"No, she's all right. She's at Vanstone's havin' tea wi' the ladies."

"What, then?"

"Look here." He reached inside his coat and withdrew a folded envelope. "A sojer from the regiment at Yelverton brought it just now. 'Tis from the War Office. I know what it says, for the sojer told me. His lordship's dead."

Christy waited under a black umbrella at the edge of the green, forty feet from the front gate of the mayor's handsome, two-story Tudor house. He and Holyoake had agreed that Anne ought not to be told about Geoffrey immediately—not at Honoria Vanstone's tea party. So William's job was to tell her there was trouble and get her out of the house; later, at the rectory, it would be Christy's job to tell her the truth.

The rain had emptied the street and shuttered the windows of the houses. John Swan's smithy smoked in the distance, and the door to the George and Dragon stood ajar, as usual; otherwise, even the shops looked abandoned. What would the villagers' reaction be, Christy wondered, when they learned their new lord was gone, barely seven months after they'd lost the old one? A troubled time was coming, and they would look to him for stability.

He looked up and saw Anne hurrying through the Vanstones' gate, Holyoake behind her. Christy stepped out from under the dripping trees. She stopped dead when she saw him, said something sharp to William. The bailiff shook his head, miserable. She started off again, ignoring the arm he held out to her. She wore her hooded cape over a dark dress; she'd come on foot, William had told him, for at three o'clock the day had been fair. Tall and slim, and graceful even dodging the puddles in her half-boots, she made Christy's heart hurt, and not with ministerial compassion. God help him, he loved her, and at this moment his mind could hold only one fact: she was free.

He met her in the middle of the street.

"Christy, what's happened? William won't tell me!"

He reached for her elbow. "Let's go to the vicarage; I'll tell you there."

"No." Dread stiffened her facial features. She stepped back. "Tell me now."

He and Holyoake eyed each other uneasily. William could have excused himself now, and Christy wouldn't have blamed him. But the bailiff didn't desert him; he stood stolid and four-square in the street, ready to do his duty.

But the hard job was Christy's, as usual. As it should be. He girded himself for it. "It's bad news. A letter's come from the Secretary of War."

"Geoffrey." She put her fist over her mouth.

He nodded. "It happened on the fourteenth of this month. There was a violent storm off Balaklava while he was on a hospital ship in the harbor. Thirty vessels went down. He was lost."

Tears flooded her eyes. She covered her face with her hands. Christy and Holyoake groped for their handkerchiefs and held them, clumsy, halfway between themselves and her. They exchanged grim looks—masculine comfort for each other—while Anne stood still and quiet, her hood and her white fingers hiding her face. A gust of wind blew a cold slice of rain sideways, and she tottered.

Christy said, "Come," and took hold of her arm. "Come home with me, Anne. There's a fire there. We can get warm." She looked at him. He nodded, holding her misty, unanchored gaze. "Let's go home," he repeated.

Her mouth made the word "home." She nodded back.

The two men fell in on either side of her, both grasping the stem of Christy's umbrella to shield her, and set off across the wet village green for home.

"Here, drink this, Anne."

She took the cup and saucer from him and put them on her lap, transferring her dry-eyed and apparently fascinated gaze from the flames crackling in the fireplace grate to the milky-brown liquid in the teacup.

"Drink it," he reminded her.

She took a sip, grimaced, and closed her eyes. "I think I've drunk more tea in the last six months than in all the rest of my life."

Christy smiled, encouraged by the remark—by the fact that she was talking at all—and sat down in the chair next to hers. He rested his elbows on his knees and clasped his hands together, frowning at his shoes and searching for the right words. "Anne," he began slowly, "the death of someone we've loved, especially when it comes unexpectedly, often seems arbitrary, even cruel if we—"

"Don't." She didn't open her eyes; her mouth made a straight, thin line. "Christy, for God's sake."

"You don't want to talk about it? All right, then we—"

"I don't want your Christian comfort. If Geoffrey's death

strikes me as arbitrary and cruel, don't worry about me blaming God for it because I don't believe in God. And don't you *dare* tell me he's in a better place."

He nodded agreeably. She couldn't see the nod, because she wouldn't open her eyes, so he said, "Very well, no Christian comfort. Let's talk about how you are."

"How do you think I am?"

"Why don't you tell me?"

"I'd really rather not."

He nodded again, not as agreeably. He picked up the poker and banged at the charred logs, sending a cloud of sparks up the chimney.

Anne put her undrunk tea on the table beside her chair. "I'm sorry. It's just that I don't know what I feel, except numb."

"That's natural."

"I suppose."

"You can't believe it yet. I can't either. It's hard to grieve when it's not real to you." She didn't answer. "If you like, I'll take care of all the arrangements for the memorial service."

"Memorial service," she said dully. She dropped her head into her hand. "Do whatever you like, I don't care."

He waited a moment before saying, "You might want to think about what the village needs. What the people have a right to expect. They've lost their squire again; they're bound to feel anxious, uprooted, worried about the future."

"Yes, yes, all right. But Geoffrey wasn't a good squire—how could they miss him?"

"It's the continuity that's been upset. Geoffrey wasn't a conscientious leader, it's true. Neither was Edward. But at least their presence provided some sense of stability, and in the absence of anything else, sometimes that's all that holds a community together."

"You hold it together." He sighed, and she said quickly, "Do whatever you like, Christy, give Geoffrey the biggest funeral they've ever seen—I tell you I don't care. I can't stay here any longer."

At first he thought she meant here, in this room. When the truth struck him, he felt a coldness seeping through the pores of his skin. "What do you mean?" he said carefully. "Where will you go?"

She shook her head, shrugged, shook her head again.

"This is your home now."

"Of course it's not. I've never been accepted here."

"That's not true. You're—"

"There's a cousin somewhere, Sebastian Verlaine. He'll inherit the title. The estate too, I suppose." She got up from her chair with quick, jerky movements and went closer to the fire. He watched her press her fingertips to the edge of the mantel in random, repetitive patterns, staring straight ahead at nothing. Her face in profile looked sharp against the dark wood, her nostrils thin and pinched. While he watched, her cheeks slowly bloomed with hot color; she opened her mouth to breathe quietly—so he wouldn't know she was crying. Then she turned her head away.

He stood up and, after an indecisive second, went to her side. He laid his hand on her back, between her shoulder blades. "Anne—"

"I don't—I don't want—"

"I know. No Christian comfort." He moved his hand to her far shoulder and squeezed it softly. She was shaking, swallowing repeatedly to keep back the tears. "It's all right," he whispered—the most useless, unwarranted piece of consolation he knew. "It's all right, Anne. It's all right."

Shuddering, she turned and came into his arms, and let him go on saying it.

28 November

A letter from Geoffrey came today. He wrote it on board the hospital ship in the Black Sea. The date is 10

November—four days before the storm that killed him. He writes of his brave exploits in the battle at Inkerman, where he was wounded in the thigh and the shoulder. They might decorate him for valor, he says.

29 November

Dreamt of Ravenna last night. I was a child again, and my mother was teaching me to swim. Woke up sobbing.

30 November

The memorial service was much better attended than Geoffrey's father's funeral. A tribute to me, says Christy. I very much doubt that.

2 December

Sleepless again. Back to normal, then. Yesterday I slept half the day, and spent the other half in a sort of daze, staring out the window, too lethargic to put my clothes on. I can't understand my mood. Moods, rather; they shift. And now—now I don't feel like writing in this book.

4 December

I've been thinking of the night when Geoffrey and I first met. Springtime; a house party in Surrey; the hostess a Mrs. Wade or Ware, some starving artist's patroness, I think. By the second day I was bored to utter distraction. I knew no one, and Papa, who was on the scent of somebody's wife by then, had forgotten I existed.

I noticed Geoffrey before he noticed me—or so I thought. As it turned out, that wasn't the case. Years later he told me that his friend Symington had pointed me out to him earlier. He already knew about Papa's inheritance, of course; indeed, that was why he got Symington to wangle him an invitation. I was immediately intrigued because he didn't look remotely like an artist to me. He looked like a man of action. His clothes were fashionable, not deliberately scruffy, and he looked healthy and well fed. And sharp-eyed, focused, not dreamy. That was seductive to me—a man with energy and physical strength, an actor instead of an observer. When he caught my eye and smiled, it didn't feel like flirting; it felt like sympathizing. Two kindred spirits swimming toward each other in a sea of dullness and inanity. Oh, foolish, foolish girl.

I can't remember what he first said to me; something well planned and perfect, I'm sure. What I remember is his impatience with (contempt for, I was to learn) all the other guests at this house party. He said funny, sarcastic things about them, to my guilty delight. He took it for granted that I was not one of them—oh, no, I was like him, a bemused outsider; our superior common sense saved us from the excesses of these limp, dismal aesthetes. And always there was the sexual implication underlying everything—that he was more of a man than these men would ever be. This I had no trouble believing. I was twenty years old and ripe for it.

I wanted him, but that isn't why I married him. He said he loved me. I've forgiven him for everything else, but that lie is the one thing I cannot pardon. Even now.

5 December

Restless, keyed up. I think I could go out now, get out of this house. I've been a recluse long enough, seeing no one but Christy—and only once, briefly, because he insisted. I wish he would come now. I could send a note— no. Better not. Oh, but if only he would come. Now that I've thought of it, I can think of nothing else.

6 December

I don't know what I feel, what I think. Is this an end or a beginning? I am at loose ends, as the saying goes. It's apt, for I feel untangled, unwrapped. Unglued. If I've been freed, I don't know from what, or for what. Especially for what.

7 December

I have money but no home.

So say the solicitors, three of them, who came from Tavistock this morning to tell me, very politely, of my fate. I'm to have two thousand pounds a year, interest on the principal sum I'm left from the estate, for as long as I live, regardless of my situation (remarriage, that means; a laughably unlikely event). But Lynton Great Hall is now the property of Sebastian Verlaine, and I am advised to seek domestic accommodation elsewhere as soon as conveniently possible.

The very thought makes me so tired, I can barely hold up this pen in my hand. I've fantasized for years that if I had money and independence, I would go to live in Ravenna. I know I was happy there as a child. Could I be happy there again? Perhaps. But I'm so tired. I simply can't bear the thought of moving.

8 December

I don't have to move. Not immediately, at any rate. A reprieve has come in the form of a letter from Sebastian Verlaine, the new Viscount D'Aubrey. The lawyers notified him of his cousin's death a few days before he was to set sail for France, where he means to begin a "sojourn," as he calls it, that will last, at the very least, half a year. "Do not disturb yourself on my account," he writes. "Upon my return is soon enough to begin thinking about your removal from Lynton Hall; and even then, I daresay I shall have no pressing need to dislodge you if it should chance you've procured no suitable accommodations yet. I'm perfectly comfortable in my London digs and wouldn't dream of turning you out until you're quite ready to be evicted."

He sounds languorous and sophisticated, which fits with what little I can recall Geoffrey telling me about him; but elsewhere in the letter he writes sincerely, even movingly, of his sympathy for my loss. He makes no hypocritical claim of missing Geoffrey, whom I gather he barely knew—indeed, I don't think they liked each other very much—but he sounds perfectly earnest when he offers his condolences to me. He's piqued my curiosity; I wish I could remember what Geoffrey told me of him. My impression is of *decadence*; and yet that hardly squares with the tone of this letter. I recall that there's money somewhere—and perhaps that's it. Perhaps the reason for the new lord's admirable magnanimity is as simple as the fact that he can afford to be magnanimous.

Cynical, Christy calls me. If he only knew the half.

9 December

I can't make out what I am; I don't know myself anymore. I go for long periods in a state of depression, and then for no reason I rise out of it into something I can only call euphoria. Both moods are unnatural, and apparently beyond my control.

It seems that, without Geoffrey, I don't know who I am. For good or ill, he defined me: I was his wife, bound to him by our mutual bitterness and disillusion. What am I now? Christy says I can be anything, not knowing that, for me, that translates into nothing at all. Freedom is vastly overrated. It hasn't released me, it's paralyzed me.

I thought I was used to loneliness. I'd made it my lover,

my best friend. But I shall die if I don't speak to someone today.

P.M.—Christy came. I could almost believe in the efficacy of prayer, since I'd been thinking of him all day. We talked easily about Geoffrey, and more frankly than we ever have before. I kept remembering the time, right after he told me Geoffrey was dead, when he held me in his arms and let me cry. I kept thinking about how that had felt. Sometimes I lost the thread of our conversation while I thought of that. I suppose you could say I was distracted.

The best part was when, after a while, we stopped talking about Geoffrey and actually spoke of other things. Like two ordinary people, friends, conversing on everyday topics, casual things, making little jokes, interrupting each other. This was enormously satisfying to me. I think I'm beginning to wake up. Could it be? The possibility that there may be life after Geoffrey tantalizes me. I don't dread this night, and I'm positively looking forward to tomorrow.

This can't last. Can it?

XII

DECEMBER LAY MUTE and gray over the quiet woods and the gaunt, naked fields. Christy tramped the muddy lane between village and Hall with no companions but a lone thrush, puffed up for warmth in the hedgerow, and one gray fox trotting across a tawny cornfield in the distance. At the last rise before the lane dipped and then flattened out in front of the manor house, he paused, searching through the somber brake of beech trees for a glimpse of the Wyck. A silver ribbon of water twinkled in the chill sunlight, and a dark-clad figure—still before; he'd thought it was a sapling—moved, halted, and moved again along the bank, toward the bridge. It was Anne.

Then the brake thickened and she passed out of sight. But her eloquent image stayed in his mind's eye, dark and lonely, the picture of solitary grief. Christy looked down at the clutch of rusty, scentless chrysanthemums in his hand, the last living things—just barely—in the Weedies' garden; he'd snatched them on his way past their cottage, deeming it a mercy killing. Now they made him ashamed. He was courting a woman whose husband had been dead for exactly four weeks. Mumbling to himself, he flung the scraggly bouquet in the dirt and started down the hill.

Anne saw him from the bridge. She'd been staring down at the sluggish, leaf-clogged stream, leaning on her forearms over the stone ledge of the arch. When she looked up, the change in her pale, expressive face from melancholy to glad made Christy's heart twist—made him wish he had his flowers back. While she waited for him, she smoothed her coat collar and gave her skirts a discreet shake; the idea that she was smartening herself up for his benefit struck him at first as incredible, then miraculous. By the time he reached her, he felt like laughing. But he pulled himself together and said good afternoon to her without unseemly enthusiasm; and in the manner of old friends, they turned to lean against the cold stone and peer down at the river together, elbows touching.

"How have you been, Anne?" he asked, having not seen her in four days.

"I've been better, Christy. Much better. I think I'm starting to come round." Sometimes she reassured him just to sidestep the question, but this time she said it as if she meant it. "Have you been all right?"

"Yes, I've been fine. Busy, but quite well." They talked about a keen winter coming, and Christmas, and a little about church business, and then Christy came to the ostensible point of his visit. "I wanted to ask you something, and you must be completely honest when you answer, not allow me or your sense of duty to influence you in any way."

"My sense of duty?" She gave a skeptical laugh. "Tell me what it is, Christy; you've got my curiosity roused."

"There's a tradition at Lynton that goes back for as long as I can remember, of opening the great hall on Christmas Day to the children of the village and their families. Edward hated it, but he always did it anyway, because he revered tradition—any tradition. He'd make a quick, formal speech to greet everyone and then disappear upstairs, never to be seen again."

"You want me to—"

"I don't want you to do anything. You're in mourning; no one would think twice if you chose not to host the occasion. For that matter, there are probably some who would censure you if you did. All I'm—"

"I want to do it," she interrupted. "It's just for the children, isn't it? Then we must have it. And I expect you're right, certain people will condemn me for not behaving like a proper grieving widow. But you know me well enough by now to guess how little that bothers me."

He smiled, thinking he did, indeed. Strictly speaking, she wasn't even in mourning now, because the velvet dress he could see under her unbuttoned coat was a dark shade of russet, not black, and it even sported a white lace collar. Honoria Vanstone would be scandalized.

"What's it like?" she asked. "Tell me what I must do."

"It's not at all elaborate. The children have usually rehearsed a Nativity play, and there's some singing, a few gifts—just little trinkets Mrs. Fruit has bought and set the maids to wrapping beforehand."

"Is there food?"

"There's fruit punch and some cakes, I think—really nothing much. You mustn't think it's going to be a great deal of trouble."

"And it's in the great hall? Heavens, how ever do they heat it?"

"Not very adequately," he admitted, thinking of the years when the children had had to leave their coats and hats on during the whole affair. Anne had her finger on her cheek and was gazing off into space. He asked her what she was thinking.

"I'm thinking it sounds a little grim. And that it could be softened, or at least warmed up a bit without too much trouble."

"Are you really certain you want to get involved in this?"

"Yes, I'm sure. I wouldn't dream of canceling it. I'll talk to Mrs. Fruit—try to, that is—" she smiled humorously, "and have her tell me what's to be done. With Christmas less than two weeks away, we'll have to start planning it immediately."

There was pink color in her cheeks and a light in her eyes that he hadn't seen in a long time. Impulsively, he reached for her hand. "I'm glad you're going to do it. It'll be good for the children, but I think it'll be even better for you."

"I'm glad you told me about it." She smiled up at him, her face open and shadow-free for once. "Oh, Christy," she said suddenly, "I forgot! Molly—the bay mare? She foaled last night. She's a hunter; Geoffrey used to ride her before he bought the black."

"I know Molly."

"Do you want to see the foal? It's a filly, and she's gorgeous."

"Show me."

Collie Horrocks, Lynton Hall Farm's head groom, was coming out of the stables just as Christy and Anne started to go in. He tipped his hat and told his mistress he was off to Swan's smithy unless she needed him. Anne said no and asked him how the foal was doing.

"She's a right corker, m'lady," he replied, puffing his chest out as if he'd sired the filly himself. "She's doing quite brave, an' 'er mum's fine as well."

"How's the black stallion, Collie?" asked Christy.

"Now, 'e could do wi' a run, Vicar, no mistake. I take 'im myself o'er the wolds when I've the time, but the lad could do wi' more, like, for he's turrible restless and pent up."

The massive old stone-and-mortar stable was only half full of horseflesh, the old viscount having been a frugal man; but he'd had a good eye, and so the animals he had bought or bred were uniformly first-rate stock. Christy walked with Anne down the straw-strewn passage between the immaculate stalls, bestowing a soft word or a pat on the nose on the curious heads that poked over the railings. Feeble December light crept in through the cobwebbed windows. The warm, close air felt good after the chill outside, and before they'd reached Molly's stall Christy was taking off his greatcoat. He'd been in the Hall stables only once or twice since he and Geoffrey had been boys; it was comforting for some reason to see that nothing much had changed.

Molly and her foal were in the roomy loose box at the end of the long barn, separated from the other horses, even from Longfellow, the proud father, for the sake of quiet and calm.

"Aren't they beautiful?" Anne murmured, raising the wooden bolt softly and sidling inside with slow, soothing movements. The foal was nursing; Molly swiveled a wide eyeball at them and whickered a welcome. "Hullo, Moll," Anne greeted her, running a hand down her sleek throat. "How are you, beautiful girl? How's your lovely baby? Oh, God, Christy," she whispered ecstatically, "have you *ever*?"

He chuckled in sympathy; a day-old foal was surely one of God's most beguiling creations. This one had her sire's sorrel color and her dam's white eye patch. "Collie's got it straight: she's a right corker," he agreed, stroking the filly's shoulder. "What have you named her?"

"Collie calls her Patch."

"Oh, you can do better than that."

"Yes, it's not very imaginative." The leggy filly left off nursing long enough to examine them with her giant liquid eyes. "But since she's not really mine, I don't think I've the right to name her anything. I'm only visiting here now."

She said it lightly, her face serene, gaze steady on the spindly foal. Christy tried to echo her tone. "Have you thought about where you'll go?"

"No. Or I should say, not to any purpose." She took off her wide-brimmed hat and ruffled her hair with the flat of her hand. "Do you want to see the stallion?" He nodded and followed her back out into the corridor.

Devil's quarters were almost as commodious as Molly's birthing stall, as befitted an expensive thoroughbred racer. But the big stallion stamped about restlessly, the hide under his glossy coat fluttering with impatience. As Collie had said, he was "pent up" and raring to go. "Before he left, Geoffrey asked me to look after him," Christy confessed, stroking the nervousness out of the black's long, aristocratic neck. "I've been busy, but that's no excuse. I'll make time to ride him."

"You'll have to call him Tandem, I guess," said Anne. "That's his *Stud Book* name, and it would never do for the minister to go flying about the countryside on the back of a horse named Devil." He grunted in agreement and they smiled at each other.

"Christy," she said presently, her smile fading, "what really happened that day you and Geoffrey raced?"

He glanced at her sharply. "What do you mean? I fell off my horse, I told you."

"But that's not all of it. Come, you can tell me now—what difference does it make?" When he still hesitated, she added, "Believe me, there's nothing you could tell me about Geoffrey that would shock me."

The stoicism in her face disturbed him. She dropped her head, pretending to examine the curry brush she'd picked up from a box in the corner. "Geoffrey forced my horse off the path," he said slowly, "because we were about to overtake him."

Anne looked up, and her eyes were shocked but not surprised. "You could've been killed."

"Yes. Or Doncaster—my horse. I don't understand it. When we were boys, he would never have done anything like that. Never."

"He changed."

"Why?"

She shook her head and dropped the brush back into the box. Without speaking, she left the stallion's stall and moved down the dusty passage toward the mare's again.

"What did you mean when you said nothing I could tell you about Geoffrey would shock you?" he pursued, taking off his jacket and throwing it on a low bench along the side of the stall. Anne had her back to him, leaning against Molly's shoulder. The foal was curled up in a pile of hay, fast asleep. Christy went closer, until he stood at Anne's back. Her head was bowed; he could see the skin of her neck, the gold strands in her pretty red hair. "Tell me," he said quietly, and she started, not having realized he was so close. "Did he hurt you? Tell me, Anne."

"I'll tell you one thing," she said in a voice so low that he had to bend closer to hear. "A year ago he hit me and I fell down some steps. We were arguing—he lost control. I broke a bone in my wrist. He's never—he never touched me again. That was the end of the violence."

Appalled, Christy reached for the hand she was resting on the mare's withers. "This one?" She nodded, not turning around. He spanned the slim, pale-skinned joint with his fingers, squeezing the fragile bones lightly. "What else?" She shook her head. "Tell me."

"Christy, don't ask me."

Still holding her wrist, he used his other hand to smooth the hair back from her cheek so he could see her. "All right. Not now. But I'm sorry you were hurt. And I wish I'd known you then. I wish I could've helped you."

She made a half-turn toward him. Their bodies were almost touching; if he was in doubt about the nature of this new silence between them, the soft intensity in her eyes answered all his questions. And then she touched the tip of her tongue to her top lip and whispered, "Christy, would it be a sin if you kissed me?"

He didn't laugh. Nor did he say what he was thinking—that for him it would be a sacrament. He didn't want to scare her. He bent his head and pressed his mouth to hers, lightly, feeling her soft breath on his face. Her lips quivered, but he kept the kiss gentle and didn't touch her, on the chance that he'd misunderstood what she wanted from him. Her hand crept to his cheek. Her mouth was warm and sweet, soft as a pillow; he couldn't keep from moving his lips over hers in a caress. Then she lifted her arms and slipped them around his neck, and he knew he hadn't made a mistake. "Anne," he murmured, joyful, and gathered her close.

They kissed in earnest, then pulled back to look at each other, full of amazement. He closed his eyes when she touched his face with her fingertips, tracing his brows, his cheekbones, the bridge of his nose. He had her pressed against Molly's sturdy flank; the horse shifted lazily, and they staggered. Laughing, they turned in slow circles until they were next to the wooden bench along the wall. Christy kicked his coat out of the way and they sank down, never letting go of each other.

"I've wanted to touch you," he confessed in a whisper, moving his lips along the underside of her jaw, marveling at how soft she was.

"I've wanted you to."

"It was wrong—"

"Then." Her fingers twisted in his hair. "Not now. Oh, Christy, this is so right."

He put his hands inside her woolen coat and slid them around her waist, pulling her closer so he could feel her breasts against him. The velvet of her dress wasn't as soft as her lips. When he kissed her this time, he parted them with the tip of his tongue, relishing her gasp of surprise and pleasure. She was trembling—so was he. She framed his face with her hands and kissed him passionately and without reserve.

"I haven't done this in a long time," she told him in a shaky voice. "I was afraid I might not like it." A smile blossomed on her lips; she leaned in to whisper against his mouth, "How wrong can a girl be?"

He took her in another long, drugging kiss, feeling like a randy adolescent with his first girl. His hands inside her coat were wandering with a will of their own, and she wasn't doing anything to discourage them. She closed her eyes and made a soft humming sound while he stroked the sides of her breasts, then cupped them, caressed the tips with his thumbs. Without a thought, he began to unbutton her dress under the lace collar—until an inkling of where all this lovely fumbling might really lead brought him back to a semblance of reason. He started to laugh. "What are we doing?"

"I don't know, but don't stop," she said in a throaty murmur that made his blood race.

It took all his self-control to take his hands off her soft, perfect breasts and put a few inches of distance between them. She was adorably mussed; she even had a straw in her hair. He removed it tenderly, then took her hands in both of his. "Anne." He made his voice serious; he wanted to be sober, so to speak, for what he was about to say, so she would know that passion wasn't all that motivated it. "Anne, my love." She bent her head to kiss his fingers. When she looked up again, he saw that there were tears in her eyes. "I love you, darling. With all my heart. It's too soon to tell you that, I know"—she shook her head—"but I have to. I love you. If you'll have me, I promise I'll make you happy."

"I'm already happy." The tears welled over and spilled down her cheeks.

He had to kiss her again. He tasted salt on his tongue and felt like weeping with her, he was so happy. "It'll have to be a secret engagement. Probably for a whole year," he said ruefully. "Even after that, we couldn't marry for a few more months, not without offending the whole—"

"Christy, stop—I can't marry you!"

The surprise in her voice was more of a shock than the words—at first. What did she think he'd been leading up to? "You can't?" he said stupidly.

"No. *No.* I'm sorry, I didn't realize you—that you wanted—that you were *proposing* to me." She made the word sound outlandish, even distasteful. "It's just—oh, Christy, I'll never marry again. I have no intention of marrying again, anyone. But *especially* you."

She stood up and backed away from him. All he could do was blink at her while she made a shaky-fingered attempt to rebutton her dress. When his wits came back, he said, "Why not?"

She looked at him as if he were a slow-witted child. "Because! You're a minister!"

He stood up, too. "It's the first I've heard that that rules out marriage." He thought that came out sounding fairly reasonable; odd, since inside his head everything was chaos.

"Christy," she said patiently, "I don't believe in God. You're a priest and I'm an atheist."

"You're an agnostic. That's—"

"No, I'm not, I'm an atheist. For me to marry you, it would be like—like St. Paul marrying a harlot." He snorted. "Or Jesus marrying Mary Magdalene." He started to laugh, but she cut him off. "How can you even consider it? It's impossible, absurd. We can't be together like that."

He spread his hands. "Then how can we be together?"

She started to pace. The mare sidestepped out of the way, sensing her nervousness. "It would be risky for you. I don't care for myself, I honestly don't, but if we were found out I suppose it could be very bad for you. They might even defrock you or whatever it's called."

The truth hit him. Just to make sure, he said, "What are you talking about?"

She stopped pacing and looked him in the eye. "I'm talking about an affair," she said boldly.

"An affair."

"Yes."

"No."

"Why not?"

"Are you in earnest? Because it's *wrong*."

"I don't see anything wrong with it! It's not adultery—we're not married. 'Thou shalt not commit adultery'—we wouldn't be. 'Thou shalt not covet thy neighbor's wife'—you wouldn't be."

He didn't know whether to laugh at her or throttle her. "Have you ever heard of the sin of fornication?"

"It's not a sin to me." She crossed her arms and lifted her chin.

"Is that so. How many affairs have you had?"

"That's not the point. If I haven't had any, it's because I haven't wanted to until now, not because I think they're immoral."

She had an answer, albeit a stupid one, for everything. "Anne, have you ever thought about this? Ever sat down and really given it any serious consideration?"

"Have you?" she countered.

"Yes, I have. In the abstract as well as the concrete."

An impish light came into her eyes. Moving a step closer, she made her voice seductive and asked, "With whom have you thought about it in the concrete, Reverend?"

He was enchanted all over again. But he kept his hands to himself and just said, "Fishing for compliments?"

"Maybe." She smiled naturally, dropping the coyness. "You want me, don't you?"

"I want to marry you."

"I can't marry."

"In time you won't feel that way. It's too soon, you're still—"

"No, you're wrong. I never wanted to marry Geoffrey either, and I was right. I never should have."

"Marrying Geoffrey was a mistake," he agreed. "Marrying me—"

"Would be almost as catastrophic. Christy, it's impossible, it's absolutely out of the question!" She pounded her fist against the palm of her hand, meaning it. "If there were ever two people who shouldn't marry each other, it's you and I. And not only because of our—ha!—religious differences. When you get down to it, we have nothing in common. I couldn't live here in Wyckerley for the rest of my life. Me, a minister's wife?" She laughed again, without humor. "Visiting the poor and the sick, having people to dinner, being nice to the bishop—all that political nonsense—"

"I can see you doing all of that."

"But this isn't my home. I—I want to go back to Italy, to Ravenna, where I grew up."

"Ravenna?" It was the first he'd heard. He tried to keep exasperation out of his tone, but it was getting harder. "Do you have people there? Family?"

"I was happy there," she evaded. "We left when my mother died, but I have memories—"

"Anne, you were seven years old!"

She turned her back on him for a moment, then spun back around. The distress in her face made him close the gap between them and take her hands. "Oh, Christy," she wailed, "it's hopeless. I'm simply not the wife for you. You know it too, I think." He started to deny it, but she put her fingers over his lips. "But we could still be together. We could still be happy." She caressed his cheek, then his lips with her fingertips. Standing on tiptoe, she kissed his mouth, whispering his name. He watched her eyes close, felt a tremor of wanting shudder through her body.

He put his hands on her shoulders and gently pried her away. She blushed. At first he couldn't believe it; he thought she must be about to cry. But she didn't cry, and the blush—her first ever, as far as he knew—was because she was embarrassed. Such a storm of tenderness seized him then, he couldn't contain it. "Oh, Christ, Anne," he mumbled, reaching for her.

But she jerked back, and now there was a holy fire in her eyes. "Oh, so it's a sin to kiss me now?" she said scathingly. "I loathe your religion. You say you love me, but you won't be my lover. How can love ever be a sin?" She brought her arms out and dropped them back to her sides. "Oh, this is completely hopeless. I'm sorry, Christy, I made a mistake. The truth is, you're too provincial for me. I can see now that we don't suit at all."

She had her hand on the door to the stall before he realized she was leaving. *Leaving*. It was a trick to move fast so he could catch her, and smoothly so he wouldn't spook Molly. He managed it, and he had the added satisfaction of seeing Anne's face go from grim to astonished in the second before he grabbed her, backed her up against the rails, and growled at her, "This is the way we kiss in the provinces." Her surprised mouth was an open target. He took an intimate, breath-robbing kiss from her, then another and another.

She wilted. Making the loveliest sounds, she found the strength to reach behind him and press her hands to his buttocks, pulling him close against her. Raw sexual heat burned him. He pulled her head back and kissed her throat with his hot, open mouth, while his fingers played over the soft swell of her bosom, teasing her, making her moan. "Marry me," he grated, taking dangerous little nips of her neck with his teeth. "Marry me, Anne." She tried to shake her head, but he wouldn't let her. "Marry me." All she got out was "Nnn," before he silenced her with his mouth. He could feel himself losing control, and at the last second it came to him that seducing Anne wasn't the solution to his problem, but to hers.

Shivering with frustration, he dragged his mouth away and rested his forehead against hers. Their mingled breaths sounded harsh and desperate, and it was no consolation at the moment to know that he'd succeeded in getting her as excited as he was; in fact, he felt contrite. Without much hope, he said, "We wouldn't have to wait a whole year. To hell with it—six months."

She shook her head and said, "No, no, no, no no."

Standoff. Their hands fell away from each other, but they didn't move apart. She looked the way he felt—drained.

"I'm going to wear you down," he warned.

"I'm going to seduce you."

"No, you're not."

"Yes, I am. If I'm a sinner and I have to go to hell, I damn well want you with me." Suddenly she smiled. "Just you. Think about it, Christy—you and me in hell. Wouldn't it be heaven?"

He stepped back, shaken. If she was the devil in disguise, he had serious fears for the fate of his immortal soul.

"You'd better run," she taunted shakily. "I'm going to get you."

He pointed his finger at her. "The bigger the sinner, the harder she falls. I'm going to get *you*."

A noise from the front of the stables made them both jump. "Collie's back!" Anne said in a guilty whisper.

Christy snatched his coat off the floor and said, his eyes rolling upward to God, *"Thank you."*

XIII

Let the heavens rejoice, and let the earth be glad; let the sea thunder and all that is in it; let the field be joyful and all that is therein. Then shall all the trees of the wood shout for joy before the Lord, for he cometh, for he cometh to judge the earth.

WHEN HE COMETH *to judge the earth,* thought Anne, *I will be in trouble. Because I tried to corrupt one of his finest creations.*

Sitting in her warm, padded, D'Aubrey family pew, she lifted her gaze from her prayer book and let it rest on Christy. He was reading the 96th Psalm, his Bible in his left hand, gesturing with his right with smooth, slow, hypnotic movements, perfectly in tune with the psalm's joyful message. His vestments were white today, in celebration of Christmas. In the light of the altar candles, his graceful robes glowed like mother-of-pearl, and his gorgeous golden hair gleamed with a radiance she could only call heavenly.

Heavenly? Good Lord. But it was true; what she thought of as his militant angel quality always seemed to intensify when he had on his liturgical garments and was backlit by candles and crucifixes. If he had suddenly sprouted wings and brandished a fiery sword, she doubted anyone in the congregation would have been surprised.

And she'd tried to seduce him. If the memory of that afternoon in Molly's stall weren't so vivid, she'd have thought it a hallucination. Seduce the vicar of All Saints? Look at him! He was reading the Collect, preparatory to the Lesson and the sermon— she could follow the liturgy now like a seasoned congregationist— and his voice rang with the absolute conviction that God's only Son was born of a pure virgin and became a man. She lowered her eyes, ashamed. If there was a God, she'd have to ask his pardon; but since there wasn't, she guessed she'd have to ask Christy's.

She hadn't seen him alone since their encounter in the stables. He'd invited her—in a *note*—to attend the adult choir's Advent program, and she went, not knowing what to expect. As it turned out, there was nothing to expect; after the singing, he disappeared. On some church business, no doubt, but she didn't want to ask Reverend Woodworth exactly what. And once he'd come to the Hall to ride Devil, but he left immediately afterward without coming to the house or trying to see her; she wouldn't even have known about it if William Holyoake hadn't mentioned it to her. Since then, nothing.

It meant he'd come to his senses, and that was a good thing. That was the best thing that could happen. Yes, yes, yes, but why did she feel so let down? All that heat, all that new, forbidden wanting, the excitement, and the hard, wrenching *denial* in the end—gone! And apparently forgotten by him, as if it had never been. Could he really have discarded her that easily? Written her off as a risk not worth taking? An occasion of sin his soul was better off avoiding? The thought was not only distressing but perversely galling. She already admired his willpower; she didn't feel like increasing the admiration by adding herself to his list of successfully abandoned temptations.

But he'd said he loved her. Oh, God. He loved her.

He didn't know her, of course; if he did, he couldn't love her. She had too much bleakness inside, too much desolation. Compared to her, he was a sun god—Apollo to her dark Diana. Oh, but he'd said it, "I love you, Anne," and so he must believe it, because Christy would never lie. So she could keep that, no matter what else happened.

But evidently he was fighting his illicit passions and winning. She should feel glad for him; that would be the Christian thing to do. But she didn't feel a bit glad. She listened to his sermon in a bad mood. It was a simple one, and short for him, on the miracle of the Nativity. He thought he gave terrible sermons, but Anne disagreed. Maybe sinners didn't suddenly fall to their knees, repent, and turn their lives around because of his power and eloquence, but she doubted if anyone's sermons accomplished that, not in any lasting way. What Christy couldn't see was that he—"manifested" was probably the word—he manifested God's teachings by his own manly, gentle, upright example. She could listen to him preach all day, because his intentions showed through so plainly. He'd told her more than once that even he had doubts at times, occasions when his faith failed him—a confession that had shocked and fascinated her. But if he did have doubts, it never showed in his sermons, during which he appeared to believe in, *glory* in, every word he uttered. That was his magic: his absolute earnestness.

The children's choir sang "Behold a Little Child" like angels, led by Sophie Deene, who still looked pretty despite the heavy black mourning she wore for her father. When the time for Holy Communion came, Anne sat still in her pew, as always, and watched Christy distribute the bread and wine to the communicants. These were the times when she almost envied people for their devout-looking, mysteriously simple belief. Christy said faith was a gift, which was not consoling since it meant God had decided not to give it to her. Did the villagers wonder and whisper about the interesting fact that Lady D'Aubrey never took the sacraments? Oh, probably. They'd whisper louder if they knew she'd never been confirmed in their Anglican religion. They'd *shout* if they knew what she'd tried to do with their pastor two weeks ago in a horse stable . . .

Christy was blessing them: "May the peace of God, which passeth all understanding, keep thy hearts and minds in the knowledge and love of God, and of his Son Jesus Christ our Lord."

"Amen."

Anne put away her prayer book and her hymnal, relieved that the service was over. She didn't know what she was going to do about Christy; but if she was going to renounce him, it would be easier to do if she didn't have to look at him.

The reprieve would be brief, though: he and forty village children and their parents were coming to her house in two hours for the annual Christmas revel.

The great hall refused to look intimate, in spite of the best efforts of every housemaid, kitchen maid, footboy, and stable lad Anne had set to work on the project. The dimensions of the vast, echoing chamber defied coziness no matter how many boughs of holly, ivy, spruce, or pine were lugged in and dutifully hung from its burnt, mile-high rafters. But with a Nativity scene complete with manger and live lambs, a Christmas tree laden with holly berries and lit candles, and a Yule log crackling in the enormous fireplace hearth, no one could deny that the place looked *festive*. As soon as the children began arriving, the distinction between cozy and festive became irrelevant in any case, and the new challenge was trying to be heard over the din.

"What can I do to help?" Miss Weedie almost had to shout. "Just give me your worst job and forget all about me." She looked tall and gawky in a dress of plum-purple bombazine that didn't become her; in fact, it looked as if it might have belonged originally to her mother. But her anxious smile was kindness itself, and Anne had grown extremely fond of her faded prettiness and the frowzy blond hair that wouldn't stay put no matter how many pins she stuck in it.

Anne looked around, feeling a bit overwhelmed. The adult residents of Wyckerley might be in awe of Lady D'Aubrey, but their children definitely weren't, and they were making free with her great hall as if it were the village green on May Day. Just then a little girl of about four barreled into her hip. Anne bore the impact sturdily, but the child toppled over backward and landed on her behind. Before she could cry, Anne knelt down and pulled her into her arms. "Well, hello!" she exclaimed brightly. "How in the world did that happen?" She kissed one sticky cheek, and the little girl smiled at her shyly. "What's your name?"

"Birdie," she mumbled.

"Birdie? That's a pretty name. Do you know what mine is?"

"No."

"No?" She made an amazed face that tickled Birdie and made her giggle. "You don't know who I am?"

"You're the Hall lady. We're to curtsey when we see you an' say 'Good day, m'lady.' " Her little snub features lit up. "I know your name," she crowed. "It's M'lady!"

Anne laughed. "I guess it is," she said, and stole another quick kiss before Birdie scrambled up and ran off. Anne rose to her feet a little wistfully. She'd known it before, of course, but until now it had never hit her with such force—one of the problems with ruling out marriage was that one also ruled out children.

To Miss Weedie she said, "It was so good of you to come. How is your mother today?"

"She's better, thank you, and asked me to tell you in particular how much she enjoyed the pumpkin soup. Miss Pine is sitting with her while I'm here."

"Then I'm indebted to Miss Pine as well."

Miss Weedie blushed. "How can I help you?" she repeated.

"You can tell me whose idea it was to give the boys whistles for presents and let them open them up before the party even begins!"

Miss Weedie, who always took her literally, looked confused, then worried.

"It was mine," Anne explained, laughing. "Collie Horrocks, our groom, is a wood-carver in his spare time, and I set him to making twenty-five whistles two weeks ago. Now I wish I'd given them out as farewell presents, so the children could drive their parents mad at *home* with the dratted things." Miss Weedie tsked sympathetically. "Well, if you really want to do something, I suppose you could start helping Miss Mareton get them quiet and organized for the Nativity play. That's the first order of business, I believe."

Immediately Miss Weedie's customary air of tentativeness fell away and she drew herself up, full of purpose. "Right, then. My lady," she remembered to add, and marched off to do her duty. Oh, of course, Anne remembered, she'd been the village schoolteacher years and years ago. She'd been Christy's teacher, in fact. Good—then she was in her element.

And there was Christy, over by the Christmas tree, sipping hot cider and talking to Captain Carnock. A little boy of about three had his arms wrapped around his left leg and was trying to climb it. He stopped talking to the captain long enough to bend over and haul the little boy up into his arms. *Well, what else?* Anne grumped to herself. Didn't it just *have to be* that he was marvelous with children?

"I've never seen the great hall looking so cheery. You've quite transformed the place, Lady D'Aubrey."

Anne turned with a start to see Mayor Vanstone at her side, looking tall, sleek, and faintly seal-like with his elegantly graying hair combed straight back from his forehead. "It's the children who've transformed it," she demurred. "I'm so glad you and Miss Vanstone could come."

"We wouldn't miss it. Everyone is in your debt for carrying on with the tradition in spite of your terrible loss."

"Oh, do you think so? It occurred to me that some might think carrying on with it showed disrespect for my late husband," she said deliberately. Indeed, she'd heard through the grapevine that that was exactly what Honoria Vanstone had been saying.

"Not at all," he denied smoothly. "It's an event the children eagerly anticipate, and only a very churlish person would construe the continuation of it as anything but a kind and benevolent act by our most beloved ladyship."

She could only agree: Honoria *was* churlish. But it was hard not to smile at his description of herself, or to ask him if he was referring to her or the Blessed Virgin. She couldn't wait to repeat this conversation to Christy.

That is, if he ever spoke to her again, about anything. Now he was across the way, helping Miss Mareton and Miss Weedie get the Nativity play youngsters in their proper places for the start of the performance. "Sorry?" she said, realizing the mayor had asked her a question.

"I say, I wonder if you might be free one evening next week. Honoria has been hoping you would dine with us—and I, too, it goes without saying. It would, of course, be a very quiet evening, *en famille,* in keeping with your state of mourning. Or, I should say," he added quickly, "with the state of mourning of all of us."

"How kind. It sounds delightful. Thank you so much." It sounded no such thing; she could hardly imagine anything more tedious. But he was the mayor, and she was still the head of Lynton Great Hall; she felt an obligation to be attentive, at least for a little longer, to the exigencies of local politics.

Not that she fooled herself that Eustace Vanstone was inviting her to dinner for the sole purpose of discussing policies and programs for the benefit of Wyckerley. This wasn't the first time he'd paid his stiff court to her since Geoffrey's death, although it was the most direct. Unless she was grievously misreading the signs, Mayor Vanstone had designs on her. She wished she knew a way to communicate to him the absolute hopelessness of his suit without causing embarrassment. And hopeless it was, and not only because she didn't fancy him. Even if she were mad for him, she would still have to decline a marriage proposal, because accepting it would make her Honoria's stepmother. Gads!

The Nativity play started. Tommy Nineways, the church-warden's son, played Joseph, and it was immediately clear that nepotism rather than dramatic talent had played a major role in the casting. Mary, on the other hand, was played by Sally Wooten—Christy tutored her brothers, Anne recalled—and except for a bad moment when she dropped the Christ Child doll on the floor, Sally seemed born for the stage. All in all, the performance was sweet and touching and very funny; more than one adult watching it had to resort to coughing into a handkerchief to smother uncontrollable laughter.

Anne's enjoyment was tempered by having to watch Margaret Mareton stand next to Christy throughout the play, whispering to him, bumping shoulders, sometimes leaning against him as if overcome with pride in her fledgling thespians. She was an undeniably pretty girl, with shiny black hair and big serious brown eyes. But Anne didn't care for her. Where was her sense of decorum? She was the Sunday school teacher, for heaven's sake; children looked up to her as a model of propriety. Why was she leaning against the vicar in a public place? In *any* place, if it came to that?

Sophie Deene led the children in carols after the Nativity play, everyone gathered round the candlelit Christmas tree. Anne joined in as well as she could, in a rusty alto that was at least an octave below the children's reedy sopranos. As loose and casual as this event necessarily was because of the children, she was nevertheless aware of the abiding stiffness with which most people still treated her, worse now because of her "bereavement." When she'd been Geoffrey's wife, she was an object of speculation and curiosity. As his widow, she was that and more; she'd become someone to whom no one knew quite what to say.

And Christy thought he wanted her for his wife. If it weren't so sad, it would be funny. She looked across the sea of singing faces at Mrs. Nineways, the churchwarden's wife, and Mrs. Woodworth, the curate's; they smiled and nodded, acknowledging her through the strains of "Good King Wenceslas." Laura Woodworth was a small, compact woman, in perpetual motion, busy as a beaver; she tirelessly visited the parish's sick, who frequently got well—so Christy said—because she bullied them into it. Emmaline Nineways was shy and retiring, a genuinely religious woman, if her attendance and demeanor at church were any indication.

Anne knew herself to be neither devout nor dynamic, and she knew as well that, deep down, the people of Wyckerley would never really come to trust her. She would end up a burden to Christy, not a help—assuming she wanted to be his wife, which she didn't.

After the singing came the present-opening, a mad, scrambling event that Miss Mareton and her helpers were hard put to keep civilized. Besides whistles for the boys and cornstalk dolls for the girls—constructed by the housemaids over a furious two-day marathon—Anne had ordered pencils and paper tablets from a stationer in Tavistock; they'd arrived yesterday, in the very nick of time. In addition, Captain Carnock had generously donated several bushels of apples, and Mr. Farnsworth, owner of Wyckerley's only inn, the First and Last, had contributed a barrel of spiced cider. The mayor's gift was a tree, to be planted next spring on the village green in the children's name, complete with plaque. But the individually wrapped cakes and candies that Lynton Hall's kitchen maids had been baking for days got the warmest reception, which ought not to have come as a surprise. "I should've made *that* the farewell gift," Anne wailed to a laughing Miss Weedie. "Now they won't eat their supper!"

A baseless fear; Mrs. Fruit and the maids barely got the food laid out on the long trestle tables before the children proceeded to devour it. If Christy had meant to say grace before the meal, their locustlike descent changed his mind. He watched the rout from a distance, hands in his pockets, talking to Captain Carnock again and looking unbearably handsome in his "full holy blacks." Honoria Vanstone was saying something to her, but Anne didn't hear it. Over the heads of two dozen people, Christy's eyes suddenly met hers. The clamor of voices died away and all the bodies around her became as insubstantial as ghosts. Neither of them smiled; the silent message that passed between them was no laughing matter. But when the odd, out-of-time moment ended and reality flooded back, she felt a grim relief. Christy wasn't ignoring her because he'd given her up. Oh, no. And none of the pain in store for them had diminished a whit. Nothing had changed. They were still obsessed.

All the contrition she'd felt in church this morning vanished, along with her good intentions. She was tired of pretending nothing had happened, tired of treating Christy as an acquaintance. Tired of his public politeness. Tired of watching women like Margaret Mareton hang on him like barnacles.

"I've just remembered something I must tell the vicar," she said abruptly, cutting Honoria Vanstone off in the middle of a sentence. "Excuse me, will you?" Not waiting for the answer, she handed her punch cup to a passing servant and made for Christy in a determined straight line.

She didn't know what her excuse was going to be until it came out of her mouth. "I've come upon a little volume of sermons in the library, Reverend Morrell. I thought it might interest you. It looks quite old. There are some notes in the margins that are quite intriguing, too," she embellished recklessly. "Would you like to see it?"

"Yes, very much," he said seriously—so seriously, she was afraid he had actually believed her. "Would you excuse me?" he asked Captain Carnock, who bowed to them both and said, "Not at all," several times.

Leading the way out of the great hall and down the paneled corridor to the library, her nerves, already tight, stretched to the breaking point. All she could think of was, What if, on top of everything else that was already wrong or probably would go wrong between them, Christy was disappointed when he found out there weren't any sermons?

She opened the library door herself and stood back to let him enter; then she closed it and stood with her back against it—barring it, in effect. He turned around in the center of the unlit, unheated room and looked at her expectantly.

"I lied about the sermons."

He wasn't disappointed. A slow smile lit up his face with the radiance of sunshine. He came toward her—and all at once she was afraid of him, because he was so beautiful. *What if he wins?* she had time to think before he touched her. Without asking, he slipped his hands inside the little jacket that went over her best mourning dress. It thrilled her so, that one act of possession, that she gasped. His arms went all the way around, and they stood pressed together, not moving, just feeling each other's deep breathing. Already she loved the hard solidness of his body, the strength in his arms; embracing him was like embracing a thick stone pillar. No, wrong image, too cold. Like embracing a tree, warm and vital and firmly planted in the ground. Unshakable.

She loosened her arms and pulled back to see his face. "I thought you were going to *get* me," she accused.

"I am." His smile shattered her, kicked the last prop out from under her. "I thought you were going to seduce me."

She licked her lips. "I am."

His smile faded. When he kissed her, any illusion that she was the one in control of this situation disappeared, like strong light dissipating a shadow. She closed her eyes and let go of herself, forgetting everything except the pleasure rising inside, soft and irresistible, the tenderest yielding. So this was it; this was what her woman's body had been made for. The revelation made her sigh, and hold on tighter so she couldn't lose it. It was as if she'd been covered with a layer of scales all her life, and Christy's touch had made them fall away. Now she felt like Eve, naked in the garden, and without an ounce of shame.

When he stopped kissing her, she felt like an opium addict deprived of her drug. "Merry Christmas," he murmured.

"Merry Christmas," she whispered back, not letting go of him.

"We can't stay here long."

She had an inspiration. "Stay for dinner. After everyone leaves, you stay."

"Can't."

"Why not?"

"The Maretons have invited me to their house."

"Margaret Mareton?"

"Her family."

"That—Sunday school teacher who can't keep her hands off you?" His brows shot up; his ice-blue eyes were pools of innocent amazement. "Do you like her?" she pressed. "She's mad for you. Well, do you?"

"Yes, I like her," he answered, maddeningly ingenuous.

"*She'd* marry you."

"She probably would."

"You know I'm jealous of her."

"I know." He brought his fingers to her cheek and softly caressed her. "It's the nicest thing that's happened to me in days. Since I saw you last."

"Why didn't you try to see me before now?"

He looked down, thinking, and she knew that whatever he was going to say, it would be the truth. Talking with Christy was not like talking with anyone else she'd ever known. "I wanted to see you," he said slowly. "Every day. Most days I couldn't because

I was too busy with meetings, commitments, the dean's visit. I couldn't get away."

"And the other days?"

He held her hands between his, their fingers pointing upward, prayer-fashion. "I was afraid," he said quietly.

His honesty gave her the courage to say, "I was afraid, too. But I wanted you to come. Every day I hoped you would." Their lips met again in a soft, breathless kiss. She was flirting with surrender, but she didn't care. "Oh, Christy, I don't want to scare you away, I just want to be with you!"

"Meet me tomorrow, Anne. We'll go for a walk."

"A walk? Yes, yes," she said quickly, "a walk. Lovely." She'd go to a public hanging if he asked her, and count it a fine outing. "When?"

"Three o'clock? We could meet at the crossroads."

"Three o'clock."

"Pray it doesn't rain," he said, a teasing gleam in his eye.

"I just might," she retorted, and she wasn't teasing at all.

XIV

1 January 1855

Christy left another poem for me in our hiding place at the crossroads. If anything, this one is worse than the first.

> God, though our lives are only smoke,
>   Although that truth we try to shirk,
> Although we travail, sick, heartbroke,
>   Let me have Anne, your finest work.

And so it goes, for several more mortifying verses. It's an awful poem, by any standards a reasonable person could apply. But every time I read it, I cry like an infant. I am a perfect idiot. How does he do this to me?

I retaliate by leaving him tracts by agnostic philosophers. (Unaccountably, there are several in the library; we found them when we cleaned it, tucked out of sight, as heresy ought to be, on a high shelf.) I doubt that they make Christy weep, though, so the exchange isn't equal.

I've decided it's just my luck that my first full-fledged love affair (no, half-fledged; but hope springs eternal) is unfolding in the dead of winter. Were it a *full-fledged* affair, I daresay we would both be dead of pneumonia by now, because of Christy's insistence that we carry it on almost exclusively out-of-doors. He won't go near the old caretaker's cottage, where we could be private *and* warm. I don't blame him; my intentions aren't honorable. So this is the only benefit of the half-fledged state of things: that we're both necessarily *clothed* at all times.

Yesterday I waited for him at the old Plym canal, a dismal, deserted, unbearably melancholy place—except that he came, and then all the dreariness was gone, just forgotten. Except for the cold! But even that had an advantage—Christy had to fold me up in his greatcoat so my teeth would stop chattering. And of course, then he had to kiss me. And so forth.

I've been thinking ever since about the *and so forth.*

God, I'm in such a state. Is this normal? Who can I ask? No one. Anyway, my feelings are too private. I doubt I could confide them in a sister if I had one. And part of me doesn't care if this is normal or not. For once I'm alive, and it's enough.

But sometimes—it's almost as if I'm ill. I can't sleep for thinking about him, I don't care anything about food, I forget things, mislay objects, lose track of time, don't hear other people speaking to me, lose my own train of thought in the middle of a sentence. I'm like a mildly retarded adult, bumbling about, useless, but so far doing no actual harm.

And I'm burning up inside. I know what I want; Geoffrey gave me that, at least—the knowledge of passion, even the experience of it. So I'm no blushing virgin. I'm a woman with, for all I know, nearly as much worldly experience as Christy.

No; unlikely. Geoffrey initiated him too, I remember now. At a brothel when they were scarcely more than boys. I don't know what to do with that information, where to put it, how to feel about it. I won't think about it.

Christy *will* be my lover. He must be. We've "sinned"

already, both of us, simply from *wanting* it so much. If I died tonight and God existed, he'd send me to Dante's Second Circle, and quite rightly, where I'd whirl round and round with Paola and Francesca for eternity, howling out my frustrated passion.

That being the case, I'd rather hang for a wolf than a sheep, thank you very much.

12 January

The feast of Aelred, Abbot of Rievaulx. I know all of them now.

Christy left a present for me at our crossroads hiding place. His poems he rolls up in cylinders and ties with a ribbon, and if they get wet he doesn't care. (I care; I love his dreadful poems with all my constant heart.) But this present was wrapped in a bit of sealskin, and so I opened it with some care, some trepidation. It was a portrait of me. A watercolor, done from a sketch he'd made last week when we went to Abbeycombe, the old Roman ruins. I'd brought some bread and cheese, and after we ate he did a quick charcoal drawing of me, head only, in his notebook. I thought nothing of it, or only that he was fast, and that he might fill it in a bit, later, on his own.

Well. I don't have to wonder anymore what he'd have become if he hadn't chosen the ministry. And I must also confess that I'm jealous. (*Here* I confess it; I'm not up yet to confessing it to him.) All my life I wanted to be an artist. I was either blessed or cursed with the objectivity to see that my father's talent, such as it was, did not pass on to his daughter, and so, after a mercifully brief disillusionment, I abandoned all hope. (Dante again.) But Christy— whoever his European teachers were, whoever discouraged him from pursuing painting for his life's work ought to be flogged, hanged, shot, quartered, tortured—words fail me.

But then, perhaps I'm biased. It's possible. And his picture is of *me*, after all. And I've not seen any of his other work. Maybe I inspire him! That makes me laugh—but self-consciously. Hopefully. Oh, I'm like a child! He makes me so giddy, so silly!

Anyway. His watercolor is so very lovely. Can this truly be how he sees me? My cheeks are hot, just thinking of it. No museum would show it, it's too flagrant, too honest. I can't describe the expression he's captured. My lips are open, just slightly; my eyes . . . hot. Purposeful, I suppose. It's half-profile, and he's stopped the movement as if with a camera. The blurriness of the outline—ah, God, I can only describe it as passionate. I can't stop looking at this picture. It's not only me, Anne Verlaine, it's the woman I can feel myself turning into. But I don't know her yet, and so how could Christy know her so well?

I shall die if I don't have him soon.

14 January

How dare he call me "a near occasion of sin"? It's the most offensive thing anyone has ever said to me, and I told him so. That and a lot more—I called him "an occasion of boring pietism." Ha! Take that, Reverend High and Mighty Christian Morrell.

15 January

He apologized. In a poem. Execrable, as usual.
All is forgiven.

16 January

I can't say the words to him. He says them to me each time we meet. "I love you, Anne." But I withhold the gift and don't reciprocate, even though I know I'm hurting him. That's the punishment for my cowardice, and it's an acute, tormenting one. I'd rather hurt myself than Christy.

I love him.

There, I've written it. Now the page is wet and blurry, because looking at those three words makes me cry. Why is it so sad? I don't know, but my heart is breaking. I feel as if my life is ending—some—fracture is occurring—

No, I don't know what I mean. But I know that if I gave him this gift, I would lose control. He would win. I can't let him win.

I tell him my reasons for not marrying him, and all he does is make fun of them.

WHY I CAN'T MARRY CHRISTY

1. The dream I've had for five years has finally come true: I'm free and financially independent. I can do anything, go anywhere, be anyone I want. I'm rich! Why would I stay in Wyckerley and be a minister's wife??

2. I'd make a terrible minister's wife. I'm a private, not a public person; I can't go around visiting the sick and clothing the naked. Corporal works of mercy would be the death of me. Imagine me entertaining the bishop!

3. People don't like or trust me. The ones who do like me are intimidated by me, I have no idea why. I don't fit in.

4. I hate the weather. Italy's the place for me, where the winters are kind and mild.

5. A minister's wife ought to believe in God. Minimum requirement.

"Anne, my dearest love, you're a coward," Christy writes in his last letter. "You've never had a home in Italy or anywhere else. Furthermore, not all men are like Geoffrey or your father, so that reservation doesn't hold water either. It's not Wyckerley that's constricting and imprisoning, it's your own fear. But you could set yourself free by choosing to stay and make a life with me. You could be happy."

And so on. I tell him *he's* the dreamer, not me, but he shunts my best, most logical arguments aside as if they were the natterings of a worried old maid. I think he's gone blind. The answer is so clear—why can't he see it? We are not suited for marriage; we are suited for love. If he doesn't give in soon, I'll go insane.

17 January

Now he's sending me the marriage vows. Think about the words, he says. He wants to say them to me in church, he says, in front of all our friends. "I, Christy, take you, Anne, to have and to hold from this day forward, for better, for worse, in sickness and in health, to love and to cherish, till death us do part."

All right, Christy, this is war. I'm going back to sending the agnostic tracts.

19 January

Touch and go today. So close, so close. I'm blushing, just thinking of it. We were at the canal, huddling under his umbrella, laughing at the curse words I shouted out at the rain. He started it, kissing me and so forth. We . . . It's hard to write it. But I want to. He . . . Ah, well. He caressed me. It was the first time—without clothes. Not *altogether* without clothes—God, I'd have frozen! But—

partly. The way he touched me, the closeness, the stark, unbearable intimacy of it—I'm shaking now, remembering. And I find I can't write it. He could have done anything. Anything.

Oh, I want, I want, I want.

THE CARETAKER'S COTTAGE, abandoned since William Holyoake had moved out of it two years ago to new quarters in the Hall's basement, was looking better and better to Christy. Especially through a haze of wet, sticky snowflakes. But he tramped past it stolidly, heading for the appointed rendezvous—the D'Aubrey family cemetery. A bleaker spot on this dreariest of days could hardly be imagined, and he was in complete sympathy now with every incredulous, insulting thing Anne had said when he'd suggested and then insisted on it as the location for their next tryst. But it was a sure bet that no one would come upon them here, and at the time that had seemed the paramount consideration. At the time. Warmth seemed the paramount consideration now, but it was too late to change the rendezvous.

His pocket watch chimed four just as he eased open the wicket in the low stone wall. A glance around told him he'd beaten her this time—a minor satisfaction; the vagaries of his schedule frequently made him late, and she liked to tease him that it was always women who bore the stigma of chronic unpunctuality. The silting snow blurred every surface; there was no place dry to sit. No shelter, either, now that winter had denuded the ancient oak trees. To keep the wind from blowing wet snowflakes in his face, he went to the lee side of the tallest monument, a granite obelisk marking the grave of William Verlaine, the fourth D'Aubrey viscount. With his back to the cold gray stone, Christy ducked his head, jammed his hands in his greatcoat pockets, and recommenced brooding.

Compared to the problems occupying his mind now, the great issues of his past—does God exist? why do men suffer? how can I console?—seemed trifling. He thought of the mental line dividing his preoccupations as B.A. and A.A.—before and after Anne.

After Anne, he was consumed with thoughts of sexual morality, sins of the flesh, concupiscence, lust, adultery, Mary Magdalene, Saint Paul—all the sidelines of the seventh commandment that heretofore had struck him as the *interesting* sins, the ones which caught the eye but which, fortunately, didn't relate to him personally. He'd been chaste since his ordination, and sincerely repented his few transgressions before that. Once in a while (before Anne), he would catch himself coveting the flesh of a comely, pink-cheeked parishioner, acknowledge it, and have faith in God's forgiveness of it. Almost as important, he would forgive *himself* for it, quite easily, with a masculine shrug and a smug, underlying assumption that he would soon be marrying one of the young parish ladies who made themselves so agreeable and available to him on a daily basis. In his thoughtless arrogance, he'd always assumed he'd choose the best of the bunch—whom, of course, he would love—and then reward himself for his years of restraint by exercising his husbandly rights with great vigor and enthusiasm.

Now there was Anne. God had sent her to test him, he sometimes believed. Was she the instrument of his soul's damnation? If so, why did she feel like salvation? It was enough to drive a man to drink.

He stamped his feet to keep them from freezing. It would be dark soon. Where was she? If she couldn't come and he had to tramp back home without seeing her—it didn't bear thinking about. With the ease of practice, his mind slipped into the well-worn memory of their last meeting. They'd played with fire that day; how they'd avoided total immolation could only be explained by divine intervention, in the form of a rising wind blowing ice-cold rain against her bare skin—and bringing them both to their senses in the proverbial nick of time.

They couldn't go on like this much longer. He couldn't, anyway. His body felt like a cocked gun with a hair trigger. Either

Anne or the devil was blurring the line between right and wrong that had stood him in fairly good stead until now. He argued with her by rote, not because he could really see anything sinful anymore about their joining. God help him, he *agreed* with her. On the few occasions when church members had confided in him that they'd broken or were thinking of breaking the seventh commandment by committing the sin of fornication, he had never been particularly shocked or morally outraged. With adulterers he had no patience, or not much; but right or wrong, unmarried men and women who engaged in consensual sexual acts with other unmarried men and women did not put his moral back up, and he habitually dealt with them gently. So. At least he wasn't guilty of hypocrisy. A paltry comfort.

Where was she? He'd arranged this meeting because he had a plan, a scheme, and he couldn't put it in motion until she agreed to it—unwittingly. And she would agree to it, he had no doubt; in fact, she'd see it as a golden opportunity to seduce him. But he had other plans.

His watch chimed half past four. The puny, grudging sunset turned the snow cover a shade of lavender-blue that depressed him and made him shiver. Anything could've happened, a dozen domestic responsibilities could've kept her away, and he was a fool to imagine that anything was wrong.

He would leave her a note. Today was Tuesday; she had three whole days to make the arrangements for what he had in mind. That should be enough. All she had to do was think up one really good lie. That was nothing compared to the elaborate fiction *he* had to come up with by Friday.

So, Reverend Morrell, it's come to this, he sneered at himself. He was going to tell lies. But—always that defensive, self-serving *but*—if the plan worked, he'd avert a whole catalog of much worse sins. So the end justified the means? Yes. In this case, yes. It did.

He fumbled his notebook and pencil out of his inside coat pocket. With frozen fingers, he wrote his beloved a note.

She found it, wrapped in his handkerchief, between the latch and the gate handle, covered with soggy snow and almost illegible. She read it by the light of the dying sun in the west and the rising moon in the east.

> *Anne, my darling,*
> *I can't wait any longer; vestry meeting at 5:30, Ludd's early dinner waiting, etc., etc.—the usual. Send the footman with a note, I don't care what we've said, I must know tonight that you are all right.*
> *Now, you must also do this. Say anything, but get away on Friday evening next, at least until midnight. Come to the rectory (after dark, like a thief in the night) and have dinner with me. Yes! Both Ludds in Bath, visiting son and daughter-in-law, bless them. I will take care of sending housemaid packing for the night. Come, Anne. Think of it: WARMTH. Hours of talk, alone, in complete physical comfort. You can't say no.*
> *I love you to distraction. Literally.*
> *Christy*

XV

Except for the smell of woodsmoke from an invisible chimney, the rectory seemed deserted. All the curtains were drawn; if there was light behind any of the windows, it couldn't be seen from the square, or the cobbled street, or the clean-swept path to the front door. Clean-swept recently, Anne noted, so a nighttime visitor couldn't leave footprints in the latest snow dusting. She set her feet down lightly, and still the noise seemed too loud in the evening hush. Ignoring the brass knocker, she used her knuckles on the wooden door panel, rapping softly. Too softly; no one came. She tried again, a little louder, and heard a stirring beyond the door. A second later it opened, a hand shot out, seized hers, and pulled her inside.

She'd have flung herself into Christy's arms, but he held her away to look at her, his face barely visible in the pitch-dark foyer. "You're here," he announced gladly.

"I'm here. I feel like a spy. Why are we whispering?"

He laughed, kissing her cold hands. "No reason—nobody's here but me. And now you." He moved closer—to embrace her, she thought, but instead he helped her take off her coat and hung it on a hook by the door. "Come into the parlor, Anne. There's a fire, and we can have—"

"Christy."

"Yes?"

"Are we or are we not alone in your house?"

"We are."

"Then for God's sake, stand still and give me a proper kiss."

He sighed. Before she could decide whether it was a resigned, relieved, or anticipatory sigh, he'd drawn her inside the strong circle of his arms. Their mouths met eagerly, his warm lips softening her chilled ones in no time. Afterward, she laid her cheek on his collarbone and murmured against his throat, "Mmm, I do love the way they kiss in the provinces."

Chuckling, he gave her a hard squeeze, took her hand, and led her down the hall to the drawing room.

This was special: they usually sat in his study after the Friday night readings—canceled this month and next because of the expense of heating the parish room in wintertime. Anne took a seat on the worn brocade sofa, leaving plenty of room for Christy to sit beside her. He did, after handing her a glass of wine, and his smile told her he knew exactly what game she was playing. They clinked glasses. "What did you say to get away?" he asked her.

She pressed the back of her hand to her forehead. "My head is splitting! I couldn't eat a thing, I need complete rest and quiet, I won't be disturbed on any account whatsoever—at least until morning." She wriggled her eyebrows suggestively. "I'm sure everyone believed me; I quite *threw* myself into it." She waved her hand in a gesture that took in the room, the whole house. "And what did you say to accomplish *this* miracle?"

"Well, when I heard the Ludds wanted the long weekend off to visit their son, I immediately began making noises about going to Mare's Head and staying the night with my deacon, Mr. Creighton—which I will do, only tomorrow night instead of tonight. This way I've gotten rid of the housemaid, who would've thought it strange if I'd banished her for two nights. Thank God it's snowing; now I can tell her I postponed the trip and muddled through in my bachelor way tonight without her."

He looked so pleased with himself, she bit back the exclamation on the tip of her tongue—*You mean all this circumspection is for the benefit of the sensibilities of one trifling housemaid?* Besides, on further reflection, she could see that one trifling house-maid's knowledge of what they were doing, innocent though it was (so far), could have catastrophic consequences for a man in Christy's position, in a place like Wyckerley. "How clever of you," she said instead, and his satisfied smile widened.

"Mrs. Ludd's left a cold supper in the kitchen for me to heat up tomorrow. I told her I'd be starving after my long day in Mare's Head, and to be sure to leave plenty. She did—I checked."

She shook her head at him in awe. "You think of everything." The guilty delight he was taking in this simple deception made her heart ache with love for him.

"Are you hungry?"

"Yes, but this is so nice, just sitting here talking. Let's not eat yet."

She'd said the right thing. He grinned and took her glass from her, set it on the low table. Her heart began to pound—until he reached for her hand and pulled her to her feet. "You've never really seen the house, Anne. Let me show it to you."

"The house? Now?"

He shrugged. "Don't you want to see it?"

"Well—all right. Fine. Let's see the house."

He showed it to her by candlelight, carrying a three-candle holder from room to room, since a brighter light could have been seen from the street through the closed draperies. It took her an unconscionably long time to figure out what he was up to. The clue came when he began to use words like "commodious" and "convenient" to describe the rectory's perfectly nice dining and living rooms. The sitting room, she learned, was "free of drafts." When he called the entrance hall "welcoming," she gave a whoop of laughter, cutting him off. "Christy, are you *showing* me the house or *selling* it to me?"

That made his ears turn red, a reaction that always delighted her. "What do you mean?" he blustered, trying to sound hurt. "I'm showing it; I thought you'd be interested."

She laughed again, enchanted by his transparency. "This is a plan, isn't it?" she accused, leaning against him. "A plot! You smuggled me in here with an ulterior motive, admit it."

"I did not."

"Yes, you did. You're trying to seduce me with a golden vision of what married life could be. Honestly, Christy, this is worse than the marriage vows."

He caved in without a fight. "All right, it was a plan. Do you mind? Would you have stayed away if you'd known?"

"Of course not, I'd have come under any circumstances, you know that. But, darling, let's not have our old argument tonight."

"Absolutely not. We won't argue about anything tonight."

"And your house is beautiful. I've always liked it."

"Really?"

"Yes, of course—but don't let's talk about me moving into it permanently, all right?"

"All right. You'd be happy, though. You could change anything you wanted. And you'd like Mrs. Ludd—"

"Christy—"

"And she'd love you. Arthur does all the gardening, so you couldn't kill anything. The kitchen's huge, I'll show you."

"Christy—"

"There's plenty of room for more servants if you want them. I always ride Doncaster, but there's a gig in the stables and Arthur could fix it up, paint it or whatever it needs, and I'd buy a nice hackney to pull it. All right! I'm finished." He rubbed his shoulder, where she'd just punched him.

Arm in arm, they ambled back to the drawing room. This time he drew chairs close to the fire, and they sat beside each other, holding hands sometimes, staring at the flames and talking. "This is so nice," they took turns saying, interspersed with exclamations of "How lovely to be together *and* warm." Christy told her the latest village gossip, and Anne realized with a slight start that, far from being boring, it all fascinated her. Old Mrs. Weedie needed some surgical treatment, unrelated to the hip she'd broken last summer (something "female," which automatically precluded further medical discussion). It was to be done tomorrow in Tavistock, at the hospital, by Dr. Hesselius. Anne had known of it for days, and offered all the assistance she could think of, including the use of the D'Aubrey coach to and from the hospital. Now Christy told her something she didn't know. "Captain Carnock took them to Tavistock today in his carriage."

"Captain Carnock?" she exclaimed, surprised.

He eyed her, weighing his words. "I'll tell you something in confidence."

"My lips are sealed."

"Captain Carnock paid a call on me last week. To ask my advice. He wanted to know what I thought of the propriety of his offering the Weedies the use of his carriage."

"The propriety?" Sometimes the intricacies of English social etiquette eluded her.

"Taking the Weedies to Tavistock for Mrs. Weedie's . . . procedure . . . will necessitate returning Miss Weedie to Wyckerley tomorrow. Alone."

"Aha. *Alone.* And what did you tell him?"

"I told him I could see nothing wrong with his kind, apparently motiveless offer."

"Apparently?"

"Apparently."

His face gave nothing away, but it set her to thinking. Miss Weedie and Captain Carnock . . . Captain Carnock and Miss Weedie. Yes. Why not? Why, how perfectly lovely! Patting her lips with her forefinger, she repeated meaningfully, "Apparently," and the gleam in Christy's eye told her he was way ahead of her. But he wouldn't say any more, so she let the subject drop, not wanting him to think she was the kind of woman who went in for idle gossip.

Rather than open the chilly dining room, they decided to have their dinner right where they were, so they pulled a table in front of the fireplace. Mrs. Ludd's prepared meal was a simple one—luckily, since lighting the stove was almost the extent of their combined cooking skills. "I always ate in restaurants in London," Anne confided, "or had my meals sent in. When my father and I lived on the Continent, we always had someone to cook for us."

"We always had a housekeeper who did the cooking," Christy said, "although my mother was definitely the one in charge. I wish you could've known her, Anne. You remind me of her sometimes."

She stopped with a forkful of peas halfway to her mouth. "I remind you of your mother?"

"You do. She had a sharp mind. Sharp tongue, too, sometimes—I told you she didn't suffer fools gladly. But inside, she was as soft as a feather pillow." He took a bite of roast pork, and added with his mouth full, "She was pretty, too."

Anne took refuge in the business of meat-cutting for a few moments while she put her thoughts, and her face, in order. That Christy thought she had a sharp mind was, of course, gratifying; that he considered her soft inside . . . she didn't know what to do with that. She found it unsettling, and inexplicably moving. Of course it was true, but she didn't think anyone knew it, not even him. Softness could so easily cross over into weakness, and she'd imagined that life with Geoffrey had toughened and hardened all that out of her.

Christy had on his "worried lion" look, as she thought of it, the noble brow furrowed, the clear blue eyes studying her. She said brightly, "Well, I don't remember my mother, but you're not a bit like my father, so I can't return the compliment. If that's what it was."

"I suppose that's what it was, although I didn't say it to flatter you."

"No," she agreed, "you wouldn't."

He frowned. "Would you like me to? I'd say flowery things all the time if I thought you'd like it. Shall I?"

"That won't be necessary." His poems, she thought in private, did quite enough on that score, and then some.

He looked relieved. "What could I do, then?" he asked, smiling at her, ingenuous as always. "What would persuade you to come round to my side of the issue?"

"I thought we weren't going to talk about this."

"I'm not arguing, just asking. Seriously, what would sway you? I don't feel as if I'm making any headway with you."

Oh, Christy, if you only knew. "Well," she said slowly, pretending to consider it. He leaned closer, alert. "For one thing, you could show me the rest of the house. My tour was incomplete. I haven't seen the upstairs." She rested her chin on her cupped palm and batted her eyelashes. "I haven't seen the room where you sleep."

"So you might marry me if you like my bedroom?"

"Never can tell." It came out a sexy purr. Where was all this shameless-hussy behavior coming from?

"I guess I'll have to take the chance," he said seriously, but his eyes were dancing. "Right after we have our coffee."

"Better say a couple of Our Fathers first, Reverend. For willpower."

"Our Father, nothing. I'd better make the Stations of the Cross."

They took their coffee with them.

On the way, Christy showed her his old nursery, whose cozy virtues he couldn't resist extolling; that their own children could grow up safe and happy here was the clear implication, but he didn't say it out loud, no doubt for fear of getting another cuff on the shoulder.

When they got to his bedroom, Anne took the candle holder

and left him leaning in the doorway while she explored. The walls were papered in green and white stripes, with tendrils of some flowery creeper winding cheerfully in and out. A thick carpet lay on the floor, and bright green draperies hung at the windows—two windows, the room being on the southeast corner. The furniture was old and dark, but not oppressive. The massive tester bed had a crocheted white coverlet over a multicolored quilt; solid, sturdy, stable, indestructible—it was the perfect bed for Christy. She could live out her life taking her rest every night in that bed. Why was it, again, that she wasn't marrying him? Sometimes she forgot. She needed to marshal her forces; if this was going to be a seduction, it was important to be clear at the start about who was seducing whom.

"This is a bit hedonistic, isn't it? I thought you'd sleep on a hard wooden pallet, with nothing but religious icons for decorations."

He folded his arms and smiled tolerantly, cocking one eyebrow. He wore black tonight—not his full holy blacks, just a black coat and trousers, and a plain white shirt. She'd grown addicted to looking at his strong, straight body, broad-shouldered and lean-hipped; she loved his golden hair, the bones in his face, his serious eyes. "You're mixing Anglican ministers with Roman Catholic monks," he explained patiently. "As you see, we have all the creature comforts here."

"Mm." She took her eyes off him to take another turn around his room. His wardrobe door was ajar. "May I?" she asked archly, and he gave a permissive wave of his hand.

He had three other coats, and four waistcoats, two more pairs of trousers, all clean and neatly pressed—courtesy of Mrs. Ludd, she supposed. Shoes and riding boots were lined up on the wardrobe floor, and an assortment of neckties hung from hooks. She wandered over to his bureau, another massive affair built of dark mahogany; on the dust-free top rested his comb and brush, a stack of clean handkerchiefs, and a little box containing his sparse supply of jewelry: one pair of jet-and-silver cuff links; two stickpins, one pearl and one garnet; and a heavy gold signet ring.

"Your parents?" She indicated two framed watercolor miniatures, and Christy nodded. She bent closer. So that was the famous old vicar, about whom she had never heard a single disparaging word. She'd thought he would look like Christy, but he didn't; he was dark, not fair, and frail-looking, and the only extraordinary thing about him was his eyes, which were light brown, penetrating, and uncannily sympathetic. Christy had been influenced powerfully by this man, may even have chosen his vocation because of him. Looking at his portrait, she thought she could understand why.

"She was pretty," he'd said of his mother tonight. Anne thought it an understatement. She was a beautiful woman, with her son's blond hair and ice-blue eyes, and an expression that was, at least in this portrait, at once loving and ever so slightly ironic. She was fond of the artist, but her face said she wished he would hurry and get on with it.

A thought struck her. "Did you paint these?"

"Yes."

"I should've known. Oh, Christy, they're lovely. How old were you when you did them?"

"Twenty, twenty-one."

"I'd like to see all of your paintings. You've kept them, haven't you?" He nodded. "Could I see them?"

He smiled, shrugged. "Someday. If you like."

"I would like." She crossed the room to his bedside table, which was covered with books and papers. Stirring the papers, deliberately nosy, she saw that they contained notes for one of his upcoming sermons. She made a shocked face. "You write your sermons in *bed?*"

"When I'm stuck. Which is most of the time."

"Oh," she exclaimed, "you're really reading it." One of the books on the table was *A Treatise on the Philosophy of Agnosticism*; she'd left it for him last week in their hiding place.

"Did you think I wouldn't?"

She hadn't even read it herself. She felt sheepish. Christy's faith was based on study and contemplation and who knew how many hours of soul-searching, while her lack of it was based, if she cared to be truthful, on not much of anything at all. "What did you think of it?" she asked in a small voice.

"Haven't finished it yet. Mostly I'm impressed by the dreariness of a man's vision of a world with no God."

"Let's not talk about theology tonight," she said hastily.

He smiled his patient smile. "All right."

She remembered—had never forgotten—why she'd lured him up here in the first place. On slightly surer ground, she moved to the middle of the bed and sat down at the edge, smoothing her palms over the coverlet. "Soft," she said—softly, giving him the full benefit of her smile. "Join me?" She raised her eyebrows, daring him.

He watched her without speaking for a long, long moment. Then he shrugged away from the doorpost and straightened his folded arms. Not smiling at all, he crossed the room to the bed, and by the time he reached her she'd stopped breathing. He put his hands in her hair, tipping her head up. "Anne," he said, and kissed her with such tenderness, she could hardly bear it. She pulled him down beside her on the bed and put her arms around his neck, and in no time at all they were holding each other, exchanging soft, glad caresses. "I've been waiting all night to do this," he confessed, and she whispered back, "Me, too." She put her hands inside his coat so she could stroke his broad back and hold him tight against her, savoring the hard, muscular feel of him, all man, all hers. While he kissed her, he whispered in her ear, words that curled her toes and took her breath away. Was there ever a man like him? She could feel her heart stealing away, deserting her side and going over to his. Uncatchable now; she'd think about it later.

He held her jaw in his cupped palms and stroked her lips with his thumbs, urging them open with a gentle pressure. A sweet, heavy longing moved over her. Their lips met in the slowest of kisses, warm and damp, as intimate as lovemaking. She wasn't sure how her hand had gotten on his thigh, but she loved the rock-solid feel of it under her stroking fingers. Christy made a soft sound in his throat and she echoed it, a low hum of sheer appreciation.

She had on a black lace jabot that buttoned down the front of her blouse. She said, "Oh," when she realized he was slowly undoing the buttons. She pulled back to see his face—faintly flushed, beautifully intent; when he looked up from his unbuttoning, she saw that his pupils had almost eclipsed the clear blue irises. He spread his hands across her chest, above the frilly chemise, caressing her skin and making her sigh. Bending his head, he put his lips on the bare top of her shoulder. She breathed in the scent of his hair, stroking it, letting it tickle her between her fingers.

He began to tug at her corset, and she could feel his thrilling impatience through his touch. Her breasts spilled out, the top of the garment pushing them up like an offering, a gift. His strong hands covered her possessively. "My darling," he murmured. "Anne, my love." She closed her eyes, giving herself up to the delicious pleasure, feeling wanton—but safe, too, because she was cherished. And she was falling, falling, the coverlet at her back, and Christy's hair a soft, sweet teasing on her breasts. She felt his lips kiss one sensitive nipple, and she arched her back, sighing his name.

"Be my wife," he whispered, trailing kisses up and down the hollow between her breasts. "Marry me, sweetheart."

"I can't. Don't ask me," she got out, eyes squeezed shut.

"Anne . . ."

"Don't ask me. Please, Christy. Be my lover."

Very gently, he slid his hands under her shoulders and pulled her up, so that they were sitting again. His eyes were downcast, hidden by his long lashes. The kiss he gave her was different this time, still tender and loving but . . . sad. "I won't ask you again," he said in a murmur, brushing his fingers across her hot cheek. "At least, I'll try not to." His crooked smile twisted inside her painfully. He whispered, "I wish you could've loved me." And then he stood up.

She blinked at him, dazed. "You . . . ." Her heart slowed, began to thud in a dull, panicky rhythm. "Oh, no," she breathed. "Oh, Christy, please. Don't—oh, don't say we can't see each other again—like this."

He faced her. Where she'd ruffled it, his hair was wild-looking; he still had two rusty spots of color on his cheeks. "I wish I could say that. I'd better take you home now, Anne."

She scrambled off the bed, pulling her loose clothes together across her chest. "Why did you touch me like that, then? Were you—were you trying to seduce me? And then—how could you stop? It's not nice of you, Christy!" She felt like crying. "It's not very gentlemanly to—to start that and then just stop, leaving me feeling this way—"

"I'm sorry, I apologize. It won't happen again."

"Oh, fine!" She tried to laugh. "That makes me feel much better!" He turned away. "Well, then, when can we see each other again? When? You said we could. When can we meet? Say right now—when." He didn't answer. *"Tomorrow,"* she urged. She was on the edge of a terrifying capitulation, taking refuge in arrangements, schedules, details.

"No, I have to go to Mare's Head."

"Early?"

"In the afternoon."

"Let's meet in the morning, then. I'll come to you—anywhere.

Or you could come to the Hall for breakfast. No one will think anything of it."

"I can't."

Panic fluttered again, closer to the surface. "Why?" He didn't answer. "Why?" He just shook his head. "Why, Christy? Don't do this to me. You could come if you wanted to!"

"No, I honestly can't."

She spread her hands. "But *why?*"

She thought he looked embarrassed. "You'll laugh at me if I tell you." She shook her head mutely. "Very well, then. I told you Mrs. Weedie's surgery is tomorrow in Tavistock. In the morning. Miss Weedie—you know what she's like; she's beside herself with worry. I've made her a promise." He took a deep breath and looked up at the ceiling. "I told her I would take on all her worries. Tomorrow morning. I told her she could set her mind at rest, let all her tension go, so she could be a true comfort to her mother. So now I have to . . ." He laughed softly, abashed. "I have to worry and pray for Mrs. Weedie tomorrow. In the morning, for about three hours, I should think."

Anne pivoted, clapping her hands to her mouth. She went to the far side of the bed, sat down, and toppled over backward. A sob rose in her throat, but a laugh overtook it and got out first. With tears streaking down her temples and running into her ears, she managed to gasp, "I'll marry you! You win, Christy, I give up. I can't stand it."

The paroxysm of despair and hilarity tapered off; she felt her emotions evening out. She twisted around, propping herself up on her elbows. "I'll marry you," she repeated, in case he hadn't heard.

She couldn't read his face; he'd withdrawn toward the door, into the shadows. "I know you enjoy making fun of me," he said in a hollow, dignified voice. "Just now, though, I don't think I want to hear it."

"Christy!" He'd turned his back on her—he was leaving. She bolted off the bed and scuttled around it. "Wait!" He stopped, standing stiffly, so tall and straight—so dear! She had to take his arm and turn him around, bodily. "I'm not mocking you," she said with urgent tenderness. "I'm sorry for all the times I ever did. I love you. I couldn't tell you before because—well, what does it matter. Christy, I love you with all my heart! I want to live with you in this beautiful house." She reached up with both hands to touch his face. "I want to have babies with you. Our children."

"Anne—"

"I'll make the worst minister's wife who's ever lived, but that's your lookout now." She stood on her toes and kissed him. "I will always, always love you, and I swear I'll never stop trying to make you happy."

Christy stared into her earnest green eyes; they still glittered from tears, and her cheeks were still wet and streaky. He wanted to believe her, but what she'd just said was too good to be true. She made an impatient sound and threw her arms around his waist. He held on tight; they were both shaking. "Just because of the Weedies?" he asked, incredulous.

"It was the straw. The damn last straw. The last damn—"

He found her lips and kissed her hard, blurring tears between their mouths—her tears or his, he couldn't have said. "Anne, you do me such an honor."

"No, it's the reverse. Oh, I love you, Christy!"

"I love you." His heart was too full to say more. He held on to her while he offered up a quick, uncomplicated prayer of thanks for this miracle. He couldn't understand how it had happened. One minute he had her half-naked in his bed, and she wouldn't marry him; the next, he was telling her about the Weedies, and she would. It made no sense—but he supposed miracles never did. He wrapped her up in his arms and lifted her completely off the floor, to celebrate.

"Oh, look at us," she cried, laughing. He turned around with her and saw their reflection in the wardrobe mirror: two giddy, black-garbed people with joyful faces.

"Look at *you*," he said, moving closer to the mirror. He put her in front of him and clasped her around the waist, beguiled by her dishevelment. She lifted a hand to cover herself, and smiled knowingly when he pulled it away. "Look at you," he said again, more softly. Blouse and chemise gaped open enticingly; the cream-colored corset barely covered her nipples. "You look like one of those bawdy ladies in a Hogarth painting." Laughing, she leaned back in his arms, a movement that swelled her bosom and stretched the corset tighter; that it still covered her at all struck Christy as another miracle. One of the lesser kind.

Anne sighed. "I don't suppose we can make love now, can we?" she said without much hope. She wasn't tempting him; she was just asking.

Impossible to think while he was watching her in the mirror. He put his head down, resting his lips in the warm hollow between her neck and shoulder, and closed his eyes. Impossible to think here, too. She smelled like flowers, and she filled his arms, fit against his body perfectly. She was his love. "Do you think I could let you go now?" He watched her lovely eyes widen in the mirror, felt her soft breathing change. "Share my bed tonight, Anne. Be my love."

She turned around slowly. Her face had gone still. She licked her lips warily. "Won't you feel guilty afterward?"

He smiled. "Don't worry."

"That's not an answer. Will you?"

"I don't know." It was the truth. He had some idea that this had to happen, that they were meant to be lovers tonight. She had been brave, and honest, and to some degree she had given in, made a sacrifice. Now it was his turn. He wanted them to begin their lives together as equals; the thought of either of them being the "winner" repelled him. "I've wanted to love you with my body for such a long time, Anne. It's what you want, too. You won't deny me now."

"But—I don't want us to do anything that will hurt you, Christy. I truly don't."

"Don't worry," he repeated. It was the best he could do. That he would pay for this somehow, sometime, was a foregone conclusion to him, but she didn't need to know it.

She studied him for a few more seconds, trying to read the truth in his face—before it occurred to her that, just at this precise moment, she might not want to know the truth. And that, if she gave him the chance, he might change his mind.

Unthinkable.

"All right, I won't," she said quickly, and stepped away from him so she could take off her clothes.

She thought he would help her, especially when she got mitten-fingered over the hooks of her corset. But he didn't; he stood still and watched, his eyes heavy-lidded, a certain dangerous, barely leashed waiting in his posture that excited her and made her clumsy. The metal fastener at the back of her skirt defeated her. She felt her cheeks heating from frustration. "Christy—!"

"Turn around."

She did, and bowed her head in patient, heart-pounding submission while he got her skirt off and her shift laces untied. Then he had to kiss all the places he'd uncovered, and she felt as if he were greeting her body, welcoming it in small bits and pieces, one at a time.

The way he touched her was unearthly sometimes; she could feel *reverence* in his skin when it caressed hers. It made her reciprocate, and think, *This is a miracle, this human lovemaking.* Making love. This was as close to divine as she could imagine being. Sacrilege, he'd say, but she felt it. The beautiful congress of their bodies was not completely right for him, she knew. It wasn't blessed in the sacrament of marriage, so it couldn't mean for him what it meant to her: glory—unexpected rapture—the deepest blessing she'd ever hoped for. She was sorry for him, she truly regretted it—but she wouldn't have stopped if she could have. *"Christy, this is so right,"* she told him, naked now, holding him in her arms.

He couldn't take his eyes off the image in the mirror behind her, of his two hands sliding slowly up and down her long, slender spine. How could skin feel this soft? Be this white? He cupped the nape of her neck, tilting her head back to kiss her, letting his other hand drift down to her soft breast. "Anne, do you know how beautiful you are?" She didn't answer, but her eyes said, *Tell me.* But he didn't have the words. "I'll paint you one day," he promised. "Then you'll know."

They kissed again. She took a deep, ragged breath. "Now you. I'm longing to see you."

He took off his clothes. She watched him, entranced, frozen in place. Self-consciousness slowed him down. His body was just his body; he was thankful that it was strong and healthy, but otherwise he didn't think of it. He hoped it pleased her.

"Oh, God."

There was no tone to her voice, so he had no idea what that meant. What was she feeling behind that hot-eyed stare? "I won't hurt you," he assured her—inanely.

She made a sound, possibly a laugh, and came out of her trance. "Oh, Christy," she whispered, "I'm so—I'm shaking, I'm so excited. Oh, hurry, let's get in bed."

He laughed with relief. They climbed into the bed in which he'd always slept alone, the bed in which his father and mother had conceived him. Was it blasphemous to think that the slow slide of his hands over Anne's bare skin was heaven? If so, he couldn't help it. He was only a man, and this was the sweetest human thing he'd ever experienced. Her silky breasts were heavy and full against his chest; it was as natural as breathing to put his mouth on her nipples and gently suckle her. They clutched each other, head to toe, their bodies' perspiration making a lovely slickness. He felt the soft brush of her pubic hair against his stomach, and his head swam. He ran his hands down her long flanks, squeezing her buttocks, trying to get her, capture her, understand her body all at once.

Impossible. He made himself slow down, concentrating on her sleek belly, touching and tasting, and now one satin-skinned thigh, perfect, perfect.

She'd lost her breath—she was losing her mind. "Hurry," she said again; "I want—oh, I want—" She wanted to know *everything*, find out *now*. She touched him without gentleness, whispering her urgency in his ear, firing him, taking them both higher. But he would not be rushed. He was on a different journey, and his slower pace only magnified her desire. Deep, drugging kisses; slow, shattering caresses; and words—she could've swooned from the things he said to her, the singing sound of passion in his voice. *This is real*, she chanted to herself. *Christy would never lie, and this is happening. I am loved, and this is happening.*

At last, at last, he came into her. She enfolded him, and they sighed together, sharing the relief and the deep wonder. Lying still, she felt the strong beat of his pulse inside her body. "I love you," they said at the same moment. And she said, "This can't be wrong," and she was weeping; she felt torn out of herself, born all over again. "Oh, Christy, you know it can't."

He kissed her mouth, moving in her, putting an end to talk. Nothing now but the wild, tender endearments and the gasping sighs, raw, helpless groans, the music of passion, graceless, unrehearsed, heartfelt. Human love, nothing divine. The peak rose up fast, she could feel it, almost *see* it, rolling in on itself, nearer, closer, the ultimate wave in her turbulent sea. She wanted it to take both of them, both together, so she told him it was coming. She clung to him, her lifeline, her mate, "Christy!"—until it swamped her.

Lovely, oh, lovely, the sweetest drowning, the endless immersion. She stopped being herself and turned into the sea, and

Christy did too, and it was all one, all vast liquid pleasure, rolling and breaking, a rough, sweet churning. From a deep, fathomless distance she heard him say, "Oh, *God,* oh, *God,*" on weary, spent breaths. Her mind came back to her gradually, in pieces. When it finally reassembled, she thought it highly likely that he meant it literally—that he was praying.

XVI

CHRISTY HAD HAIR all over his body. Fine pale blond hair, soft as a baby's, lightly fleecing his arms, his chest, his long, handsome legs. The only hairless places Anne could see, after a meticulous survey, were his belly and his buttocks. And the tops of his shoulders. And those soft places on his inner arms, where she liked to kiss him.

I wish summer would come. The thought came to her out of the blue as she sat on her heels, naked in Christy's bed, gazing down at him as he slept. She had a bright, vivid picture of him, naked, lying in a sunny, grassy meadow. She saw herself kneeling above him—as she was now—sprinkling him with flowers. Adorning him. Decorating him with buttercups and daisies, marsh violets and forget-me-nots. She'd make a crown of clover and plait it in his hair. Stick foxgloves and scarlet pimpernel between his toes. A little wreath of speedwell for his navel. And for his cock, something most special . . . Ah, she had it. Of course. Hearts-ease.

A yawn overtook her soft smile. Lying down beside him, she covered his golden body with the quilt and snuggled close, sighing with contentment. A minute later she was fast asleep, dreaming of flowers.

He'd only been gone a few minutes. He'd left her sound asleep, a warm, enticing mound huddled under a heap of bedclothes.

She was even more enticing now. The fire he'd rebuilt had warmed the room in his absence, and she'd thrown off all the covers. He crept closer on silent stocking feet. He set the tray he'd brought from the kitchen on the bedside table and eased down beside her, careful not to shake the mattress. She looked like a runner in profile, lying on her side, all her elbows and knees bent at different angles. A naked runner. He had an urge to stroke one finger down the long, graceful curve of her backbone—but he resisted, fearful of waking her; he wanted to look at her a little longer. Everything about her was beautiful to him, from her red-gold hair, vivid as a flame across the pillow, to the pink soles of her long, skinny feet. Candlelight flickered over her lily skin, gilding it, and he could feel its unearthly softness again even though he wasn't touching her. One out-flung arm coyly hid the tip of her breast, and her topmost thigh shielded the curly nest of her pubic hair. A discreet pose, classic in its way. If he were painting her, he would lessen the discre-tion. He'd leave the light exactly where it was but lift her left arm a half-inch higher, so the rose-colored nipple showed. Yes. And he might shift the angle of her bottom, paint it in three-quarter profile, because—well, just because. He smiled, and couldn't re-sist trailing his fingers in a feather-soft circle around her left but-tock. She didn't stir. She had a cleft on either side of her spine, a subtle indentation just big enough for his thumb; he pressed it there, lightly. The toes on her right foot twitched. What an in-triguing reflex. He tried it again, with the same result. He was looking around for other sites that might connect—her shoulder blade and her chin, who knew?—when she opened her eyes, turned her head, and saw him behind her. Her sleepy, instanta-neous smile went straight to his heart.

"Oils," he told her. "Definitely oils. Even sleeping, you're too strong for watercolors."

"What?" She put her hand inside his dressing gown and rubbed his chest.

"Will you let me paint you, Anne?"

She blinked up at him dreamily. "I presume you mean in the nude."

"Of course."

"Mmm. Won't that get you excommunicated or something?"

"We won't show it to the bishop." He said it with a smile, but he wasn't really ready to joke about the consequences of his relationship with Anne, morally or professionally.

"You can paint me if I can draw you," she decided, rolling over. "I'm best with pen and ink, and I've got an idea for a nice pastoral pose. You and a lot of flowers."

"All right."

Her eyes twinkled—mischievously, he thought. She gave his lapel a tug, pulling him down so they could kiss. It was a soft, slow, comfortable kiss, the kind he imagined married people shared when they were in love. Delightful thought. How could he wait a year to marry her—maybe more? Terrible thought.

"I'm starving."

She had a fondness for double entendre, he was learning; he studied her face, but apparently she meant this statement literally. "Good," he said, "because I've brought you sustenance."

She looked awed. "Do you have any flaws, Christy? Any at all?"

"You'll find out when you taste what I made you."

Roast pork on big pieces of bread, smeared with butter and grated horseradish; potatoes, mashed up in cream and reheated on the kitchen stove; a little salad made of the watercress that grew year-round along the banks of the Wyck; and an ancient bottle of Chambertin from his father's tiny cellar—good or bad, they would find out together.

They ate it in bed, Anne wearing one of his shirts, and midway through she pronounced it all delicious, the best meal she'd ever eaten in her life.

"Does this mean I don't have any flaws?" he wondered.

"None that I've been able to discover. But you must have

some, everyone does, and I'm looking forward to ferreting them out. Over the next fifty years or so." They kissed, in a sort of lips-toast, and went back to their feast, both smiling.

"I don't make very much money," Christy said presently. "I think of the rectory as my home because I was born and grew up here, but it really isn't; it's part of the income from the ecclesiastical benefice. It'll pass to the next incumbent when I'm gone."

"Well, then," she said carelessly, "nobody can say I married you for your money."

"No, but they might say I married you for yours."

"Nonsense. No one who knows you could think that, Christy, not for a second."

He didn't answer. He thought people would think, and probably say, any number of things once their engagement became known. But there was no sense burdening her with that at this early stage.

"Anyway, I expect you'll be a bishop in a few years," she said airily, biting into one of the apples he'd brought for dessert.

"I will, will I?"

"A man with no flaws has got to rise, it's a law of physics. How do you get to be a bishop, by the way?"

"The prime minister nominates you and the queen appoints you, subject to a formal election by the cathedral chapter."

"Oh, Lord, I'm going to have to learn what all that means, aren't I? Cathedral chapter, benefice, incumbent. Canons and deans. Advowsons."

"Candlemas, Martinmas, Michaelmas," he threw in. "Whitsuntide. Rogation Day."

She slid down on her pillow in mock despair. "Exegesis, eschatology. Apostasy."

"Saint Swithin's Day."

"Oh, no, you made that up."

"Not a bit. July fifteenth. They say if it rains on Saint Swithin's, it'll rain for the next forty days."

"Well, that I don't doubt. And that's another thing, Christy, I *hate* the winters here."

He shook his head sadly. "Not much I can do about that."

"No, but at least I want credit for the sacrifice I'm making."

He set his empty plate down and rolled onto his side to face her. "I'll give you credit. I'll give you all the credit you know what to do with." He reached across her to pull her closer. "I'll keep you warm, too."

"I wouldn't doubt that, either," she said breathlessly. Her mouth, when he kissed her, tasted of apple. She shimmied down lower in the bed until her head was off the pillow entirely, inviting him. Her hands coasting over his skin felt like warm flames. "What time is it?" she murmured, her voice sultry.

"Late."

"How late?"

"Three, three-thirty."

She smiled. "That's early. Nothing stirs at the Hall in winter before six. We've got three whole hours."

"Time enough for you to finish telling me your life story."

"Pardon me?"

"The thrilling conclusion."

"*Now?*"

"Unless you don't want to." He pulled a stray strand of hair out of her eyes and tucked it behind her ear. "You needn't tell me. But I know something was wrong between you and Geoffrey, something worse than the trouble I'd expect between two people who didn't suit and didn't love each other. Something you won't speak of."

She broke their gazes to stare past his shoulder at the ceiling, and her eyes were cloudy with indecision. She sat up. She plumped her pillow and tidied the bedclothes over her legs, turning the quilt back and folding the top of the sheet over it in her lap, running her hands pointlessly across the wrinkle-free coverlet. "I was going to tell you," she said at last. "I kept putting it off.

It's just—I guess I'd have chosen some other time, some other place. But I've been using that for an excuse not to tell you for too long, and this is probably as good a time as any."

"It is so painful, then?"

"It's . . . unsavory." She turned to him earnestly. "But nothing can spoil *this,* can it, Christy?"

"No, nothing can spoil this."

The trouble left her face; she smiled at him tenderly. "No," she agreed. "So. Well, then, where did I leave off? I believe Geoffrey had just left me for the first time."

"Anne, don't—" He stopped.

"What?"

"Never mind. Go on. No, nothing, go ahead." He'd been about to say, *Don't use that terrible dry, brittle tone, because it hurts me to know how badly you were hurt.* But she had to tell it her way, and if it helped to put that sardonic distance between herself and her story, he wouldn't ask her not to. "Geoffrey had left," he prodded when she didn't continue. "How did you live in London all by yourself? Did he send you money?"

"Occasionally. How did I live? Not very well. He'd left me in a flat in Holborn with one surly servant and no friends. At first I naturally gravitated toward the London art set, but that soon became awkward."

"Why?"

"Because the men wanted to seduce me and the women— not coincidentally—didn't trust me. I was weary of their self-absorption anyway; I had only drifted into that world out of inertia."

"What did you do with yourself?" He poured more wine into her glass and handed it to her.

"My main preoccupation was trying to find enough money to pay the rent. I tried painting, but as I've already told you, I didn't have enough talent. I started a biography of my father, but couldn't find anyone interested in publishing it. I—" she heaved a sigh, as if she were already tired "—wrote a few little memoirs, 'Life with My Father in Provence,' that sort of thing, and sometimes people even bought them and paid me for them. I kept a journal, a diary—still do, in fact."

"What about Geoffrey's father? Wouldn't he help you?"

She looked at him rather pityingly. "You knew him better than I, Christy. What do you think?"

"Did you ask him?"

"Yes, once. His written reply was a very short, very blunt refusal. In essence, he advised me not to darken his door again. I'd made my bed, et cetera." She took a sip of wine and set the glass down with a little clatter, her movements stiff from old anger.

"So you were on your own."

"Quite."

"And yet you didn't take a lover?"

She raised her eyebrows at that. "No, I've told you."

"Well, forgive me for saying so, darling, but that doesn't sound very sophisticated to me. That sounds—why, that almost sounds *provincial* to me."

She rolled her eyes, trying not to laugh. "I can see I'm not going to live that down for a long, long time."

"No, but I'd have thought a true Continental sophisticate like you would have taken lovers while her husband was away. But you didn't."

"I could have," she said defensively.

"I'm quite sure of that."

"I was invited to do so more than once."

"Why didn't you?"

"Certainly not because I thought it was morally wrong."

"Certainly not."

She sighed again. "Oh, Christy, I don't know. Lack of energy? I'd been betrayed. Geoffrey hurt me very badly."

He picked up her hand and began to trace its outline against the coverlet on his raised thigh. "Wouldn't that be all the more reason to have an affair? A kind of revenge?"

"I thought of it."

"But you didn't," he persisted.

She hesitated. "There was a man." Another pause. "Two men, in fact."

Immediately he was sorry he'd raised the subject. "You know, Anne, maybe I don't need to know this after all."

"Oh, no, you asked me, and now you're going to have all of it, the whole sordid story." But she squeezed his thigh, telling him it wasn't going to be that sordid. "There was a man, an old friend of my father's. I'd known him most of my life; I thought of him almost as an uncle. When Geoffrey left me, I went to him for advice. He gave me money immediately—a hundred pounds, I think it was. Well—I daresay you're ahead of me already in this story—it wasn't long before it became clear that this was not precisely a loan. Or I should say, he wasn't interested in being paid back *in kind*; he had a different *tender* in mind, so to speak." The brittle tone was back, barely veiling the bitterness underneath. "That hurt me. It felt like another betrayal. After that, I was leery of helpful-seeming men. I stayed to myself. I got a cat," she said with a short laugh. "I formed friendships with women in my neighborhood—most of them in remarkably similar circumstances—and we helped each other whenever we could. And Geoffrey did send money occasionally. The time passed. Then he came home. He was ill and—"

"Wait." He kept his gaze on her fingers, bending them backward and forward, pretending absorption in their amazing flexibility. "I believe you forgot the second man."

"Ah. That was nothing. Really."

"The whole sordid story," he reminded her softly.

"All right, then. I was half in love with him," she said, speaking quickly. "He was a sculptor. My marriage was an impediment

234

at first; but then, as it became more and more impossible—I didn't even know where Geoffrey was, or if I'd ever see him again—I came close to acquiescing in an affair with this man. I didn't, though, and the relationship ended. About which I certainly have no regrets now." She took her hand back and faced him. "Something held me back, Christy. I didn't know what it was—I thought perhaps I was a cold woman, incapable of giving myself in that way. But it's not true, and I know now why I couldn't take him for my lover."

"Why?"

"Because he wasn't you. I didn't love him enough. There won't ever be anyone for me except you."

They reached for each other and held on tight for a long, wordless embrace. Christy's heart felt swollen. Love and gratitude streamed through him, and a profound humility. "I'm blessed," he said, and Anne whispered back, "I *feel* blessed." He thought that was a fine start.

She pulled away, dashing a hand at her shiny eyes. "I've not quite finished the whole sordid story. And—" she gave a forced laugh "—believe it or not, it gets much worse."

He shifted onto his side and put his arm across her lap. "Tell me."

"Geoffrey came back, after being away for more than two years. He looked—I can't describe to you how much he'd changed. He'd been in Burma, he said, where he'd contracted malaria. He'd lost his *hair,* he—looked like an old man, his speech was slurred, he had lumps and swellings all over his body." She closed her eyes, as if to block out the memory, then opened them again quickly, as if that hadn't worked. "I didn't like his doctor, I thought he was a quack, but we couldn't afford anyone better. The drugs he took only made him sicker. I truly thought he was dying. It went on for months.

"But—gradually he started to get better. When he was out of

bed and almost normal again, the doctor, the—*quack* I didn't trust and couldn't stand, told me something Geoffrey had made him promise never to tell. Something that probably saved my life."

A premonition chilled Christy; in its aftermath he wondered why he hadn't guessed the truth before now. He didn't move or speak. He knew exactly what she was going to say.

"Geoffrey didn't have malaria. Why he lied, or how much longer he'd have kept lying—I don't even want to know. What he had was syphilis. There was no telling exactly when he'd gotten it, but since I wasn't infected, and since it had already progressed well into the second stage, the doctor concluded it must've been very soon after he went away."

Christy pulled her closer. "Sweetheart," was all he could think of to say.

"I found out why the medicine was making him as sick as the disease—sicker. He was taking chloride of mercury."

"My God."

"There was nothing else that would work, the doctor said, and it did seem to be helping; most of his symptoms went away and he swore he was cured. He even found another war to fight, someplace in India this time. But then he fell ill again, and they said it was mercury poisoning. And his disease came back—he wasn't cured at all. That's when he gave up his captaincy and came home for good. Or so I thought."

"So when you first came to Wyckerley—"

"He'd recovered again, to some extent; he was as healthy during the months you saw him as he'd been since he first fell ill. Once again, he said he was cured. He was taking a different medication, iodine of potassium, and it seemed to be doing him good. Perhaps he was cured, I don't know. Now we'll never know."

She leaned forward and put her head down, next to his, and

spoke softly against his temple. "The second time he came home, Christy, it was absolute hell. You can't imagine—I don't even want you to know, not all of it. I've already told you about the violence—some of it. Enough. It was the drinking as much as the sickness that made him act like a madman sometimes. I've never seen anyone suffer as he did, physically, of course, but even more from despair. Just utter hopelessness. Soldiering was his life, and he couldn't do it anymore. He couldn't control himself, and his erratic behavior had thinned his circle of acquaintances until he was down to rotters like Claude Sully. I think he could see himself decaying, literally decaying, piece by piece, falling apart. The pox was—*racing* through him. It can go fast or slow—I've become something of an expert on it, as you can imagine—and Geoffrey's case was one of the quick kind. If he'd lived, I don't know what would've become of him. I doubt that he was cured. How they could have let him back in the army is a mystery I'll never understand."

They lay quiet for a time, softly touching, listening to the fire in the grate. Finally Christy said, "I don't know what I could've done or what I could've said. Nothing, probably. But I wish you had told me. Or he had. I just wish I'd known."

"I couldn't have told you then."

"No, I don't blame you."

"But you're right—it would've been better if you'd known. Geoffrey loved you, Christy, in his way."

"Do you think he did?"

"I know it. And I don't know what you could've said or done either, but I think you might've helped him. It was such a dreadful secret, and I was such an unsatisfactory confidante. You would never ask, and so I must tell you that we were never intimate again after our short-lived wedding trip. And—he wanted me. But I—couldn't—give him anything. My body was the least of it. I couldn't give him *anything* of myself, there was no love in me. I was his reluctant nurse, nothing more, and the bitterness between us was an absolute nightmare. And I could add guilt to my nightmare because . . ." She took a deep breath. Tears welled in her eyes, and she said on a near-sob, "Because at the end, I think he loved me. Oh, God." Christy gathered her up, and she wept against his chest as if her heart were breaking. "I think he did—he never said, but I think so—oh, Christy—"

"Shh," he soothed her, holding tight, rocking her a little.

After a time, she grew calmer; she stopped crying, and used his handkerchief to wipe her cheeks. "I've never admitted that, even to myself, until this minute. I must've been trying not to believe it. It makes everything worse."

"No, Anne, it doesn't. If Geoffrey's life at the end was hellish, then loving you must've been the only good thing left for him. How can that be anything but a blessing? It might've been a desperate love, maybe even twisted, but because it was love, it must have been gentle and good-hearted as well. You can be grateful for that. And glad for Geoffrey, not heartsick."

She turned in his arms to embrace him. "I love you, Christy," she said, and the tears were back—he could hear them in her voice when she hid her face in his neck. But her open mouth felt hot on his skin, and her hands were making short work of the buttons down the front of the shirt she wore. "Make love to me." Bare-breasted, she yanked at the belt of his dressing gown and dragged the cloth away, then lay down on top of him. Searing heat flared in him, and he resigned himself to the knowledge that passion between them was going to be unpredictable and out of his control. *God help me,* he prayed automatically, but it wasn't sincere: He didn't want help. All he wanted was Anne.

She put his hands on her breasts. He kissed her while he fondled her, her body arched over him like a bow, but he had to stop when she began the soft, slow squeeze of her thighs around his rock-hard erection. "God!" he ground out through his teeth, and she threw her head back and laughed with lusty, uninhibited gladness. The sound freed him from the last restraint, and he reached for her, wanting to hold her against his heart, overcome with love.

But she glided out of his grasp. Sliding down his body, she made a curtain of her hair and caressed him with it, softly, back and forth, brushing his skin like cool silk scarves. Bent over him, she slipped her hands under his buttocks. The tantalizing hair-caress became more intimate, immeasurably more exciting, and now it was her lips and her cheeks she was nuzzling him with, humming softly with her own pleasure. He made a strangled sound when he felt her tongue circle the sensitive tip of his penis. She took him into her mouth, and he made a grab for her knees, his body jerking in stunned reaction. "Anne," he groaned. "Oh, Jesus—Anne—"

She lifted her face; her eyes were shining with love and the thrill of power. "It's not wrong," she whispered. "Do you think this is wrong?" All he could do was shake his head. She laughed her sweet, purifying laugh again, and this time he laughed with her. She made a soft, slick-walled tunnel with her hands, and pleasured him with it until he couldn't take any more.

Sitting up, he lifted her so that she was kneeling, straddling his hips. They kissed while she guided him into the warm cleft between her legs. Her surprised gasp fired him; he wanted to take her even higher, make her wild. Pulling her head back, he trailed kisses down her neck to her breasts, and thrust deep, deep inside her while he grazed his teeth across her hard little nipples, making her cry out. She felt like liquid flame in his arms, pliant and fiery, nurturing and consuming.

Holding tight, he tumbled her backward without losing their intimate joining. The edge neared. He set his teeth and slowed his rhythmic pumping, grinding himself against her. He murmured her name as he kissed her again and again, losing himself in sensation, blind and aching, so close to bursting. And then her sweat-sleek thighs slowly clamped around him. Her head fell back. Like a starving man, he feasted his eyes on the face of his beloved while she climaxed. She made no sound except for a low grinding in the back of her throat, but her lips thinned in a pained-looking grimace and her head twisted fitfully on the pillow. To give her pleasure this intense felt like a miracle; he'd have thanked God for it then and there—but the deep, gentle pursing of feminine flesh around him banished every thought that wasn't carnal. Crushing her to his chest, he pulsed into her in time to her slow, deceptively patient rhythm, groaning, trying not to hurt her, unable to stop until he was drained and empty.

When it was over, he couldn't speak at first, only hold her. Her eyes were closed. The tears on her lashes didn't surprise him; nothing so intense as that had ever happened to him, either. "My love," he was finally able to say. "Beautiful Anne, I love you."

"I love you," she whispered. "Oh, Christy, so much. So much. It frightens me."

"Why, darling?"

"Because I can't think of anything but God that could make me feel like this. It's not natural." She heaved a deep, tragic sigh. "I might have to convert."

"I feel so guilty."

Anne stopped beside the banks of the Wyck, in the shadows cast by the bare alder branches in the graying dawn. Hoarfrost glimmered on the sere winter grass, and over the river a milk-white mist curled. Christy lifted one heavy wing of his greatcoat and folded her inside it, pulling her next to the warmth of his body. "Why, love?" he asked.

"Because you have to go home now and worry all morning about Mrs. Weedie, then ride to Mare's Head and do whatever it is you have to do there—"

"Meet with the deacon."

"Meet with the deacon—while I'm going to tell Mrs. Fruit my

headache is worse, not better, and then go to bed and sleep all day long." She barely stifled a yawn against his chest; she was drooping with fatigue. "Poor, poor Christy."

He chuckled, kissing her temple and giving her a squeeze. "I don't mind. How will you get inside, Anne, without being seen?"

"I left the front door unlocked. I'll just walk in and go upstairs to my room. No one will see me, and if they do, I'll say I've been out for a walk."

"At half past five in the morning?"

"They may not believe me," she conceded. "But they'd never in a million years guess what I have been doing." She laughed, but he didn't join in. She found his hand and held it. "You hate this, don't you? All the secrecy and the lies."

"It's not what I'd have chosen."

She decided to shock him with the truth. "I can't help it—I *do* like it. It makes me feel alive." He smiled at her, but a bit wanly. "I know you wouldn't have chosen this way, and it makes me love you all the more because you did choose it, for my sake. Christy, *please* don't be sorry."

"Don't worry about me."

He'd said that before. She touched his cheek with her gloved fingertips. "You're not going to suffer now, are you? To—to *atone* for what we did?"

He took her hand and kissed the palm through her glove. "Sweet Anne," he murmured. "It's possible that you can't have everything."

"You mean I can't have you, *and* have you without your guilty conscience." He only smiled. "But if God is truly loving, why would he mind what we did? Whom did we hurt?" He didn't answer, and she knew it was hopeless: he was going to worry and think and ponder over everything no matter what she said. Which was another reason she loved him so much. She sighed. "You won't stop caring for me, will you?"

"You know the answer to that."

"And we can still be together, can't we? You'll come to me, won't you, Christy? In the old caretaker's cottage? I'll make up some excuse for why I want it aired out, the fireplace cleaned and so on. I don't know why I'll say I want fresh linens and blankets on the bed, though. But leave all that to me," she assured him hastily, seeing that the subject was making him uncomfortable. If subterfuge and little white lies were sins, she would gladly take them on for him, and suffer any consequences Christy's God might have in store for her.

"Well," she said on another sigh. "I guess I'd better go in now." But she didn't move, and he didn't let go of her. She whispered against his throat, "I love you. Please don't have so many second thoughts."

His arms around her tightened. "I've told you, you mustn't worry about me. I'll find my way."

"But—"

"You make me happy, Anne, not unhappy."

She closed her eyes in relief. That had been her only worry. He'd gone to the heart of it, and now everything was perfect.

Except that they had to say good-bye. "Kiss me," she begged, standing on tiptoe. "Make it last."

He did his best, but she was already missing him a second after he let her go. "I know what 'sweet sorrow' means now," he told her with a sad smile and a last caress.

She stepped out of his arms and moved reluctantly toward the bridge. There she turned, just to look at him again. "Write me a poem," she called softly, on an impulse. "Leave it in our place."

He cocked his head, judging her seriousness; he was suspicious of what she thought of his poetry, although she'd never told him. "What about?"

She held out her arms, telling him that was obvious. "About sweet sorrow!"

He looked arrested, then thrilled. He stood straighter and called back, "Yes—all right, I will!"

She blew him a kiss. Hurrying across the bridge, she muttered under her breath, "Good Lord, what have I done?"

XVII

2 February

It must be love: I don't even hate the weather anymore.

I'm looking out my high sitting room window at the smoke-gray treetops and the colorless fields, the grim cloud-piles banking on the horizon, and I'm thinking there's beauty in this dreary landscape, and an austere kind of comfort. It makes me shiver a little, but the sensation isn't the least unpleasant. It's all in the eye of the beholder, isn't it? A prosaic thought that's never seemed truer to me. I believe I could be happy today in a Dartmoor Prison cell.

If you turn a gem in your fingers and view it from another angle, all its facets change. Same stone, different perspective. All my doubts, fears, and reservations about marrying Christy remain—no miraculous broom from on high has come down and swept them away—but they don't defeat me any longer. They're challenges now, not obstacles.

Case in point: Wyckerley. Amazing how my impression of the village has changed now that I know it's to be my home, probably for the rest of my life. I see the narrow streets and thatched-roof houses in a new, gentler light, I admire the neat orderliness of our village green, I take pride in the blocky Norman solidity of our church, and I have a downright proprietary fondness for the rectory. My house. My garden, my sycamore tree. My front walk, my parlor. Mrs. Ludd will be my housekeeper, and her husband will be my gardener, groom, and odd-job man. I'm so delighted by this humble prospect, I don't know what to do with myself. Lynton Hall, as much as I've grown to love it, has never felt like mine, not even remotely. First it was Geoffrey's, now it's Sebastian Verlaine's. But the vicarage, which will always and forever be Christy's, is by some transcendent piece of good fortune going to be mine too—because he's so keen on sharing it with me, I suppose. I am unquestionably the luckiest woman in all of Devon. All of England, make that. Oh, hell: the world.

The other worry which hasn't gone away but doesn't prostrate me anymore is my agnosticism. I understand now that it's based on nothing more solid than my father's example (his contempt for religion was profound; he never set foot in a church except to paint it) and my own resulting prejudice and ignorance. I've stopped giving Christy atheistic tracts, and now I ask him about his faith, what the basic tenets are of the Church of England, etc. I learn, but my mind still resists. If faith is indeed a gift, it's still being withheld from me.

But I'm starting to think that believers are better off than nonbelievers if only because they have something to live by besides self-interest. Then why not simply join them? If I can't accept all of it yet, maybe I will in time, little by little. Religion doesn't do any *harm*; at least Christy's brand doesn't, because there's no hypocrisy and no secret motive of control or power underlying it. And so I ask myself, why not? In the absence of anything better, why not embrace it? It isn't as if I would be relinquishing any hard-won, deeply felt principles of my own.

6 February

Christy told me the most important lesson his father taught him was not to be afraid of passion in religion. "The church needs lovers," said old Reverend Morrell. "To be a priest is to be in love." I'm beginning to wish I'd known this man.

8 February

Christy has just left me—I'm flush with love. But there's still room for exasperation.

I wormed out of him why we must wait until November—*November!*—to announce our engagement. Stupid of me not to have guessed sooner: it's not himself he wants to protect, never mind that he's the one whose sterling reputation is important—vital, you might say, in his line of work. No—it's me! He wants to avoid a scandal for *my* sake! And nothing I can say budges him from this noble but infuriating position. But he's not heard the last from me on the subject, oh no, not by a long shot. If I can't marry him for a year, I'll torment him for a year.

14 February, Saint Valentine's Day

Christy left me another poem. Sometimes I wonder what he takes me for.

Thy lips are like a thread of scarlet, and thy speech is
     comely.
Thy temples are like a piece of a pomegranate within
     thy locks.
Thy two breasts are like two young roes that are
     twins, which feed among the lilies.
Thy lips, O my spouse, drop as the honeycomb: honey
     and milk are under thy tongue; and the smell of thy
     garments is like the smell of Lebanon.

I wrote him one back:

A bundle of myrrh is my well-beloved unto me;
   he shall lie all night betwixt my breasts.
His mouth is most sweet: yea, he is altogether lovely.
This is my beloved, and this is my friend, O daughters of
   Jerusalem.

But, of course, now I'll never know if he meant to pass the Song of Solomon off as his own work indefinitely. Probably not. More likely, he thought to wait for me to praise his poem and then spring it on me—"Aha! It's from the Bible!" I'm mildly irritated that he thinks me so ignorant I wouldn't recognize it. I'm an agnostic, not an illiterate.

18 February

We argued again. (In our way; Christy's the only man I've ever known who argues completely without rancor. Which is not always as estimable as it sounds; sometimes he wears me right into the ground with his infernal patience and fair-mindedness.) As usual, I had to bully him into discussing the subject at all. He wants to mull it over in private, and I want it out in the open in all its unsavory splendor: his guilty conscience. I don't tell him how much it hurts me that he still has moral qualms about what we do—but only because I know he already knows.

He agrees that our loving each other is right; where we digress is over the rightness of the physical expression of our love. I've stopped calling him "provincial" (too many chances for that boomerang to come back), but it's clear to me that it's our very different backgrounds that make us see this issue in such different lights. Then, too, as he always points out, if he makes an exception in his own case, how can he preach chastity and continence to his congregation? How can he look an adolescent boy in the eye and counsel him it's wrong to seduce virgins, or visit brothels, or steal away with his sweetheart and copulate in a haystack before the wedding? How can he tell Farmer So-and-So that his affair with Widow Such-and-Such is a sin?

I tell him it's *not* a sin, and I don't know why he'd want to tell them it is anyway. (This is about the time he throws up his hands and mutters things that sound like "pagan" and "godless"—always without rancor, though.) If Farmer So-and-So is married, I say, then maybe it is wrong; but if they're both free, where's the harm? Anyway, Christy and I *will* marry, eventually. Where does it say we can't love each other with our bodies? Show me the line in the Bible! (He can't.) Aren't we human? Didn't God give us our human bodies, flesh and blood and bone? *He* made us want each other—how could he turn around and make our loving union a sin? Et cetera, et cetera.

And I've been reading up to buttress my argument. I found something in Saint Augustine: "Love, and do what you will." Exactly. Exactly.

Of course, Christy knew that quote already and countered, after a fashion, with another of Augustine's: "Give me chastity and continency, but not yet." He says that means the saint believed that chaste moral behavior is superior to unchaste, he just wasn't fanatical about it. As far as I can see, that's where Christy stands too. Or would, if his bloody conscience would let go of him. I love his conscientiousness, his rectitude, his righteousness—but sometimes I want to take him by the scruff of the neck and shake them all out of him.

22 February

Today we made a pact: no arguing, no speaking of the future at all, in fact—just enjoying each other in the too-short time we could steal to be together. Oh, what an afternoon. I could have died in his arms quite happily, and counted my life worthwhile. Blessed.

The caretaker's cottage, the caretaker's cottage. I love the very syllables! (I would tell Christy to write a poem about it, but I tremble to think of the consequences.) After we're married, I think we should sneak back into the cottage on every anniversary (assuming it's vacant), just for old time's sake. Such happiness. Such content. When I'm an old lady, I will remember these afternoon trysts and midnight rendezvous, and no matter what my life has brought me by then, whether glad or tragic, full or empty with loss, I'll look back and say it was enough. I had Christy, and we loved, and it was enough.

Bless him, he's still reticent about our meetings, the secrecy, the stories we have to tell to be together. But once we are, once we're finally alone in our snug little hideaway, he's everything any woman could dream of in a lover. And I'm in a perpetual state of anticipation. Presumably this will pass. Presumably my body will settle down in time, as it gets used to this—this—indescribable experience. For now, though, I quite literally live for the hours when we can be together.

It's odd. I never considered myself a particularly carnal person before. Sex has always interested, not repelled me (which sets me apart from quite a number of respectable Englishwomen), and yet I never dwelt on it much. My only model was my father's example (vigorous, insatiable) and that of his many mistresses, some of whom I liked, one or two of whom I even loved—briefly, before they were supplanted by new ones.

But now it's as if I've turned into another person. I hardly know myself. It's not that I'm out of control; I still have all my faculties. If anything, my mind is sharper than usual, as if a veil between the world and me has been lifted, and I'm seeing, hearing, and feeling everything clearer than usual, unfiltered. It's my woman's body that's come into its own. I yearn. I long. Oh, say it—I lust. I've become a sexual being. I can go into a trance while reading a book, gazing out a window, eating a solitary meal, and become nothing more than a great lump of my own flesh, dying for release and fulfillment. Sexual fulfillment. Christy's awakened me. I love him for many things, and I'm not ashamed to say that that's one of the chief ones.

And by God, it's no sin. And deep down, I think he agrees with me. For once I'm right. He's smarter than I, but this time, poor man, he's a step behind.

27 February

The second-to-last day of the shortest month of the year. Not short enough, however; I wish they all had ten days, or two, until November!

I'm invited to the Weedies' this afternoon, for tea with the old ladies. I have it on good authority that Captain Carnock walked Miss Weedie home from church last Sunday. I wonder if the captain has also been invited for tea today; if so, I'll be able to judge for myself the progress of this fascinating, although glacially slow, courtship.

But the real *draw*, as it were, is that Christy's coming. I absolutely adore these public encounters, when we pretend we're nothing more than cordial acquaintances, the vicar and the lady of the manor. He *doesn't* like them—of course, he wouldn't—and I suppose it's a flaw in my character that I do. Oh, but they're delicious! Sometimes I send him hot looks over a teacup, just to watch his beautiful cheeks burn. (Childish, I know, but I can't help it.) And once, dining with Dr. and Mrs. Hesselius, I took my shoe off and tickled his ankle with my bare foot under the table. I thought he would spill his soup in his lap. Afterward, he gave me a stern talking-to, but I don't really think his heart was in it. Mine certainly wasn't when I promised never to do it again.

By HALF PAST THREE, the disappointing possibility that Christy wasn't coming to the Weedies' tea party had turned into a virtual certainty.

Despite that blow, Anne couldn't help enjoying herself. It was, so to speak, another turn of the gem in her fingers, she decided as she sipped tea and ate scones with clotted Devon cream. Armed with her secret knowledge of the new relationship she would soon have with people like the Weedies and Miss Pine and Mrs. Thoroughgood, she was seeing them all in a different light. Gone was the uneasiness she'd always felt because of the social barrier they'd unilaterally thrown up between themselves and her while she was Lady D'Aubrey. Now that she was going to be plain old Anne Morrell, the minister's wife, everything had changed. Changed so radically, in fact, that she was left to wonder how unilateral the barrier erection had really been. Was it possible she'd unwittingly contributed to the social atmosphere that had kept these kind people at a distance? Unconsciously acted the part of the viscountess because that was what was expected of her? A fascinating thought. It would have dismayed her if she hadn't known that that time had passed. A new day was dawning, and she found it at once frustrating and titillating that she couldn't tell them so.

"More tea, my lady?" Miss Weedie urged shyly, and smiled with pleasure when she said yes. Anne couldn't get over the transformation in Miss Weedie. It wasn't just the new dress— a soft wool crepe in dusty rose that was not quite but almost *stylish*—although that alone was cause for wonder. Even more surprising than the rose wool was the aura of exhilaration that hovered around her blooming cheeks and fluttering hands. Her graying blond hair looked more disheveled than usual, as if her excitement were coming out through her scalp and disarranging her hair, strand by strand.

The cause of all this pretty perturbation could only be Captain Carnock, big and bluff and blocky in his tan tweeds, and looking like a great shaggy mastiff in a roomful of tiny, well-behaved terriers. Even his voice seemed to rattle the dishes on the tea-table. His eyes followed Miss Weedie wherever she went with her teapot, and he inclined his massive body to catch every shy, infrequent utterance that passed her lips. Anne found herself observing the intriguing ritual with the same rabid interest that Mrs. Thoroughgood and Miss Pine were trying not to show. Old Mrs. Weedie, who ought to have been the most avid spectator of all, was, alas, largely oblivious to the romantic melodrama unfolding in her small living room. She'd recovered from her surgery, but she was still chair-ridden from her broken hip. From her comfortable place on the settle by the hearth, she nodded and dozed, slurped her tea and clicked her teeth, and conferred the same vague, placid smile on every remark she happened to hear.

"He says he's a *magistrate,*" Miss Pine repeated, kindly trying to include her old friend in the conversation.

Mrs. Weedie cupped her good ear. "Who? A hatchet blade?"

"A *magistrate!* Captain Carnock!"

"A retching cough? Oh, dear." She sent the captain a sweetly sympathetic look.

"A judge!" Mrs. Thoroughgood shouted at her. "Just got appointed! Sitting at the next quarter session!"

"Oh," Mrs. Weedie said, enlightened, "a *judge.* Well, I declare, isn't that something. My, my." Her chin sank to her chest; she fell asleep.

Miss Weedie rushed over and snatched the empty cup from her hand before it could slip to the floor. "I'm sure we're all very glad for you, sir," she said softly, blushing, massaging the cup in her fingers. "I'm sure you'll make a wonderful justice of the peace."

"Well, I thank you for that, Miss Weedie," the captain boomed, looking pleased and proud. "I take it as an honor and a serious responsibility, and I intend to do my best."

"Will we have to call you 'Your Worship' from now on?" Mrs. Thoroughgood inquired playfully.

The captain threw back his head and laughed. Miss Weedie laughed with him, as if she found his good humor irresistible. "Plain old 'Captain' is still good enough for me. Vanstone wears a wig, you know, but I don't plan to. Scratchy things; plus I'd look like a damned fool." His bulbous cheeks turned bronze. "Oh, say, I do beg pardon."

The old ladies tittered and coughed behind their hands, pretending they were shocked. But Anne suspected they liked his bluffness, and actually welcomed his refreshing male crudeness into their decorous female midst, like fresh air in a room that's been shut up too long.

Four o'clock came, the unvarying hour in Wyckerley when all tea parties came to an end. Saying her good-byes at the cottage door, Anne recalled a conversation with Christy, before she'd agreed to marry him, in which he had repeatedly insisted that she was wrong about the residents of the village feeling respect but no real warmth toward her. Now that she was seeing them through new eyes, she was ready to accept at face value the words of gratitude and gladness Captain Carnock and the old ladies expressed for her company. More important, she was letting go of her own reserve and allowing her fondness for these kind people to show through, unrestrained. Small wonder that they all parted with true affection, and even the bashfully bold suggestion from Miss Weedie that in the future Anne might like to call her Jessie.

A most satisfying afternoon, thought Anne, standing in the lane beyond the Weedies' sallow winter garden. Except that

Christy hadn't come. Silly to worry about him; half a dozen ecclesiastical chores could've kept him away. She missed him, though; she hadn't seen him in three whole days. She felt off-kilter, out of rhythm, when that much time passed between their meetings. The prospect of trudging back to the Hall now in the gathering twilight depressed her. Did she have to? Giving her skirts a resolute shake, she turned around and began to walk west, toward the rectory.

The Wyck was a chatty companion as she went on her way up the High Street, nodding and returning the bows of all who acknowledged her. Her black-garbed, unescorted figure was a familiar sight by now and no longer excited the notice it once had, thank goodness. She passed a row of cottages, the town hall, the First and Last Inn, Dr. Hesselius's house. The sweet smell of new malt followed her past the George and Dragon's open door. Swan's smithy, the center of village gossip and a source of current intelligence as reliable as a newspaper, was crowded with the usual gang of philosophers and hangers-on—perchers, Christy called them. The ones lounging on benches stood up when they saw her; everyone doffed his hat and bowed to her, and she thought Tranter Fox winked. What a funny little man. She quite liked him; Christy did, too, even though he never went to church and liked to boast about what a great sinner he was.

Strolling past the mayor's pretentious Tudor mansion, she saw the front door open and Honoria Vanstone step out, followed by Lily Hesselius. *Oh, bother,* thought Anne, trapped; now that she'd decided to find out Christy's whereabouts by going directly to his house and asking, she had no tolerance for frivolous delays, and there was nobody in Wyckerley she considered a more frivolous delay than Honoria Vanstone.

"Why, Lady D'Aubrey, what a delightful surprise," exclaimed that lady when she saw her.

"Delightful surprise," echoed Lily, Honoria's constant companion these days. The two ladies unfurled their parasols together, never mind that the wintry sun had already slid behind the trees into gray oblivion. While they exchanged stiff chitchat about the weather and various village events, Anne mentally took note of Honoria's interesting ambivalence toward her. She wasn't as unctuous and flattering as she once had been, and it had started immediately after Geoffrey's death. Anne was still Lady D'Aubrey, but it was common knowledge that Sebastian Verlaine was the new viscount, as well as the new owner of Lynton Great Hall—so where did one place in one's social scale a widowed viscountess with no visible property? Honoria's confusion was amusing, but only to a degree; she was such a disagreeable person that Anne couldn't even enjoy her at an ironic distance for very long.

With Honoria, she'd learned, there was always a point to the most trivial conversation, and she got down to the point of this one as soon as the pleasantries were decently out of the way. With an arch, artificial smile, she asked, "What news do you have of Sebastian, my lady?"

Sebastian? What impudence. "Nothing of any great moment recently," Anne answered, and couldn't help adding, "I wasn't aware that you were acquainted with my husband's cousin." Indeed, it was her understanding that Geoffrey himself had met Sebastian Verlaine only two or three times in his whole life.

Honoria at least had the grace to blush while she said, "Oh, yes, we met as children—many years ago now, of course, but I shall never forget it. Sebastian—Lord D'Aubrey—was visiting at the Hall with his parents."

"Oh, I see. So you met him at the Hall?"

There was a short but telltale pause. "Mm, the Hall, quite," she said, suddenly vague, and immediately changed the subject. Silly old goose, thought Anne, irritated; Honoria had probably "met" the future viscount in the street; they might have fought over a ball or a mudpie, maybe jumped puddles together for twenty minutes. And for that, he was henceforth and forever going to be "Sebastian" to Miss Vanstone.

"We're off to Miss Carter's shop to buy ribbons before it closes," piped up Mrs. Hesselius, as if it were the most delightful outing she could think of. Which it probably was. Of the two women, she was even sillier than Honoria, but for some reason Anne still had hopes for Lily. Christy had confided once that she was a terrible flirt and that she led poor, sweet Dr. Hesselius a merry chase—a circumstance which didn't inspire an excess of sympathy in Anne's harder heart; men who married pretty, flirty, much younger wives usually got what they deserved, in her opinion. Still, Lily wasn't all bad. Silliness without malice was an easy sin to forgive; and for all Lily's frothiness, Anne sometimes caught glimpses of a quick mind that, given time, might grow into a thoughtful one. The time would be shorter once she realized she could do better than to cast her lot with the likes of Honoria Vanstone.

"You're in a hurry, then," Anne said, relieved that the meeting was ending so quickly. "I won't keep you standing in the street."

She said good afternoon and parted from them before they could ask her where she was going—not that such a thing could stay a secret for long in Wyckerley. She didn't doubt that a dozen people saw her continue up the street, cut the corner across the soggy green in front of Christy's house, walk up the flagged path, and knock at the front door.

Mrs. Ludd answered. She had flour on her apron and ashes on her forehead—still there from the Ash Wednesday service. The sacrilegious thought crossed Anne's mind that if she'd known she would miss Christy this afternoon, she might've gone to the service this morning, and at least gotten the imprint of his thumb on her forehead.

"Hello, Mrs. Ludd. Is Reverend Morrell at home, by any chance?"

"Why, no, he's not, m'lady," she said with a hasty curtsy. "He went to Mare's Head for a noon christening. I thought he mighta gone direct to Weedies' if he was running late."

"No, he didn't; I've just come from there."

"Well, I hope nothing's gone wrong with that Draper baby. Elly Draper's lost three infants before now, two girls and a boy, all from general neshness of constitution. It'd break her heart to lose another." The two women clucked their tongues and shook their heads in sympathy for Mrs. Draper. "Do you want me to give the vicar a message, m'lady?"

"Yes, if you would. Say I stopped by to have a word with him about a letter I received from the new viscount. It concerns the disposition of the glebe land." This was true; she had had a letter. "Tell him I'll be at home this evening if he would care to stop by and discuss the matter. It's rather important." This was not true; Sebastian's letter had said, in essence, that she could do whatever she liked with the glebe land.

"I certainly will," Mrs. Ludd said, impressed.

"Thank you." She smiled at her future housekeeper, thinking it was a lucky thing that they liked each other, and took her leave.

The church clock was striking half past ten as Christy stabled his horse, and when he crept in the back door to his house, there was no one waiting up for him. Mrs. Ludd had left a light in the kitchen, a plate of food in the still-warm stove. He almost didn't see the scribbled note, folded under the candleholder on the deal table.

So. Anne had come. The message made him smile—the sweet duplicity in it. But he was glad he'd missed her today. He had a choice to make, and seeing her would only have clouded his judgment. Without taking off his coat, without touching the food—Mrs. Ludd must've forgotten that he was fasting today—he went back outside, closing the door softly behind him.

It was the first of March, windy and a little too warm; pneumonia weather, his mother would have called it. In the high, cloudy sky, a moon rode but no stars. Spring was a faint but definite intimation in the odor of turned earth and the rustle of some burrowing creature in the garden humus. Deliberately skirting the cinder path that led to the sacristy, Christy walked around the church to the main portal—because tonight he was entering it as a man, not a priest. The familiar smells of stone and still air and dying flowers greeted him. The only light came from the tall altar candle, shrouded in red glass, a warm but lonely glow. His footsteps echoed quietly on the stone floor of the nave aisle; he sidled into a middle pew and sat down, shivering a little in the sudden cold.

He tried to clear his mind. At first nothing came to him but the prayer he'd been praying all the way home from Mare's Head: "Thank you, God, for saving the Drapers' child; please keep him safe."

Thank you, God. Please, God.

Gradually the dark and the absolute stillness brought a measure of peace. He thought of Anne. If he were a Roman Catholic, he could go to a fellow priest and confess his sins, unburden his conscience in private. For the first time, that option appealed to him—interestingly, since before it had always seemed to him an intrusive, nearly offensive interpretation of the sacrament of penance. Now he could see some advantages—privacy, intensity, and immediate results: absolution.

The trouble with absolution was that it implied reformation. The sinner resolved to sin no more. But Christy's love affair with Anne had never felt like a sin, not in his deepest heart, and resolving to love her no more felt like the vilest sacrilege. Was that Satan's work? He smiled to himself, thinking how angry she would be if she knew he entertained such thoughts. In truth, he'd never had much use for Satan, and the concept of evil had always been more of an abstraction than a reality, something infinitely harder for him to take on faith than the existence of a merciful and loving God.

Anne joked that he and she were like Jesus and Mary Magdalene. A perverse analogy, since he made such a miserable stand-in for Christ—but what about her? Did God see sinfulness in one of his creatures who could not believe? Who did no harm, who lived a good, kind, gentle life, but could not believe? No—impossible; Christy felt it deeply, that Anne was God's child as surely as anyone was. Then how could loving her be wicked?

Slipping from the bench, he sank to the hard wooden kneeler and covered his face with his hands. He felt as if he were on the brink of a conclusion to the chaos in his soul. He wanted to be silent and still in his heart, to hear God's message, if there was one.

Noise. Confusion. He prayed the written prayer for guidance: "Grant us, in all our doubts and uncertainties, the grace to ask what thou wouldst have us to do, that the Spirit of wisdom may save us from all false choices, and that in thy light we may see light, and in thy straight path may not stumble."

The tower clock struck eleven. In the quiet expanse of time after the last toll, Christy prayed out loud, "God, I don't know if I'm still your servant or not. I know how easy it would be to delude myself, but lately I've been feeling that you're not displeased with me for loving Anne, that I'm still doing your will—as imperfectly as usual, but still your will. Approximately. Help me to see the difference between what you want and what I want. Help me not to confuse them. I want to see the truth. I need your guidance, Lord, to know what's right and what's my own wishful thinking. Please help me. Show me the way."

His mind stayed a jumble. "Please, God," he prayed, more a chant than a prayer, eyes shut, hands clenched together. "Show me the right way. Please, God. Is it a test? Is Anne a trial you've sent me, or a free blessing? If she's a blessing, help me to know what I've done to deserve it."

No answer came. *Please God, please God,* he began again, to drive the noisy debris out of his brain. "Why doesn't it feel like a sin to love her with my body? Give me the wisdom and humility to know what's right. I thought I knew, but since she's come I'm not sure if I know anything at all. Help me."

Except for the intermittent tolling of the clock, he would not have known if time passed or stood still. The small light on the altar, the one he'd thought was dim, burned like a red sun in his eyes, even when he covered them with his hands. His knees went numb, then his fingers, then his toes. All the while he listened, listened. Sometimes God spoke softly, and he couldn't afford to miss the news. Close to dawn, the early chirp of a chaffinch roused him from some kind of revery. Hedge sparrows twittered in the ash tree outside Saint Catherine's window. Christy lifted his head from his crossed arms. Silver dawn light was invading the black shadow-corners; the white of the altar cloth gleamed palely, the brightest object he could discern, brighter even than the candle now. And something had settled inside him. He would pray again, pray forever, in the hope that it was true, not self-deception, but for now it seemed right. For now, that was enough. "Thank you," he prayed, too exhausted for joy. That would come later, too.

2 March

I'm—I don't know what I am. I'm—no, I really don't know.

A letter's come from Christy. He's decided we're not committing a sin when we make love. He says he's made a pact with God. He wants to announce our engagement to the world (meaning the Ludds, and whoever else will get the word out with dispatch and discretion) on Easter Sunday, and to hell (expletive mine) with public opinion. I would rejoice, I *do* rejoice, except for the codicil, the condition all this good news comes attached to.

I see that Christy's God is very wily, very clever. We're to have our hearts' desire, but there's a price. I look at the words in the letter again and again, trying to rearrange them so they don't say what they say. But they always do.

Thunderation! (The worst oath I have ever heard pass my beloved's lips.) Hell and damn! Balls! I wish I knew more curses; at times like this, I feel the deprivation acutely. Journal, are you ready?

He's giving me up for Lent.

XVIII

"CHRISTY SHOULD PAINT THIS," Anne said out loud—talking to herself again. She frowned down at the half-finished drawing on her lap. She'd chosen the wrong medium—which seemed obvious in retrospect; trying to capture sun-shot daffodils on the far bank of Wycombe Cleave with a pencil and a piece of charcoal was a pretty silly thing to do, and a gross overestimation of her artistic abilities. "Christy could get it, though. In watercolors. Right at this moment, the way the flowers are filling up with sun like teacups."

She heaved a sigh and wrote "Wycombe Cleave" at the bottom of the page in her sketchbook. She liked the words, if not the picture they were meant to describe. They sounded so English. A cleave, William had told her this morning, was a place where a river ran through an avenue of trees. Which was exactly what the Wyck did here, down the center of a long copse of larches, not half a mile from the Tavistock toll road. It was a lovely spot, but she wouldn't have known it existed if Christy hadn't asked her to meet him here at three o'clock. It seemed as if every day she discovered a new point of interest or beauty or enchantment in her adoptive neighborhood. How could she ever have thought of Wyckerley as a lifeless backwater? It was a mistake that said less about the village than it did about her state of mind, then and now.

Another turn of the gem.

She stretched her arms up over her head to ease the slight

stiffness in her shoulders, blinking at the sky through the bare branches of the tree at her back. After two days of steady rain, it was finally fair, radiant in fact, with bees droning and turtledoves cooing, everything in creation budding, blossoming, and bursting. This morning she'd seen robins, skylarks, blackbirds and sparrows, starlings building a nest in the dovecote, pheasants feeding in the plowed fields. Primroses and cinquefoil were in bloom along the lane, and new green buds were showing on the hawthorn and the wild rose. Right now, two magpies who had forgotten she was there were building a nest directly over her head in the larch tree. They made a noisy diversion—and a handy excuse for laying her sketchbook aside once and for all. It was simply too beautiful to go on pretending she was usefully employed.

Something drew her gaze to the spot where the mossy footpath disappeared in a bend among the trees. Seconds later Christy strode around the turn, swinging an ash sapling for a walking stick. She didn't move at first, just basked in the luxury of looking at him, resigned by now to the reckless leap in her pulse rate. But then she couldn't contain herself. Jumping up, startling the busy magpies, she brushed at her skirts and smoothed her hair. No need to pinch her cheeks; she could feel the flush in them, growing warmer the closer he came. His dear face lit up when he saw her. His knee-high leather gaiters were spattered with mud; he'd taken off his jacket and thrown it over his shoulder. He looked so handsome in his shirtsleeves and unbuttoned waistcoat, his neckerchief untied and flying in the breeze, that she had to lean against the rough trunk, actually feeling weak in the knees.

He veered off the path and started up the shallow rise to her secluded spot under the larches. He'd been visiting needy souls in the southern reaches of the parish. "I thought you'd be on horseback," she greeted him from twelve feet away, beaming at him.

"I lent Doncaster to Reverend Woodworth. His pony's lame, and he needed to go to Swallowfield for a christening."

"That was awfully nice of you. How many miles did you walk today?"

He shrugged, coming to a stop in front of her. "It's a good day for walking." He had the same idiot's grin she knew she had, and he was looking her up and down as if she were a mutton chop he was about to bite into after a long, difficult fast.

"And how many souls did you save?"

"All of them. I left 'em singing hymns on their knees, praising God for the miracle of salvation."

"Think of that. A satisfying day for you, then."

"Ah, well. Not entirely."

She batted her eyes at him. "What's missing?"

The game was up as soon as he touched her. Kissing Christy was serious business these days; she couldn't afford to waste a second through frivolous talk or lack of concentration. He had her pressed against the tree, his hands on her waist. She flung her arms around his neck and kissed him passionately and exuberantly—and thoroughly, since this kiss might have to last her for days.

"You are delicious," she sighed, nibbling on his top lip, not letting go of him. "I missed you so much. I thought it would never stop raining. *Two whole days.*"

"I know. It felt like forty to me." He stroked her hair, bringing a handful to his nose to sniff, and then to his lips to kiss. "You're so pretty, Anne. I love it when you wear your hair down like this."

"I know," she said, shiny-eyed. "That's why I do it." She caressed his face, his hard cheekbone and the light stubble of beard on his chin. They dared another kiss, this one slower, sweeter. And more devastating: they broke away at the same time, taking their hands off each other with the same reluctance. She could have said, *Why are we doing this, again? Explain it to me one more time*—but what was the point? It was one of those things she was never going to understand.

"What's happened? Tell me everything you've been doing," he charged her while she bent to gather up her scattered belongings—sketchbook and pencils, reticule, straw hat and shawl. So she told him about all the petty household dramas that had been unfolding at the Hall in the last two days: the politely worded reminder from the butcher and the chandler that their bills were long overdue—because Mrs. Fruit had forgotten to pay them; the latest instance of the housemaid Violet Cocker's amazing impudence, and Anne's increasing temptation to let her go; the shepherd's helper William Holyoake had hired at Lady Day, who spent too much time in the kitchen flirting with the scullery maid; William's dilemma over whether to try Early Flourballs or Thompson's Wonderfuls when hay-sowing time came; Anne's invitation to dine with Dr. and Mrs. Hesselius next Thursday; and what she thought of the book she was reading these days, *Walden, or Life in the Woods,* by an American with a French name.

They held hands as they went along the path toward home, confident they wouldn't be seen because, Christy said, nobody ever came this way, but keeping a careful eye out anyway. "Now tell me what *you've* been doing," she invited, having exhausted her fund of domestic tidings. "Did you visit today with anyone I know?" His pastoral work intrigued her, in part because he kept so much of it to himself. Once they were married, she hoped he wouldn't be quite so discreet, but for now she often had to settle for the most sweeping generalities—"Mrs. Mooney is having a difficult time of it these days with Mr. Mooney," for example, when she knew for a fact that old Mooney had gotten blind drunk and set the privy on fire with his wife in it.

"Do you know Enid Fane?" Christy asked. She shook her head. "Her brother's in Dartmoor Prison, so I write a letter to him for her once in a while."

"Can't she write?"

"She can, but she says her letters never come out sounding right. So I talk to her, find out what's been happening with her, what's on her mind, and then write it down for her. When I read it back, she always says, 'Why, Vicar, ee've got it fair perfect, I never knowed I'm havin' such a interesting life.'"

Anne laughed, pressing her cheek to his shoulder. "What's her brother in gaol for, if I may ask?"

"A variety of petty crimes, all related to drink. He'll be out in a few months."

"Do you ever go to see him?"

"Him and a few others from the parish, yes, sometimes. I've gone as guest chaplain for Sunday services at the prison, too."

"That sounds a bit grim."

"Grim doesn't begin to cover it, believe me. I feel sorry for any man who ends up in Dartmoor, no matter what he's done. Or any woman."

"Are there women there, too?"

He nodded. "Pitiful, wretched creatures, Anne. Don't ever break the law, will you? Whatever you're tempted to do, I can assure you it won't be worth it."

"I'll try to remember that." They stopped in the angle of an L the river made, a shadowy spot overhung with the budding branches of willows. "Once we're married, no one would dare to arrest me, though, even if I became a master criminal. I'll be Mrs. Christian Morrell, the minister's wife, which will immediately convey legitimacy to my existence. I'll achieve the ultimate in respectability overnight."

"So Lady D'Aubrey isn't respectable?" he asked interestedly, folding his arms and leaning against a thick, waist-high willow bough.

"Oh, the title is. It's the lady herself who raises the occasional eyebrow."

"Do you really believe that? I thought you'd gotten over such feelings."

She smiled to reassure him. "It's just that I know what was said and thought about me here in the beginning. People were even surprised to find out I was English—they thought I'd be Italian, or half-Italian. From some cloudy sort of *artistic* background, too—definitely not respectable, possibly even decadent. At the worst, the new viscountess was a fortune hunter who had snared their absent heir apparent with her foreign, immoral wiles."

"You're exaggerating."

She laughed. "Yes, but not much."

He put his hand on her shoulder. "You're always telling me how beloved I am, the esteem in which I'm held by my congregation. I wonder how it is that you can see that about me, but you can never see the affection the people of Wyckerley have for you. They had no love for Geoffrey, Anne. Even before he went off to war, he'd made his mark on them. Believe me, because I'm privy to all this," he said seriously. "It was you they learned to look to, and it's you they look to now."

"Even though I'm to be replaced soon?"

"Even so."

She took his hand and held it to her cheek. "If what you say is true, then we're *equally* afflicted with an inability to know our own worth."

"I suppose we are."

"Well, I guess there are worse things."

"Much worse—we could *overestimate* our value to the world."

"Mm," she said doubtfully. "But is that worse? Think how much happier we'd be in our overweening arrogance."

He laughed, and reached for her. She went into his arms eagerly, and they stood quietly for a while, listening to the chuckle of the river. "Lord, I'm so lucky," Christy said presently.

"Why?" she asked leadingly, smiling with her eyes closed.

"Because my best friend is also my lover."

Not lately, an irreverent voice in her brain retorted. But to Christy she said, "I was just thinking the same thing."

"What would you like to do most after we're married?"

This was one of their favorite topics of conversation lately. "The very most? Walk down the High Street holding hands with you," she answered unhesitatingly.

"I should think we could do that once we're engaged."

"Really?" She was thrilled. "What else could we do?"

"Well, if you took Susan Hatch for a maid-companion, I don't see why we couldn't go to Exeter for an outing."

"I've only been through Exeter on the train. You could show me the cathedral."

"There you are—what could be more respectable?"

"Christy, what if we met *by chance* in Tavistock one day? I'd be there for the Corn Market, and you'd . . ."

"I'd be visiting the rural dean."

"That sounds respectable. We'd meet on the street. Naturally, we'd start walking together."

"We might pass a bookseller's shop. We'd go in and browse together."

"How perfectly lovely. Then we'd go and have coffee somewhere."

"Maybe even a meal," he said boldly.

"Think of it—actually eating together in public!"

"What I can't wait to do is show you the Devon coast. We could take a pony gig to Plymouth—"

"Wouldn't we have to be married for that?"

"That's what I mean, after we're married. We'd stay in a hotel—"

"A hotel," she breathed. It sounded like heaven on earth.

"And we'd take walks along the coast, exploring. There's a little fishing village called Luton Water about an hour's walk from Devonport. It's on a cliff overlooking the Channel, with a hundred and thirteen stone steps leading down to the shingle beach."

"Ohh."

"We could have a picnic in the sand."

"We could wade in the sea."

"We'd meet people, take up with them the way travelers do. Have a meal with some nice couple in a restaurant—"

"And then say good night and go up to our own room."

Words failed them.

"You've never been to Cornwall or the Scillies," Christy rallied to point out. "We could go on the train for a few days. St. Austell, Penzance, Mount's Bay, whatever we like."

"I want to see Wales someday, too."

"Llandudno—they say the beach is beautiful."

"The Cardigan Bay."

"The abbey at Tintern."

They were overcome again.

"Christy, how could heaven be any better than this?" She pressed her ear to his chest and closed her eyes, the better to listen to the strong beat of his heart.

"Don't ask *me* a question like that."

She could tell he was smiling. She wanted him so much at that moment; she let the lovely, unbearable longing well up inside, standing quite still so he wouldn't know.

But he knew. "This is even harder than I thought it would be," he said, sounding a little hoarse. "And I thought it would be sheer hell."

"Don't worry. Everything's going to be all right." One of the curious things about this horrible forty-day abstinence was that she always did her best to help him keep his vow. Not once had she deliberately tried to tempt him.

"I think it's so hard because I know what I'm missing. If we'd never made love . . ." He trailed off.

"No."

"No," he agreed, on second thought. "It wouldn't be any easier."

She lifted her head. "Christy, I'm so in love with you."

The tenderness in his eyes melted her. "I shouldn't even kiss you. You don't have to do anything—you're a walking, talking temptation." She didn't argue, didn't even answer; she knew he was going to kiss her. "The wonderful thing is that you don't even understand any of this. But after—after—"

"After the shock wore off."

"Right—you haven't once argued with me about it. Do you know how grateful I am for that?"

"Why do you think I'm doing it?"

He smiled, but he wouldn't let her tease him out of what he wanted to say. "I don't know what I've done to deserve having you. Sweet Anne, you're in my heart. You're my delight—my heart's desire." He lowered his mouth to hers in the gentlest kiss.

She loved his soft breath on her cheek, the warm skin of his neck where she touched him, under his collar. His hands coasting lightly, lightly, up and down her spine. They shifted the angle of their mouths, shifted the mood. Hunger now—her breath quickening, his hands tightening on her waist, pulling her closer. She made a sound low in her throat, a purr of pleasure, and a warning. *Be careful.* But the slow slide of his tongue had her opening her mouth for him, welcoming him, light-headed from the taste of him. She stepped closer, wanting the pressure of his hard chest against her breasts, then wanting more. *Careful.* The hot, slick kiss deepened, and she was falling too fast. *Must not.* She made herself turn her face away, shivering from the heat of his open mouth gliding softly along the line of her jaw.

"It's character-building," he muttered against her neck. "We don't have to stop yet."

She realized she had the shoulders of his shirt wadded in her two clenched fists. Relaxing her hands, she smoothed the wrinkled white cotton over the bunched muscles of his upper arms.

"This is not character-building," she got out between unsteady breaths. "Christy, this is torture."

Foreheads touching, they wailed in unison, "Three more weeks," then groaned piteously.

They walked home the rest of the way with their arms around each other. When they reached the crossroads, they lingered, delaying the moment of parting as long as they could. Their secret hiding place was a hollow chestnut stump, a few feet from the main road in a thicket of gorse and straggly heath. "I left something for you," Christy told her as they stood in the lane.

"Did you? I haven't been to look, because of the rain. Is it a letter?"

"No, it's nothing at all. Really," he demurred when she started into the weeds to retrieve his gift, "it isn't anything. Don't go, the grass is wet. I'll get it for you."

She waited while he waded into the tangled brush. They might need a new hiding place one of these days—she noticed they were beginning to wear a path. He bent down to retrieve something from the mouth of the stump; she caught only a flash of yellow before he whipped it behind his back and returned to the road, wearing a sheepish look.

"It's nothing," he repeated, standing in front of her. "Not even worth bothering with."

"Let's have it." She extended her hand, and he brought out his present: a sad, wet, wilted bouquet of very dead coltsfoot. She laughed, at Christy and at his silly flowers, but her throat caught and she was moved by a powerful emotion. "Did you come out in the rain to leave them for me?"

He shrugged. "Had my umbrella."

"Oh, God, I have to kiss you right now. No, I mean it, I have to. Where can we go?" The only place was at the edge of the oak trees, twenty yards away where Lynton's wooded parkland began. Stifling laughter, they walked up the road as fast as they dared, careful not to run. With a last glance around to make sure the coast was clear, they sidled into the trees, feeling like guilty poachers. Acorn husks crackled noisily underfoot. There wasn't much cover; they had to go in a fair ways before the bare trees shielded them from the road.

Still clutching her bedraggled flowers, she came into Christy's open arms with a laugh and a sigh. "I am absolutely mad for you," she told him between soft kisses all over his face. "You make me feel like a girl again. A very silly girl who's off her head most of the time."

"Yes, and you've reduced me to this. Stripped my dignity away like a banana peel. Me, a man of the cloth—"

She kissed him on the mouth to shut him up—and in no time at all they were back to the dangerous stage, exactly where they'd left off. "This has *got* to stop," Anne said with insincere firmness, ignoring the fact that she'd started it.

"Not yet, though."

"No, not yet." She let herself go, let him do what he wanted, leaving it in his hands. Oh, the aching sweetness of this!—the deep, yearning kisses and the soft-hard touching, the whispered words of love and desire. But then, quite suddenly, Christy froze. Ah, well, she thought, tottering on the edge between frustration and fatalism; it had to end sometime, didn't it? She pulled back to tell him so, and saw his face. It was blank and staring, rigid with shock. Jumping back in a panic, she spun around.

Someone was watching them.

"Holy Mother of God," breathed Anne. It was Mrs. Weedie. And she was stark naked.

Christy recovered first. "Find her clothes, Anne," he said quietly, then moved past her toward the old lady with smooth, unhurried steps, trying not to frighten her. But she seemed to crumple up the closer he came; when he reached her she'd sunk to her hands and knees in the damp leaves and was peering up at him fearfully. "You're too big," she cried, cringing away. Her gray hair had come halfway out of a bun on top of her head, and a long lock of it fell almost coyly over one of her small, flaccid breasts. Christy went down on his knees beside her. When he put his hand on her shoulder, she fell to her side and drew her knees up, wrapping her bony white arms around them. "Too big!"

"Anne," he said again, and she finally reacted. Creeping forward, heart pounding, she found a white flannel nightgown and one cloth slipper on the ground a few yards away. She went a little farther toward the road, and something red caught her eye, hanging from the low branch of a spindle tree; it proved to be a quilted dressing gown, with most of its buttons torn off or hanging by threads. She snatched it up and hurried back to Christy.

He and Mrs. Weedie were having a conversation. She called him "Bobby" and kept asking him if he was home for good now. He spoke to her with gentle jocularity, soothing her with his voice as well as his words, and she smiled at him and put her hand on his head, ruffling his golden hair as if he were a toddler. He'd put his jacket across her lap, but she seemed completely unaware of her nakedness and didn't even try to cover her bosom. Christy sent Anne a helpless look, and they changed places.

She must not have been naked for long; she wasn't shivering and her skin was cool but not cold. "You're not Jessie," she accused, while Anne struggled to get her arms into the sleeves of her nightgown. It was a lot like dressing a small child—no cooperation.

"No, I'm . . . I'm Anne." The situation was odd enough already; bringing *Lady D'Aubrey* into it, she felt, would only increase the absurdity.

"Do I know you?" Mrs. Weedie inquired politely.

"Oh, yes," she assured her, pulling a dead leaf out of her tangled gray hair. "We're neighbors, you and I. And very good friends."

"Are we? I'm so glad. Now, where's Bobby got to? There you

are, you bad boy. Help your mama up, it's time to go home. What are you doing out in these wet woods with—with—" Her lips quivered; she looked ready to cry. "I can't remember your name."

"It's Anne. We're friends."

Her face cleared. "Anne," she repeated with relief. Christy knelt down again and lifted her up in his arms. Anne put the lone cloth slipper on one of her cold feet and tied her own handkerchief around the other. "Ready to go home, Mama?" Christy asked softly.

Mrs. Weedie put her head on his shoulder and smiled.

Miss Pine was coming down the Weedies' front path as they turned in at the gate. Hatless, hair awry, she looked worn to a frazzle. "Saints, you found her!" she cried when she saw them. "Jessica!" She whirled and ran back to the door, throwing it open. "Jessie, she's here, the vicar's found her!"

Miss Weedie bolted past her, red-faced, apron strings flying. "Oh, thank God!" she exclaimed, while grateful tears ran down her cheeks. "Is she all right? Where was she? Mother, are you all right? Come in, put her by the fire. Oh—Lady D'Aubrey, I didn't see you!" Even in her distress, she remembered her manners and dropped an awkward curtsey.

"I think she's all right," Christy told her, setting his burden down carefully on the cushioned settle beside the hearth. "But you might want to send for the doctor anyway, just to be sure."

"I'll go," Miss Pine said immediately, and scurried out.

Blankets were brought, tea poured, soup heated, new slippers put on the invalid's feet. Anne stood quietly by while Christy explained how he'd found Mrs. Weedie. He didn't tell any lies, but he left out a few particulars, such as her own presence from the beginning. She didn't doubt that he would wrestle with his conscience later.

Mrs. Thoroughgood came, and several other ladies of the parish, members of an informal search party that had been scouring the neighborhood for the last half hour or so. Miss Pine came back with Dr. Hesselius, who said he'd run into the constable on his way and informed him that all was well. Christy carried Mrs. Weedie up to her tiny bedroom on the second floor, where the doctor examined her and gave her a sleeping potion. When he came down, he pronounced her tired but not much the worse for her adventure. Neighbors and friends began to drift away. The excitement was over.

Anne lingered uncertainly, then said good-bye to Miss Weedie—who thanked her profusely for coming, as if she'd done her an honor—and went outside. But she loitered in the gloom outside the cottage gate, waiting for Christy. After about ten minutes he joined her.

They stood in the middle of the street, in plain sight of any passersby, two acquaintances having a parting chat. Except that neither knew quite what to say. It was all so extraordinary—Anne wanted to talk about everything, but there wasn't time now. "So she's really all right, is she?" she said at last. "Lord, I hope she doesn't catch cold."

"No, I think she'll be fine."

"Poor Miss Weedie, this must be so hard for her. I wish I could do something to help."

Christy shook his head in sympathy. "There's not much anyone can do." He looked at her speculatively, then said, "Captain Carnock's asked her to marry him." He interrupted her glad exclamation by adding quickly, "She's refused him."

"What? But why?"

"Because of her mother. She says she can't leave her."

"Oh, but can't she—"

"It seems the original proposal didn't include Mrs. Weedie. The captain's added her on since then, but for Miss Weedie it's too late. She says he's just being dutiful now, and she won't take advantage of his good nature. She's adamant."

"Why, what utter rot," Anne exclaimed wonderingly. He raised his eyebrows at her. "No, but really, Christy—isn't it too nice of her? Too delicate? And none of my business, I know. All right, I'll shut up, before you say you're sorry you told me. But really—" He raised his infernal brows again, and she subsided, with a put-upon sigh.

He clasped his hands behind his back and bent toward her a little, tall and priestly in his dark blue coat and trousers, his forehead creased with earnestness. Who would guess that an hour ago he'd had her up against a tree trunk, kissing her, and whispering words in her ear that could make her blush right now if she cared to think about them. "What's the moral of this day's interesting events, Anne? What lesson have we learned from them?"

This must be how he quizzed the Sunday school children on their catechisms. She laid her index finger on her cheek, pretending to think. "Mm . . . never kiss the vicar unless you're sure you're alone?" He sent her a severe look. "That's wrong? All right, I give up."

"The lesson," he pronounced, "is that you and I are not really having such a bad time."

"We aren't?"

"Compared to other people's troubles, yours and mine are embarrassingly trivial. Well, mine, anyway; I won't speak for you."

"Best not."

He lowered his voice. "The one and only imperfection in my life at the moment is that I can't take you to bed."

"You call that *trivial?*"

He looked up at the sky, as if praying for patience. "What I am trying to—"

She cut him off with a gay laugh. "Oh, Christy, don't you think I know how lucky we are? I've found my life's mate. I love you more every day, and I'm so happy it frightens me. Poor, poor Miss Weedie, my heart breaks for her. All the things keeping you and me apart—in three weeks they'll be gone, and you'll be mine again, and I don't know if I can—*live* with pleasure and contentment that strong. Oh, my." She took a step back, whispering, "Say good-bye, Christy, before I start to cry!"

Somewhere in the lane behind her, a cottage door opened and closed. She didn't dare turn around. Christy tipped his hat to someone, looking over her shoulder, and the effort he was making to look grave and ministerial restored her composure—so much so that now she felt more like giggling than weeping.

"Well, good night to you, Lady D'Aubrey," he said loudly, with an elegant bow—hand on his heart and everything. "Shall I see you on Saturday at the church bazaar?"

"You shall, Reverend Morrell. You might see me sooner if you come to the bridge tomorrow night. Or the caretaker's cottage if it rains."

A most unclerical grin split his face. "Your servant, my lady." He took her outstretched hand, and for a second she thought he might kiss it. But he only bowed over it as he gave it a slow, intimate squeeze.

Her heart fluttered. "You're driving me stark staring mad," she murmured to him as they were both turning away. It halted him in midturn. She kept going and walked away from him without looking back. As she went, she imagined him standing in the street, staring after her. Going a little mad too, she hoped.

XIX

Come, ye sad and fearful-hearted,
With glad smile and radiant brow:
Lent's long shadows have departed;
All his woes are over now.

CHRISTY WAS DOING his best to look priestly, or at least serious and thoughtful, while the men's choir sang the hymn before the Gospel; at all costs, he had to hold in the wide, moronic grin that kept trying to take over his face. Joy was a commendable emotion at Eastertide, but laughing out loud at the Sunday morning service would be decidedly *de trop,* as Anne would say, especially in the celebrant.

It would help if he could stop looking at her, but he couldn't. She looked more than beautiful, she looked . . . *angelic* in her Easter gown of rich midnight-blue. Today was the first day she'd been out of mourning in public for five months. Tongues would wag, but neither of them had it in them to care much anymore.

That she, not spiritual appreciation of the risen Christ, was the source of his euphoria made him feel guilty, but not excessively so. Today it was easier to believe God was rejoicing with him because the long Lenten abstinence was over. Forty days and forty very long nights. There had been times when he was sure it would've been less difficult to give up food than Anne; maybe water, too. But he'd persevered. Now it was over, and tonight they would come out of hiding and announce their engagement. Alleluia, indeed.

The last strains of the hymn died away; the choir members resumed their seats in the stalls. Christy read the Gospel from the chancel, and the congregation sat down. He had a simple sermon prepared for this Easter morning. He mounted the pulpit steps without trepidation or anxiety. The church was the Body of Christ, and the faces looking back at him from the nave of All Saints were his best friends; his heart felt swollen with love for every one of them. Without notes, he began to speak.

Anne listened with breathless attention. She'd heard him preach numberless times by now, on procrastination, pride, loneliness, parental neglect, forgiveness, the universality of suffering—but she had never heard him preach like this. He'd taken his text from Ezekiel, the passage about the valley of dry bones. His message was the usual one for Easter—joy in Christ's Resurrection and hope for life eternal. But he'd hardly begun before she knew she was listening to something out of the ordinary.

She sensed a new attentiveness in the audience, too; everyone sat up straighter, and it seemed as if even the babies stopped squirming. Christy's vestments were white—for joy. He began with simple word-pictures, homely parables to illustrate his theme. He kept his gestures subdued, sometimes leaning forward, sometimes straightening suddenly to his full height, as if upraised by the power of his thoughts. His voice was low, clear, penetrating; it seldom rose, and when it did, it wasn't from loudness as much as feeling. Even so, his words stirred her because of what seemed a deliberate *repression* of emotion, all the more powerful for his obvious restraint. Everything came together; everything meshed. She was witnessing the conjunction of eloquence with deep moral earnestness, and she was profoundly moved.

I could pray, she thought when it was over. *I actually feel like praying.* She wanted God the way Christy had him, personally, like a soul's mate, its other half. And when most of the congregation stood up and went to the altar to receive Holy Communion, she wanted to go with them. *I'm jealous,* she thought, in awe and wonder. *Oh, Christy, wait till I tell you.*

He liked to greet his congregation after Sunday services in his plain black clothes, not his vestments. Every week she watched him say the last blessing and then exit stage left, so to speak, into the sacristy—only to appear on the church steps seconds later, it seemed, vestment-less and not even breathing hard. It was either magic or impressive sprinting skills, and it was amusing to imagine the children starting rumors of miracles and transformations, tales that would intensify over the years and become full-blown, self-sustaining myths.

Today was no different: there he was, waiting for her—Lady D'Aubrey, due to her exalted station, was always first to file out of church—and they shook hands with even more decorousness than usual, both enjoying the last few hours of pretend-formality because it was so close to being over forever. Oh, but she wanted to kiss him! Not allowed. Wouldn't be, not even after they were married, not on the church steps, for heaven's sake. But she was a woman deprived; she wanted her man. Forty days and forty—nights; an unladylike expletive came to mind, and the wickedness of it made her smile at Christy in a way that had his ears turning pink. *Oh, I love you!* she told him with her eyes, then let go of his hand to move discreetly aside so others could speak to him.

She waited on the first landing—in a few minutes they were going to walk together to Mayor Vanstone's luncheon party—watching him covertly while she exchanged Easter greetings with her neighbors and friends. She was especially pleasant to Margaret Mareton, whom she quite liked now that the Sunday school teacher was completely out of the running for the minister's hand. Thomas Nineways annoyed her more than usual, because she knew he was a thorn in Christy's side; but his wife, quiet and unassuming, with a wit so dry it could blow away in a stiff breeze, intrigued her as a possible friend. She was surprised to see William Holyoake walk away with one of the Swan sisters on his arm—Cora or Chloe; she could never keep them straight. She'd never thought of Holyoake as anything but the bachelor bailiff of Lynton Hall Farm, a man with no life outside his work, who might even find the company of young ladies somewhat tedious. Which showed what she knew. Still—sturdy old William and a *Swan sister?*

It was a perfect day, with storybook clouds in a blinding blue sky, birds singing, tree buds sprouting. The village green had never been greener, and the children just let out of church were already sporting on it, giddy as mad hares. Anne watched them over Mrs. Thoroughgood's stooped shoulder, exchanging small talk with the old lady while a bewitching fantasy teased at the corners of her mind—of her own child, hers and Christy's, playing on the green while they watched fondly from a window in the vicarage.

A coach moving slowly up the High Street caught her eye; it was coming from the direction of the Hall, and from this distance it looked like the ancient D'Aubrey barouche. Since that couldn't be, she kept her eye on the steadily moving vehicle, and stopped hearing what Mrs. Thoroughgood was saying to her when she recognized first the two chestnut hackneys pulling the coach and then the driver—Collie Horrocks, her own groomsman. How extraordinary. She hadn't ordered the carriage, and yet here it was, stopping in the road at the very base of the church steps. Mrs. Fruit must've misheard her when she said . . . when she'd . . ..

The carriage's freshly painted green door was thrown open from the inside and a pale hand came out to turn down the step. *It's a dream,* thought Anne, watching the long, tan-trousered legs swing out over the threshold. Geoffrey held on to the door when he jumped down to the ground and kept one hand on the handle, swaying a little while he scanned the crowded church steps.

Her vision dimmed. She turned jerkily, looking for Christy, and found him as if at the end of a long telescope, paper-white and staring. Around her, she heard gasps and broken-off exclamations. Geoffrey saw her. He had on a stovepipe hat. He snatched it off with a mocking flourish and made a short, shaky bow. His grin was ghastly. He threw his arms out at his sides, Christ-like, and croaked into the horrified silence, "He is risen!"

Captain Carnock saw her stagger, and caught her before she fell. His kind, worried face looming above her was the last thing she saw.

"Did I ever tell you, darling, about the time my father locked me in this cupboard?"

From across the room, Anne watched her husband drum his heels against the door to the low side cabinet on which he was sitting. She didn't answer. She was trying to hold on to a delusion that if she didn't speak to him, she could keep him from being real.

"I don't remember how old I was; small, though, to fit in here, eh?" He gave the wood a hard smack with his boot. "Guess what my childish crime was. Come, darling, guess. You won't play? Very well, I'll tell you. I was *impudent*. Yes! Can you conceive of it? Lost to memory is the precise form my impudence took on that occasion—a facial expression, a certain tone of voice, perhaps. But I do recall the cupboard. Oh, yes, my recollection of that is quite, quite unclouded."

Anne swallowed a sip of brandy and tried not to shudder. Odd—she was drinking, but Geoffrey wasn't. Water; he was drinking water, glass after glass, as if he were parched, but so far no alcohol. Odd.

He got up and went toward the table in the middle of the drawing room; on the way he stumbled and almost lost his balance. "More for you, darling?" he asked while he poured another glass of water from the silver pitcher.

She stared at him in veiled horror. He'd gained weight, at least thirty pounds; his corpulent body looked sluggish and unco-ordinated. His hair, once dark and sleek, had turned motley shades of gray, and grew out of his dry scalp in random patches.

When she didn't speak, he toasted her with his glass and drank down the contents in a few noisy gulps. He was out of breath when he finished, and it took him a moment before he was able to say without panting, "Well, my love, did you miss me while I was gone?"

She passed her hand over her eyes, steeling herself for speech. "What happened to you, Geoffrey? Where have you been?"

"Which didn't, he noted, quite answer the question," he said with a facetious twist of his lips. "What happened? Why, you'll hardly credit it, but I lost my memory. Amnesia, they call it. From the Greek, you know, for 'forgetfulness.' I've been in an army hos-pital in Hampshire for the last four months."

"I don't believe you."

He shrugged. "Nevertheless, it's—it's true." He leaned heavily against the table; sweat beaded suddenly on his forehead and under his nose.

"Are you sick?" she asked sharply.

"No, no." But he went to the sofa and sank down on it heavily. "It's nothing. Just the excitement of coming home to the arms of my loving wife."

She couldn't look at him anymore. His body, his voice, his face, everything about him repelled her; she felt nauseated by his very presence. "Do you want anything?" she forced herself to ask. He looked at her strangely. "I'll ring for the maid if you want something to eat."

"No, I don't want anything to eat. Tell me, darling, how have you been? Tell me every little thing you've been doing."

She felt like a thin sheet of glass. She wanted to scream and scream, scream the house down. But she was listless, too; bone-weary. She couldn't summon the energy to get up and walk out of the room. Maybe they would both die here, entombed in the drawing room, done in by their own inertia.

"How's Devil? Tell me that, at least."

She blinked at him, as if he'd spoken in a foreign language. Far away, she heard a knock, then footsteps, voices. Violet stuck her sharp little face in the doorway, her nose twitching, avid for news. "Reverend Morrell's here," she announced.

Geoffrey tottered to his feet. "Christy," he said with real pleasure, and hobbled to meet him in the center of the room. "My God, look at you."

Christy's blue eyes skittered over her for only an instant, long enough to make her heart contract. He looked ill. Speechless, he shook Geoffrey's hand, trying so hard to smile.

If she stayed, she would break down. Her voice was a too-high trill. "Will you excuse me?" She got up from her chair stiffly, like an old lady. When she tried to say more, her throat closed. She looked at Christy helplessly. He couldn't speak to her either, she saw. With her head down, she got out of the room.

"Well, well, sit down! Have a drink? Or tea, I'll ring for it if you want."

"No, nothing. I can't stay, I just . . ." He trailed off, hardly knowing what he was saying. He kept seeing Anne's ruined face, and he couldn't string two sentences together. Why had he come here? To see her, of course. Now she was gone, and he must pretend he'd come to see Geoffrey.

"How are you?" he finally managed to say, sitting down in the chair she'd just left. Geoffrey looked ghastly, worse than ever before.

"I've been a little unwell." He giggled—a terrible sound—as if conscious of the understatement; then his puffy, paste-colored face sobered. He poured out a glass of water from a pitcher on the table and carried it to the couch. "The old curse flared up again while I was out in the Crimea. Malaria, you know. Gave me a run for it this time."

What if Christy told him he knew about the syphilis? Geoffrey might welcome that, be relieved to have it out in the open. But he couldn't speak.

"Place looks different," Geoffrey said, gesturing at the room with his glass. "Can't say how exactly. Anne's done well, better without me, I daresay. Thanks for looking after her, by the way. Mean it. Good show."

Unable to acknowledge that, Christy said, "Has she told you about tenants from the Hall helping to cultivate the glebe lands this spring?"

"What?" He rubbed the heel of his hand against his eye socket. "Yes, something in a letter, I think. Lifetime ago. I'd forgotten."

"We'll talk about it later."

"Later, right-ho. How's Devil?"

Christy couldn't make sense of the question. He stared uneasily, his heart pounding.

"My horse!"

"Oh, Devil, yes—I—I've been calling him Tandem."

"The bloody hell you say. Do you ride him?"

"Yes, yes. Not as often as I've meant to, but between Collie and me we keep him in pretty good trim."

"Good, that's good. He's a cracker, isn't he?"

This was intolerable; the conversation was becoming more absurd by the second. He felt full of a sick, baffled rage. "What happened to you?" he blurted out. "We thought you were dead."

"Yes, sorry about that. A misunderstanding." When he smiled, Christy saw that his gums were a livid purple. The hand holding the water glass wobbled; he had to steady it with the other, and finally he set the glass down on the floor at his feet. "Listen, Christy," he said in a rush, and the mockery in his voice was suddenly completely gone. "Do you know what happened at Inkerman?"

"Inkerman? Yes—"

"I mean, do you know what it was *like*? No, of course you couldn't. It doesn't matter what you've heard or what you've read in the newspapers, you couldn't know what the fighting was like there, the unbelievable—the brutality of it, the beastliness. It was hand-to-hand combat at the end, and it wasn't a battlefield, it was an abattoir." His body was bowed in half, leaning forward, his eyes bright black with intensity.

"You were wounded, we heard."

"Shoulder and thigh, both from the same Russian bayonet. Before he could kill me, my corporal cut his head off." Again the chilling, high-pitched giggle. "That wasn't—that wasn't—that wasn't what did it. Something happened to me. I was afraid. First time. But—not normal fear, the kind any soldier feels in the heat of battle." He wiped his hand across the sweat on his forehead and tried to slow his words. "I mean paralysis. Not being able to move or speak. *Paralysis*. Do you understand?"

"Because you were ill, your disease. You were—"

"No, not because of that! That came later. This was different. After I was wounded, I knew I couldn't go back, couldn't fight again. *I could not*. And they'd have sent me back, no question of it. My wounds weren't serious enough to get me invalided out for good."

"The letter from the War Office said you were on a hospital ship in the harbor when the storm struck."

He nodded quickly, over and over. "Shut the door, would you?"

Surprised, Christy got up and closed the door to the drawing room.

"No one knows this, not even Anne. It's a secret." Geoffrey told the rest in a fast, eerie whisper. "My ship went down in the storm, but somehow I made it to shore. I was naked—I took the clothes off one of the corpses on the beach. That's when it hit me that nobody knew who I was! See? So I let myself be found, babbling like an infant, claiming I'd lost my memory. Everything was in chaos, you can't believe what it was like. No one knew me—what was left of my regiment was on the other side of the peninsula. So there I was, wounded and incoherent, possibly insane. Five days later they shipped me home."

"Home?"

"To Portsmouth. I've been in an army medical barracks in Fareham since December."

Christy tried to absorb it. "But why? Why didn't you tell them who you were? Why didn't you come *here*?"

He slumped in his chair, as if telling the story had exhausted him. "Why?" he said irritably. "I've just told you why, weren't you listening? Isn't that your bloody *job*?" He looked down at his left hand, which was clenched in his lap like a claw. "Little bit of stiffness," he muttered, catching Christy's eye. "From the . . . from the wound. Say, you wouldn't tell any of that to Anne, would you? All I said was that I'd lost my memory. She didn't believe it, but she can't prove otherwise." His attempt at a playful smile crumpled. "I don't want her to know the truth. You won't tell her, will you, Christy?"

It took him a few seconds to be able to say, "No, I won't tell her."

"Ah, I knew you wouldn't."

Beyond the window, the setting sun was shining in Christy's eyes. "Why did you leave Fareham?"

Geoffrey hesitated. "Actually, they asked me to leave." He looked away. "They found out about me having malaria, you know, and told me to clear out. They think it's catching, the bloody sods. Gave me ten pounds and a suit of clothes and wished me the best of luck." His laugh was hideously artificial. "It was like—like leaving the Bodmin gaol after a period of penal servitude. But it was time to go. I needed . . . I needed . . .." He looked lost. "I needed to see my wife. My friends. Friend," he amended, with a terrible wistfulness.

"What will you tell the military authorities? They still think you're dead." It seemed that all Christy could do was ask questions.

Geoffrey began to squeeze his left hand with his right. "I'll tell them my memory was miraculously restored after I left hospital. Ha, ha! Like my wife, they probably won't believe it, but do you know, I'm a wee bit past caring."

Christy found himself on his feet, hearing himself saying, "I must go. I'll come again, but I have to go now. Call on me any-time, if I can—if you need anything from me—" He broke off stupidly. What could Geoffrey need from him? What could he give?

Geoffrey was looking at him strangely. "Go, then," he said, an-gry again. He patted the sofa cushion next to him. "I'm going to lie down, I think, have a little nap before dinner."

Christy stopped at the door. "Shall I stop by Dr. Hesselius's house on my way home? Ask him to come and have a look at you?"

"God, no. No more doctors. I've got my little pills." He patted his waistcoat pocket. "I'm just tired, that's all. It's been a moving and emotional day for me. Odysseus back from his travels, don't you know." He uncovered his teeth again in another travesty of a grin. "The analogy breaks down, though, since my wife as Pe-nelope leaves a certain something to be desired, don't you agree?"

Christy went out without answering.

Geoffrey's memorial marker was as far away from his father's tombstone as the small confines of the family burial ground allowed. Last November, Anne had thought he'd have wanted it that way.

D'AUBREY
Geoffrey Edward Verlaine, 6th Viscount
B. 12 Mar. 1823   D. 5 Nov. 1854
At rest now.

At rest now. Not exactly. How he would relish the macabre irony of this stone when he saw it. She hoped she was nowhere around when that happened; most of Geoffrey's humors depressed her, but his bitter, sardonic one laid her the lowest.

Come to me, Christy, she prayed with her eyes closed, but when she opened them he wasn't on the gravel path, or coming over the crest of the hill from the house. The sun going down behind the dark trees looked cold and indifferent in the whitish sky; she shivered, and pulled her shawl tighter around her shoulders. *Please come, Christy.* She sank into a lifeless revery.

It grew colder, darker, but she didn't stir. There was still a chance. The crunch of stones made her lift her head. She put her hands to her cheeks and rose from the chilly stone bench, feeling hope surge inside. He came toward her, through the gate she'd left open for him. But he stopped on the far side of Geoffrey's marker and came no closer.

She felt the warm, welcoming blood drain from her face. She held out her hands, whispering, "Can't you touch me?" He didn't answer; his beautiful eyes were dark with misery. "My God, Christy—can't you even touch me?"

"Anne."

In that one word, she thought she heard pity. She turned her back on him, covering her eyes. After everything, this was the worst. Christy's hands, suddenly holding her shoulders, were no comfort. She shrugged away, hugging herself. She hadn't wept before. Now hot, stinging tears clogged in her throat, her chest—everywhere but her eyes, which were quite dry.

"Don't, Anne," he begged, touching her again. "For God's sake."

Her head shot up; she whirled on him. "For *God's sake*? Don't talk to me about your God, Christy. This is his punishment on us, isn't it?"

"No, I don't believe that."

"I do! I loathe your God. Hateful, cruel, vengeful—"

"No." He had her by the arms, trying to hold her still. "Anne, listen to me."

"We sinned, Christy, and this is his retribution. Because we loved each other!"

"Stop it, you know it isn't true."

"Prove it, then. Kiss me." She grabbed at him, past caring about the anguish in his eyes or what it might cost him to touch her now. "Damn it, damn it," she muttered, incoherent, frenzied, shaking him in her anger and frustration. His cold mouth came down, silencing her. She pressed closer, holding his head. Now the tears were blinding her. She pushed her tongue between his teeth, sharing the taste of salt, frantic to arouse him. She found his hand and pressed it to her breast, hard. His breathing grew harsh and ragged, but he stood still, not flinching, enduring it for her sake. She fumbled her own hand between them and touched him through his trousers; he came alive in her palm, and she knew a grievous victory. "Take me," she commanded in a hoarse whisper; she was trembling so hard she could barely stand. "Take me on top of his bloody grave!"

He would have. She could see it in his eyes, feel it in the desperate clutch of his hands on her body. Even if it meant the destruction of his own soul, he was going to do it, give her what she thought she needed.

She pushed him away while she still could, holding him off, stiff-armed, shaking her head over and over. The suffering in his face cut like a dull knife. "Go away, Christy," she ground out, empty and exhausted again. "You're a terrible failure as a sinner, aren't you? There's probably a special place in hell for your kind. The petty, no-account sinners, hardly worth God's attention."

290

He shut his eyes tight. "I love you," he said.

A sob in her throat almost strangled her. "What good does it do? There was never any hope for us, it was always a dream, a joke. I wish I'd fallen in love with someone else, not you. An ordinary man, who would run away with me now so we could be happy." She whispered, "But you won't, will you?"

"No," he said, hollow-voiced. "And you wouldn't either."

"If you think that, then you don't know me at all!" At that moment she believed it. "Oh, God, Christy, leave me alone. I can't look at you anymore." He held her gaze for one more excruciating minute. Then she was reduced to begging. "Please go. *Please.*" He started to speak. "Don't tell me again that you love me! I can't—I can't—" She spun around, fists clenched in the air in front of her face. When she turned back, he was gone.

XX

Dearest Anne,

By now I should know what to say to you. After two days, I should have precise thoughts to convey, orderly sentiments, a plan. It can't be that I haven't pondered the situation deeply enough. No, I assure you it can't be that. And picture this, Anne: the very Reverend Christian Morrell, swilling port wine all alone at his desk, until he passes out cold on top of an old sermon. Perfect, isn't it? How you'd have laughed at me last night for my one ludicrous attempt at debauchery. I'm a little drunk now, to tell you the truth. Mrs. Ludd is quite beside herself. I've had to lock the door so she can't keep fluttering in and gibbering at me. But it's wearing off, I can feel it. No matter; it wasn't a very effective anesthetic anyway.

One thing that's come to me clearly—relative to anything else, I mean—is the unlikelihood of my remaining in the ministry. I don't see how I can keep on with it. I can't picture it, cannot imagine myself continuing in the role. "Role" is a revealing word here, isn't it? I used to dream quite often that I wasn't a real priest but an imposter, and that I'd been found out. And now it's come true. It seems to have come true. But I don't know for certain. I don't really know anything at all.

Except that I must stop rambling. You can see how my

wretched sermons got out of hand, can't you? Only with them, I couldn't even blame it on an excess of drink.

Anne, I keep seeing you, your face and your bitter tears, the way you couldn't even look at me. There's so much pain in me now, but I swear I would take yours too if I could. I swear it. But I can't do anything for you. None of my numberless other failures weighs on me as heavily as this one. This is the one that's driven me to drink. And despair.

God is punishing us, you said. I don't want to believe that, but I wonder if you're right. It feels true. The evidence points to it. You said there was never any hope for us, it was always a dream. If it was, it was a pure, blameless dream from the start. A God who would punish lovers—punish you, Anne, for the generosity of your heart—my spirit recoils from that God. He's too hard to love, and I've failed at it. I can't serve him.

But what am I if I'm not a priest? Believe it or not, even now I find myself praying. I break off in anger—but then there's truly nothing, no alternative to sustain me. You're stronger than I am. You've never claimed to have faith, and yet you lead a "Christian" life in every way that matters. For me, nothing makes sense anymore, none of the verities and absolutes I used to believe in help me. I've lost my way. And when I think of the pieties I once would have offered as consolation to anyone suffering the same desolation I feel, I want to smash things with my fists and shout blasphemies in God's face.

I've been thinking about my father, and how his faith never deserted him even when he lost everything—his wife, his health, finally the work he loved. He was deeply spiritual, the gentlest man I've ever known. I wanted to be like him, Anne. I'm in despair when I measure how far

I've fallen from that goal. I can't help anyone, I'm as hollow as an empty box inside. I would stay here, I swear I would stay if I thought I could help you in any way, be any kind of legitimate friend to you. But I'm afraid I'd hurt you more. God knows there's nothing I can do for Geoffrey. And I don't believe I can go on for long pretending I don't love you. Anne, it's best if I go. If you don't agree now, only think of how it was between us when we were together last. Remember that pain. And now I'll risk your scorn and recommend Reverend Woodworth to you if a time should come when you need—don't laugh, my darling—guidance of a spiritual nature. He's a good man, and he has the advantage of me now: he believes in his own counsel.

I'm afraid Geoffrey is very ill. He's unstable as well, emotionally chaotic, and yet I don't really think he's a danger to anyone—you, I mean. If I thought otherwise, nothing could make me leave you. But if anything should happen, if you ever need advice, help, even sanctuary, Robert Polwin is not only a friend I trust but also a man of judgment, means, and discretion. I've spoken of him before—he's the rector of St. Stephen's church in Tavistock; I'll add a note with his address at the end of this letter. Please, Anne, do not hesitate to call on him for anything, if ever the need should arise.

Two days ago you didn't want to hear that I love you. You must read it now. It's the last time I'll be able to tell you. I wish I could see you, hear your voice, hold you close. I don't regret anything we did. I'll always love you, always believe you were my salvation. If I could think of a way for us—

But I can't, not an honorable one. And despite what you said, I know you wouldn't choose any other, not in the end. So we're both cursed, equally. Again. My dearest love, once I'd have said I'll pray for you. Now I can only say I'll never forget you. Or stop loving you.

Christy

TIME TO LIGHT a candle. She couldn't remember what she'd just written in her journal, and the room had grown too dim to read the words. Was it that late? No, now she remembered—it was raining. Everything was a cold shade of gray. Inside and out, no color, and no sound but the dripping gutters and the wind. She was startled by the sound of the match striking, blinded a little by the dazzle of the flame. She blew the match out and set it in the base of the candleholder, moving the candle closer to her journal.

It seems incredible now; my stupidity embarrasses me, it was so complete. I honestly thought I was free, and that I had been allowed to have some happiness. I'm choked with chagrin at my arrogance. Christy Morrell was off-bounds to me from the beginning, but I defied the laws of God, man, nature, who knows what, and took him for my own. I'm suffering for my dangerous, God-insulting presumption. I must be made to pay.

She took a swallow of sherry and tried to remember if this was her second or her third glass. "Third, if you can't remember." The gruff, barely recognizable sound of her own voice jolted her. Shuddering, she set the glass down and pushed it to the edge of the table, out of reach. She took up her pen again.

If only I could leave Geoffrey. But I can't. He's sick, and I'm cursed with a conscience, surely the cruelest "gift" God ever distributed in his fun-loving omniscience. Oh, thank you, Lord; how can I repay you? With my life? Will that satisfy you? No? Too bad, and to hell with you. I despise your gifts, your ubiquitousness and your omnipotence, all that nonsensical claptrap I came so close to swallowing. So close! Oh, poor Christy—to think I envied him his faith! I wonder if he'll realize it before I have a chance to tell him—that God is a very sad, very distasteful joke on us all.

She looked up, arrested by a sound—footsteps on the stairs. Susan again, on another of her mercy calls. *Can't I get anything for you, m'lady? Sure you don't need yer shawl? What about a nice hot cup o' tea?* Anne couldn't even make herself smile anymore.

But no—the tread was light, but it wasn't Susan's; too slow. Violet's? She closed her journal, using her pen to mark her place. Before his head bobbed above the top stair, she knew it was Geoffrey.

He'd come here only one other time. The memory of that violent encounter had her pushing her chair back and getting to her feet. The room spun once before it steadied. Too much sherry, she chided herself; too little food. The candle on her little writing table wavered in the rippling air currents her movements made, and Geoffrey made when he came in the room. He had a piece of paper in his hand. An envelope?

In three days, she hadn't gotten used to his physical appearance. She'd seen him ill before, once she'd even thought he was dying, but she'd never seen him like this. The stairs had winded him. He leaned in the threshold of the doorway and leveled his flat black stare on her while he caught his breath. She found she couldn't speak to him. Couldn't say anything.

"What are you doing? Hm? Writing a letter?"

She shook her head. "Nothing. I'm not . . ." It was so hard to talk. "I was just sitting here. I'm not doing anything."

He moved closer to the candle. His face looked like a skull.

"Look what I've got." He waggled his envelope at her. "Don't you want to see it? It's a letter."

"What is it?"

"A letter, I said. It's to you. Want it?"

She was afraid to look at the white square in his hand. His face was ghastly, but she kept her eyes on it. Something was happening. Something awful was unraveling.

He threw the envelope on the table in front of her. *"Take it."* His voice, suddenly violent, made her jump. "Come, you'll want to read it. I know I did. When I realized who it was from, I couldn't wait."

Her skin froze; her blood felt like icy slush in her veins. She stared down at her own name in Christy's straightforward handwriting, honest and undisguised, and the heartbreakingly trusting "Personal" he'd scrawled in the corner.

"Open it!"

Geoffrey had already opened it; the plain red seal was broken, the angular flap gaping loosely. Her body felt numb, but her hands were shaking badly as she pulled two sheets of Christy's cream-colored vellum out of the envelope. The words swam; her eyes skimmed the pages wildly. "Dearest Anne"—"the unlikelihood of my remaining in the ministry"—"your face and your bitter tears"—"I want to smash things with my fists and shout blasphemies in God's face"—"I'll always love you, always believe you were my"—

Geoffrey grabbed the letter out of her hands. She screamed when he began to tear and rip at it, shredding it to pieces. He stamped on the jagged scraps fluttering to the floor. His face turned a vivid scarlet. She slipped into the old fear of him, began to back away toward the window. Spewing curses, he came at her.

If she hadn't been so frightened, if he hadn't been so angry, she might have fought him off, because he was weak, ill, uncoordinated. She saw the hand he raised to hit her in time to dodge or turn away—but he struck her in the face with all his strength, and the force of it slammed her head against the wall. Her legs buckled. She slumped to the floor, and prayed it was over.

It wasn't. On his knees beside her, he muttered, "Bitch, oh, you rutting bitch," and shook his fists at her. She threw her hands up for a shield, but he batted them aside and grabbed at handfuls of her dress, pulling her down, away from the wall, until he had her flat on her back. His teeth were bared; the fetid smell of his breath brought her close to retching. His hurtful fingers pulled and shoved at her clothes until he had her breasts bared, and then he sprawled on top of her, kicking her legs apart with his knees. "I'll make you like me," he panted, trying to kiss her. "You'll be just like me. Anne, Anne, Anne." He brought his open mouth to her throat and bit down while he struggled with her skirts, yanking at the cloth and hauling it over her knees. He had her arms pinned between them. She freed one and pulled his head back by the hair. Tears were spilling down his cheeks. He stopped cursing her. She heard him say, "I'll make you love me," while he mashed her breasts with his hands.

The fight went out of her. He was fumbling at the front of his trousers. Her legs trembled, but she let him press her thighs apart. He wasn't hard yet; he had to use his own hand to get his erection. When he pushed into her, they both cried out, a harrowing sound she knew she would never forget. "Sorry, I'm sorry," he rasped, with his face buried in her hair. "Oh, God, I'm so cold."

She put her hands on his shuddering shoulders and held him. He was weeping, hardly able to get his breath. He couldn't climax; his painful thrusts quickened, but he began to pound the floor with his fist, vicious blows full of pain and rage. His full weight was suffocating her. "Stop, Geoffrey. Stop it now." She took his face between her hands and lifted his head. The dark, unimaginable suffering in his eyes defeated her. They rolled to their sides together, and she held him while he sobbed against her breast.

When he calmed, the rain beating against the window became the only sound in the dark room. *I ought to feel more,* thought Anne. *More than this coldness.* At least Christy's God would be satisfied now, for she'd gotten what she deserved. After all the years of coldness and rejection, Geoffrey's disease and his defilement were to be her punishment. Her just deserts. Everything was gone now, her last hope finished. Then why couldn't she feel anything?

Geoffrey had begun to shudder uncontrollably. He pulled her to a sitting position and began trying to fasten her dress and brush her skirts down over her legs. She held still, waiting, numbed into a weird state of bemusement, while he pulled her wild hair back from her face with his shaking fingers, gentle now, almost loving. He moaned when he got to his feet. Her shawl lay across the table; he brought it back, with the sherry decanter and her half-finished glass, and tucked it carefully around her shoulders. He offered her the sherry next. She was close to vomiting; she shook her head. He drank it himself, and another glass after that.

"You can't get it, you know."

She stared at him blankly. His cheeks were a hectic pink; he was holding the glass in both hands to steady it. "What?"

"You can't get the pox from me." His chattering teeth clacked together like bones. "I'm not contagious any longer, I've gone— I've gone—beyond that stage." He must have seen skepticism in her face. "It's true. I swear it. If you don't believe me, ask the army doctor who threw me out of Fareham."

She sank against the wall behind her, waiting to feel relief, but she didn't feel anything. The peculiar numbness wouldn't go away.

Geoffrey set the glass on the floor and reached for one of her hands. His shook so hard, she covered it with her other one and squeezed it tight. He smiled at that, looking down at their clasped hands. "So. Do you love Christy? Do you? You can tell me."

She whispered, "I love him. I'm sorry. We thought you were dead."

He took a long, slow breath. With nothing but gentleness in his voice, he said, "I am dying. The doctor said a year or two, but it's going to be less. It's going to be considerably less."

She whispered, "Oh, God," exactly like a prayer. Oh, hopeless, hopeless.

He bent his head and put a soft kiss on the back of her left hand, then her right. He laid his cheek against her palm. She reached up to stroke his hair, but he sat back before she could touch him and staggered to his feet, stifling another groan.

"Don't go."

He turned in the doorway. They looked at each other in astonishment, as if neither could credit what she'd said. Geoffrey put his hand over his heart and made her a short, unsteady bow. "I thank you for that, darling," he said in a parody of his old voice, the ironic one. "Do you know, that's going to make it ever so much easier."

After he was gone, she shut her eyes and listened to the rain. The strange detachment persisted; she floated in it for a time, thankful for the painless, neutral hum in her head. Her body ached, but even that was filtered through some kind of stuffing around her, an extra layer of skin, keeping her at a safe, kindly distance from the too-real.

It didn't last. *Do you know,* he'd said, *that's going to make it ever so much easier,* and finally the import of that began to penetrate the friendly fog. *Ever so much easier. That's going to make it.*

Make it easier.

Oh, dear Jesus.

She got up too fast; she had to hang on to the window ledge while the vertigo subsided. Holding her head, her fingers found the tender swelling in back, where she'd hit the wall. Not serious, just a bump, but she needed the table's support to cross the room, and the banister's to get down the narrow servants' stairs to the second floor.

He wasn't in his room. She met Violet on the first floor landing. "Where is he?" she demanded. The maid looked at her stupidly. "My husband, where is he? Have you seen him?"

"I saw 'im go out. Had his guns, 'e were goin' huntin'."

"Hunting!"

"Now that *is* peculiar, in't it, this rain an' all—"

With an oath, Anne pushed past her and took the steps at a run. In the front hall, she called back, "Which way did he go? *Which door?*" and Violet pointed, wide-eyed, to the formal, seldom-used front door at Anne's back.

The rain had slowed to a drizzle. The river flew past in a torrent under the stone arch of the bridge, the rush of the water drowning out every other sound. Geoffrey was nowhere. She called his name, but only once; the roaring Wyck made her voice useless as a whisper. Snatching up her skirts, she made a run for the stables.

She saw Collie Horrocks through the misty rain, crossing the stable yard toward her, huddled under his mackintosh. When he saw her, his pudgy face registered surprise. He had his hand on the dripping brim of his hat when the boom of a gunshot made him leap into the air. Anne didn't scream. Collie whirled around, staring at the black, gaping doorway to the stables. She reached him before he could move. "Get William! Go and get him!" she shouted in his face. Too stunned to speak, the groom spun away and bolted toward the house.

A lamp was burning at the far end of the passage that ran the length of the stables. Deep dread made her heart pound, her skin go clammy-cold with fear, but she put one foot before the other and forced herself to walk past all the stalls to the last one—Devil's. As she neared it, a shadowy form rose from the straw-covered floor. Stark terror froze the scream in her throat.

Geoffrey jolted when he saw her. He threw his rifle down and pulled a pistol from his belt. Behind him, the black stallion lay on its sleek side, not breathing, a bloody hole through its temple.

Shock and relief made her light-headed. "Dear God. Geoffrey, what have you done?" She stumbled toward him, reaching out for the wooden gate that separated them.

"Don't come any closer." He lifted the pistol and pointed it in her face.

She gasped. "What—what—"

"Turn around and walk out, Anne."

"No. Why? What are you going to do?" But she knew. She pulled the gate back, but halted when she heard the deadly click of the hammer.

"If you try to stop me, I'll have to shoot you too," he said, and she believed him. His voice sounded calm, but his eyes were black and crazed. "Turn around."

"Geoffrey, don't, this isn't the answer, please, please don't."

"It's the perfect answer. I won't rot away like a corpse, one bloody piece at a time. This is quick and clean, a soldier's death." His hand on the gun wavered; he started to cry. "Turn around."

"God! Geoffrey! I'm begging you!"

He wiped his cheek with his sleeve. "Tell Christy good-bye for me. He's a good man. You'll make each other happy."

"Listen to me—I won't leave you, I swear I won't leave and I'll take care of you, it'll be all right—"

"If you don't get out, you'll have to watch."

"Geoffrey!" He turned the barrel of the gun around. She screamed. She saw him open his mouth wide before she squeezed her eyes shut and covered her head with her arms. The sound of the shot deafened her, as if it had gone off in her own head. She was on her knees on the hard floor and someone was brushing by her. Through half-closed eyes and the barrier of her crossed arms, she caught dark, dreadful, unconnected images of bloody flesh and bone, before William Holyoake's body cut off the grisly view. She bent over, gagging, and pressed her forehead to the ground.

She must have fainted. Rain on her face revived her; she found herself outside, under the sloping roof of the well, half-lying against the cold bricks. The bailiff's strong arm was around her shoulders. She turned her face into the wet wool of his coat and cried.

"Did he hurt you a'tall, m'lady?" She shook her head but didn't look up. "I've sent the lad for surgeon, but I'm afraid 'is lordship's dead." She tightened her grip on his sleeve, burrowed deeper into his coat. As long as she could block the dreadful image of Geoffrey's face from her mind, she could control the nausea. William gave her his clean, neatly folded handkerchief, and she buried her nose in it; the everyday smell of soap and sunshine helped to steady her a little. He kept patting her back, a soft, consoling pressure. "I'll go an' get Reverend Morrell myself, shall I?"

She looked up at that. Something in his voice arrested her. She searched his plain, honest face for a sign that he knew.

"Shall I go for Vicar, m'lady?" he repeated.

"No." Her head fell back against the damp brick of the well. "There's nothing for him to do here, William," she murmured, so tired all of a sudden, it was an effort to move her lips. Later she might feel differently, but for now Geoffrey's death was a catastrophe, not a liberation.

For the first time, she noticed Collie Horrocks standing behind Holyoake's shoulder; Susan and Violet stood next to him, huddling in the drizzle, their faces stiff with shock. And here came Mrs. Fruit, with a shawl over her head and her hands in her apron, crying, "What's happened? What's happened?"

Despair was swallowing her up a little at a time. The thought of moving, the thought of speaking, of making choices, giving explanations—

She couldn't. It was too much. When the bailiff started to

help her to stand, she reached for his wrist and held onto it. "Oh, William, go and get Christy," she begged him, defeated. "Tell him to come right away."

In his study, Christy was filling a box with his belongings. He'd closed the door so Mrs. Ludd couldn't see; he hadn't told her yet that he was leaving, and he didn't feel up to dealing with her reaction to the news, which was bound to be dramatic.

The ecclesiastical living included not only the vicarage but most of the furnishings in it as well, so he wouldn't be taking much with him. He'd decided to leave most of his books for the new incumbent, his sermons as well—for all the good they would do him—and so only *things* were going into the box: pens and paper, a few pictures on the wall, a vase he'd made out of papier-mâché for his mother twenty-five years ago. He was finished in no time, and the scantiness of his collected personal possessions dismayed him. The study had always been the heart of the house to him, his favorite room, a place of endless variety, stimulation, enrichment. The fact that everything in it besides his books and papers fit into a small wooden box came as a rude surprise.

Another instance of his thoughtlessness and complacency, he supposed. For years he'd taken for granted that he would live out his life in this comfortable old house, and that the sparse but well-loved belongings he'd inherited from his parents would pass down to his own children. But that was another unconsidered dream, and he was sick to death of self-discovery.

He was keeping a list for his curate, Reverend Woodworth, adding to it as new thoughts occurred to him. One came to him now. He crossed to his desk and wrote,

5. Miss Sophie Deene would welcome sound, unbiased counsel on mgmt., etc., of Guelder mine. Wd. not ask for it (too proud, too convinced of her own competence—

which, at twenty yrs. old, she may overestimate), but might accept it. Her uncle tries to bully her. To resist him, she sometimes goes too far in opposite direction. My advice— be open to unspoken requests for help.

He read over what he'd written before that.

1. Be alert for trouble in Pendrys family. Go often, despite unenthusiastic welcome. Martin is in a delicate phase; has agreed to stop drinking, but may backslide w/o constant encouragement.

2. Keep careful eye on Mrs. Lloyd. Taking loss of husband deceptively well, but I fear it's a mask and she may sink into despondency. Urge to attend penny readings, etc.

3. Miss Weedie appreciates visits esp. now that her mother is such a trial to her.

4. Nineways will pester you mercilessly re. St. Catherine window. Resist tactfully. "Support" in vestry he brags of is nonexistent, consisting solely of Brakey Pitt.

There were twenty, maybe thirty more things he could write down on Woodworth's list. For an ex-clergyman whose letter of resignation lay on his desk, sealed in an envelope and ready to post, he was doing a rather poor job of making the break. But— should he say something about Anne or Geoffrey, or both of them? He picked up the list—and threw it into his desk drawer, slamming it shut with suppressed violence. It was finished. And he was the last man on earth to advise his curate or anyone else on what to do for the Verlaines.

He wandered to the window. The monotonous patter of the filthy rain on the glass echoed his mood. Anne must have received his letter by now. The need to see her was like a sharp ache inside, as real as a wound that wouldn't heal. Now that he'd resolved not to see her before he went away, his mind was tormented with idiotic daydreams of the future. In one of them, he went to London to try his fortune at being a painter, the only thing he'd ever shown any talent for besides racing horses. He became an artist (of unknown repute; the dream was unspecific on that), and Anne left Geoffrey and followed him to the city. They lived together in a garret, impoverished and wildly happy— or in a Mayfair mansion, wealthy and wildly happy.

It was a childish, embarrassing fantasy, unworthy of him and certainly of her. But, God, how could he just let her go? What would become of them if they lost each other? Yesterday he'd known exactly why betraying the man who had once been his best friend would be a sin, but today the reason eluded him. He told himself it was good that he was leaving soon, before his weakness made him rethink his so-called principles and convinced him that staying would not be the act of monumental dishonesty he knew in his heart it would be.

The clip-clop of a horse's hooves on the cobbles broke in on his black thoughts. He recognized Dr. Hesselius' pony gig through the sooty drizzle, and he sighed when he saw it stop directly in front of the house. The doctor jumped down from the seat and, without tying the horse, raced up the front walk to the door. Christy thought of all the times this had happened before, that he and Hesselius had rushed off together to work on some poor parishioner—the doctor on his body, Christy on his soul.

But he wasn't in that line of work anymore. Souls were no longer safe in his keeping. You'd be a fool to ask a bankrupt for a loan, and you'd be crazy to ask Christy Morrell for spiritual comfort.

Hesselius began to pound at the door. Dragging his feet, Christy unlocked his study door and started down the hall. Mrs. Ludd, coming from the other side of the house, beat him to the door. Hesselius bustled in, dripping rainwater on the rug. "Is he here?" he asked sharply, then spied him in the dim corridor. "Christy, thank God you're at home!"

"What is it?" he asked, fatalistic, but alarmed in spite of himself by the doctor's urgency.

"There's been an accident at Guelder, a cave-in. Miners are trapped. I don't know how many, and one's dead already. You can come with me in the buggy or—"

"I'll ride," he broke in. "It'll be faster."

They spun away from each other and ran, Hesselius for his gig, Christy for the stables and Doncaster.

XXI

GUELDER MINE LAY NORTH of Wyckerley and south of Dartmoor, close by the uppermost reaches of the Plym, into which the mine's mammoth, steam-powered pumps constantly drained water. Darkness was closing in when Christy reined his muddy, sweating horse to a halt beside the only tree on the rubble-strewn hillside, and some of the men gathered in straggly, dejected-looking knots around the mine's outbuildings had begun to light lanterns. From one such group, a miner detached himself and came toward Christy as he crossed the yard, hurrying around the piles of machinery and planks, attle and rock. He recognized Charles Oldene, one of his parishioners, and stopped to wait for him.

"Bad business, Vicar," Charles greeted him—snatching off his sodden felt hat. "Not but what it could be worse, but 'tis bad enough."

"Are men still trapped underground, Charles?"

"No, they come up, and all but one unhurt—Thacker, a man you may not know, for 'e's Methody. It were thought he were dead, but 'e ain't, only burnt from the steam. He's over to the changing shed now wi' the other parson, waiting for surgeon."

The "other parson" was Mr. Snodgress, the Wesleyan preacher from Totnes. Christy said, "Dr. Hesselius was right behind me; he should be here any minute. But what's wrong, Charles? If the men are safe, why does everyone look so stricken?"

"Because there's one left down, Vicar, and 'e's lost."

"Lost? Why?"

Charles hung his head and said haltingly, "He's in a bad place, the whole blinking mine's falling down around 'im. He's alive and can't be got up. We've had to leave 'im."

"My God. Who is it?"

"One o' yours, Reverend. 'Tis Tranter Fox."

Behind the main engine room with its tall, smoking chimneys was a smaller building the miners called the countinghouse. Yellow lamplight spilled from its windows, throwing a weak blur on the darkening mist. Inside, the principal room was empty, but the door to a smaller office behind it was ajar, and through it Christy saw Sophie Deene and three other men in earnest conversation. Sophie's distraught face lightened a little when she saw him; she got up from behind the wide oak desk that had been her father's and came around it to greet him. "I'm glad you've come," she said in a low voice, holding out her hands.

They were ice cold. "I've heard about Tranter," Christy said quietly. "Is there nothing that can be done, Sophie?"

She shook her head. "Nothing, Jenks says." Jenks was her mine captain. The other two men in the room were Dickon Penny, the mine agent, and Andrewson, the grass captain. "We'll send a crew to try to get through from behind the pump wall, but they'll never be in time."

Christy turned to Jenks, a stocky, compact miner with a fierce black beard. "Can no one get near him, then?"

"No, Reverend, the risk is too steep. I'd not send any man close to him."

"And I won't let Jenks go, either," Sophie said bleakly. "It's an unbearable situation—better if Tranter had been killed outright." She blinked tears out of her eyes, unashamed, while the men around her shifted from foot to foot and stared at the floor.

"Is he injured?"

"No, and that's the hell of it," Jenks burst out, then mumbled an apology. "He went into a vogal—that's a cavity, like—to eat his croust at two o'clock, and when the core changed at three, Martin Burr, his partner, thought it would be a great lark to leave him where he lay—he'd fallen asleep, you see, which he always does after dinnertime, as almost every man knows. The new core went down and began stoping the lode, not knowing Tranter was just beyond the wall a matter of feet from where they were working. What Martin didn't know was that 'twas time to lay a charge to sink the new costean."

"Which still would've been all right," Andrewson put in, "except there was a raw new man on the gang, and he laid his powder too close to the pump shaft housing. It blew, and Fox's wall caved in atop him and the stamping mill. Then the mill's steam engine exploded, and half the gallery came down on top o' the men, who lay trapped until they were excavated out just now. The man Fox is beyond them and unreachable."

"Barely," Jenks gritted. "You can hear him across the rubble in what's left of the gallery. There's not a mark on 'im. Now I'm praying for another cave-in, for he'll die without water in three or four days, and that's a far crueler way to go."

"There'll be a cave-in," Andrewson assured him grimly. "We'll not have to wait long, nor him neither."

Christy was appalled. "But why can't you get him? If you got the others out, why not Tranter?"

"The second blast blew away the mill's pestle, and now it's jammed against all the rubble blocking his way out. Even if you could get to him, which you can't, nothing could dislodge that iron rod. And that's the end of it."

Sophie had covered her mouth with her hands. Her lovely blue eyes glittered; all the freshness and good humor Christy was used to had gone out of them. She'd never lost a man in her brief tenure as the owner of Guelder, and Tranter's plight was an unkind baptism. Christy put his hand on her shoulder and said gently, "It's not your fault. You know it's not, Sophie. Now, I must go down and try to speak to him."

Everyone gaped at him. Sophie found her voice first. "But you can't! It's too dangerous, Jenks says so. No one can get near him, Christy, not even you."

"It's true," the mine captain agreed, "it's too close to coming down, everything within thirty yards is collapsing strut by strut—can't you hear it?"

He'd heard something, a deep, distant rumbling every now and then; he'd thought it was the steam pumps, at work fathoms below the surface. "Nevertheless, I must go to him. You said you could hear his voice across the ruined gallery, which must mean he could hear mine. Is the ladder down to his pitch still intact?"

Jenks nodded reluctantly. He spread his legs in a bullish stance and stuck his chin out. "No one can get near him, I'm telling you. If you shouted, he could barely hear you now. It don't make sense to go down there, as much as I wish it did."

Jenks was afraid, and ashamed of his fear—which Christy never doubted was justified. "It may not," he said levelly. "But if you would guide me down to his level, Mr. Jenks, I would be grateful to you. I wouldn't ask you or anyone else to go closer." He spoke the rest to Sophie. "I must go, though. I've no thought of saving him—that's in God's hands now. But Tranter's in need, and I hope you won't refuse to let me go. I would never tell you how to run this mine, Sophie, because that's your job. In terrible times like this, my job funnels down to one small, narrow thing, and I have to do it. And you mustn't deny me."

She shook her head wordlessly. She mouthed, "No, I would not," then said more clearly, "But God keep you safe, Christy!"

Outside, the waiting men watched as Christy and Jenks trudged across the yard toward the fenced entrance to the main shaft. When they realized the two men intended to go down, the miners hurried over, eager for news. Christy saw that Ronald Fox, Tranter's father, was with them, and stopped so he could speak to him.

"You're never going down, are you, Vicar?" Charles Oldene asked in amazement. To Jenks he said, "You'd never take 'im down there, would you, Captain?"

Jenks spat on the ground. "It ain't my idea, and I ain't doing it willingly."

Ignoring them, Christy went nearer to old Fox, who had grown so feeble of late that he needed two canes to stay upright. "Sir, I'm going down to speak to Tranter," he said in a loud voice, bending down to the little man's level.

"Eh? Gettin' 'im out?" All the wrinkles in his wizened face suddenly lifted with hope.

Christy shook his head sadly. "No, sir, I can't bring him out. I'm going down to *speak* to him."

"Oh, speak." The despair returned. "Well, he'm a good lad deep down, an' 'e main't go straight to the smoky place if 'e 'ears yer holy words. You d' tell un 'is da says farewell, an'll join 'un as soon as may be somewhere in the great 'ereafter." His face closed up like a bunched fist; he couldn't say any more.

Christy had never been down in a copper mine before. Most of the miners in Devon were Wesleyan Methodists, but a few, like Tranter, belonged to Christy's parish, and he knew from them a little of what to expect. Heat and hard going, mainly, and then dirt and damp. Jenks gave him a miner's hat—padded felt, heavy as a helmet, with a candle stuck in the band with a piece of clay—and led the way down the first long, nearly perpendicular ladder. In a parallel shaft to the left, the huge beam of a steam engine could be seen as it rose and fell, straining at the heavy volume of water it lifted ceaselessly from the sump far below. At the bottom of the third ladder, Jenks stopped on a wooden platform to let Christy catch his breath. "We're at the twenty-five level, Vicar. Fox is at seventy."

Not used to thinking in terms of fathoms, Christy had to calculate. They'd come a hundred and fifty feet straight down, with another two hundred and seventy to go before they reached Tranter. Already he could feel the muscles in his calves vibrating. The short, stocky captain wasn't even breathing hard, and a minute later he swung out onto the next ladder. Christy followed, grasping the clay-caked sides and trying not to think about how endless a two-hundred-and-seventy-foot fall would be in the pitch black.

It wasn't a straight drop, though; at forty fathoms, they stepped off another ladder and turned into a level side gallery, sixty feet long and barely wide enough for two men to pass abreast. The heat was becoming severe, and Christy felt glad that he'd left his coat at the shaft entrance. He was grateful for his hat, too, when more than once it cushioned him from a stout blow caused by the odd lump of solid rock protruding from the six-foot ceiling.

The going was not only rough, it was dangerous. "Mind here," Jenks threw over his shoulder repeatedly, alerting him just in time to the presence of a thin, shaky, slippery plank of wood, the only covering over some dismal trap-hole leading to nothing but deep, dark disaster. At length, after ceaseless walking, stooping, creeping, and occasional crawling, they came to another ladder, shorter than the ones that had brought them to this depth, that led down another shaft to another gallery. This happened four or five more times before the long ladders began again. Christy was soaked with perspiration, sucking in gulps of the hot, unhealthy air when Jenks stepped off the last ladder and told him Tranter's pitch lay at this level, in a wider excavation beyond the next gallery.

"Shall I go on by myself?" Christy asked, noticing that Jenks seemed unwilling to proceed.

"Don't be daft," he snapped, then ducked his head. "Beg your pardon, Vicar," he muttered.

"It's all right, Mr. Jenks. You know, you're not at fault for what happened here." He hadn't meant to say that; something in Jenks's manner had prompted it. A moment later, he understood why.

"I am, though," the captain said stiffly, speaking to the black, dripping wall straight ahead of him. "In a way. I'm the one that told the gang to costean so close to the mill. 'Twasn't safe, and I knew it. I didn't tell Dickon or Miss Deene because I knew they'd be against it. But I thought it was worth the risk. And now look what's happened."

Christy could barely see his face in the weird shadows cast by the candle in his hat. "Perhaps that was bad judgment," he conceded quietly. "You couldn't have prevented the second explosion, though, and Tranter would still be trapped, wouldn't he?"

The captain sighed. "Aye. But Bob Thacker wouldn't have got scalded by the steam, and without the sinkholes the flooding's made between us and Fox, mayhap we could've gotten to him earlier. Even gotten him out, for all I know."

"Maybe, but you—"

"I ain't looking for any comfort, Vicar. Meaning no disrespect, I know what I done, and I've got to live with it." With that, he pushed past Christy and started down the narrow shaft. "Now I'll take you to the closest place a man can safely go, and leave you for five minutes to your prayers. After that, we must be away."

Without answering, Christy followed him.

Seventy feet later, they came to a stop. "Oh, sweet Christ," Jenks whispered. " 'Tis much worse now." He took another candle from his buttonhole, lit it from the one in his hat, and held it aloft. By its weak white flicker, Christy saw what he meant.

They were standing at the low, smoky entrance to hell. The smell of hot metal and gunpowder was so strong, he could taste it in the back of his throat, see it floating, cloudlike, in the dirty air. Through the fog, the dark shapes of twisted iron and splintered wood jutted at every angle, like tombstones in an underground cemetery. The red metal wreckage must be the stamping mill, or what was left of it; the scattered timbers were joists and ceiling supports, and the remains of the wooden housing around the water pump. Over half the gallery was simply gone, crushed under the weight of the fallen solid-rock ceiling; the rest was a broad ruin of metal, granite, soft ore, and timber, chest-high in places, underwater in others. Over everything a scalding mist of steam still hissed, spewing out the last of the pressurized water in the broken mill's boiler.

Numbed, Christy asked, "Where is he?"

Jenks held his candle higher and pointed. "Yonder. You can't see the place from here in this light, 'tis too far away. He's walled in and can't be reached for the hazards in the way. What's left of this ceiling won't last much longer, and then he'll be tombed up proper." He turned aside, as much to avert his face as to attach his extra candle to the wall with another lump of clay. Then he cupped his mouth and hollered, "Hullo, Tranter Fox! Can you hear me?"

Immediately an appallingly faint voice called back, "Hullo! Hullo, Captain. I can 'ear you!"

"Reverend Morrell's come down with me! He wants to speak to you!"

Christy winced when nothing but silence greeted this, imagining what Tranter must be thinking right now: that if the vicar was here, he must be doomed indeed. Jenks couldn't stand the silence, either; backing out of the shattered portal, he mumbled, "You'll be wantin' privacy. I'll come back in a short while, Vicar." Christy watched his dim form recede into the black.

He knew little of mines or mining, but he knew enough to see that a hundred perils lay between him and the invisible wall beyond which Tranter was trapped. He also knew that bellowing out spiritual consolation from this distance was out of the question. He had to go closer.

The weakening spray of steam was no longer deadly, but it was still an obstacle. To avoid it, he abandoned the thought of moving toward Tranter's vogal in a straight line and instead struck out to the right, close to the only wall that remained completely intact—so far. His candle had barely been adequate in the long, unobstructed shaft, with a sturdy guide to lead the way; here it was almost useless, illuminating a sharp-edged hindrance a few feet before he collided with or cut himself on it. When he wasn't scrambling over hulking tangles of contorted metal, he was knee-deep in hot water, holding on to whatever was nearby to avoid sliding on the slippery, unsteady mud underfoot. Fox yelled out something he couldn't hear, and he called back, "I'm coming! Hold on a minute!" But it was slow going, and much longer than a minute before he'd covered another six feet.

"Vicar?" the miner called again, his voice still distressingly faint. "Ee don't care t' be comin' too close! The whole roof's fallin' in, an' there'm sinkholes underneath to suck you down to hell!" Christy smacked his shin on sharp metal, muttered to himself, and kept coming.

Two blind, faltering steps later, a sinkhole to hell nearly swallowed him whole. His own outflung arms were all that saved him from sliding straight down to oblivion. With no sturdy handholds within flailing distance, he had to haul his body out of the chest-high pit using only his arms—even his feet were useless against the walls of the narrow, slick-sided tube of muddy stone. He'd no sooner hoisted himself out and half-fallen, panting, onto the wet rubble, when a harsh, splintering sound from above made him cover his head with his arms. Something struck him hard between the shoulder blades; he grunted in pain, listening to the thud of falling wood and rock all around him. When the sounds subsided, he looked up. Miraculously, his candle hadn't gone out; his body ached, but he wasn't injured, and nothing much seemed to have changed. He murmured a prayer of thanks and set off again toward Tranter's wall.

At last he could go no farther: with only about eight feet between himself and the collapsed vogal, the way was blocked by the great iron pestle of the stamping machine, cantilevered upward on Tranter's side by the fallen weight of its own engine. "Can you hear me?" Christy called, sinking to the addle-strewn floor and resting against the rusty metal bulk of the pestle.

"Aye, Vicar, I hear fine, but ee're a fool fer creepin' this close to me, no offense, what wi' the—"

"Reverend Morrell, where are you? Reverend Morrell!"

"Here," Christy shouted to Jenks. "Go up without me, Captain! I know my way back, and I'll follow as soon as may be."

Jenks's reply was so profane, Christy felt glad the man was a Methodist and none of his spiritual responsibility. They shouted orders and refusals to each other across the murky wasteland for another minute or two; then, with a final outburst of obscenity, Jenks fell silent and—presumably—went away. The candle he left on the wall at the gallery entrance was like a lit pinprick in the pitch-black distance, a feeble beacon offering little light and less hope. Christy turned his back on it and drew his prayer book out of his pocket.

He and Fox no longer had to shout at each other to be heard. "Your father's above," he told the miner, in something close to his normal voice. It seemed monstrous to be this near and not be able to help him.

"Is he? Tes a bit nasty fer 'im t' be out an' about. I hope he's well wrapped."

"How are you, Tranter? Are you injured?"

"A couple o' snicks, and I've breaked a finger on my left 'and, but naught else."

"What's it like where you are?"

"Small." Christy could imagine the wry look on Tranter's monkey face. "I can't stand. I can sit wi' my legs straight out, but I can't lie flat. Got air, an' now I can see gray instead o' black on account o' yer candle. Before, 'twur dark as a blathering sack."

"Miss Deene says she's sending a crew down to begin excavating from the other side. If they can get through the wall behind you—"

"They'll find a bag o' dry bones fer their trouble. I helped pick, hammer, blast, an' break this lode yer standin' in, Vicar. Three of us together digged out six inches on especial good days."

"But if they use explosives—"

"Then they'll kill me all the sooner. Same if they tried blasting the great pestle out there that's flush wi' this tomb I'm in—except that'd kill everybody instead o' only me."

Christy was silent.

"Beggin' yer pardon, yer grace, but what the ruddy hell 'ave ee come down 'ere for?"

"To talk to you."

"Well, thur were no need fer that. If tes my soul ee're that anxious after, you of all men oughter know tes a lost cause and there bain't any help for it at this late day."

"Do you truly feel that way, Tranter? That God has abandoned you?"

"Tes more me that's abandoned him, like."

"Then the case isn't so dire. Are you afraid to die?"

"Naw. Every man dies."

"That's true. But he doesn't have to die alone."

"If ee was thinkin' o' lingerin' down 'ere an' waitin' whilst I draws my last gasp—"

"I didn't mean myself. You can have God with you if you want him."

"Well, now, I bain't just so sure o' that. Me an' God, we bain't what you'd call close."

"Do you ever pray?"

"Me?" He laughed uneasily. "Whatever should I say to a great gaffer like the Lord?"

"Whatever's in your heart. The things you hope for, the things you fear."

There was a long silence. At the end of it, Tranter said quietly, "I'm scairt to die. I lied before. Christy?"

"Yes?"

"Oughtn't I to confess or something?"

"You can if you want to."

"You can forgive me, can't you?"

"Yes."

"Well, then I'll do it." Another pause. "I'm a loose, low man, a miserable blinkin' sinner an' no mistake. I've breaked every commandment in the book. Do I 'ave to say 'em out loud?"

"No."

"Good, for I ha'n't the heart."

"Are you truly sorry for your sins?"

"Sink me if I ain't!"

"Then they—"

"But . . ."

Christy waited, then asked, "What is it?"

"Well, Christy, let's look on it straight. Don't the Lord know I'm only repentin' because I know tes my last chance?"

He almost smiled. "I expect he does."

"Well, don't 'e care? If he knows I'm only confessin' on account o' I'm scairt out o' my mind, don't that make 'im suspicious? Don't it make 'im take it all wi' a grain o' salt, so to say?"

He sighed. "God isn't like us, Tranter. He doesn't hold grudges or keep score. What God is—he's love. That's it, that's the simple truth of it. He can come to us at the end of our lives and tell us we won't die unloved. Our death gets swallowed up in love. It goes with us as we cross over, it's waiting for us on the other side. If you can believe that, you can let go of your fear."

"But how can it be? *How can it be?*"

Christy heard the desperation of the well-meaning unbeliever in Tranter's hopeful, hopeless question, and he thought of Anne. "Listen to me," he said with quiet ferocity. "God had a son, and he sent him into the world to face down evil. His enemies took him and hung him on a cross and killed him. And now the bond between God and us is the love of a father for his children. It won't pass away; it's a love that endures forever. It includes you and it includes me."

"Do you believe it?"

"I do. I believe it." And he did.

"Christy, am I forgiven?"

"If you repent, you are forgiven."

Tranter grew quiet. The minutes stretched, and Christy fancied it was a peaceful silence until he heard the soft, unmistakable sounds of weeping. "Tranter? Talk to me."

He heard a thudding sound, as if the miner were striking out at the rock prison around him. "How can I die like this?" he burst out. "What if it's slow? I'm scairt I'll go mad before I die. What if I lose control o' myself? I can't die in this little hole, slow, breath by breath. How could this happen to me? How can God do it to me, Christy? How can I bear it?"

He said the only thing he could think of. "I won't leave you alone. You're a good man, a strong man. I've always respected you, Tranter."

"That's a bloody lie."

"No, it's the truth."

"But I'm a *sinner*."

"Do you think that makes you unloveable? I love you, and I'm only a man. Think what God's love for you is like. You've a good heart. You honor your father, you work hard and steady to support him. You're as kind to him as a mother to her child. What man have you ever hurt? What woman? Your sins are the easiest to forgive, because they're the sins of excess, the sins of a full heart.

"I can't tell you dying is easy. God has sent you a trial—I can't tell you why. But he's with you right now, just as I am. You're not alone. You're forgiven, and you're loved."

Another lengthy silence. Christy took the candle out of his

hat and stuck it in a crevice under a piece of broken metal. "Tranter? What are you thinking about?"

"One thing I'm thinkin' is that if you don't hurry an' get yer saintly arse up to grass, Vicar, we could be crossin' over into the next life 'and-in-'and."

Christy chuckled. "What else?"

"I'm thinkin'. . . . I wouldn't mind singing something. A hymn, like."

Christy's eyebrows shot up. "I didn't know you were a singing man."

"Oh, aye, all Cornishmen are great for singing."

"I thought it was all Welshmen."

"Nay, Cornishmen. So what might be a good song, Vicar? For this particular situation, so to say."

He thought. "Do you know 'Abide with Me'? A young priest wrote it as he was facing his own early death. We've sung it in church, but you may have forgotten it," he said tactfully. "I'll start it off." He cleared his throat and sang,

> Abide with me: fast falls the eventide;
> The darkness deepens; Lord, with me abide.
> When other helpers fail and comforts flee,
> Help of the helpless, O abide with me.

Tranter knew the hymn. In a fine tenor voice, he sang out every slow, solemn verse.

> Hold now the cross before my closing eyes;
> Shine through the gloom and point me to the skies;
> Heaven's morning breaks and earth's vain shadows flee:
> In life, in death, O Lord, abide with me.

The last note faded away in the rock chamber. In the new silence, Christy began to pray, and he knew Tranter was praying with him. The words came to him easily, humble and heartfelt, as simple as the words to the hymn. It seemed strange that he could feel profound sadness and profound peace at the same time, both equally, neither disturbing the other. He didn't pray for a boon; he prayed for the ability to accept God's will with humility, and he prayed for the grace to minister in his name with thoughtfulness and courage. Most of all, he gave thanks to God because his way was clear now. Everything had been revealed.

"Get up, Christy! Get up, *now!*"

The panic in Tranter's voice made no sense until a soft groaning sound finally registered, several notes lower than the lessening hiss of steam that Christy's ears had long since grown accustomed to. There was no other warning except a light shower of dust, gentle as snowflakes. The sudden rip of wood sounded like a gun exploding in his ear.

"Get under something! Duck!"

But there was no cover. The heavy pestle might save him if he could wedge his body under the spare foot of space between its lower end and the rubble beneath it—or it might crush him to death even sooner than the giant beam that was splitting directly over his head. Christy flung himself sideways and buried his head in his arms. "If God is for us, who is against us?" he prayed over the roar of breaking timbers. "For I am sure that neither death, nor life, nor angels, nor things present or to come, nor powers, nor height—" Something struck him on the back of his wrist, momentarily stunning him. "Nor height, nor depth, nor anything else in all creation will be able to separate us from the love of God. Tranter! Can you hear me?" No answer. The ceiling was collapsing all around him. He curled into a tighter ball. "Father," he prayed, "into thy hands I commend my spirit."

Rock and wood pelted him; he gritted his teeth to bear the pain, and waited for the last one. A deafening boom, loud as a cannon, came from his left, and the ground shifted sideways. No, it wasn't the ground—he realized it as his body slid backward helplessly, scraping across sharp addle and slippery clay. The stamping mill pestle had moved, and when he uncovered his head and peered over the long iron cylinder, he saw why. The huge ceiling beam had come down on top of it, and the crushing weight had shifted the rod's angle fifteen degrees higher on the far end.

Tranter's end.

"Tranter!"

Cursing was all the answer he got—joyous, hopeful curses punctuated by the *smash, smash* of boot heels against rubble. He knew it was boot heels, because just then one came crashing through the wreckage that the pestle had been wedging against Tranter's premature grave. Another boot followed. Before Christy could think about scrambling up and trying to help, the little miner slipped and slithered through a child-size hole in the heaped tangle of metal and ore, clambered to his feet, and let out a whoop of pure jubilation.

Christy began to laugh. Nothing hurt; everything was perfect. "Bleeding miracle!" he shouted back at Tranter, echoing him. With the nimbleness of a ballet dancer, the miner negotiated the obstacles that still separated them, and they fell into each other's arms like long-parted lovers.

"Yer candle's still lighted," Tranter marveled, plucking it from the rubble. "A good thing, for we'll need it and *another* miracle to get safe out o' this hellhole, Vicar, beggin' yer bleedin' pardon fer my bloody bleedin' language!"

"Don't mention it!"

Jenks's candle, forty feet away through a veritable minefield of hazards that had only worsened in the cave-in, illuminated the way out. "Take 'old o' my shirttail, Christy, an' follow along behind me. Step where I step, an' whatever ee do, don't look up,"

Tranter advised. "If the Lord changes 'is mind, we might get brained anyway betwixt 'ere an' that candle."

It was a definite possibility, one that ought not to be dismissed. But Christy couldn't believe it. There was no accounting for it, but somehow he knew they were going to be fine.

XXII

ANNE COULDN'T LET GO of Christy's horse. The big animal was tethered to a tree within sight of the engine house and the other outbuildings, around which twenty or so miners and their families were keeping a quiet vigil. The rain had stopped; a warm wind was blowing the mist away. Through the lingering fog, she could make out Sophie Deene, pacing in front of the mine office with her head down, arms folded tight across her middle. That was her way of dealing with the awful, unbearable anxiety. Anne's was to hang on to Doncaster's thick mane like a lifeline. And keep out of sight, so no one could look at her.

A man broke away from one of the huddled groups close to the engine house and moved toward her. She recognized William Holyoake's tall, broad frame, and stood straighter, waiting for him. But she didn't let go of Don, and the fine, calm animal never moved, never twitched a muscle. So unlike Geoffrey's high-strung stallion. Dead now, with a bullet through the brain. Like Geoffrey. She clutched harder at the horse's bristly mane, so the terrible, body-wracking shudders couldn't start again.

"What news, William?"

"Still nothing, m'lady. Miss Deene asks again that you please come inside the mine office where you can be dry."

"Thank her for me. Tell her I should only be in the way." That was true, but the real reason was because she only had eyes for the lantern-lit mine entrance thirty yards distant and couldn't have borne anything obstructing the view. "How long since he went down?" She already knew the answer, but she was sick of solitude and needed to share her misery with someone she trusted.

"Nearly an hour now, m'lady."

A low rumble from deep in the earth froze her in place. "It was worse that time," she whispered. She dropped the horse's mane and reached out for Holyoake's arm. "He's got to come up. It's suicide to stay down any longer!" The bailiff nodded once and bowed his head, too respectful of her, too discreet to acknowledge the naked fear she didn't have the strength to hide anymore. She wondered again if Holyoake knew everything. She suspected that he did. Curious, after all she and Christy had done to keep their affair a secret, that the idea didn't trouble her. In fact, at this moment she took a measure of comfort from it. It helped her feel not quite so alone.

"Word's gotten out everywhere about 'is lordship, m'lady. Some have asked me to convey their sympathies to you—Miss Deene and Dr. Hesselius, as well as some o' the common folk, miners and their families and whatnot."

"I suppose . . ." She took a deep breath and tried to order her thoughts. "I suppose it must be a great shock to them. They lost Geoffrey once before, and now they've lost him again."

"Aye," he said slowly. "But 'tis really yourself they've got feelings for now, m'lady. They say 'tis not fair and a great tragedy that you must suffer so again. They asked me to say that you're in their hearts an' in their prayers."

Tears stung behind her eyes. "I'm blessed to have such friends."

"Aye," William agreed softly. "Indeed, I think you are."

Another low, trembling sound came from the mouth of the mine, just under the throbbing of the pumps, and this time it didn't fade away after a few seconds. Anne came up onto her toes, her fingers digging into Holyoake's sleeve like talons, when the next sound was a muffled boom, deep-throated and sustained. She gave a frightened cry and stumbled forward, compelled to go closer to the source of the dreadful noise, even though it meant showing her ravaged face in the murky lantern light. Men and women made way for her, snatching off their hats and bowing, greeting her with subdued shyness and respect. They kept their distance, but she fancied they were being kind, not remote. A lonely, forlorn affection for them welled up, warming her.

Sophie had stopped pacing and was in the midst of a fierce-looking conference with one of her subordinates. No one was allowed to go down in the mine until Christy and the man who had gone with him came back up, and the miners were clustered around the fencelike wooden scaffolding that surrounded the main shaft entrance, waiting. The ominous subterranean roar had ceased; once again, the only sound was the steady, monotonous driving of the water pumps in the engine house. Overhead, the high chimney stacks puffed steam that evaporated immediately in the misty air. It wasn't cold, but Anne pulled her hooded cape tighter around her shoulders. Holyoake stood at her back, and she felt grateful for his strong, silent presence. But she was coming apart inside; if there wasn't news soon, she was afraid she would break down.

Footsteps on the ladder. Holyoake came around to stand beside her. She took his hand unthinkingly and crept nearer, shivering with hope and dread. She couldn't see anything past the shoulders of the men crowding around the mine entrance. Then someone called out, "It's the captain!" She dropped her head and shut her eyes tight, whispering, "Thank God. Oh, thank God."

The miners cleared a path for Sophie, who met the captain at the top of the ladder. Anne waited for Christy to come up behind him.

". . . wouldn't listen," she heard Jenks saying to Sophie, and then the words "some privacy." She felt Holyoake's hand under her elbow, supporting her as she took a shaky step closer. "So I waited, and when I come back he was gone."

"Gone!"

"Aye, gone. Somehow he got at least halfway across the gallery while I'm down-shaft waitin' for him. It ain't my fault, and there wasn't nothing I could do on my own to get him back. I waited as long as I could, half an hour almost, then I started up to get fresh men to help. I was at the fifty-fathom when I heard it go. Had to be the whole damn gallery. Had to be."

The fog closed in. Anne swayed. Holyoake caught her and kept her from falling.

A man called out, "Are they dead, then?"

"I don't know," said Jenks.

Sophie was issuing orders. Anne heard her as if from a great distance away, vaguely aware that men were dispersing, moving off toward the changing shed. *Are they dead, then?* The ground came as a hard, damp surprise on her knees, but the act of kneeling felt completely natural. Natural, too, to fold her hands and bow her head, and then to pray. The words came to her as easily as a child's prayer, simple and unconsidered, unself-conscious. *Please, dear God, don't let him be dead. Christy's your finest work, your best creation, don't take him away. Please, God, give him back to the ones who need him. Think how much good he can do here. Give him back to us, please, God, because I'll do anything, just give him back, oh, God, I'm asking you on my knees . . .*

The words wouldn't stop. Fluent, utterly sincere, she kept praying, and from somewhere an absolute conviction came that she was heard. She felt that there was a God, and it was Christy's God, loving and kind, merciful and forgiving. She felt herself giving up, giving herself to him; a heavy weight seemed to lift, rise up, fly off. *Your will and not mine,* she prayed, the way Christy did. *Into your hands, Lord. Your hands.*

A noise made her lift her head. Looking around in amazement, she saw that other people were on their knees too, hands clasped, praying with her for their minister. She saw Jenks and three other men in miner's gear, waiting at the shaft entrance, ready to descend, listening intently.

Steps—the noise she'd heard was steps. Steps on the ladder.

"Hold up, Christy," came a querulous voice in a thick Cornish accent. "Tedn seemly for a layman to 'ave that much wind left on the last ladder. Hold up, I said! Wait for a poor tutman, or my mates'll rag me hollow!"

Shouts of relieved laughter rang out all around, punctuated with hearty exclamations of "Thank God! Oh, thank God!" William Holyoake, who had been on his knees beside her, pulled Anne to her feet and gave her a hard, swift hug—then blushed to the roots of his sandy hair. He took her arm in a respectful clasp and started to move her toward the others crowding around the scaffolding—but she hung back. He sent her an understanding look and left her, going up alone.

Through the bobbing heads, she saw Christy emerge and step off the ladder. He had on a miner's hat, and he whipped it off with a flourish and threw it in the air. People cheered. Lamplight fired his golden hair; his teeth gleamed bright white in his sooty face, and she thought he looked like the dearest, dirtiest angel God had ever made. Everybody wanted to touch him. Tranter Fox came next, looking like a little black elf, and a frail, tiny old man rushed forward to embrace him. Then his mates gathered round, and she heard their rough backslaps on Tranter's skinny shoulders, gentler ones for the broader back of Reverend Morrell. She could have gone to him then, but she stayed where she was, feasting her eyes on him. She didn't forget to thank God for saving him.

William went closer, whispered something in his ear. She watched his body go rigid. His eyes found hers. There was a breathless moment of sweet, fierce connection—before someone got in the way, and the tension broke. She backed up slowly, never losing sight of him. People were drifting away in clusters, talking and laughing with relief and excitement. Now Christy was speaking to Sophie Deene. Anne saw him gesture in her direction, saw Sophie nod in understanding. He was telling her he must go and console the widow, she knew. And then he turned away from the remains of the crowd and came toward her.

She wanted to throw her arms around him and never let go. Instead, they took hands. "William has just told me about Geoffrey," he said, and all she could do was nod. "Are you all right?"

"I need to be alone with you."

"Yes." His voice, his eyes, everything said he needed it, too. "Will you ride Don with me, Anne?"

"Yes," she answered, and they moved together to his patiently waiting horse.

A three-quarter moon rode in the gaps of cloud the warm wind blew. Spring was a subtle perfume of budding trees and newly turned earth. From a hedgerow came the twitter of a willow wren who'd forgotten to go to bed. Doncaster trod the worn, moon-dappled path at a sedate pace, and Christy thought of the day, a year ago, when he and Geoffrey had raced along this same abandoned track. A lifetime ago. Anne turned in his arms, and he moved his lips from the crown of her head to her temple, hearing her soft sigh. Neither spoke. The deep quiet between them was soothing, healing. Necessary.

A trickling stream came and went at intervals alongside the path, widening under a willow grove at the edge of the woods. Christy reined the horse to a stop, slid off his bare back, and reached up to help Anne dismount. He took Don's bridle off so the horse could graze, then knelt down by the creek and began to scrub the dirt from his face and hands. The ground was damp; Anne took off her cloak and spread it out on the grassy bank. When Christy finished bathing, he turned to find her sitting close by, watching him. Still without speaking, he sat down beside her. She gave him her handkerchief—his was filthy—and he used it to dry his wet face.

Leaning lightly against his shoulder, she murmured, "You're all right, aren't you, Christy? Not hurt or anything?"

"No, no. Nothing to speak of."

"What was it like? How did you get Mr. Fox out?"

"I didn't do anything." He told her about how the ceiling had collapsed, freeing Tranter from his rock cell.

"I agree with Mr. Fox," she said when he'd finished. "It *was* a miracle."

"It was . . . a wonder," Christy conceded, taking her hand.

"Were you afraid?"

"Yes."

"I was wild. When Jenks came up alone, I couldn't—I felt—I thought I'd lost you, Christy, and there aren't any words to tell you how that felt. It was the worst thing that's ever happened to me." She brought his hand to her cheek and held it there for a moment, then put her lips on the beating pulse in his wrist. She sent God another fervent *Thank you*.

The moon rose higher. The stream made a soothing gurgle, and somewhere in the treetops an owl hoo-hooed, but otherwise the night was intensely still. Anne dropped her head when she felt Christy's fingers at the back of her neck, caressing her. "Tell me about Geoffrey," he suggested, and gradually, haltingly, she began to speak of what had happened. She told him about everything except one thing—that last act of love. And it had been an act of love, no matter that it had begun in violence and desperation. She couldn't regret it; she could only be grateful for it, now that Geoffrey was gone and she couldn't help him anymore. She would tell Christy about it someday—perhaps—but for now she would bear the secret weight of it alone, because she was strong enough.

"My God," he whispered in distress when she told him that

Geoffrey had found out about them. "It's my fault, I shouldn't have sent the letter to the house. I'm sorry, Anne, I don't know what to say to you."

"It hurt him," she said truthfully. "But it's not what drove him to take his life. The doctor had told him he was dying, and he didn't want it to happen slowly—piece by piece, he said. And at the end, Christy, he forgave us. He loved you, truly he did. And me. I know he forgave us." She put her arms around him and held him close.

A feeling of peace stole over her, a gentle closing of the circle. She felt as if she and Christy were in a quiet space, an out-of-time interval between the past and the future. But he was solid and real, no illusion, his hard body warm and vital in her arms. She slid her fingers into his sooty hair, molding the noble shape of his skull, massaging his scalp. With a sigh, she laid her head on his shoulder, breathing in the earthy scent of him, the salt tang of his skin.

It was he who pulled away first, somewhat hastily. In the dimness of the moonlight, she thought he blushed when she asked him what was wrong. He drew a pattern with one finger on the satin lining of the bit of cloak between them. "I'm a bit . . . I'm feeling a little . . ."

"What?"

He was looking down, but she thought he might be smiling. "Ever since I saw you, I . . . it's something about coming up from the mine, realizing I wasn't going to die after all . . ." He stopped, and she stared at his bowed head, bewildered. Then he looked at her, and he was definitely smiling. "Sweetheart, I'm randy as a goat, and there's not a thing I can do about it."

It was her turn to blush, something she never did. And she couldn't think of anything to say—another first. She felt like laughing because of the gladness rising up inside, pure happiness, overwhelming relief because their bodies, at least, weren't constrained anymore by mourning and trouble and guilt.

Christy leaned over and kissed her softly, lingeringly. She'd have held on, made love with him right here, right now, but he straightened—he'd always been the strong one—and said with great seriousness, "Anne, there's something I have to tell you, something that happened to me when I was down in the mine. I learned a lesson about myself. A revelation."

"What, Christy?"

"I don't know if you'll like this or not, but—it's turned out that I'm a minister after all. There's no help for it. I've . . . I've consecrated myself to it." He said the word self-consciously, as if he thought she might mock him for it. "I've found my way back, through my own weakness and powerlessness. I'd lost my faith, but I've got it back again, and now it's as if everything's become clear. I know what it is to be blessed, and to bless others. Can you understand this at all? My service to God can be free, because I've been given the grace to see the joy at the heart of things. I'm not afraid anymore. I've felt what God's love is like, truly felt it. No—I'm not saying it right, it's too—"

"I *do* understand," she exclaimed, taking his hands and holding them against her heart. "Oh, thank God, Christy, thank God. The worst was thinking I'd stolen your life's work from you, destroyed it for you. I couldn't bear it! Oh, thank God." She used his knuckles to wipe the tears from her cheeks. He started to kiss her again, but she pressed him back. "I have something to tell *you*."

"What?"

At the top of a deep, steadying breath, she said, "I prayed for you. Tonight. I knelt on the ground with the others and prayed with them. That you would be saved. I didn't just mouth the words, or bow my head and pretend. I prayed to *God*, Christy. Your God. Maybe . . . my God. I believed."

He smiled. "Did you?" He looked unimpressed. She thought he might even be humoring her.

"No, I mean it, I *believed*. And—I believe now. Not the way you do, but in a way I've never felt before. It's a start, don't you think? Stop smiling at me like that. I'm serious! I think I've been converted!"

He looked at her for another moment. Then he laughed. He fell on his back and laughed until the tears streamed down his face. She was nonplussed—insulted—amused. When he finally stopped laughing, she lay down beside him, propping her head in her hand. "I'll need a lot of spiritual instruction, though, or I might backslide." She traced his lips with her fingers, outlining the curve of his smile. "Good thing I'm marrying a minister, isn't it?"

"Mmm. A daily challenge for me. Humility guaranteed for a lifetime." He took her caressing hand and kissed it, with such tenderness that she ached. "I love you, Anne. I'll cherish you for as long as we live."

Through tears of happiness she made a shocked face. "Longer than *that*, I hope. The minister I marry has to cherish me for *eternity*."

XXIII

Casa La Cima
Ravenna, Italy
22 April 1856

My dear Lord D'Aubrey,

By now you must be well settled in at Lynton Hall. If so, you may have reached the stage of questioning whether your inheritance was the boon you quite reasonably expected or, in fact, a *reversal* of fortune. If it is any consolation, I had the same misgivings when Geoffrey and I moved into the Hall. All I can tell you is that the place has a way of growing on one. The drafts and the dampness never quite become *charming,* but one gets used to them, after a fashion, and gradually learns to appreciate the subtler pleasures of country house living. I would enumerate them for you, but half the fun lies in discovering them for yourself.

You write of the sudden and unexpected retirement of your housekeeper, Mrs. Fruit, as a misfortune. My dear sir . . . how can I put this kindly? I'll only say that, even if you can find no suitable replacement, even if you go housekeeper-less indefinitely, your household has just taken a giant leap forward in efficiency and smooth running. Far from being a tragedy, that kind old lady's departure is the godsend I once prayed for but lacked the heartless courage to effect myself by direct action.

ANNE TAPPED THE END of her pen against her lips, wondering if she wasn't taking too flippant a tone with the new viscount. They'd never met, but she'd received numerous pieces of correspondence from him over the last year or so, in which *he* had always adopted a most casual manner of address. Indeed, there was a certain world-weariness in his tone that intrigued her. Warden Nineways had felt morally obligated to write a letter telling Christy that the new viscount entertained "unchaperoned London ladies" at the Hall, "at all hours of the day and night." Anne would have taken this news with a sizeable grain of salt, considering the source, except that not long afterward a corroborating note had come from no less a font of reliable village gossip than Mrs. Ludd, who hinted quite broadly that Lord D'Aubrey was an out-and-out rake.

Well, what if he was? Anne didn't care if he brought down and bedded every lady in London and then started on Manchester, so long as he treated his tenants fairly and responsibly. A point in his favor was that he'd agreed to accept the newly vacated post of justice of the peace, and would be joining Mayor Vanstone and Captain Carnock on the bench at the next quarter session. That didn't sound particularly rakish. Unless he was doing it for a lark. Well, she would find out in time. William Holyoake would know the truth about his new master, and the only trick would be worming it out of him, for one of Holyoake's most honorable and annoying qualities was his discretion.

Thank you for your most kind and helpful suggestions regarding sight-seeing and points of interest in Ravenna. As a matter of fact, I know the city already, having spent the early years of my childhood here when both my parents were living. It is exactly as beautiful as I remember it, and my husband, who has been abroad but never to Ravenna, is as enchanted with it as the fiercest loyalist could wish. At this very moment, he's in Saint Maria Maggiore Cathedral, looking at early Christian marble sarcophagi with a monsignor we met on a tour yesterday. Poor Christy: whenever these kind priests discover he's an Anglican minister, they immediately drag him away to view antiquities. He has some interest in them, to be sure; but let's face it—

She lifted her pen, amazed at the indelicacy of the sentiment she'd been about to confide to Viscount D'Aubrey: *Let's face it, a man on his honeymoon has other things on his mind besides the tombs and relics of ancient saints.*

She put her arms over her head and stretched luxuriously. Perhaps she would finish her letter later. That was the trouble with Italy: it made one worthless and lazy. It sapped one's ambition. She got up from the little table she and Christy were using for a writing desk and walked out through the open shutters to the wooden balcony. Past the neat courtyard and the lovely terraced gardens below lay the sail-dotted Corsini Canal, and beyond it, too far away to see, the Adriatic. They had been here for three weeks, on a honeymoon that ought to have begun four months ago, after their Christmas wedding. But Anne had wanted Christy to see Ravenna in April, the way she remembered it best, and so they had delayed their trip. She thought of how they had both worried—she much more than he—that their marriage would scandalize the good people of Wyckerley, coming a mere eight months after Geoffrey's suicide. But as it turned out, no one minded; everybody was happy for them. (Well, maybe not Thomas Nineways, but what was one man out of hundreds?) People saw the logic in it, too. They had, after all, waited more than a year since the news of Geoffrey's "death" in the Crimea. And Sebastian Verlaine's arrival had, as it were, turned Anne out of her own house; how silly to move somewhere else for a few months just to observe the proprieties, when it made so much more sense to go directly to her new husband at the vicarage.

Lost in her thoughts, she didn't see the man in the courtyard below until he whistled to her softly. And, sun-blind, she didn't recognize Christy until she'd jumped back into the shadows and folded her arms across the front of her negligee. He wagged his finger at her as she crept back out into the light. She blew him a kiss. "I thought you'd never come," she called out softly. He shook his head and cupped his ear. Louder, she said, *"I missed you."* He smiled, and her whole world tilted a little sideways. When he took off his hat, his hair looked like burnished gold in the warm sun, his skin a healthy, handsome shade of bronze. He had on his new suit, his "honeymoon" suit, the one they'd decided he could probably never wear in Wyckerley because it was too decadent. It was white, for one thing; and for another, it was linen. Worst of all, the cut wasn't English, it was *foreign*. Ah, but he did look handsome in it, she thought with a sigh. And they'd decided they would come back to Italy every few years, God willing, if only so that Christy could wear his decadent white suit.

"I've brought wine," he called to her in a loud whisper, holding up a paper-wrapped parcel.

"Oh, lovely."

"And some fruit."

She put her hands together prayerfully. "Wonderful—I'm starving." He shook his head in pretend-amazement. They'd eaten lunch only two hours ago, before he'd gone off to his sarcophagi and she'd lain down for a nap. She had an idea what her appetite and her persistent sleepiness might signify. But she wasn't absolutely positive, so she wasn't saying anything—yet. Oh, but God, it was like capping a volcano, so intense was her longing to tell him the miraculous news! Two more weeks. In two more weeks she'd know for certain, and *then*—She hugged herself, feeling shot through with happiness.

He sent her a jaunty salute with his hat and walked off around the pensione, beyond her line of sight. She wandered to the dressing table and sat down, thinking she really ought to do something about her hair. Who was this pretty, pink-cheeked, slightly blowzy-looking woman staring back at her? Could this really be Anne Meredith Verlaine Morrell, lately of Devon, who used to hide away in an attic sitting room and jot down her bitter, caustic thoughts in a journal? Who had taken solitary walks to faraway, abandoned places so that no one could look at her? Who had been so lonely that she'd fantasized long conversations with servants, then been too languid and debilitated to initiate them? It didn't seem possible, so complete was the transformation. This woman, this *girl* in the mirror looked as if her biggest worry was which flower to put in her hair for an afternoon of shopping, or whether she would make love with her husband before or after dinner, or both. She smiled at herself, abashed and delighted. Then the key turned in the lock, and she turned to smile at her husband.

Christy stopped in his tracks when he saw her. She was sitting in a pool of sunlight at her dressing table, brushing her hair, wearing the filmy green dressing gown he'd bought for her in Bologna. She was so beautiful, she hardly looked real. *This is my wife*. He had to tell himself that once in a while; otherwise, it didn't seem real either. He set his packages down, except for one, and went to her.

She lifted her arms for his kiss. "How were your saints' coffins?" she asked. She smelled of lilacs and jasmine, and she made his head swim.

"Deadly. All I could think of was that you were here in bed by yourself and I was in a cold, damp crypt with an eighty-year-old priest. Something seemed awry." Standing behind her, watching her in the mirror, he gave her his gift. He loved the pleased, feminine expectation in her face as she unwrapped the flowers, and the surprised delight when she saw them. "They're beautiful," she sighed, burying her nose in the bright bouquet of fuchsias and arum lilies he'd bought in the flower market. She took his hand from the top of her shoulder and kissed it softly, then leaned her head back against his stomach. "Thank you. I love them."

Her hair was still warm from the sun. He slid his hands into it, twining the red-gold curls around his fingers. "You're beautiful," he said, and watched her eyes close, her smile widen. "Do you know, Anne, the light is perfect for finishing your portrait."

Her eyes flew open. "Now?"

He shrugged and gestured to the bed, where the afternoon sun was softening the white of the pillows to a mellow rose-gold.

She tapped a finger to her lips. "It's certainly taking you a long time to finish this painting. Why is it you can't seem to make any headway, I wonder?" He hummed noncommittally, hiding a smile. "All right, then," she said—daring him. She stood up slowly, holding his gaze in the mirror until the last second, and then walked to their big iron bed. Throwing back the rumpled sheets, she got in bed and took up the pose—back against the mountain of pillows, legs drawn up and to the side, head in half-profile, chin dipped slightly. He watched her pull on the ribbons that held her dressing gown closed and slip the garment down over her shoulders. Her white silk nightgown buttoned down the low front. She undid each button slowly, dreamily, not looking at him, as if she were alone in the room. Then she pulled her arms from the sleeves and lifted her head, smiling directly at him. Naked to the waist.

Sometimes, incredible as it seemed, he was actually able to work on the painting. More often, though, his watercolors dried up before he could use them, which was why this portrait was only half finished after two whole weeks of pretend-painting.

He went to his easel and swished a brush around in the murky water jar. Anne's pose was pensive and provocative, innocent and erotic. Like her. He was painting her in pastels, all whites and pinks and subtle flesh tones. If he ever finished it, it would definitely not be among the souvenirs of their trip he planned to show to the members of the vestry when they got home.

She had a watchful, worried look in her eyes while he took off his coat and hung it on the back of a chair. "Christy?"

"Yes, love?"

"Are you really going to finish it now?"

He looked up in feigned surprise. One of the joys of his life was teasing his wife. "Shouldn't I?" She didn't answer, and he moved toward her slowly, staring at her intently, while her cheeks took on a delicate apricot tinge. He sat down beside her on the bed. "This isn't quite right," he said seriously, adjusting a flounce of lacy silk at her waist. His fingers brushed the warm white skin over her ribs, and he heard her breath catch. "Turn your head a little." He touched the side of her neck, drawing her hair back from her bare shoulder. She was breathing softly through her mouth; she had to wet her lips with the tip of her tongue. "Don't move." He leaned closer to adjust a pillow.

"Christy," she whispered. "Don't finish it now."

"Shh. This isn't right, either."

"What?"

"This." He touched the tip of her left breast, and she gasped. "That's better," he murmured, watching the pink tip tighten and swell. "But . . . it was darker before. *Couleur de rose,* as we said in art school."

"Christy . . ."

"And shinier, too, as I recall. It must've been wet." He lowered his head and touched his tongue to her nipple. She gave that same enticing, high-pitched gasp, and when he took her breast deeply into his mouth, she moaned—softly, so the German couple in the next suite couldn't hear. Her hands cupped his temples, holding him gently to his task, and when he raised his head to look at her, she was smiling with her eyes closed. And she was the most beautiful woman he'd ever seen.

Her nightgown and robe were tucked modestly around her ankles. He gave the cloth a soft yank and began to pull it over her knees, her thighs. "What are you doing?" she asked on a pleasure-filled sigh. "Aren't you painting me?"

"I've got a slightly different position in mind." And he pulled the long, silky leg nearest to him up and over his knees, letting it dangle over the side of the bed.

Her half-closed eyes flew open, revealing shock. "Very—*wanton*, this pose," she managed, breathless again, cheeks flushing.

"Now I want you to put your head back." She obeyed as soon as he slid his slow hands along the velvet skin of her inner thighs. Pressing her legs apart, he caressed her with a soft, teasing touch, then deeply, watching the fascinating expressions that came and went in her face. All at once she inhaled sharply. She arched her spine, and he took the blatant offer of her breasts with his mouth, suckling her strongly. He felt her hands clamp around his shoulder blades, felt the muscles of her thighs clench and relax in subtle spasms, and reveled in her long, silent, liquid unraveling.

Her body went limp by slow, sweet degrees; she dropped her damp forehead on his shoulder. "How lovely," she told him, between soft, panting breaths. "Christy, you're so . . . mmmmm."

"Sweet Anne," he whispered. "I can't seem to get enough of you."

She slipped her hand inside his white linen waistcoat to feel the strong pounding of his heart. Under his shirt, every muscle was hard and straining, telling her his effortless-looking self-control wasn't altogether what it seemed. She smiled to herself, anticipating what was going to happen next, and began to slide the buttons open down his shirt—slowly, not hurrying at all. "You must be warm," she murmured, her cheek still pillowed against his shoulder. "You can't paint me in this." She got to the last button and tugged his shirt out of his trousers.

"No, indeed," he said huskily. "An artist needs freedom of movement."

The skin over his flat belly was soft as a child's, but not as soft as the light fleece of golden hair that covered it. She put her lips in the hollow of his collarbone while she stroked her hand across his chest, humming with pleasure and returning excitement. Not so patient now, he shrugged out of his shirt and waistcoat at the same time and dropped them on the floor. He bent his head and put a hot, wet kiss on her navel, making her squirm, before he slid out from under the tangle of her legs and stood up. She stretched like a cat, watching him unfasten his trousers, feeling sultry and irresistible. She shimmied out of her bunched-up nightgown and negligee, then slid down farther in the bed, admiring her husband's tall and gloriously naked body. All that blond hair and all that lovely skin, covering all those beautiful muscles. Sometimes it didn't seem possible that she was married to a *minister*.

Sinking down beside her, he put his hands in her hair and spread it out on the pillow, making a fan with his fingers. "Oils next," he said, and he had that intent look again in his beautiful blue eyes. "Rich reds and golds, maybe a little florid and overdone; something after Titian, I think. Although your figure isn't quite as . . . generous." She pouted her bottom lip until he thought to add, "Thank heavens," and gave her bosom a soft, appreciative squeeze. She thought of asking him if he had just thanked God for her breasts, but decided against it. He'd take the question seriously, and the last thing she wanted to get into with him right now was a theological discussion.

"I used to think of you sometimes as Man in Michelangelo's ceiling," she confided. He looked amused. "Because of the hair." She reached up to touch it, and he turned his head to kiss her palm, then each of her fingertips. "And sometimes . . ." She'd never told him this before. "Sometimes I thought of you as the lion in Rubens' painting of Daniel. The worried one with the gorgeous eyes."

His delighted laugh tickled her; she laughed with him, admiring the faint flush of pleasure and embarrassment that crept into his fair cheeks. Raising up on one elbow, she put her lips on his throat, breathing in the clean smell of him. His strong arms came around her, supporting her. She moved her mouth to his ear and murmured a soft, frank suggestion—because he was deliberately giving her time to recover, and his laudable self-restraint wasn't the least bit necessary.

He smiled a slow, anticipatory smile that stole her breath away and made her skin tingle. She wound her arms around his neck and let him lower her to the pillow, holding on while he stretched his long, powerful body beside her. The hair on the heavy thigh he threw over hers tickled; she parted her legs for him, wanting more of that sensation. With his mouth and his hands, he found all her secret places, and then he kissed her breathless. When he braced over her, she reached between them to guide him home herself. At the last second, she whispered, "Christy, are you sure you don't want to finish the painting?"

For an answer, he lifted his head and growled like a lion.

From their balcony, Anne and Christy could see the sun come up over the canal at dawn, and at twilight they could watch it sink beyond the ruins of the basilica of Saint Apollinare. It was beginning its westward descent now. Time to dress for dinner; they were going to Paulo's, their favorite trattoria, to eat mussels and lobster outside in the garden. But they lingered in a corner of the balcony, arms entwined, too lazy and satisfied to move. They hadn't lit the candles in the room yet; the darkness behind and the gathering dusk all around shielded them from the view of anyone who might be passing in the courtyard below. Good thing, because they were both in their dressing gowns, barefooted on the still-warm floorboards of the balcony.

Anne popped a grape in her mouth and took a sip of Dolcetto, the wine Christy's monsignor friend had given him this afternoon for a present. "Did you read Mrs. Ludd's letter yet?" she asked.

"Not yet. What did she say?"

"Well, for one thing, she said Captain Carnock had a dinner party for eight people, including the mayor and Dr. Hesselius, and Miss Weedie came *unescorted*."

Christy said, "Hmh," in a thoughtful tone.

"He served sherry and port, and Miss Weedie drank one glass of each."

"How does she *know* these things?" he marveled, a rhetorical question each of them had asked the other about their housekeeper any number of times.

"She says if the captain doesn't declare himself soon, he and Miss Weedie may find themselves the target of irresponsible gossip."

Christy nearly choked on his wine. When he stopped chuckling he asked, "What else did she say?"

"She said Sebastian Verlaine is a degenerate—but I already told you that."

"Hmh."

"She said Reverend Woodworth gives a nice, earnest sermon, but they're nothing like yours and everyone misses you." He put his arm around her and dropped a kiss on her temple. Sharing his pleasure with her—so typical of him, she thought, squeezing him back. "Oh, and Thomas Nineways told the vestry he wants to commemorate the Feast of the Holy Innocents this year with a church procession of all the male babies in the parish."

"That would be a very *slow* procession," Christy noted, and they chortled together, imagining it.

"Arthur's finished planting the garden. She didn't mention the fact that I, his employer, am not allowed to do anything but weed and water it."

"Poor Anne. The vegicide wife."

"Quite. And she said it's a great shame we won't be home for the May Day festival because the children have planted a new tree on the green, I've forgotten what kind, and everybody expects it to burst into flower right on schedule. That's assuming the weather and the Blessed Virgin cooperate."

He smiled, and she followed his gaze out over the darkening water to the lavender-gray clouds piling up in bands above the horizon, like striations of ancient granite. The color of south Devon in the spring was a rich reddish-brown, not quite like any other place she'd ever seen. The hedges bordering the fields would be greening now, creating that lovely patchwork-quilt effect the county was famous for. She could picture the cottages on the High Street with their new spring coats of daub or whitewash, the heavy thatched roofs that made them look as if they'd grown out of the ground where they stood. The sheep would be dragging their long, dirty wool around the pastures like damp mops, and at Lynton Hall Farm, William Holyoake would be hiring extra men to help with the shearing.

"I spoke to Father Croce about our trip to Rimini," Christy mentioned. "He said we can either travel by train from Bologna or hire a diligence and go directly from here. Either way, it's a whole day's journey. It'll be too cold for sea-bathing, he says, but the temple of Malatesta will keep us occupied for days."

Anne nodded absently. The Weedies' garden would be coming into full glory soon. Lily Hesselius had suggested at a church meeting once that the village ladies organize a spring garden contest, with the winner being allowed to display her prizewinning flora on the church altar for the entire month of May. Poor Lily, a relative newcomer, had had to be told that there was no point in that because the Weedies would win effortlessly, no one would dare compete against them, and their flowers already graced the altar for at least eleven, quite possibly all twelve months of the year. Anne could see it now, tumbling with hollyhocks and hydrangeas, sweet peas and canterbury bells. In a few weeks the honeysuckle and white jasmine would bloom, climbing the old plum trees beside the path. Peonies and heliotropes came next, tall, sweet-smelling stock, lavender and marigolds—and moss roses, banks and banks of them, spilling over everything by the end of May—

Christy had asked her a question. "What, darling?"

"I said, should we come back along the coast again, or go inland a bit and see Cesena and Forli?"

"Ohh . . . whatever you like. Or we could wait and decide later."

"Did you read the bit about Rimini in the guidebook I left out?"

"Hm? No, I didn't get a chance yet. I'll look at it tonight." That reminded her—the penny readings were starting up again at the rectory hall. Reverend Woodworth had begun with "Elements of Morality" by Mr. Whewell, which was all very well, but attendance had fallen off alarmingly after the first night and she worried about the program's future. Last fall, she'd read *The Count of Monte Cristo,* thrilling Wyckerley, if she said so herself, to its toes. She'd tried a tactful suggestion to Reverend Woodworth that something more on the order of *The Deerslayer* might hold his listeners' attention better, but he'd been immovable. Maybe when they got home she could suggest something to Mrs. Armstrong by Poe, or one of those Brontë women, to revive people's spirits . . .

"Anne?"

"Hm?"

"Where are you?"

"What? Oh, sorry. Woolgathering, I guess." She sent him a contrite smile, but when she turned to stare out over the water again, he touched her cheek and made her look at him. His hair was adorably tousled—from her fingers, a little while ago in bed; he looked wonderful in the damson-colored silk dressing gown she'd given him for a wedding present. But his brow was furrowed and his eyes looked troubled.

"Would you rather we didn't take the trip tomorrow? We can stay here if you prefer, it doesn't matter a bit to me."

She opened her mouth to exclaim that of course she wanted to go to Rimini, they'd been planning it for days—and after that she wanted to go on all the other side trips they'd mapped out, to Comacchio and Lugo, the mineral springs, the Umbrian Apennines. Then she heard what he'd said—"it doesn't matter a bit to me"—and she realized that it was the simple truth. He'd come on this trip, had suggested it himself, in fact, purely to please her.

"Darling," she said slowly, smoothing her fingertips along the inside of his wrist, "are you having a good time?"

"Yes, of course," he answered immediately, "the best. Aren't you?" She hesitated, and he faced her in alarm. "Anne, what's this? Aren't you enjoying yourself?"

"Of course I am—it's heaven on earth, it's *paradise,* one would have to be mad not to love all this." She gestured at the sky, the harbor, the lights of the city twinkling on, their beautiful, sexy bedroom in the quaint old pensione. "But . . ."

"But?"

"But . . . don't you want to go home?"

He was floored. He couldn't speak.

"Aren't you the least bit homesick? Just think what it's like now, Christy—they're sowing barley in the fields, and the cattle have been let out to graze, it's almost sheep-shearing. The hedges are all blooming—the flowers—oh, skylarks everywhere! And the evenings are getting longer—think of the walks we could take. Don't you worry about everybody? I know Woodworth's a brick, but he's not you, and everybody misses you, Mrs. Ludd said so. What if someone has a genuine moral crisis? Where will you be? Where will *they* be? You say Nineways is harmless, but what if he pulls off some sort of *coup* while we're gone? What if he gets them to initiate public confessions, or stonings, putting people in the old stocks and throwing rotten—" Christy was laughing, so she broke off to laugh with him. "I know you did this for me," she resumed while he was still snickering, "and I adore you for it—"

"Did what?"

"Came on this trip. You thought it would make me happy because it's the only place I was ever able to think of as my home. And I *am* happy, truly I am—but—I've found out in this beautiful city that I was wrong. I'd been making it up in my head, pretending it meant something to me so that my childhood wouldn't seem so empty, so pitiful." He ran his thumb very gently along the side of her neck, but she didn't need consoling. "Christy, this is what I've learned: that my home is with you, and that I love it. And I can't wait to be there with you. This has been coming over me for days, and tonight, I don't know what's happened, but it's—irresistible. Next February when I can't get warm, next March when it won't stop raining, I'm going to kick myself for saying this, but I'm saying it anyway." She smiled up into his amazed face. "What I'd like to do is go home."

Christy laughed again, because his heart was making his chest tickle, and laughing seemed to be the only way to scratch it.

"You aren't angry, are you? I guess we'd lose the deposit we gave the hotel in Rimini, and you wouldn't get to see the Saint Francis temple or—"

"Don't be an idiot," he said tenderly. "I feel the same. I love it here—who wouldn't—but frankly, we could've gone to Newcastle and I'd have loved that, too. Or the Hebrides in January. Anne, you are . . ." The right words eluded him. But she looked so expectant, he marshaled his wits and made an effort to say what he felt. "You are . . . my delight. When I think there's no possibility that I could love you more or that you could be more lovable, you always surprise me. Always. You'd think I'd have learned by now, the lesson's become so routine."

"Oh, Christy."

"You've changed my idea of how things are supposed to unfold in the world. This earthly realm."

"How did I do that?"

"Well, this is supposed to be a vale of tears."

"Is it?"

She was trying not to smile. He couldn't blame her—it was impossible to be serious in this rare and blessed moment. But someday he would say it better, tell her what he really meant. "At the very least," he plowed on, "it's supposed to be a trial."

"A trial? Is it really?"

"What it's *not* supposed to be is heaven. That comes later, see? Earth now, heaven later."

"I think I've got it."

They put their arms around each other. "You scare me sometimes," he said truthfully. "If I'm this happy now, what's going to become of me later?"

"Christy, that is such a strange thing to say. Lucky for you, you've married the right woman, because I know exactly what you mean." She gave his ear a soft kiss and pulled away. "We could stay another day or two if we want. Now that we know we're leaving, there's no real hurry, I guess."

He nodded agreeably. She could've said, "We could stick pins in each other," and he'd have nodded agreeably. He was enthralled. Then he noticed she was frowning.

"So," she said, "you'd like to stay? It's all right, I just—"

"No! Do you want to go?"

"Do you? I just thought, since we've *decided,* we might as well—"

"Absolutely. Let's pack."

She laughed. "Shouldn't we eat dinner first?"

"Dinner! Right you are." He'd forgotten he was starving.

"And then . . ." She screwed up her face in a unique Anne-expression, one he liked but didn't see very often; it signified intense inner struggle and emotional turmoil, processes she normally kept to herself.

"What?"

"Then . . . maybe I'll tell you something. It's a secret. I shouldn't, but . . . I might have to. Otherwise I might explode. Oh, God, Christy, I love you!"

Her exuberant hug knocked him back a step. "I love you, too," he said, laughing again. What a day this had been. *Thank you,* he thought, in a prayer that was becoming as automatic as breathing, and nearly as frequent. "We'll start for home tomorrow," he decided, holding her close. "We'll go have dinner, you'll tell me your secret, we'll pack, and tomorrow we'll go home."

"Home," she said, beaming at him.

And that's exactly what they did.

Author's Note

When the idea for Christy and Anne's story first came to me, I never considered that theirs might be the first of *three* tales set in Wyckerley. But as the village began to fill up with more and more people—people I was starting to like—I found myself extremely reluctant to say good-bye to everybody after only one book. And I wanted to know: Is Sebastian Verlaine really a degenerate? How will Sophie Deene manage the copper mine all by herself? Will Miss Weedie ever marry Captain Carnock? Can't something be done to find William Holyoake a true love?

Clearly, Wyckerley had more stories to tell.

The second in what is now the Wyckerley Trilogy, *To Have and To Hold,* is Sebastian's story—and yes, it turns out he is a shade on the decadent side. Rachel Wade, the housekeeper he hires to replace Mrs. Fruit (bless her, she finally retired), is a convicted felon, just out of prison for murdering her husband ten years ago. Their love story begins in obsession and ends in healing and understanding, and it intrigued me from the moment the idea first came to me.

Sophie Deene is so pretty, so dutiful, so *good,* I had a perverse compulsion to throw lots of trouble her way. In the third book, *Forever and Ever,* trouble comes in the shape of Connor Pendarvis, a handsome, insolent Cornishman who shows up in Wyckerley one day, claiming to be a simple miner. He turns out to be a great deal more. When Sophie learns the truth, there's hell to pay.

Their relationship is stormy, to say the least, but love wins out handily in the end over pride and misunderstanding.

The middle decades of the nineteenth century were the golden age of rural England, the idyllic time before the agricultural boom faltered and working people had to leave the country for jobs in the industrialized cities. Thomas Hardy immortalized the period in *Far from the Madding Crowd,* and Wyckerley and St. Giles' parish take their inspiration from that sweet, melancholy book. It's my hope that you've enjoyed spending time with Anne and Christy, and that you'll want to return to Wyckerley, as I did, to hear Sebastian's story, and then Sophie's. For myself, even knowing that they're all busy living happily ever after, I'm *still* finding it hard to say good-bye!

Happy reading.

Patricia Gaffney

If you've fallen in love with Wyckerley, don't miss the other marvelous novels in Patricia Gaffney's beloved trilogy. Return to the place where enchanting romance and unexpected passions meet. . . .

To Have and To Hold

and

Forever and Ever

NAL Trade Paperbacks
Coming in Spring 2003

Turn the page for a special early preview . . .

To Have and To Hold

"But it is too rude of you, Bastian! How can you send me away like this? Don't you like Lili anymore?"

"I adore you," Sebastian Verlaine avowed, prying away the grip of his mistress's tiny white hand, clamped to his thigh like a nutcracker. Through the carriage window, he watched the chimneys of Lynton Great Hall, his dubious inheritance, recede behind a screen of ancient oak trees. He couldn't help liking the look of his new house. But it was hard to sustain admiration for its rough granite grandeur when he thought of everything that was broken, peeling, crumbling, smoking, or leaking, and how much even rudimentary repairs were going to cost him.

"And have we not had a nice time? Did we not play lovely games in your new *baignoire*? Eh? Bastian, listen to me!"

"It was paradise, my sweet," he answered automatically, kissing her fingers. They smelled of perfume and sex, an essence he wasn't capable of appreciating just now, at least not in any way that required virility. Enough occasionally was enough, and four days and nights in the intimate company of Lili Duchamps was, as the lady herself would put it, *plus qu'il n'en faut*—more than enough.

"*Oui, paradis,*" she agreed, insinuating her index finger between his lips and tapping his teeth with her fingernail. "Put off your silly men's business and come to London with me. We have never made love on a train, *oui*?"

"Not with each other," he conceded after a second's thought.

He bit down on her finger hard enough to make her snatch it away and glare at him. It would have been amusing to say, "You're beautiful when you're angry." But it wouldn't have been true.

"Oh, you are cruel! To send me off all alone to—to—*Plymouth*—" she made it sound like Antarctica—"and make me ride on the train to London all by myself—*c'est barbare, c'est vil!*"

"But you *came* by yourself," he pointed out reasonably, "and now you just have to do everything in reverse." Past her lavishly styled, champagne-colored hair, he watched the quaint parade of thatched-roof cottages glide by as the carriage bumped and rumbled up Wyckerley's cobble-stoned High Street. The cottages were charming, he supposed, with their fat dormers, profuse gardens, and pastel fronts; but his aesthetic appreciation was tempered by the thought that his own tenants probably lived in half of them. Then they weren't so charming; then, like the manor house, they were just a lot of old buildings that needed his money and attention.

"But *why* can you not come with me? Why? Ooh, I hate you for this!" She drew back her hand, but he grabbed it before she could strike him. By now he knew her shallow tempers; she rarely caught him off guard anymore. "Take care," he said in the soft, menacing tone with which he'd originally seduced her; the fact that it still worked was one reason their affair was growing stale. "Do not try my patience, *ma chère,* or I'll have to punish you."

The lurid flare of excitement in her eyes made him laugh—spoiling the mood. "Oh!" she cried, thumping him on the chest with her fist. "Beast! Cad! Ungrateful bitch!"

"No, darling, that's *you*," he corrected, holding her hands still in her lap. Lili's English wasn't fluent, and sometimes she called him the things her own spurned lovers must have called her. "Now, kiss me and say good-bye. Justice is waiting for me."

"Who? Oh, your silly court business." Suddenly her peevish scowl lifted. "I know—Bastian, I will come with you and watch!"

"No, you will not." The good souls of Wyckerley already worried that their new viscount was a degenerate; one look at Lili and their worst fears would be confirmed. He wanted to save them from that, or at least delay the awful truth a little longer.

"*Mais oui!* I want to see you in your black robes and your *perruque*, sending poor criminals to the *guillotine*."

"Ah, darling, what charming blood lust." He leaned across the carriage seat, intending to retrieve his walking stick. Lili intercepted the move by seizing his hand and pressing it to her powdered white bosom, inhaling to inflate it to the maximum—a needless augmentation of an already prodigious endowment. In fact, Lili's bust was what had first attracted Sebastian, four months ago at the Théâtre de la Porte, where she'd made her debut in *Faust* as the living statue of la Belle Hélenè—a good role for her because it didn't require her to speak. Despite her reputation as one of the most heartless of the *grandes horizontales*, she'd proven an easy conquest: one intimate supper at Tortoni's, absinthe afterward at the Café des Variétés, and then the *coup de grace*, a pair of diamond eardrops in the bottom of a bottle of Pontet-Canet—*et voilá,* they were disporting themselves on the black satin sheets in her gaudy rue Frochot apartment. She'd been his mistress ever since, but she wouldn't be for much longer. They both knew it—how could they not? They were professionals, he as keeper, she as kept; they knew how to recognize the first stirrings of ennui before it could blossom into full-fledged contempt.

With a little shimmy, Lili got her left breast into the center of his palm; he felt the nipple harden into a warm little peak. She uncovered her teeth in a carnivorous smile and slipped one of her knees over his.

The carriage had just stopped at the entrance to Wyckerley's exceedingly modest town hall, or "moot hall" as they still called it, inside of which two magistrates and who knew how many "poor criminals" were waiting for him to help dispense justice in the petty session. Pedestrians were passing on the street, staring openly at the new D'Aubrey brougham, while above, the coachman waited patiently for his lordship to alight. Satisfying Lili didn't take long, Sebastian knew from experience, and sending her away happy would be the better part of discretion. But the logistics, not to mention a disinterest that might be temporary but was nevertheless profound, defeated him. With a sigh, he gave her luscious breast a soft farewell squeeze and withdrew his hand.

Predictably, her eyes flashed with anger—"eyes like multifaceted marcasite, their soft glance more stimulating than a caress," according to a so-called critic in one of the Paris theater revues. Not so predictably, her dainty little hand drew back and slapped him hard across the cheek; he barely caught her wrist before she could do it again. "*Pourceau,*" she spat, her long-nailed fingers curving into claws. "*Bâtard.* I loathe you." But the lascivious look was back, and it grew heavier, lewder, the harder he squeezed the bones in her wrist. All at once the carnal gleam in her eyes irritated him. They'd played this game too often, and now he was mildly repelled by it, not aroused.

She must have seen his disgust; when he pushed her away she made no protest, and except for one brief, longing look at his cane, she seemed to be through with violence. "*Au revoir,* then," she said airily, pulling up her low bodice, patting her hair, every inch the insouciant *coquette* once more. "Darling, how do you say '*je m'embête*' in English?"

"*I'm bored,*" he answered fervently.

"*Exactement.* So I will leave you to your so *bourgeois* business affairs. When you are next in London, you must do me a great favor, Bastian. *S'il vous plaît,* do not come to see me."

360

"Enchanté," he murmured, privately amazed that she was letting him off this easily. The Comte de Turenne had been foolish enough to break off his liaison with Lili while dining at the Maison d'Or, and she'd retaliated by dumping a plate of Rhine carp *à la Chambord* in his lap.

He opened the door and sprang down to the pavement, breathing deeply of the unperfumed air. "John will take you to the posting inn where the Plymouth mail coach stops, Lili. I'd let you have my carriage, but then, how would I get home?" He gave a Gallic shrug, enjoying the tightening of her carmine lips. "You'll be fine," he said more kindly. "John will wait with you and see that you're safely ensconced and on your way." He reached into the inside pocket of his frock coat and withdrew a jeweller's box. He flipped it to her in a quick underhand lob she couldn't have been expecting. But with the dexterity of a cricket ace, she threw her hand up and caught it—*chunk*. Like lead to a magnet, Sebastian analogized; or a lure to a great, hungry bass. "I wish you well," he said in French. Less truthfully he added, "I treasure our time together. You may be sure I'll never forget you."

Mollified by the gift more than the words, she lifted her chin and her theatrical eyebrows in what she no doubt intended to be a regal look; he could imagine her practicing it in front of one of the dozen or so mirrors in her garish boudoir. "Good-bye, Bastian. You are a terrible man, I do not know why I put out with you."

He grinned. "That's put *up* with me, darling—although your way is closer to the mark." She was softening, she was all but ready to forgive him. To forestall her, he swept off his hat and made a low, fatuous bow. *"Adieu, m'amour.* Be happy. My heart goes with you." Before she could respond, he slammed the door, sent John a discreetly urgent look, and backed away to the curb, keeping his hand on his breast as if overcome with feeling. The carriage jerked away, and he had a last glimpse of her scowling face, cheeks just beginning to flush with anger as she realized he was mocking her—for whatever else Lili might be, she wasn't stupid. But it scarcely mattered now, and all he could feel as he watched the coach turn the corner and disappear was relief.

Forever and Ever

The tower clock on All Saints' Church struck the quarter hour with a loud, tinny thud. Connor Pendarvis, who had been leaning against the stone ledge of a bridge and staring down at the River Wyck, straightened impatiently. Jack was late. Again. He ought to be used to it by now—and he was, but that didn't make his brother's habitual tardiness any less aggravating.

At least he didn't have to wait for Jack in the rain. In typical South Devon fashion, the afternoon had gone from gray to fair in a matter of minutes, and now the glitter of sunlight on the little river's sturdy current was almost blinding. It was June, and the clean air smelled of honeysuckle. Birds sang, bees buzzed, irises in brilliant yellow clumps bloomed along the riverbank. The cottages lining the High Street sported fresh coats of daub in whimsical pastel shades, and every garden was a riot of summer flowers.

The Rhadamanthus Society's report on Wyckerley had said it was a poky, undistinguished hamlet in a poor parish, but Connor disagreed. He thought the authors of the report must have a novel idea of what constituted poverty—either that or they'd never been to Trewithiel, the village in Cornwall where he'd grown up. Wyckerley was friendly, pretty, neat as a pin—Trewithiel's opposite in every way. Connor had been born there, and one by one he'd watched his family die there. Before he was twenty, he'd buried all of them.

All except Jack. Here he came, speak of the devil, swaggering a little, and even from here Connor could see the telltale glitter in his eyes; it meant he'd recently downed a pint or two or three in Wyckerley's one and only alehouse, the George and Dragon. But his thinness and the gaunt, gray concavity of his cheeks stifled any reproach Connor might have made, and instead he felt that squeeze of pain in his chest that overtook him at odd times. Jack wasn't even thirty yet, but he looked at least ten years older. The doctor in Redruth had said his illness was under control, so worrying about him made no sense. Connor told himself that every day, but it did no good. Fear for his brother was as dark and constant as his own shadow.

"Don't be glaring at me," Jack commanded from twenty feet away. "I've brought yer ruddy letter, and there'm money in it, I can tell. Which makes me the bearer o' glad tidings." Producing an envelope from the pocket of his scruffy coat, he handed it over with a flourish. "Now where's my thanks?"

"I'd say you've already drunk it." But he said it with a smile, because Jack could charm the red from a rose—and because he was right about the envelope; it had a nice, solid heft that said the Pendarvis boys wouldn't go hungry tonight in Wyckerley.

"Open it up yonder, Con. Under the trees. Cooler."

"Are you tired, Jack?"

"Naw. What I am is *hot*."

Connor said no more, and they ambled toward a clump of oak trees at the edge of the village green, opposite the old Norman church. But it was warm in the afternoon sun, not hot, and he knew it was the support of the iron bench under the oaks Jack wanted, not the cool shade.

"So," said Jack, spreading his arms out across the back of the bench, "how much 'ave the Rhads coughed up this time?"

The plain envelope had no return address. Connor opened it and thumbed through the banknotes inside the folded, one-page letter. "Enough to cover the note of deposit I've just signed for our new lodgings."

"Well, that's a relief for you, counselor. Now you won't get pinched for false misrepresentation o' personal fiduciary stature." Jack chortled at his own humor; he never got tired of making up names for laws and statutes, the sillier sounding the better.

Connor said, "I had to pay the agent for the lease of six months. Thirty-six shillings." It wasn't his money, but it still seemed a waste, since they wouldn't be in Wyckerley past two months at the most.

"What's our new place like, then?"

"Better than the last. We've half of a workingmen's cottage only a mile from the mine. We'll share a kitchen with two other men, both miners, and there's a girl who comes in the afternoons to cook a meal. And praise the Lord, we've each got a room this time, so I won't have to listen to you snore the glazing out of the windows."

Jack cackled, going along with the joke. There were times when he kept Connor awake, but it was because of his cough and the drenching night sweats that robbed him of rest, not his snoring. "What do they say about the mine?" he asked.

"Not much. It's called Guelder. A woman owns it. It's been fairly—"

"A *woman*." Jack's eyes went wide with amazement, then narrowed in scorn. "A woman," he muttered, shaking his head. "Well, ee've got yer work cut out right and proper, then, 'aven't ee? The radical Rhads'll be aquiver wi' joy when they read yer report this time."

Connor grunted noncommittally. "The woman's name is Deene. She inherited the mine from her father about two years ago, and she owns it outright, without shareholders. They say her uncle owns another mine in the district. His name's Vanstone, and he happens to be the mayor of Wyckerley."

"Why'n't they send you to that un? The uncle's, I mean. Tes bound to be far better run."

"Probably, and there's your answer. The Society hasn't

employed me to investigate clean, safe, well-managed copper mines." No, but the selection process was still fair, Connor believed, if only because conditions in most Cornish and Devonian copper mines were so deplorable, there was no need to doctor reports or tinker with findings. Or pick a woman's mine over a man's in hopes of finding more deficiencies.

He put the envelope in his pocket and clasped his hands behind his head, blinking up at the sky.

The June afternoon was lazily spectacular, and he couldn't deny that it was pleasant to sit in the shade while butterflies flickered in and out of sun rays slanting down through the tree leaves. In a rare mellow mood, he watched two children burst from a side door in the church across the way and run toward the green. A second later, out came three more, then four, then another giggling pair. Shouting, laughing, they skipped and ran in circles and tumbled on the grass, giddy as March hares. He'd have thought Sunday school had just let out, except it was Saturday. The children's high spirits were contagious; more than one passerby paused in the cobbled street long enough to smile at their antics.

Half a minute later, a young woman came out of the same door in the church and hurried across the lane toward the green. The school teacher? Tall, slim, dressed in white, she had blond hair tied up in a knot on top of her head. Connor tried to guess her age, but it was hard to tell from this distance; she had the lithe body of a girl, but the confident, self-assured manner of a woman. He wasn't a bit surprised when she clapped her hands and every shrieking, frolicking child immediately ran to her. What surprised him was the gay sound of her own laughter mingling with theirs.

The smallest child, a girl of five or six, leaned against her hip familiarly; the woman patted her curly head while she gave the others some soft-voiced command. The children formed a half circle around her. She bent down to the little girl's level to say something in her ear, her hand resting lightly on the child's shoulder.

"Look at that now, Con. That's a winsome sight, edn it?" said Jack in a low, appreciative voice. "Edn that just how a lady oughter look?"

Where women were concerned, Jack was the least discriminating man Connor had ever known; he liked *all* of them. But this time he'd spoken no more than the truth. This woman's ivory gown, her willowy figure, the sunny gold in her hair—they made a very beguiling picture. And yet he thought Jack meant something more—something about the long, graceful curve of her back as she bent toward the child, the solicitousness of her posture, the *kindness* in it that took the simple picture out of the ordinary and made it unforgettable. When Connor glanced at his brother, he saw the same soft, stricken smile he could feel on his own face, and he knew they'd been moved equally, just for a moment, by the perfection of the picture.

She straightened then, and the little girl skipped away to a place in the middle of the semicircle. The spell was broken, but the picture lingered; the image still shimmered in his mind's eye.

She took something from the pocket of her dress—a pitch pipe. She brought it to her lips and blew a soft, thin note. The children hummed obediently, then burst into song.

Smiling encouragement, her face animated, the music teacher moved her hands in time to the melody, and every child beamed back at her, eager to please, all wide eyes and happy faces. It was like a scene in a storybook, or a sentimental play about good children and perfectly kind teachers, too good to be true—yet it was happening here, now, on the little green in the village of Wyckerley, St. Giles' parish. Mesmerized, Connor sat back to watch what would happen next.

The choir sang another song, and afterward the teacher made them sing it again. He wasn't surprised; smitten as he was, even he could tell it hadn't been their finest effort. Then, sensing her charges were growing restless, she set them free after a gentle admonition—which fell on deaf ears, because the shouting and gamboling recommenced almost immediately.

"Looks like a litter o' new puppies." Jack chuckled, and Connor nodded, smiling at the antics of two little towheaded boys, twins, vying with each other to see who could press more dandelions into the hands of their pretty teacher. Heedless of the damp grass, she dropped to her knees and sniffed the straggly bouquets with exaggerated admiration. Her way of keeping their rambunctious spirits within bounds was to ask them questions, then listen to the answers with complete absorption.

Just then the curly haired little girl, clutching her own flower, made a running leap and landed on the teacher's back with a squeal of delight. The woman bore the impact sturdily, even when the youngster wound her arms around her neck and hung on tight, convulsing with mirth. But gradually the laughter tapered off.

"She'm caught," Jack murmured when some of the children crept closer, looking uncertain. "The lady's hair, looks like. Edn she caught?" Connor was already on his feet. "Con? Wait, now. Ho, Con! You shouldn't oughter—"

He didn't hear the rest. Impulsiveness was one of his most dangerous failings, but this—this was too much like the answer to a prayer he'd been too distracted to say. He took off across the green at a sprint.

No doubt about it, the teacher was caught. "It's all right, Birdie," she was saying, reaching back to try to disentangle her hair from something on the little girl's dress. "Don't wriggle for a second. No, it's all right, just don't move."

Birdie was near tears. "I'm sorry, Miss Sophie," she kept saying, worried but unable to stop squirming. The music teacher winced—then laughed, pretending it was a joke.

The other children eyed Connor in amazement when he squatted down beside the entangled pair. Birdie's mouth dropped open and she finally went still. The teacher—Miss Sophie—could only see him out of the corner of her eye; if she turned her head, she'd yank the long strand of hair that was wound tight around Birdie's shirtwaist button.

"Well, now, what have we here?" he said, softening his voice to keep Birdie calm. He shifted until he was kneeling in front of the teacher, and reached over her bent head to untangle the snarl.

"It got stuck! Now I can't move or I'll hurt Miss Sophie!"

Around them the children had gathered in a quiet circle, curious as cows. And protective of their teacher, Connor fancied. "That's right," he agreed, "so you must hold very, very still while I undo this knot. Pretend you're a statue."

"Yes, sir. What's a statue?"

A breathy laugh came from the music teacher. He could see only her profile and the smooth angle of her neck. She had cream-white skin, the cheeks flushed a little from exertion or embarrassment. Her eyes were downcast; he couldn't be sure what color they were. Blue, he thought. "The stone cross at the edge of the green, Birdie," she said, amusement in her low voice. "That's a sort of statue, because it never moves."

"Oh."

The snarl was stubborn, and Connor was as anxious as Birdie not to pull Miss Sophie's hair. "Almost got it," he muttered. "Two more seconds." Her pretty hair was soft and slippery and it smelled of roses. Or was that the sun-warmed linen of her dress?

"There are scissors in the rectory," she said, speaking to the ground. "Tommy Wooten, are you here? Would you go and ask—"

"Out of the question. I'd sooner cut off my hand than a single strand of this beautiful hair." And if that wasn't the most fatuous thing he'd ever said in his life, he wanted to know what was.

She sent him a twinkling, sideways glance, and he saw the color of her eyes. Blue. Definitely blue. "Actually, I was thinking you might cut off the *button*."

"Ah, the button. A much better idea."

"Shall I go, Miss Sophie?" asked a reedy voice behind Connor's shoulder.

"Yes, Tommy."

"No, Tommy," Connor corrected as the last strand in the tangle finally came loose. "Miss Sophie is free."

She sat back on her heels and smiled, first at him, then at the children gathered around; some of them were clapping, as if a performance had just concluded. Her laughing face was flushed, her hair awry—and she was so stunningly lovely, he felt blinded, hindered, too dazzled to take it in. He remembered to take off his hat, but before he could speak—and say what?—she turned away to give Birdie a strong, reassuring hug.

"Did it hurt?" the little girl asked her, patting her cheek worriedly.

"No, not one bit."

She heaved a great sigh of relief. "Look, Miss Sophie, here's what I was giving you." She held out one bent daisy, the stem wilted, the white petals smashed.

Sophie drew in her breath. "Oh, *lovely*," she declared, holding the flower to her nose and sniffing deeply. "*Thank* you, Birdie." The child blushed with pleasure. Then she was off, anxious to tell her friends about her adventure.

Now that the drama was over, the other children began to wander away, too. Connor was still on his knees beside the teacher. "Thank you," she said in her musical voice.

He said, "It was very much my pleasure." They both looked away, then back. He put out his hand. She hesitated for a second, then took it, and he helped her to her feet.